The Leo Conversion

The Leo Conversion

David Smith

With best wishes,
David Smith

DODD, MEAD & COMPANY · NEW YORK

Although the place names and locations in this story are real, any similarity between characters and real people is purely coincidental.

The quotation from *Sweeney Agonistes* from *Collected Poems 1909–1962*, by T. S. Eliot, is reprinted by permission of Harcourt Brace Jovanovich, Inc. and Faber and Faber Limited. Copyright 1936 by Harcourt Brace Jovanovich, Inc.; copyright © 1963, 1964 by T. S. Eliot.

Library of Congress Cataloging in Publication Data

Smith, David, 1936–
    The Leo conversion.

    I.   Title.
PZ4.S6447Le   [PS3569.M51718]   813'.54   80-13316
ISBN 0-396-07854-0

I'll convert you!
Into a stew.
A nice little, white little,
missionary stew!
T. S. ELIOT, *Sweeney Agonistes*

Conversion a.F. *conversion,* ad L. *conversion-em* turning round, n. of action from *convertere* to turn round . . . **7.** the action of (illegally) converting or applying something to one's own use . . . **14.** translation into another language . . . **16.** substitution of or exchange for something else . . .

The Oxford English Dictionary

For
MARY and HANK
and the
HAMDALA GANG.

Prologue

JOSEPH SIMHANI wiped the sweat from his brush moustache. Although the Peugeot's speedometer registered eighty kilometers per hour and all of the windows were open, there was hardly a trace of breeze from the languid African air that hung over the savannah. For a few minutes he had removed his yellowing Panama hat to let some air onto his balding head, but he felt awkward with it off and he replaced it. He had lost the hat band months earlier and he determined now that he would have a new one made when he reached Maradi. Maybe he would get a new hat. But he liked this one and, besides, he doubted that he could get one of as good a quality this far north. Perhaps in Spain. Or Algiers. The idea of Spain made him smile.

He held the steering wheel with his left hand and unwound the gold wire-framed glasses from his nose and ears. His eyes were burning from the early morning sun and he wondered whether he should wear sunglasses. He never had. The brim of his hat was enough protection except when he drove, and he seldom drove this far. He rubbed his eyes and ran the front of his glasses over his jacket. Then he replaced them. As he did, he saw a caravan, perhaps twenty or thirty camels long, silhouetted against the horizon. And the small station house at the Niger border crossing. He could feel his pulse quicken.

1

He knew he had nothing to worry about. No one took the border checks seriously. They were more form than substance and the Nigerian immigration agents this far north were inexperienced and artless. No one could stand the desert heat for too long and only new recruits were stationed here. Even if something were to be found, some bottles of beer and a few shillings would solve the matter. Of course, the usual contraband was radios, cigarettes, hashish, or tires. And most of it was smuggled on camels or lorries, not in sedan cars. He thought briefly about the visa—or, more precisely, the absence of one, but he knew it would not be a problem.

Corporal Ibrahim Adamawa had just finished wiping a cloth over his shoes. Although it was impossible to keep the desert's dust off them, he felt it was as important to look efficient as to be efficient. Besides, the shoes were only four months old. There was a knot in one shoelace, where it had broken two days before. Corporal Ibrahim reminded himself to have someone purchase new laces for him in Kano. He was pleased when the Peugeot pulled up to the gate. He liked to meet people crossing the border and he liked to be working. He was surprised to see that the eyes of the driver were almost even with the top of the steering wheel. Europeans were not usually that short.

Joseph Simhani gained confidence as he saw Corporal Ibrahim come toward him. The officer could not have been more than nineteen or twenty. Without the uniform, he would have looked like a schoolboy. Simhani removed his passport from the inside of his jacket.

"Good morning, sir. You're our first border crosser today. You're traveling early. Good idea. You'll miss the worst of the sun if you're not going too far. May I see your passport, please?"

Simhani handed the corporal his passport. He would have liked to have gotten out of the car to stretch the tightened muscles in the small of his back, but he did not want to do anything to prolong the stop.

"I don't see a visa stamp, sir."

"My goodness, I forgot that I would need one. I'm just going

2

up to Maradi for a few hours. I'll be returning this afternoon. I've been through here many times. Your predecessors used to let me through when I forgot the visa. My business is active. I do not always have time to think of these formalities. Usually I am able to provide a small token of appreciation for the immigration officer's helpfulness."

"I see." Corporal Ibrahim looked down at his shoes. Already they were becoming dusty. He thought about wiping them against his trousers and then decided not to. "What do you usually provide?" Ibrahim smiled kindly.

"I have some beer in the back seat. I'm a provisioner. Mineral waters and spirits. I service many of the cold stores and rest-houses in the north. I am thinking of expanding into Niger. May I offer you a bottle?"

"I cannot drink on duty, sir."

"Immigration officers must get thirsty as well as the rest of us."

"Police, sir. Nigerian police. The immigration officer is still sleeping."

Simhani could feel his heart pound. "Police? What are the police doing here?"

"Special assignment, sir. There was a theft at the Jos Museum a few days ago. We are taking special precautions. Could I see the contents of the boot, please?"

"I really am in something of a hurry."

"Won't take long, sir. You should exercise your legs anyway. It's no good to be sitting for so long. I exercise every morning. Keeps the blood circulating."

The corporal stepped back two paces as the door swung open.

Simhani walked around to the back of the Peugeot and inserted the key. Ibrahim raised the lid.

"Just my suitcase and some sales literature. Wine in that box. Say, would you prefer a bottle of wine to the beer?"

"No thank you, sir. Would you mind if I opened your suit-case?"

Simhani could feel the pulse throbbing first in his neck and then in his temples. He loosened his tie and unbuttoned the top of his

3

shirt. "You'll only find clothes in there. And hair tonic."

The corporal snapped open the case and lifted two layers of shirts. "A lot of clothes."

"I keep this bag in the boot in case I am delayed in my travels."

The corporal reached below a layer of underwear. "What is this leather case here?"

"Nothing of significance. Only business papers."

"Perhaps I had best look."

"Perhaps," Simhani said softly, "you had best not." The corporal was only half-turned around when the small-caliber pistol exploded against his stomach. He fell forward onto the Peugeot. Simhani pushed his body to the ground and did not wait to close the boot.

I STOOD in the center of the funeral hut staring at Muntaka's body propped up in the heavy oak chair. At that moment I wasn't thinking about Muntaka's death—instead, I wondered where the hell they had found that chair.

The seat, wide enough for two Muntakas, was some thirty inches from the floor, and the back ended about a foot above Muntaka's head, like the spire of a French cathedral. The front legs, thick, and thick with dust, ended in the shape of lion's claws. From the sides of the back of the chair two gargoylelike creatures shot out slim, dusty tongues, as if to catch the small black flies that circled Muntaka's head. The flies had been attracted to the scene either by the smell of death or by the perfume that permeated the air.

Muntaka's body, clothed in a robe of pale blue with intricate white embroidery that looked like Arabic script, was placed erect in the chair. His bare feet did not reach the small red, gold and blue oriental rug on which the chair rested and, to keep them from dangling, they had been placed on two large, leather-covered books. I tilted sideways and strained in the candles' light to see the titles of the books. I could read only one: "Defeat in Hausaland."

Muntaka's green-black sinewy hands rested gently on the front of each armrest. His eyelids had been shut and his face had the tranquil, bloodless look of death, except for a slightly sardonic twist to the mouth. At first I felt inclined to straighten the lips. But since Muntaka was vaguely related to the late Sardauna of Sokoto, the smile seemed appropriate. In any case, I didn't feel much like touching a dead body.

Two days had passed since I had learned of Muntaka's death. When the young soldier approached me on the train, I was looking out at the crowd of hawkers, beggars, travelers, and pickpockets jammed together on the Ibadan station platform. As the corporal touched my left shoulder, I snapped my head part way around and saw the black hand and khaki sleeve. Startled, I shot straight up, bumping my right shoulder on the low overhead rack.

The soldier said, "I am very sorry. Mr. Stevens, I presume?"

I replied that my name was James Stevens.

"You are James Stevens number three?"

"Yes. I'm James Stevens the third."

"Come with me, please."

It was only as I was walking down the corridor of the train that a slight feeling of sickness swept through my stomach. By the time I reached the steps down to the station platform the sickness had changed to a mild wave of fear. As I stepped off the train and saw a chance to run and disappear into the crowd, the fear had changed to mild panic. *I* knew I had done nothing illegal, but did *they* know it? I felt the right side of my jacket for my passport. It was there. I knew there was nothing wrong with the visa. And I knew I wasn't smuggling anything—unless someone had slipped something into my suitcase along the line. I felt in my pocket for the suitcase key. Jesus. I began to sweat. It wasn't there. Then I remembered that I had transferred it to my money belt. I felt along my midsection and pressed the hardness of the metal against my stomach.

It could be someone looking for a bribe. "Your visa doesn't have the red stamp." "It doesn't?" "No." "How much is the stamp?'' ''Fifty naira.'' Do I pay it or stand on principle? Screw the bastards. . . . I'll pay it.

The soldier was behind me. As we moved off the railway car he had put his hands on my shoulders and turned me toward the front of the train. He said nothing. As we glided through the maze of people, I looked around to catch someone's eye. I would nod, or wink, or try to convey terror. *Yes, I saw the white man on the station platform shortly before midday. There was a soldier behind him. The white man had been arrested. His face showed fear.* But no one noticed me. The soldier moved to my right side, took my arm, and maneuvered me toward the station house. As we reached a side door, the soldier opened it and said, ''This way.''

The room was an office of some sort, but there was nothing in it to suggest that it was connected with the railway station. It was small, just barely large enough for two old wooden desks, three slat-back chairs, and a rusted, dust-covered file cabinet. A chubby Yoruba, wearing a short-sleeved white shirt and a bifurcated moustache that forked out from each nostril, sat at one desk, facing the door, in front of a faded, water-stained photo of the late prime minister. On the desk was a glass of silt-colored tea, a greasy newspaper wrapped around what was probably the Yoruba's lunch, and a single tan-colored file folder, decorated by a thin red ribbon tied to the upper left-hand corner. The folder was new. There was a small electric fan on the Yoruba's desk, but it wasn't turned on. The room smelled of sweat and spoiling chicken.

At the second desk was an army officer. His khaki shirt was opened at the neck and he was wearing his cap. He stood up as we entered and I noticed small drops of water on his temples. His shirt looked like he hadn't been wearing it for more than a few minutes. The Yoruba's was stained with perspiration at the armpits and stomach.

''Mr. Stevens?''

''Yes.''

7

"Your passport, please."

Son of a bitch. The handing over of the passport, I knew, was the beginning of the end. The young soldier was standing with his back to the door.

The officer looked only at the first two pages of the passport. He looked at my photo and then at me, and then back at the photo. He made no attempt to find the stamped visa. Then he handed the passport back to me.

"A cable has arrived for you, Mr. Stevens." He took a folded sheet of paper from his shirt pocket. Without unfolding it, he looked at the paper briefly and then handed it to me. "I am sorry for its contents." He paused briefly. Then he said, "I have been instructed by the commander of the Ibadan barracks to deliver it to you."

The first soldier said, "There were only two white men on the train. I had no difficulty locating Mr. Stevens."

I sat down in the chair by the door, unfolded the sheet of paper, and read the ten words. "Mallam Mohamed Murtala Muntaka dead. Proceed Bernin Gwari via Zaria." It was signed "Adamu Waziri, Provincial Commissioner." I shook my head and read it again.

The officer moved from behind the desk and came toward me. "I have been directed by the commander of the Ibadan barracks to suggest that you continue north by train. I have instructed the engineer to wait for you. You will be met at the station at Zaria by a driver from the Ministry of Works. He will escort you." Then the officer put a hand on my shoulder. He looked down at me and said, "I am sorry for the loss of your friend. I lost my brother in the war. May God give them rest."

Two minutes after I returned to my seat, the train started up.

Had the news of Muntaka's death come earlier, before I had arrived back on the west coast of Africa, it would have been easier for me to deal with. It had been four years since I had seen him and my memories had either been blurred or exaggerated well beyond what could have been the truth. But here on the train

8

moving slowly northward through Ibadan and Ilorin, across the river Niger, through countless small villages, through Minna and Kaduna, he was coming back into focus. He was a small man, nine-tenths flowing white robes and turban, his face like a groundhog peering tentatively through the side of a snow-covered hill. His pale blue eyes, which seemed to float under a veil of quicksilver, sat incongruously over protruding cheekbones covered thinly by weather brown-black skin and between ears too large for his small head. His turban was of white linen and cheap white gauze reminiscent of a World War I field hospital.

Muntaka was the chief judge of Kano and Senior Advisor on Islamic Law to the military government. Four years earlier he had served as investigating magistrate in a homicide case involving an Englishman found lying naked, under mosquito netting, on a bed in room C-24 at the Central Hotel. A bronze-handled knife had been implanted in the center of the Englishman's chest and his mouth had been stuffed with a pair of silver-plated, battery-operated Japanese Ben-wa balls. The remote control had been turned to the ''on'' position, half of the Englishman's teeth were broken, and the battery, like the Englishman, was dead. As the youngest and most expendable assistant in the Manhattan D. A.'s office, I was sent to Kano to determine whether there was sufficient evidence to require the extradition of a young American woman to stand trial for the murder.

Four weeks turned into five months as I played Watson to Muntaka's Holmes. What began as a simple case of murder developed into the unveiling of a criminal network involving child prostitution, pornography, and the trans-Saharan drug trade. In the evenings Muntaka and I took long walks, during which we shared what he had learned about the *shari'a* at Al-Azhar University in Cairo and what I had learned about the law at Yale. During the days, when we seemed to be making no progress with the investigation, I would sit with Muntaka as he heard cases in court, study the Hausa language under his tutelage, or, under an arrangement made by Muntaka, lecture on the law of crimes at the police college.

9

The combination of the two of us seemed preposterous at the time and even more so in retrospect. But we ended up pictured together on the front page of *Gaskiya*:

JUDGE AND YOUNG AMERICAN
SOLVE CENTRAL HOTEL MURDER

The chief alkali of Kano, Alhaji Mohamed Murtala Muntaka, and James Richard Stevens the third, on secondment from the office of the criminal prosecutor of New York, USA have brought to a successful conclusion their investigation of the July 4 Central Hotel murder. Three suspects were arraigned early yesterday before the Grade A Magistrate's Court. Muntaka and Stevens, both of whom narrowly escaped death at the hands of the defendants in a brothel on the outskirts of Sokoto, will be honored. . . .

We did, I suppose, complement each other in a number of ways. Toward the end of our partnership Muntaka acknowledged this for the first, and last, time. Quoting Martin Chuzzlewit, he said, "Mallam Stevens, we are the two halves of a pair of scissors when apart; but together, we are something."

Muntaka was then in his Charles Dickens phase. In the corner of room C-24 at the Central Hotel the Englishman had kept a large steamer trunk filled with a complete set of the works of George Eliot, Charles Dickens, Thomas Carlyle and J. W. P. Jasprot, one of the most prolific pornographers of all time and the author of such well known works as *School for Virgins*, *Sighs and Thighs*, *Couch d'Amour*, *Tools of the Trade*, and *A Maiden's Knee*. Thinking that the books might contain some clue to the identity of the murderer, Muntaka and I divided them up, he taking the Eliot, Dickens, and Carlyle, and I taking the remainder.

I had planned to fly to Kaduna to visit Muntaka for a few days after finishing a joint venture negotiation in Lagos for my law firm—the D. A. had lost the election eight months earlier—but Muntaka had written that I should take the train from the coast rather than fly, even though it would take twenty-four hours longer. "You should travel by train to reacquaint yourself with the smells and sounds and visions of my country," he wrote. "Africa should be entered like a beautiful woman—slowly, and with all senses at the ready." The fellow sitting next to me had a body odor that would have stopped a rhinoceros and he talked nothing but ragtime all the way from Lagos to Ibadan. He was unemployed and I seemed to represent some sort of opportunity that he shouldn't pass up. The cable from Adamu Waziri cast a cloak of sadness over the remainder of the journey north.

The funeral hut was a small round structure of dried mud and clay, with straw roofing. Like most of the other buildings in the small village, the mud and clay of the hut blended imperceptibly into the dust of the street. Seated outside were several women of varying ages and I took them to be Muntaka's wives, holding vigil. A few children played nearby, but at a respectful distance. It was noon and the heat was so intense as to be almost visible.

I moved through dark, musty-smelling curtains, heavy with the clay of the village. As I brushed them aside, dust rose and a small lizard, about four inches long, slithered down from the top of the doorway and into the room.

The only light was from the two candles that stood on a small table next to Muntaka's chair and bits of sunlight that knifed in through holes in the curtains behind me. As my eyes adjusted to the darkness, I could see that the floor was covered with flower petals and that a heavy, faded drape that could not have belonged to the dark and airless hut covered the rear wall. The drape was the color of rotting plums. The lizard moved leisurely through the flower petals, skittered up the books, over Muntaka's bare feet, and then disappeared behind the chair. There was no one in the room but Muntaka, me, and the lizard.

The smell of the flowers attacked my nostrils and buried itself sickeningly in the pit of my stomach. I tried to overcome the nausea by focusing on Muntaka's body. It occurred to me that I had no idea how old Muntaka was—or had been. Then I noticed that Muntaka had extremely large toes. The toenails looked clean, almost manicured. How did a man his size end up with such large toes? Probably from wearing sandals. I wondered if he would be buried barefooted. I wondered what the books were. Maybe they would be buried with him. Damn, why the hell did he have to die, anyway? If only we could spend one more day together—just talking, that's all. I tried to hold back the tears, but I couldn't. *Okay, Muntaka, so I'm crying. Who the hell cares?* Then, out loud: "Damn it, Muntaka." As I spoke, I realized how alone I was in that goddamned mud coffin. Where was everybody? Where was *any*body? Why was I the only one here? What the hell was I doing in this pseudocrypt a hundred miles from the nearest American consul? How did he die, anyway? I began to sweat. I looked around and couldn't see any light through the curtains. I thought for a moment that the entrance had been blocked off. In semipanic I turned and moved across the dirt floor to the curtained exit.

Then, a voice.

"Wait, Mallam Stevens, we have many things to talk about."

I whirled around. There, standing in front of that ancient chair that must have been brought by some old colonial officer from the old manse in Sussex, was Mallam Muntaka.

"Holy shit."

"Reports of my death, as your Will Rogers said, are greatly exaggerated." Muntaka stretched his arms out from his sides and folded his robe back toward his shoulders. He smiled broadly. Three front teeth were missing. The others were stained to a burnt orange.

"That was Mark Twain. Will Rogers said, 'All I know is just what I read in the papers.' "

"I always get those two confused. You read something in the papers?"

"No. No. I'm just telling you what. . . . Damn it, Muntaka, what is this?"

"So. You do not think that my premature death and rebirth are amusing?"

"Amusing? Christ, Muntaka, you scared the shit out of me."

"You have the wrong prophet. It is Mohamed Muntaka."

"This isn't funny."

"I thought it was somewhat diverting. No, perhaps you are right. I am sorry. But it has become necessary for my death to occur. Or at least to appear to occur. You have read my obituary?"

"Obituary? What obituary?"

"In the *Nigerian Times*. I wrote it myself."

"You wrote your own goddamned obituary?"

"Under the circumstances, I seemed the most appropriate person to do so."

"Yes. I suppose you're right."

"Every man should have the opportunity to write his own obituary. Only he is in a position to determine what was significant in his life—what is worth recording and what is not. Moreover, Mallam Stevens, it gives a man a chance to see what he has done. If he does not like his obituary, he has an opportunity to do something that would make for a more interesting one."

My clothes were completely drenched, there was almost no air circulating in the hut, and I was beginning to find it difficult to breathe. But I couldn't move. I stood there like a tourist from Muncie listening to Muntaka talk like a character from Disneyland. "Fourscore and seven years ago, our forefathers. . . ." "Look, Alice, he's talking!" "Looks real, doesn't it, George?"

Suddenly, Muntaka rushed toward me. I flinched and he threw his arms around me, holding me with great strength. I embraced him in return. His robe smelled musty. How the hell long had he been sitting there?

Finally, I stepped back, looked at him, and said, "Muntaka, have you gone mad? What the hell are you—we—doing here?"

"I have been asked to undertake a special assignment on behalf of the government."

"An investigation of the funeral industry? It's been done."

"The recovery of a work of art."

"What're you talking about?"

"A manuscript dating from the thirteenth century disappeared from the museum at Jos two weeks ago. The government, until now, has been unsuccessful in retrieving it. Rumors of the market are that the manuscript—a dozen pages of fine parchment—has been, or will be, taken north where it will be sold."

"And the government has put *you* on the case?"

Muntaka looked pained. "It is widely known, Mallam Stevens, that I am the leading Arabic scholar in this country. Few men could identify the authentic documents. I am one."

I shrugged. "What's this got to do with your funeral?"

"The government is anxious that it not be known that I have been sent in pursuit of the manuscript. Reports of my death may cause our adversaries to be less cautious."

"How valuable is it?"

"In monetary terms, the parchments may have a value of several hundred thousand pounds. In spiritual and historical terms they are beyond valuing."

"If they're so valuable, why were they put on display? If I remember right, the security at Jos is lousy."

"They were not on display. A hand-drawn copy of the manuscript—of considerable craftsmanship—*was* put behind glass at the museum, but the manuscript itself was kept in a safe. Unfortunately, the safe proved not to be particularly safe. The manuscript was stolen. The copy was untouched."

"You have any idea who'd want something like this?"

"As you know, African art has recently attracted much attention in Europe and the United States. Six months ago, at one of the art auction houses in London, a Benin bronze figure of one of the Oba's hornblowers was sold for an amount in excess of one hundred and fifty thousand pounds. Just three months ago a terracotta of the Nok culture, two thousand years old, was sold in the same auction house for two hundred thousand pounds. It is suspected that the piece was recently discovered in a small village and left the country illegally. But this cannot be proved. Prior to 1939 the export of national antiquities obtained legally was not forbidden.

"It is now illegal for *any* items of antiquity to be taken from the country without an export license. For a number of years we were successful in controlling the exodus of valuable items. But in the last decade a well-organized smuggling trade, operated by Afro-French citizens of the countries to the north, has developed. Foumban, the capital of the Bamum tribe in Cameroon, and Fort Lamy in Chad have, until recently, served as entrepôt centers for stolen art. Dealers from Paris, Geneva, Beirut, and Rome came to these centers to make purchases. The trade through the entrepôt towns has been curtailed somewhat by the police of Nigeria, Cameroon, and Chad, but it has proved impossible to stop the flow entirely.

"*Theft* of objects of value is rare. Most often pieces of value are purchased from villages or from the private collections of former colonial officers, missionaries, or Lebanese businessmen and then smuggled from the country."

"Why the manuscript, Mantaka? Why not something else?"

"The thief knew what he was doing. The manuscript was the most valuable item in the museum. It is of great physical beauty. The Arabic script is at once delicate and powerful. The parchment is of the finest quality. But the pages are not simply objects of art. They are documents of great historical value. The script is of a medieval Arabic dialect not well known today and the manuscript has not been fully translated. But enough is known to indicate that it preserves one of the most important missing links in the history of Africa. It is likely that this document is the only one from this period still in existence."

"You think it's likely to end up in Foumban? Or Fort Lamy?"

"No. Our informants, Mallam Stevens, tell us that an attempt may be made to sell it through a dealer in Maradi. I expect, however, that the manuscript is of too great a value to change hands in Niger. I think we shall find it in one of the great black markets to the north—perhaps in Marrakech. Still, one cannot be sure. Thus, we shall have to proceed slowly, and trace the route of the thieves, like foxes following a deer."

"You say 'we,' Muntaka. Who's going with you?"

"Why you, of course, Mallam Stevens. You."

"Oh no you don't, Muntaka. The last time you talked me into one of your escapades I nearly lost my balls. My psyche is permanently scarred."

"The military governor has suggested your name."

"The military governor? Hell, Muntaka, he doesn't know me."

"The small part we played in solving the Central Hotel murder has given you some degree of notoriety. The governor was much impressed by what he has read and heard of your role in solving the case."

"Heard? From whom?"

"Me." Muntaka moved the index finger of his right hand back and forth across his nostrils.

"Forget it, Muntaka."

"So, it's all set?"

"All set? Look, Muntaka, I'm a lawyer, not an international adventurer. You don't need me, you need Mr. Moto."

"Who?"

"What you do not seem to realize, Muntaka, is that I have a job. If I'm not back to the firm by next Tuesday, Winslow, Wallace, Wilson, and White are going to be looking for a new associate. Christ, I've only been with them six months."

"The fact that all of the partners in your firm have names beginning with the letter *W* should give you some cause for reflection."

"They're all dead."

"Who?"

"Winslow, Wallace, Wilson, and White."

Muntaka raised his eyebrows and shrugged. "So, they shouldn't miss you."

"Funny, Muntaka. Look, I need the work. Thanks anyway."

"And in three years you have become very pale. You shall find another job."

"Muntaka, I'm not quitting my job just to go camel riding with you in Timbuktu."

"Not Timbuktu. We would take the straight northern route

16

through Maradi, Zinder, Agadez, Ain Salah, and Bechar into Morocco." Muntaka paused and raised his grey-black eyebrows again. "We could, of course, go through Timbuktu on our return. It is, as you know, my ancestral home. It is not much out of the way if we leave from Taroudant in southern Morocco."

I ran a hand through my hair and then across my eyes and face. I was tired, my bladder was about to explode, and the heat and Muntaka were beginning to wear me down. I was having a difficult time thinking.

"Muntaka, my bladder can't take too much more of this."

"I, too, must pass water. We may use the corner. It will soak into the ground." As we pissed in unison against the wall of the hut, Muntaka said, "It is wonderful how much better one can feel after relieving one's bladder."

" 'Tant pis, tant mieux,' as the French say."

"So, you have not forgotten that language. Good. It will be most helpful in the countries to the north. I shall take lessons from you. It is settled then?"

"Is what settled?"

"You are coming with me."

"Muntaka, I'll see you later. I need some air." I headed for the exit. Muntaka followed, first retrieving the two books on which his feet had rested some time before. I swept the dusty curtains aside.

"I am afraid, Mallam Stevens, that there is no choice."

"What do you mean, no choice?" It was hotter outside than in the hut.

"To put it bluntly, Mallam Stevens, I need your help."

"What's wrong with the police? Nigeria has a whole god-damned police force, Muntaka." The street was deserted.

"I need the assistance of someone who can move unobtrusively and who is, like myself, a man of resources. You, Mallam Stevens, are a man of resources. Untapped, perhaps, but nevertheless there. I also need the assistance of someone whose instincts and motives are known to me."

"Instincts and motives? I thought you were looking for a

17

manuscript. You look, you find, you bring it back to the museum."

"It is the unexpected I am concerned about, Mallam Stevens. It is how a man reacts to the unexpected that may ultimately influence one's quest." Muntaka put his left hand to his head and rubbed his eyes. He rested his thumb and index finger against his nostrils and pulled on his nose. Then he said, "It will also be helpful, Mallam Stevens, that you are a man of little religious conviction."

"What's *that* supposed to mean?"

"I state it merely as a matter of fact. It will be helpful that you have no religious alliances. It is possible—although only possible—that the documents may be of interest to others than my government and collectors of antiquities. I can tell you no more than this at the moment. You must take my word, Mallam Stevens, that I need your assistance and that your aid may be the difference between success and failure." Muntaka threw his opened hands out beyond shoulder-width. "Have I ever misled you?"

"In fact, yes."

Muntaka tilted his head and shrugged. "In minor things perhaps. You'll come with me?"

It meant, of course, that I'd lose my job. Even if I had a job waiting when I returned, they'd fire me the moment I walked in the door. "Oh, I was just off searching for a stolen Arabic manuscript. Nothing much." "Good, Stevens, that's fine, the firm can always use a little more experience in stolen Arabic manuscripts. Here's a raise. By the way, where's the Kingsley deposition in the Twentieth Century case?" Screw 'em. They wouldn't understand any of this. The question was, was *I* going to understand any of this?

Muntaka stood in front of me smiling. Then slowly, involuntarily, my face broke into a wide grin. I laughed. "Okay, Muntaka, you win."

"I am very glad. Here, I would like you to have these." Muntaka handed me the books that had served as props for his feet back in the hut. "I have brought them especially for you. They are concerned with explorations of the Sahara and the old Soudan. They shall give more meaning to your travels."

"So, you knew I'd accept your offer?"

"It does not come as a surprise to me." Muntaka stepped back a pace and looked at me. "The journey will do you much good. And it will be extremely useful to me to have your assistance while my wound is healing."

"Wound? What wound?"

Muntaka pushed back his robe from his right shoulder, revealing a large bandage. "Four days ago I received a bullet through the chest muscle just below the collarbone. The bullet, I am told, came from a small handgun."

"Bullet? You mean someone took a shot at you?"

"I left the emir's court late Saturday afternoon, after spending the day with him. I am, as you know, his financial advisor. I hold the honorary title of the Mutawali. I went into the walled market behind the emir's palace to purchase a half kilo of kola nuts. As I was paying for them, I felt a sharp pain in my shoulder. The impact or the shock knocked me to the ground. I was, I believe, unconscious for several minutes. I lost an amount of blood, but the loss was not serious."

"Damn." I swallowed hard. "Who the hell would want to kill you, Muntaka?"

"Who can say? Still, it is possible that it is someone who does not wish that I pursue the stolen manuscript."

"And you want *me* to go with you? Look, Muntaka, whoever shot at you the first time is bound to try again."

"Our adversary, whoever it may be, may believe that I am dead. The obituary and my funeral may divert his attention. Nevertheless, my chances of staying alive will be much improved if you are with me."

"And mine will be much improved if I'm not." Muntaka raised

his eyebrows expectantly. "But you haven't given me much choice." I shrugged my shoulders and then took a deep breath and let it out slowly.

Muntaka put his arm around my shoulders as we walked away from the hut. "We shall need a day to get organized. I shall arrange for you to stay at the government rest house. You should get some sleep. We may have a long journey ahead of us."

"You're not being very optimistic, Muntaka."

"We shall have to be very fortunate to intercept the parchments before they leave this region."

"Then why waste our time? Let's head for Morocco, make a few inquiries, sit in a pool, and wait for them."

"We cannot be sure of the destination of the manuscript. Or of the motives of our adversary. Moreover, it is very important that we move quietly, and with caution. The people from the area south of the Benue have a saying. You would do well to remember it."

"What's that, Muntaka?"

Muntaka raised his right hand, palm down, to the front of his chest and moved his fingers and hand slowly to the right, in a stalking motion. Then he clenched his fist. "Softly, softly . . . catch the monkey."

I SAW the Greek for the first time the following morning at the Zaria rest house. I noticed him because he and his companion were the only two non-Africans in the dining room. They were sitting at a corner table. The Greek wore a dark green suit that looked too hot for the sub-Saharan climate, and thick-framed tinted glasses the color of dead leaves. His bushy hair was a shade darker than his khaki complexion. He studied me for a moment as I walked in, and then returned to his conversation with his companion. I had the impression that they were talking about me, but I couldn't be sure.

I saw him for the second time late that afternoon in the market of the old town. Muntaka's driver, Ibrahim, needed the day to make a final check of the Land-Rover and Muntaka had to put a few affairs in order. I spent the morning and afternoon walking, to reacquaint myself with Zaria. By four-thirty I had reached the meat and poultry market in the walled part of the city. More than a dozen vultures were lined up along the corrugated tin roof that protected chickens, hanging by their necks, and slabs of meat from the sun. The raw slabs were covered with flies, and five or six cats were licking the blood that dripped down from the lynched chickens. Behind one of the long meat-covered tables a thin young man, wearing a pair of blue shorts and nothing else, slept, his head resting on a large piece of beef.

Two women broke into argument just behind me and I turned to see what was going on. As I did, I saw the Greek. He was alone and, as he saw me, he turned and began bargaining with an old lady over some pieces of dried fish. I wondered if he was staying at the rest house and, if so, what he wanted with dried fish.

Fifteen minutes later I was at the inner circle of a small group of men, women, and children crowded around a young man of twenty or so. He was sitting on a crate and was wearing khaki shorts, a dusty bowler hat, and a mischievous smile. He was performing magic tricks on the small wooden table in front of him. Each trick was accompanied by a line of patter that, in Hausa, sounded more intriguing than it probably would have in English.

"Here we have a common box of matches. But what good are matches when there is nothing to cook? It is better to have a box of something to eat. One must only say the magic words, 'haba, babba, ba ka ba ni babba taba ba,' and the box of matches is converted into a box of peanuts." The boy gestured quickly and the matches did, indeed, become peanuts.

"Oos" and "Ohs" came from the audience.

"Here we have a simple, flat balsa stick, given to me by an old man from the Orient, farther away than Yola. You will notice that there are three holes in the stick. Here, I shall place this large wooden match (one of the few that I have that has not become a peanut) in the third hole from the end nearest you. I say the magic phrase, 'Haba, babba, ba ka ba ni babba taba ba,' and you shall see that the match has jumped to the second hole." And it had.

At the moment that the match jumped from the third hole to the second hole, the Greek's bushy brown hair and tinted glasses appeared across the circle just over the shoulder of a fat woman wrapped in a green and red cloth. As I looked up, the hair and glasses moved out of view behind the fat woman.

More exclamations of mystification from the audience.

"You should not be without these magic tricks to mystify your friends and relatives. Even your head man will not be able to know how you have performed these tricks. Do you have a cousin

22

whom you wish to go back home after staying too long in your house? Tell him you will turn him into a peanut if he does not leave. Only two shillings and these amazing tricks and impressive instructions will be yours. You see this cigarette? I shall light it. It is Senior Service, but one can use any cigarette. I prefer Senior Service."

The Greek's head bobbed back into view and then his hand. The late afternoon sun reflected briefly off a piece of metal near the Greek's shoulder.

"I now take this lighted cigarette and place it, lighted end first, into this handkerchief. And, 'haba, babba,' the cigarette has disappeared and there is no hole in the handkerchief."

In seconds the flash of metal was gone and I saw only the upper half of the Greek's head.

"Can you afford to be without this magic? If you buy this bag of six magic tricks now, I shall give you, at no cost, this amazing money-maker. I take a plain piece of paper and roll it into this small machine. I say the magic words and . . . it has become a five shilling note, more than twice what you pay for the bag of tricks. You recover your money and multiply it once you have mastered the technique."

Then the sun glanced off the metal for the second time and my focus blurred for several seconds. As the flash of reflected sun disappeared, I saw that the Greek had been holding a thirty-five-mm. camera just above the fat woman's shoulder. It was impossible to tell whether he had taken a picture of the young magician or me.

Business became lively. I bought four bags and gave two of them to the two pot-bellied ten-year olds standing next to me. I shoved the other two into the pockets of my bush jacket. The Greek disappeared into the crowd.

That evening I ate alone and then went into the bar for a beer before bed. There was no one else there except the Ibo barman, and I stood at the bar for my first beer. Ten minutes later several men, all Nigerians, had entered and the Ibo was too busy to talk. I took my second beer to a small table in the corner and sat alone. I was deep in thought when I was interrupted.

"Pardon me, would you mind if I joined you?"

I looked up, slightly startled. The man behind the voice was a Lebanese, or a Syrian, about ten years older than me. He was wearing dark blue trousers, a white jersey opened at the neck and leather sandals, without socks.

"Am I coming apart?"

"Pardon?"

"Please sit down."

"I hope you do not mind my coming to your table. I have been alone at the rest house for several days and have had no one to talk with. I hope you do not mind. My name is Georges Daboul."

"Not at all. I'm Jim Stevens. I'm glad for a little conversation myself. Where are you from?"

"I have lived in Nigeria for the last twenty years. I have owned three cold stores here and in Katsina and Sokoto. I am leaving the country tomorrow. Back to Lebanon, where I was born."

"For a holiday?"

"No, I am leaving Nigeria for good. As you may know, many of us who did not take citizenship have been forced to sell our businesses to Nigerians or to take them as partners. I could have taken a partner, but I do not see much future in it. So I sold out completely. I did not do too badly. The government has not been unhelpful in the transfer."

"After twenty years it must be tough for you to leave."

"For me it is not so bad. For others, who have been here longer, or who have no family elsewhere, it is more difficult. Some will stay and bring in the Nigerians. Others will pool their funds and buy larger businesses unaffected by the decree." Daboul stopped talking briefly to order a whiskey and water. "Still, it could be much worse. We have been lucky that we have been able to sell our businesses or take in new partners. For the Greeks in the Congo and the Indians in Uganda, it has been a less fortunate situation. We are, nevertheless, all in the same boat. We

24

are the Jews of Africa. It was only a matter of time that our stay would no longer be welcomed. What brings you to Nigeria, Mr. Stevens?''

''A friend and I are planning to travel through the north. I was here about four years ago and I'm interested to see what changes have taken place.''

The bartender brought Daboul's drink. Daboul wrapped the fingers of both hands around the glass.

''There have been many changes and there have been no changes. How long do you plan to remain in Niger?''

''Niger? I didn't mention Niger.''

Daboul took a swallow of his whiskey and water.

''Oh, I am sorry. You said that you are traveling in the north with a friend. I had assumed that you would be going into Niger. It is not a pleasant place to be right now, I understand. Many people from the desert are coming into Niger to the refugee camps. The rats have followed. There are many deaths. Many of the desert people travel south in search of food. Many arrive at the camps too late.'' Daboul took another drink. ''Death is always an unpleasant thing. Death which comes at the end of one's quest is the most unpleasant of all. The landscape in Niger cannot be an inviting one. You would do well, Mr. Stevens, to save your visit for another time.'' The Lebanese looked at his watch and consumed the rest of his drink. ''I had not realized that it is so late. I am leaving tomorrow. I have much traveling to do and I must rise early. Good luck to you.''

''Good luck to *you*.'' We shook hands and he left. I ordered two more beers, thought about our conversation, and then headed for bed. Whose death had he been talking about?

We had left the rest house at noon. Ibrahim was to take us to the border between Nigeria and Niger. From there I would take over the driving and Ibrahim would head for his home village for an extended leave. We had traveled some twenty-five miles when Muntaka leaned forward and tapped Ibrahim on the shoulder. ''We shall stop at the prison.''

25

About two hundred yards down the road Ibrahim turned onto a bumpy, unpaved track leading toward a large open gate. A half-dozen scrawny chickens scampered out of the way of the big wheels and disappeared into the thick dust raised by the Land-Rover.

The erratic wall surrounding the inner compounds of the Katani prison was made entirely of packed mud and I could see grass growing out of several sections of it. At the far end, in an area shaded by several large palm trees, two gray goats balanced themselves on a section of wall that could not have been more than a foot wide. One nibbled at the stray pieces of grass growing out of the wall and the other stretched his neck out to reach for one of the palm leaves that hung nearby. He was having only limited success.

At the gate were two tall, bow-legged sentries armed only with batons and small machetes. They were dressed in red berets, gray shorts, and truncated blue and red jackets that ended just above the belt line. Their bare black legs, almost violet in the sun, were spotted with orange dust. The two guards snapped to attention as Muntaka and I approached. Just inside the doorway a third guard sat next to a large book containing the names and times of arrival and departure of visitors. The last visitor, I noticed, had been Shehu Ismaeli, the provincial chief of police. I remembered him and would have liked to have seen him, but Mallam Shehu had signed out about twenty minutes earlier. The guard greeted Muntaka with the respectful "May your life be prolonged."

Muntaka said, "I am bringing my friend Mallam Stevens in with me."

"That will be all right but you both must sign the big book."

The signing completed, Muntaka led the way through the courtyard into the central section of the prison. We passed through an unguarded doorway and into a long, dimly-lit corridor. At the beginning of the passageway Muntaka stopped and turned toward me. His face was grim. "I am afraid, Mallam Stevens, that we have a visit to make that is unlikely to be pleasant. I would like you to pay close attention to what you see. You should attempt to record in your mind as much as possible."

"Who're we seeing?"

"I do not know."

"What do you mean you don't know?"

"Come, I shall show you what I mean." Muntaka turned and once again led the way. Halfway along the corridor he stopped and said, "You have a handkerchief?"

"Yes."

"You may wish to keep it at the ready."

Muntaka turned the knob of a door to our right. The room was marked "Mortuary."

The stench of decaying flesh hit me before I was into the room. I gagged and swallowed, trying to push saliva to the back of my nostrils. Then I began to breathe through my mouth. I started to gag again, found my handkerchief, and put it to my face.

In the far corner of the long, narrow room was a man sitting at a small plain wooden table. He was dipping bread into a bowl of stew. He raised his eyes as we entered, wiped his mouth on a sleeve, and stood up. Smiling, he came toward us, his arms out-stretched.

"Alhaji Muntaka. It is good to see you." He clasped Muntaka by both shoulders and Muntaka clasped him in return. I wondered what it was that would have brought Muntaka to the prison morgue in the past. I wondered what brought him here now.

"Mallam Danjiki, permit me to introduce my colleague Mallam Stevens."

We shook hands. Mallam Danjiki was tall and thin, some six inches taller than Muntaka and me. His face was narrow and there were thick blue tribal scars at the crest of each cheekbone. His eyes and smile were bright, not at all what one would expect from a prison mortuary attendant. He wore a khaki robe with a small white insignia in Arabic script. A bit of stew clung to the corner of his mouth but after a few minutes he captured it with his

27

tongue. He sucked air through his teeth, first the left side, then the right, to catch other remnants of his lunch.

"Well, Alhaji Muntaka, you are here to see the body of the Levantine. Major Muhamed informed me that you would be here. He did not say what day. The body arrived on Sunday. It is over here."

Mallam Danjiki moved to the left side of the room. The wall contained several large drawers and Danjiki pulled the large metal handle of one. The drawer, fully extended, was about six and a half feet long. The Levantine was about a foot and a half shorter. A block of dry ice had been placed between his feet and the end of the drawer. He was fat, and the sides of his body touched the sides of the drawer. Folds of wrinkled flesh hung from the stomach. The body was completely hairless.

The opening of the drawer containing the Levantine contributed a unique odor to the mortuary. The nakedness of the body surprised me and it was only as I saw it that I realized how hot it was in the room. My shirt was drenched with sweat. I wondered how a body—dead or alive—could last in here for more than a few hours.

Muntaka said, "Could we see his belongings?"

"We have saved everything but the clothing. The clothing has been burned. It was suspected at first that it was cholera that he had contracted in Niger. But it now appears to be something else. The medical technician is continuing tests."

At the mention of cholera I stepped back two paces. "Niger?" I asked. "What are you doing with a body from Niger?"

"The Levantine is a citizen of Nigeria. He holds a Nigerian passport."

Danjiki went behind the table at which he had been eating and brought out a small, gray metal box. It was unlocked and the clasp was broken. Muntaka took it and emptied its contents on the table.

There were only four items: a black, continental wallet, a Nigerian passport, a set of rosary beads with a small plastic cross, and a small, white envelope.

28

"That is all there was?" Muntaka asked.

"There was undoubtedly more but one cannot expect anything of value to survive the passage from Dakoro to the Katani prison. There is a ten shilling note in the wallet. The wallet is seldom taken, only the money. The ten shillings are left to avoid the obvious. If the wallet were taken, questions would be asked. The rest of the Levantine's money is undoubtedly in the hands of a representative from the police or military of Niger. It is quite unlikely that the money remained intact to the border. They are vultures. The beads, as you will observe, are those of a Christian, not one of Moslem faith. They would be shunned by a Moslem and would not be stolen by a Christian for fear, I expect, of divine retribution. You will note from the passport that the Levantine wore eyeglasses. There were no eyeglasses with the body.

"I am surprised that the shoes remained," Mallam Danjiki continued. "They are quite new and handsome." Mallam Danjiki raised the bottom of his robe. "I have taken them for myself, since the Levantine will not need them. They are quite close to my size. You will note that the Levantine's feet are surprisingly long and narrow for a man of his stature."

Muntaka picked up the passport. He looked at the first two pages for several minutes and then leafed through the others. He handed the passport to me. The Levantine's name was Joseph Simhani. The passport had been issued in 1969 and was due to lapse in two months. The photo showed Simhani wearing wire-framed glasses and a small moustache. He no longer had the moustache. I wondered whether he had shaved it off or whether it had disappeared, along with the rest of his body hair, as a result of the disease he contracted in Niger. He had been born in 1939. The man in the coffin looked twenty years older.

Muntaka was examining the contents of the envelope.

"What do you have there, Muntaka?"

"It does not appear to be anything of importance. It is, apparently, two pages of a book. The printing is in a foreign language. You recognize it?" Muntaka handed the pieces of paper to me. One was jagged on two adjoining sides, as if it had been torn

29

carelessly from a book. It was the bottom half of a page; the other side was blank. The second page was intact. It contained one paragraph and was apparently the last page of a chapter.

"It's written in Latin, Muntaka."

"You can read it?"

"Afric et vitae initium et educationis meae bonam partem debeo. . ."

"I mean, can you translate the Latin?"

I looked at the text briefly. "Africa and life. . . ." Damn. "No." Four years of Latin down the drain.

"A page from the Christian Bible, no doubt," Muntaka said. "Books deserve more care than that. It would be a blasphemy to treat the Koran in such a manner." Muntaka turned to Mallam Danjiki. "Do you mind if we take the pieces of paper with us?"

"I suppose that there can be no objection. I was told by Major Muhamed to give you full cooperation."

Muntaka handed the envelope to me. I put the torn pages into the envelope and shoved it into my pocket. As I did, Muntaka said to me, "Do you notice anything peculiar about the passport?"

"Simhani no longer has a moustache and the body in the vault looks a good deal older than the man in the photo. Jesus, Muntaka, it must be ninety degrees in here."

"But, do you have any doubt about Mallam Simhani and this man being the same?"

"No. I suppose not. Everything else matches; the height listed here seems about right. Five feet one inch. The disease, whatever it was, must have aged him." My body felt like it was melting.

"You notice nothing else?"

"Simhani expired two months before his passport."

"You see nothing strange in the immigration stamps?"

I leafed through the passport again. Six pages were marked. Two pages bore the exit stamp from the airport at Lagos in 1970, stamps for Lebanon, and a return stamp for Nigeria. Two other pages showed a Nigerian exit stamp dated 1971, stamps for the Central African Republic, and a return stamp for Nigeria. One page showed a Central African Republic visa. The fifth page showed a trip six months earlier to Italy and exit and entrance stamps for Nigeria. A sixth page showed an exit stamp for Niger, with the hand-written notation, "décés," and an entrance stamp for the Nigeria border station, with the notation, "deceased."

"You notice nothing strange, Mallam Stevens?"

"He's done a bit of traveling."

"What is to be noted, Mallam Stevens, is that there are no immigration stamps for Mallam Simhani's voyage northward *into* Niger."

I leafed through the passport again. "You're right. What's it mean?"

"It means, Mallam Stevens, that Mallam Simhani smuggled himself—and perhaps items of value—across the border. The questions are 'Why?' and 'What?' "

A S we drove north Muntaka said, "We shall spend two nights in Katsina. The ministry has made arrangements for you, Mallam Stevens, to remain in the rest house there. You will remember that it is a pleasant place and the food is good. I shall stay with my brother-in-law in the old city. Ibrahim will outfit the Land-Rover tomorrow. The next day we shall visit the commissioner to pay our respects and to obtain papers to assist us in crossing the border. It will be faster than waiting for visas from Lagos. The bureaucracy there is unbelievable. If we need visas for the countries to the north, the consulate in Maradi will act quickly. We shall make a brief stop in Daura before heading for the border. Ibrahim will leave us in Katsina. You, Mallam Stevens, shall then show me whether you have forgotten how to drive on African roads."

"Katsina's your original home, isn't it, Muntaka?"

"I was born here and my father was born here. My grandfather was born in Rio Muni. His father came from what is now called Mali, in the area just west of Timbuktu. My grandfather came north to Katsina in 1872. He married a Fulani girl and my father was born shortly thereafter. My birth came later."

"When was that?"

"Before you were born."

I assumed that Muntaka was twenty or twenty-five years older than I, but I really didn't know. Muntaka had an intense sense of privacy and enjoyed cloaking himself in a subtle air of mystery. I first encountered this side of him as we traveled to Sokoto in the northwest corner of the country to investigate a number of rumors in connection with the Central Hotel murder. Muntaka had asked his driver to stop en route at a small village on the edge of Sokoto Province. After the car had pulled up in front of a mud compound, Muntaka alighted, went to the trunk, and took out a large burlap sack which he carried into the compound. He emerged some twenty minutes later. When I asked casually who lived there and what was in the sack, Muntaka replied, "Do not ask me about such things in Dauchi and I shall not ask you such things in New York."

The mystery surrounding Muntaka was reinforced by his reputation for purportedly performing a series of secret "jobs" for the premier, the sultan of Sokoto, and several emirs. It was rumored, for example, that in 1940, when the emir of Wurno died and certain factions threatened to prevent the emir's son from coming from his school in Cairo to be installed as the twelfth emir, Muntaka was asked to serve as a decoy. He reportedly flew to Cairo, disguised himself as the emir's son, and diverted opposition forces while the real son flew to Wurno and was installed. The story had Muntaka concluding his job by evading pursuers in the maze of intricate passageways that make up the vast Wurno market. I tended to disbelieve most of the story. When I asked Muntaka about it, Muntaka would simply smile and say, "There are too many stories."

We arrived at the rest house about seven that evening. It had been a tiring trip, even though Ibrahim had done all of the driving. It had been hot and dusty and by body ached. Muntaka and Ibrahim dropped me in front of the main building of the rest house, with my one bag, and they left, to return in two days when Ibrahim would turn over the Land-Rover to me. I went into the rest house office.

"My name is James Stevens. I have reservations."

"Looking at you, so do I. You must have had a long trip." The rest house manager—an efficient-looking, middle-aged woman probably from the area around Jos—checked the book. "Oh, yes, Mr. Stevens, we received the cable this afternoon. Sometimes cables move more slowly than letters—or travelers. We have a place for you in number six. I'm afraid you will have to share it since we are overbooked tonight. I have told the Englishman, Mr. Worten, to expect you. I hope you don't mind."

I took the chalet key and walked with my bag over to number six chalet. Worten was sitting in a wicker chair on the small screened-in porch. He got up and came forward.

"Worten here. You must be Stevens. Understand we're shacking up together here tonight. You'll have the place to yourself tomorrow. I'll be gone before you're awake. Not usually this crowded this time of year. Or never used to be. Something of a nuisance if we both need a bath. *You* certainly do. Not much hot water in the tank. Never mind, though, I'm glad for the company. What line of work are you in, Stevens?"

I set down my bag. "I'm a lawyer—from New York City. What about you?"

"Schoolbook salesman. Here, sit down." I took the other dusty, wicker chair. "Singleton's *Geography of West Africa.* That sort of thing. Sell to the secondary schools and teachers' training colleges. Actually, most of the buying is done in Kaduna by the Education Ministry. Really up here to see my old stamping grounds."

"You've spent some time here before?"

Worten smiled. "I was D. O. up here for eight years before I was transferred to Yola. Late forties, early fifties." He was quiet for about thirty seconds. His eyes were half-closed and his thoughts were obviously carrying him back a couple of decades. He was a big man—over six feet—thinning gray hair, rusty complexion, somewhere in his early sixties. As a young district officer he had probably made quite an impression. I tried to imagine him in his white shorts and white bush shirt directing the building of a small dam, or in white trousers and red cutaway jacket with a sword at his side on ceremonial occasions. It was another time. I could sense the sadness that Worten must have felt for those lost days.

Suddenly Worten rose. "I say, how would you like to take a small walk with me while it's still bright?"

"Sure. Where are we going?"

"The D. O.'s house is—or I should say was—a couple hundred yards behind the rest house area. I'd rather like to take a look at what's left of it."

We walked down to the main rest house building where the dining room, office, and small bar were located and took a well-beaten path around the building and through the compounds containing the living quarters of the rest house staff. We walked about a hundred and fifty yards through a grassy area. A young boy of about twelve, a smile on his face, walked by us. He was carrying a large dead rat by the tail.

Worten, who was several yards ahead of me, stopped. "Well, here it is."

"Here's what?" I couldn't see anything except a field of grass.

"Over here. My bathtub."

And so it was. A large tub, probably six and a half feet long, half-hidden by grass, covered with mud, and partially filled with dirt, grass, and weeds.

"Took many a bath here. My houseboy carried hot water from the storage tank, which was over there, at the beginning. Later we put the tank on the roof and piped it down. Heated by the sun, of course. Had this tub sent down from Bristol. Took two years to get it, but it was worth it. Beats those canvas tubs, particularly if you're my size.

"Bedroom was over there," he said, pointing. "Kitchen was there. Kept a horse over there. Seems like a long time ago now. Country's come a long way. I don't mind saying I was sorry to leave. Didn't think these chaps would do it on their own. But they haven't done badly. Wonder if the little bridge we built down at the Musawa River crossing is still there? Should be. We used the best timber. Brought it all the way up from Makurdi. Didn't know much about bridges at the start. Colonial Office sent out a little book, *How to Build Bridges in the Tropics,* or some such thing. Did a damn good job, actually. Only took three months. A damn good job. I don't get a chance to build many bridges now." Worten smiled. "People were awfully nice up here.

"Very little trouble when I was D. O. Oh, we had our problems. A few machete killings. Women trouble. But nothing like down in Tiv land. They killed two A. D. O.s there. Neither one over twenty-two. Both just out of Cambridge. Made us all a little edgy, that. All the D. O.s and A. D. O.s got handguns after the killings. I became rather good. Won top prize at the club tournament for three years running. Not much good with a handgun anymore. Not much . . ."

Worten stopped himself as if he had gotten into a subject he hadn't intended to talk about. Our eyes met briefly and then he said, "Those were rather heady days."

"Where were you before coming to Katsina?"

"Gusau, Gombe, Birnin Gwari, Dutsin Mai. Out here twenty-three years altogether. Gombe was my first post. Twenty-one, just out of university, out to save the continent. Did most of my touring on horseback. I was over in Gombe last week. Not much changed, actually. No one there I knew, of course. The old village head died eight years ago. Nice old fellow. Certainly was damn good to me." Worten paused and looked out across the field. "Say, I think I'll just poke around here a while longer. No need for you to stay unless you care to. You might want to get first crack at the hot water before dinner."

I wandered back slowly, wondering what it must have been like to tour the bush on horseback, build bridges, wait two years for a six-foot-six bathtub, be D. O., and then become a schoolbook salesman.

When I got back to the rest house I took a long shower. I was drying my hair as I left the bathroom and I walked straight into the corner of Worten's suitcase, which he had placed on a small wooden stand meant for something else. The suitcase fell to the side, spilling the contents on the floor. Two of the items were a short-barreled revolver and a small box of thirty-eight-caliber bullets. The possession of handguns is illegal in Nigeria, as in many African countries, and I wondered how Worten had managed to get the gun and bullets through customs. Maybe he had borrowed them from a friend in Nigeria and planned on some target shooting. It would have been crazy to try to bring a gun in through the airport. Three paperback novels had fallen out of the suitcase and I noticed two others next to Worten's bed. There was no other bag in the room except mine and it occurred to me that I didn't see any schoolbooks.

Worten and I ate dinner together. It was not bad but it was the same dinner the rest house had been serving every Tuesday night since it was built in the 1930s—steak and kidney pie, boiled potatoes, and vanilla custard. It didn't matter that now most of the rest house guests were African administrative officers on tour. Old habits die hard. Besides, many of the Africans had studied in England—either at university or for government short courses— and actually learned to *like* steak and kidney pie, boiled potatoes, and custard.

After dinner we moved into the small bar presided over by an Ibo bartender of about twenty-five. There were five small tables in the room and three stools at the bar. A BOAC calendar hung in the middle of one wall. A Kingsway calendar hung behind the bar. One showed March. One showed April. It was May. Oilcloth curtains hung on the two windows. Overhead a ceiling fan turned slowly.

There were three other persons in the room besides Worten, me, and the bartender. In one corner, sitting by himself, was a large Hausa man who looked almost the size of Worten. He wore a white robe with blue trim and a matching cap. His dark face was serious. I hadn't seen him in the dining room. At another table were two Europeans. One, solid and ruddy from years of drinking in the tropics, wore wide khaki shorts that revealed thick, muscular thighs and blue boxer underwear. His white shirt was open at the neck. The other, tall and slender, wore pressed slacks and a white shirt and tie. I ordered two bottles of Star beer for Worten and me and carried them to one of the tables where Worten had taken a seat.

"How long do you plan to remain in Katsina?" Worten asked as I sat down.

"Just 'til Wednesday. A friend and I are planning a small trip into Niger for a couple of days. I've never been over into the French territory."

"Not much to see up there. Mostly desert. Maradi isn't much of a town—or wasn't fifteen years ago. Probably get a good dinner and good wine, though. You've got to give the froggies credit for that. Border was closed for a few days last month, you know. Two men killed on the Niger side just inside the border."

"I hadn't heard about that. What was the trouble?"

"Don't know exactly. Just the odd rumor. Something about an Arabic manuscript."

MUNTAKA and Ibrahim were at the front of my chalet, with the Land-Rover, at seven o'clock the next morning. When Muntaka knocked on the door it took me a few moments to get my bearings. My last memory was of riding through the desert on camelback and coming to a small oasis consisting of a few palm trees, a pool of water, and one tent. As I dismounted, one of the senior partners of my firm, dressed in a long black robe, a turban around his head, emerged from the tent. He asked me for the Kingsley deposition in the Twentieth Century case. I went to the saddlebags on the camel and pulled out a sheath of papers and handed them to him. He handed them back. They were all in Arabic.

I put on my pants and opened the door. "Christ, Muntaka, what are you doing here so early? I thought you weren't coming until nine."

"Ibrahim has found a person driving to his home. The lorry leaves at eight-thirty, so we must make the transfer now. You can return to bed after we finish. As it happens, we shall not be able to leave until the day after tomorrow. Something has arisen that demands my attention. Ibrahim will show you what you need to know about the car and where things are packed. If you are fully awake by then, you and I shall have breakfast together."

I put on a shirt and shoes and went outside with Muntaka.

The Land-Rover was in good shape. The tires looked relatively new and there was a good spare. There were enough tools to build the car from scratch, if I had had any idea about how to do it, and we had enough canned goods to last us a long time. There were several large containers of water. We also had cots, a canvas tub, a water filter, several hats, a large supply of kola nuts, and four cases of beer. With all this, only half of the back of the Land-Rover was filled. One person could sleep in the back, if necessary.

"Muntaka, you have enough kola nuts here to last you a lifetime. What the hell are you going to do with all of them?"

"What I do not consume, I shall offer to acquaintances."

"Don't you think you better cool it with kola nuts, Muntaka? There aren't likely to be too many seduceable young women between here and the Mediterranean."

"I shall leave the younger women to you, Mallam Stevens. Your tastes still reflect the callowness of youth. I prefer women of maturity. In any case, it has not been scientifically proven that the kola nut is a sexual stimulant."

"The point is that you *think* it's a stimulant. It comes to the same thing."

"A dozen or so a day will not be cause for alarm, Mallam Stevens."

"If your reputation precedes you, Muntaka, it's going to be plenty cause for alarm. The whorehouses had better be well stocked. They're going to have a tough time keeping up with your nuts."

"Humorous, Mallam Stevens. Humorous."

The Land-Rover was beautifully fitted out. Ibrahim was a professional and he had not missed a thing. He gave me a few last-minute instructions and then said goodbye. Muntaka gave Ibrahim several bills and embraced him.

There were a few people in the dining room of the rest house,

40

and the aroma of kippers filled the air as we entered. Another remnant of colonial days.

"Our first stop Friday," Muntaka said, "will be the provincial commissioner's office. It will be necessary for him to issue us papers so that we may cross the border. It should not take long. Then we shall proceed to Daura for a brief stop."

"Why Daura?"

"I shall inform you when we arrive there. We shall cross the border just north of Daura. Our first stop in Niger will be near Maradi, where we must make some inquiries. Perhaps our quest will end there. I suspect not. But what we learn there may shorten our journey. Perhaps you should return to bed after we finish our meal and sleep through to Friday morning. We shall leave at daybreak to avoid the heat."

As Muntaka left me in front of the dining room, the chalet boy appeared. "Sir, the manager asks if you would be willing to move to chalet number four which has one bed. Your chalet is needed for two men coming in this evening."

I said that I wouldn't mind moving. We walked to number six and I collected my belongings with the help of the boy. We walked to number four together. As he set my bag down on the bed, the chalet boy said, "There is, sir, only one problem with this chalet."

"What's that?"

"There is a snake living in the W. C."

"What?"

"There is a snake which is now making his home in the pipe connected to the toilet."

"What do you mean?"

"There is a snake, sir. It was reported by the previous occupant."

"Well, how the hell am I supposed to use the toilet?"

"Very carefully, sir."

"I can't stay here with a damn snake loose." I reached for my suitcase. "Get me back to number six."

41

"I cannot, sir. The manager will not permit it. But do not worry. Audu has gone to the market to find the snake man."

"Snake man?"

"The man who gets snakes and spiders out of roofs, and drain-pipes, and W. C.s. It is quite common, sir."

I sat on the front steps, waited for the snake man, and practiced a few of the magic tricks I had picked up in the market. Then I took a look for the first time at the two books Muntaka had given me back at the funeral hut. The first, *Defeat in Hausaland,* was an account of the nineteenth-century holy war that led to the entrenchment of Islam in northern Nigeria. The second was entitled *The History and Description of Africa and of the Notable Things Therein Described,* by one Leo Africanus. I began to leaf through the Leo Africanus volume so that I could at least tell Muntaka that I had looked at one of the books. I found myself reading more of it than I had intended. The book turned out to be an account of the author's travels from North Africa, across the Sahara, into what is now Nigeria, and along the river Niger. It was almost precisely the route that Muntaka and I would be taking—in reverse—if whoever we were following was going to be as evasive as Muntaka thought.

What drew me into the book was the translator's introduction. The book had been written in Arabic or Italian sometime in the early sixteenth century. John Pory had translated it into English in 1600.

Give me leave (gentle Readers) . . . to call to your remembrance some few particulars, concerning this Geographicall-Historie and John Leo the author thereof.

Who albeit by birth a More, and by religion for many yeeres a Mahumetan: yet if you consider his Parentage, Witte, Education, Learning, Emploiments, Travels, and his conversion to Christianitie; you shall finde him not altogither unfit to undertake such an enterprise; nor unwoorthy to be regarded. . . .

Moreover, as touching his exceeding great Travels, had he not at the first beene a More and a Mahumetan in religion, and most skilfull in the languages and customes of the Arabians and Africans. . . . I marvell much how ever he should have escaped so manie thousands of imminent dangers. And (all the former notwithstanding) I marvell much more, how ever he escaped them. For how many desolate cold mountaines, and huge, drie, and barren deserts passed he? How often was he in hazard to have beene captived, or to have had his throte cut by the prouling Arabians, and wilde Mores? And how hardly manie times escaped he the Lyons greedie mouth, and the devouring iawes of the Crocodile?

I was into Leo's description of Marrakech when a donkey-drawn wagon pulled up to the front of the chalet. A skinny man in short pants and rubber boots held the reins. A houseboy from the rest house sat beside him. On the side of the wagon was a hand-written sign in three languages: Hausa, Arabic, and English. The English read:

> *Baba Dangizo, Viper Sniper.*
> *I grasp your asp or take your snake.*
> *Also spiders. Reasonable rates.*

A hand-drawn snake encircled the sign. At the lower left-hand corner was written, in Hausa:

> *Advice on ridding your house*
> *of vermin, snakes and spiders.*

In English, just below the Hausa, were the words:

> *Drainpipe, eaves and privy counsel.*

Mallam Dangizo came into the chalet with the houseboy and, without a word, headed for the bathroom. He emerged a few moments later and went to his wagon. He returned with a fishing pole, a live mouse, and a net. He went into the bathroom, placed the mouse on a large hook, and submerged the mouse in the toilet. He asked the houseboy for a chair. The boy brought one and Mallam Dangizo sat down. He said to us in Hausa, "This will take some time. You should both leave."

The houseboy left the chalet and I sat on the front steps wondering whether Leo, who had escaped "so manie thousands of imminent dangers," had ever encountered snakes. He had. In Fez he saw people "who carrie dauncing apes up and downe, and have their neckes and armes all entwined with crawling snakes."

And among the Atlas Berbers in the mountains of Ziz, south of Fez

> there happeneth a certaine strange and incredible matter, for there are serpents so familiar with men, that at dinnertime they will come like dogs & cats and gather up the crums under the table, neither will they hurt any body, unless they be offered some iniurie. [The snakes] have been known to suck the breasts of women whilst asleep, and retire without offering any further iniurie.

Swell.

I went back to practicing the magic tricks.

An hour later, Mallam Dangizo appeared on the porch. In his net was a snake about twenty-four inches long, with a bulge halfway down its gullet. The fish line was still in the snake's mouth. Mallam Dangizo spoke to me in Hausa. "That will be fifteen shillings."

"Don't look at me," I said. "See the manager. Are you sure there aren't more snakes in there?"

"The pipe is very narrow. It is not likely. If you see another, you may send the houseboy to fetch me. The fee for the second trip is only one-half. Fifteen shillings for the first trip. You must pay it."

"I'm not paying you anything. I just moved into this chalet. The snake is the responsibility of the management."

"The custom is fifteen shillings from the occupant, fifteen shil-

44

lings from the management. It is worth much more. Snakes can be very dangerous. Should I put the snake back?"

"Christ, no." I reached for my wallet. I handed him fifteen shillings.

Mallam Dangizo folded the two bills neatly in half and placed them carefully into a long leather purse that hung from his belt. He hitched up his pants. The fish pole and net were held between his upper left arm and his body. The snake, which I had thought was dead, began to wriggle at the end of the line.

"The mouse," I asked, "is it dead?"

"Who knows?" Mallam Dangizo smiled, moved the fishing pole to his right hand and the net to his left, and headed for the manager's office.

Supper was liver and boiled potatoes. I was still hungry when I finished and decided on a couple of beers before bed. Sitting at the bar was a big, burly man in white shorts and a blue shirt. He was about thirty-five. His hair was brown, but very much lightened by the sun. I sat next to him and ordered a bottle of Star.

"Good evening."

"Good evening." The Irish accent surprised me.

"I'm Jim Stevens. I'm staying at the rest house."

"And I'm Cornelius Nunn, of the White Fathers. You can call me Neil."

"You're a missionary?" I started on the peanuts.

"Yes. I've been out here ten years. Too bloody many. The sun is beginning to get to me. I need a nice quiet parish in the mountains, or a mansion by the sea." He took a long swallow of his Guinness.

"I thought you were probably with Public Works. You look like you spend a lot of time outdoors."

"I might as well be with the bloody DPW. I've spent the last six months supervising the building of our new missionary school. I've done half the roof myself and painted most of the dining hall. We're trying to save on expenses. I wish they'd given a course in

45

roofing at the seminary. Do you know anything about roofing?"

"My grandfather had shingles when I was a boy."

Nunn stared at me for a moment and then laughed. "Not much bloody help. Well, anyway, it's not what I had in mind when I entered the priesthood. I don't seem to be saving too many souls. Things would be different if I could lay my hands on ten thousand pounds. You with a company out here?"

"No, I'm just here for a short visit. I'm seeing some old friends and doing a bit of looking around."

"Well, I hope you enjoy your visit. Stay away from the whores down by the Sabin Gari, though. Only God knows what diseases they have waiting for your pecker. Take a brief vow of celibacy. But not for too long. One shouldn't be celibate or poor unless one is forced to be."

We talked and drank beer for about an hour. Then he looked at his watch. "Well, I must be going. Have a lot to do before Saturday."

"What's Saturday?"

"A group of us are going up to Niger to see if we can help with the refugees. I understand that things are not very pretty up there."

"Say, Father Nunn . . ."

"Neil."

"Neil. I wonder if you could do me a favor?"

"What's that?"

"How's your Latin?"

"As good as the next priest's."

"I have two half-pages or so of Latin that need translating."

"What is it?"

"I haven't the foggiest. Nothing important. I'm just curious."

"Sure. Can you come by the mission school tomorrow just before noon?"

"I'll be there."

We said goodbye. I finished my beer and two others and headed for the john and bed.

46

I was at the school at eleven forty-five. I needed some exercise and decided not to take the Land-Rover. I borrowed a bicycle from the houseboy at the rest house and had no trouble finding the mission about two miles from the edge of town, on the main road south. The series of one-story buildings that made up the mission and school were white and the reflection of the sun off the buildings was so bright that I had to avert my eyes. As I biked into the dusty courtyard I heard the priest's voice.

"Hello, there. I'll be down in a minute." At the top of a ladder was Father Nunn hammering nails. As he came down he said, "This is the vacation period. Students are all away. Very quiet here." He dropped the hammer at the foot of the ladder and led the way into a small office. He took two Guinness Stouts from a small refrigerator, opened them, and handed one to me. He watched the clock on the wall as the two hands rested on the twelve. Then he said, "Just in time." He took a long swallow. "First beer of the day. I try not to touch the stuff before midday. You have the text you want translated?"

I took the envelope from my pocket, removed the two torn pages, and handed the envelope and pages to him. He looked at the pages briefly. Then he said, "Where did you get these?"

The tone of the question surprised me. There was, I thought, a slight trace of accusation. Or did I imagine it? I wondered if I had made a mistake coming here. What the hell was I worrying about? The guy was a priest. But I decided not to mention the morgue or Simhani. I couldn't mention Simhani without explaining more than I wanted to get into anyway.

"A friend of mine came across them. He's just curious."

The priest's manner became casual again. He sat down behind his desk and I took the chair opposite. He examined the papers for a few minutes and said, "The Latin is twelfth to sixteenth century."

"You recognize it?"

The priest hesitated for a moment and said, "No. No. It's nothing I've seen before."

47

"Would you mind writing out a translation for me? My friend would be grateful."

Father Nunn took a piece of plain white paper from a drawer and began writing. He paused from time to time, longer than I would have thought necessary. He was finished in twenty minutes and handed the translation to me.

The first page read:

Nor am I unaware how much my own credit is questioned when I myself write so homely of Africa, unto which country I stand indebted for the best part of my education. Although in this regard I seek not to excuse myself, but to appeal to the duty of a historiographer, who is to set down the plain truth in all places, and be responsible for the flattering or favoring of any person.

But all men do most adopt that place, where they find least damage and inconvenience. For my own part, when I hear the Africans spoken evil of, I will confirm myself to be a man of Granada; and when I see the nation of Granada disapproved, then I will profess myself to be an African. But herein the Africans shall be more obligated to me; for I will only record their principal and well-known vices, omitting their smaller and more tolerable faults.

The second page read:

in the time of my youth. Likewise I will set down my last voyages to Constantinople, from Constantinople to Egypt, and from there to Italy, in which journey I saw diverse and sundry islands. All which my travels I mean (by God's help) to be returned forth into my own country.

The priest looked at me. "Do you have any idea what this is from?"

"No. Do you?"

Father Nunn fingered the Latin pages, looked at them again, and then moved them to the side of his desk. "They don't seem to be from the church writings, although it's possible that they're from a journal kept by one of the early missionaries." He paused. "Yes, I suppose that's it. If you would like, I'd be glad to hold onto the pages and check with some of the brethren. There's a priest in Kafinfachi who knows more about this business than I do."

"It's not worth the trouble. Anyway, I'll be leaving here tomorrow."

I folded the translation and put it in the pocket of my bush jacket.

"Would you care for another beer? I need one."

"Okay."

The priest opened two more bottles, muttered "cheers," and took a long swallow. I followed suit.

"Who are you visiting here?"

"An old friend of mine. An alkali."

"What's his name? I know quite a few of the judges in this area. Church law is something of a hobby of mine and there are a number of parallels in the Islamic system. I've had a few good talks with the alkalis over warm Fantas."

"Muntaka. Mohamed Murtala Muntaka. He is also known as the Mutawali."

The priest raised his head slightly and lifted his eyebrows. I remembered Muntaka's charade back at the funeral hut too late and I wondered if I had made a mistake.

"Mohamed Muntaka?"

"You know him?"

Father Nunn glanced briefly toward the corner of the room where several dozen newspapers were piled. Then he looked back. "No. No. For a moment I thought it sounded familiar but I was thinking of someone else." The priest took another drink. "Those are common names. He from around here?"

"Originally, I think. Sits in Kano mostly."

"I see. He taking you across the border?"

"Might. We don't really have definite plans."

"Well, maybe I'll see you in Maradi."

"I'll buy you a beer if you do." I looked at my watch. "Well, I

49

guess I'd better get going. I appreciate your taking the time to see me. I suppose you have to get back up on the roof.''

''It's time for my noon nap. Too hot up there now.''

I stood up. I patted the pocket containing the translation and said, ''Thanks for this.''

''No trouble. Glad to help.''

As we shook hands I noticed the torn pages and envelope on the corner of the desk. I retrieved them, placed the torn pages in the envelope and the envelope in my jacket, and said goodbye to Father Cornelius Nunn.

I was about a mile from Father Nunn's school when I heard what I thought was the sound of a gun. I had been pedaling at a leisurely pace along the dirt road, toward the rest house. The sun was too hot for much faster movement and the Guinness Stouts had made me sleepy. The report sounded just as a large lorry bearing a hand-painted sign over the cab that read ''How You Benz'' passed me in the opposite direction. As the truck went by, it kicked up some dirt and small rocks and something ricocheted off my left shoulder. For a moment I thought I had been shot and I nearly lost my balance as I went into a brief skid. I recovered and realized that the sound I had heard must have come from the lorry. But I had thought it had come from behind me.

I looked back to see if there was anything to the rear and I saw a figure on a motorbike about fifteen yards behind. The driver of the motorbike was dressed in black, with what appeared to be a dark knit sailor's cap on his head and a dark cloth wrapped around his nose and mouth, like a grade-B desperado. Neither the black outfit nor the face covering surprised me. Many young Africans, nurtured on too many American cowboy movies, affected pseudo-Western outfits. The motorbikers were among the vanguard. Others wore face masks to protect themselves from the dust and sand. The road ahead was relatively clear, with only an occasional pedestrian, donkey cart, or vegetable stand to the right side. As I began to pick up speed, I felt a slight twinge in my shoulder. I put my right hand diagonally across my chest and massaged my shoulder muscle. As I brought my hand back, I saw that the fingers were covered with blood. I turned my head to the left to look at the shoulder and saw the rip in the jacket, the red splotch, and the motorbike at the same time. The front wheel of the motorbike was about two yards away from my rear wheel.

My shoulder began to feel hot and a sharp pain started shooting into my arm. The combination of the pain, the hot sun, and the beer was making me dizzy. But I had only a mile to go before I reached the rest house and I kept pedaling. Suddenly, I heard the clash of metal against metal and felt the motorbike curve into my rear wheel. I was off the seat of the bike and into the air. In flight I skidded over the back of a donkey and across a wooden table that had been covered with plantain, yams, and red peppers. I landed on a large, fleshy woman, the softness of whose breasts, on which my head landed, probably saved my life.

The woman screamed and I lay on top of her, dazed, like a sunbather on an air mattress. Then I felt myself being turned over and saw the masked motorbiker. He was lifting my jacket off my left shoulder, which was now completely covered with blood. I thought at first that he was going to take a look at my wound. Instead, after he lifted me and took the jacket part way off, he pushed me forcefully onto my left shoulder and began to lift the jacket off my right shoulder. The shock of pain brought me to full consciousness and I knew then that I was being robbed. I brought my right fist up sharply against his face and he rocked backwards. As he did, a pistol fell from inside the waist of his pants. I grabbed it and, without meaning to, fired it above my head. The woman screamed again and the biker jumped to his feet and ran to his scooter. I remember noticing, just before I blacked out, that he had been wearing gloves and that I had only assumed wrongly that he was an African. I also remember wondering whether he was after my bush jacket, my wallet, or something else.

WE left the rest house at seven o'clock the next morning. Our first stop was to be the office of the provincial commissioner, whose headquarters, attached to his home, were just on the outskirts of town, heading north.

On the previous afternoon the rest house manager had washed my wound, which had turned out to be a half-inch gash just to the left of my neck, and had bound it with gauze and adhesive tape. The rear tire of the bicycle had been twisted out of shape and the bell and horn had been torn off, but the frame was only scratched. I gave the houseboy eight pounds to repair the damage.

"I am afraid," Muntaka was saying, as he rolled down his window, "that the American cinema and the weaponry not confiscated after the civil war have combined to make this a more dangerous world to live in. It is a shame that there was no occasion to apprehend the hoodlum. But, of course, we must be grateful that you were not injured more than you were. I have always avoided bicycles myself."

"By the way, Muntaka, I have a translation of the pages found on Simhani's body."

"You did it?"

"No, my Latin's too rusty. But now that I have the translation I see that I probably could have worked it out."

"That always seems the case for languages one does not know well. The language is clear once we have the meaning. Who prepared the translation?"

"A priest I met at the rest house bar. I was on my way back from his mission school when the accident took place."

"You had the pages and translation with you when you were attacked?"

"Yes."

"Did you tell the priest where we had found the pages?"

"No. But he asked about you."

"He connected me with the pages?" There was a faint trace of alarm in Muntaka's voice.

"No. He asked who I was traveling with and I told him. He said that he knew a few alkalis, but not you."

"No harm, I suppose. But the fewer people who know that I am still alive, the better."

As I was about to reach into my pocket for Cornelius Nunn's scribbled translation, Muntaka said, "Stop here." I pulled the Land-Rover up in front of a large white building. A simple wooden sign read "Provincial Commissioner."

The commissioner jumped from his chair as we entered his office. He was a slight, medium-sized man just a bit taller than Muntaka and me and closer to Muntaka's age than mine.

"Alhamdulillahi. Allah be praised. Muntaka, is that you or your ghost? I thought you were dead." The commissioner came around his desk and clasped Muntaka's arm and hand. "You do not look dead. You look no worse than usual. What is the meaning of the obituary I read some days ago? Was that you or someone with your name?"

"You liked it?" Muntaka smiled and raised his eyebrows expectantly.

"What?"

"The obituary."

"What do you mean did I like it? How can one like an obituary?"

"I mean did it read well? Was it interesting?"

The commissioner shrugged. "It was all right. It was somewhat exaggerated. You may know some parts of the *shari'a* but you are not an 'expert.' "

Muntaka looked at me and then back at the commissioner.

"Some think I am. But, no matter. The obituary was a mistake. We have come," Muntaka continued, trying to change the subject, "for documents of transit."

"There seemed to be several mistakes."

"I refer to the fact of my death. Not the contents of the article. Journalists are generally unreliable." Muntaka looked at me. I shrugged. "Never mind. Here, let me introduce you to my dear friend Mallam Stevens."

The commissioner took my hand and arm as he had done with Muntaka. "I am pleased to have you here. Come sit down."

Muntaka and I took chairs at the front of the commissioner's desk. He went behind it and immediately began the ritual of traditional Hausa greetings. Muntaka echoed them.

"Well, Muntaka, it is good to see you again. I am, I must confess, pleased to see that you are still among the living. We have the honor of your presence very infrequently these days and I thought that even those rare visits had come to an end. May I ask the purpose of the obituary? I assume that it is a device for misleading your creditors." The commissioner smiled and winked at me.

"I am on a special mission for the government. It was thought that my demise, however temporary, would assist the enterprise."

"So, the government has asked you to look into the theft of the Jos Museum manuscript?"

Muntaka looked startled. "How did you know that?"

"I did not know it. It is a matter of simple deduction. The theft of the manuscript has attracted some notoriety. It is obviously an item of some value. You have misled a number of important persons into thinking that you are an expert in classical Arabic. The document has undoubtedly been smuggled out of the country. The route is likely to have been north, rather than south. You and

Mallam Stevens are seeking papers to assist in crossing the border into Niger. You have not been unknown to have taken on special assignments for the government in the past. Thus, I conclude that you are pursuing the manuscript and thief. Or thieves.''

"Perhaps, Mallam Wadama, we should retain you as a consultant.''

"He can take my place,'' I said.

"I am too old for playing at such games. So, of course, are you, Muntaka. But it is in your blood. I hope that you do not plan to infect Mallam Stevens with a similar disease.''

"Mallam Stevens and I are taking a short trip into Niger. I assume that you can arrange for permits to assist us in crossing the border.''

"So, we are back to the documents of transit. Here. It will take just a moment.''

The commissioner reached into the top drawer of the large desk and took out two pieces of paper. At the top of each, in large letters, I could make out the words "Laissez Passer.'' He asked me my full name and wrote it on one document and Muntaka's name on the other. He signed both with a large flourishing signature and blotted the signatures with paper glued to the curved underside of a handcarved crocodile. He reached into the top drawer again and after a few moments his hand emerged with two red, star-shaped seals. He affixed one to each document.

"There you are. That should do it.'' He handed both documents to Muntaka, who put them in a pocket inside his robe. "Now that that is taken care of, perhaps we can sit for a while and share some drink.'' He rang a hand bell and one of the old men who had been sitting at the front of the house came in.

"Bring Fanta for my two guests and me. Also some ground nuts for the white man.'' The messenger disappeared into the back of the house and reappeared in a few minutes carrying six bottles of Fanta orange. He opened all six bottles and placed two in front of each of us. A large plate of peanuts was put in front of me and a dish of kola nuts was put in front of Muntaka and the commissioner.

We sat in silence for a few moments and then the commissioner repeated the traditional Hausa greetings. "How is your health? How is the health of your family? How is the health of your kinfolk?" Again silence.

Then the commissioner said, "By the way, Muntaka, what is that bulge next to your arm? You have not taken to wearing a shoulder holster, have you?"

Muntaka put his left hand to his chest. "Oh, that. I am afraid that it is a bullet wound. Nothing serious, but I shall have to wear the bandage for some time."

"So, someone has finally taken a shot at you. This is a dangerous sport you are playing, Muntaka. You carry a gun?"

"No. Of course not. I know nothing of handguns."

"Tell me about the theft from the museum, Muntaka."

"There is little to tell. The manuscript is of some historical value. The parchments are also objects of some beauty. The government hopes that they will be recovered."

"And they have assigned you to the task. This cannot be an ordinary manuscript."

"As I say, it is of some historical value."

"So, you are not telling me more?"

"I intend no offense. It is best, sometimes, for one's own protection, that some things be left unsaid."

The commissioner smiled. "I am curious, but not offended. I have known you too long for that, Muntaka. What has he told you, Mallam Stevens?"

"No more than he's told you, Mallam Wadama."

"As I suspected. Our mutual friend Muntaka prefers to proceed in his own good time, with his own methods. I have learned that it is best to be tolerant. Each man is entitled to develop his own style in life. Still, Muntaka, I hope that you are not leading Mallam Stevens into anything that you cannot handle."

"We are taking a trip northward. There is little to be apprehensive about."

"You have told him of the killings at the border?"

I looked at the commissioner, then Muntaka, and back at the

commissioner. Muntaka and the commissioner were looking at each other. "What killings?" I asked.

The commissioner stood up and went to a small table by the front door. He picked up a newspaper.

"You read Hausa, Mallam Stevens?"

"Some. Muntaka taught me a few years ago."

The commissioner folded the newspaper to a quarter its size and handed it to me. "Here. Read this."

The article referred to two killings at the Nigeria-Niger border. The police thought that it was a matter of "takarda ruzuma."

"What the hell's 'takantar ruzuma,' Muntaka?"

"So, you have lost the Hausa I spent so long finding for you. Perhaps it's with your Latin."

" 'Takantar ruzuma,' " the commissioner said, "means nothing. 'Takantar rakumi' means camel dung. That's in the article?"

I read the line again. "It's 'takarda ruzuma.' "

"Packet of papers, Mallam Stevens, packet of papers."

"The article says that there were two killings at the border and that the police were looking for a packet of papers."

The commissioner smiled. "What do you make of that, Muntaka?"

"I am not familiar with everything that goes on within the police establishment, or at the border."

"You do not think, Muntaka," the commissioner said, "that the police were looking for your manuscript?"

"It is possible."

"One of the deaths was that of a policeman. It takes an item of some importance to cause someone to kill a police officer."

"Before the war I would have agreed with you. But today there are too many weapons at the loose. Many have learned to pull a trigger at the smallest offense."

The commissioner leaned back in his chair. "I do not mean to interfere, Muntaka. You undoubtedly know what you are doing. Nevertheless, permit me to give you some advice. We are about the same age, but on occasion I feel that I am an uncle to you. I

57

sometimes sense that your craving for adventure oftentimes interferes with your judgment. I hope that you are not planning to draw Mallam Stevens into something that you cannot control."

Muntaka shrugged. "Mallam Stevens can take care of himself." Turning toward me, Muntaka said, "You know, of course, that the commissioner is one of the great horsemen of the north. He has many trophies."

The commissioner threw his hands out, shoulder high, in a gesture of resignation. "So, Muntaka, you do not wish to discuss the manuscript. It is unfortunate. Perhaps there is something for you to learn."

"What do you mean?"

"But it is doubtful. There is little that others can tell you."

"You have some information?"

"First, tell me about the manuscript."

"This is a delicate mission, Mallam Wadama. It is best for all of us that the nature of the mission not be discussed."

The commissioner looked hurt. "I have known you for some time, Muntaka. You have come to me for documents of transit. You ask me for information in my possession. You know me as a man of discretion. You do not trust me?"

"It is not that. You know me too well for that to be true."

"So Muntaka, it is the Meshiva manuscript that has been stolen."

Muntaka stiffened and then leaned forward, apprehensively. "You have heard this?"

"No." The commissioner held his right-hand shoulder high, palm out. "Don't worry, Muntaka, it's simply a matter of more deduction. You have confirmed what I suspected. It shall not go beyond this room."

"Meshiva?" I asked. "What's that?"

The provincial commissioner leaned back in his chair again and looked disapprovingly at Muntaka. "So, you have *not* told the young man about the manuscript."

"Enough. Each thing in its own time."

The commissioner sat up and then leaned forward, his hands folded across the desk. "Meshiva, Mallam Stevens, was a thirteenth-century rabbi."

Muntaka looked uncomfortable.

"Rabbi?" My voice was louder than I had intended.

"A religious leader of the Jews."

"I know what a rabbi is. He was in Africa?"

"So, your knowledge of African history is as incomplete as your knowledge of the manuscript." The commissioner stood up and began to lecture. Muntaka and I sat there like schoolchildren. "Between the fifth and thirteenth centuries, a number of Jewish, or Berber-Jewish, empires rose in the western end of the Soudan, along the Niger River. The great Ghana empire, in the area north and east of the country we now call Ghana, was ruled by mixed Jewish-Berber tribes up to the ninth century, when they were overthrown by the black Soniké tribesmen. In the period following the tenth century, the Arabs replaced other Jews and Berbers as rulers in this area. But pockets of Jewish rule persisted. The Arabs were more tolerant of the Jews than of the Christians. When they swept into Morocco, Christianity was wiped out. But the Jewish colonies remained. There are, today, perhaps more than a hundred thousand Jews in Morocco. And, of course, your friend Muntaka and I may possess Jewish blood."

Muntaka grimaced. "It is better not to jest of such things, Mallam Wadama."

"I do not jest, Muntaka. You know as well as I that it is thought in some quarters that the Hausa tribes are descended from the black Berbers and Jews. The idea does not make me uncomfortable, Muntaka. The Jews are a worthy race."

"I do not contest the nobility of that particular race. Or their religion. It is simply that, at my age, I am not prepared to begin to believe that I am other than I have always led myself to believe. We are black Arabs."

I decided to move them off the subject. "What about the rabbi Meshiva? What's he got to do with the manuscript?"

"It is thought by some, Mallam Stevens . . ."

Muntaka interrupted. "You say you have information, Mallam Wadama?"

The commissioner looked at me and shrugged. "All right, Muntaka. Some weeks ago, on the same day as the killing of the policeman at the border, a man of Lebanese—perhaps Syrian, but I think Lebanese—extraction was in my office. He sat in the same chair that you, Mallam Stevens, are in now."

"There must be a number of Lebanese who come through here," Muntaka said.

"This man was looking for a document of transit."

"You gave him one?"

"I could not. He was unknown to me. The Laissez Passer is reserved for individuals I know directly or for those who have been vouched for. Otherwise, it would be meaningless."

"You learned his name?" Muntaka looked toward me and then back at the commissioner.

"I saw his passport but I did not commit his name to memory."

"This is all you have to tell me? It is suggestive, nothing more."

"Yesterday, a second man of Lebanese extraction was here. He asked whether the other man had been here within the last few weeks."

"How did you know he was asking about the other man if you didn't get the first man's name?" I asked.

"The first visitor was of a distinctive stature. The second man described him. He was short. Shorter even than you are, Muntaka. He had a square moustache and wore glasses with a wire frame. His feet seemed too long for his legs. The second man referred to him as 'Simhani.' "

Muntaka leaned forward in his chair.

"Did you get the name of the visitor of yesterday?"

"He did not give it, and I did not ask. This information is useful to you?"

"Can you describe him?"

"Thirty-five, perhaps. Medium height. He spoke Hausa, so he

60

undoubtedly has lived in this area for some time. Pleasant type. Wore shorts and sandals. He was with another man."

"You can describe him?"

"I saw him only through the window. He waited in the car. He had bushy hair and dark glasses. And a suit jacket. I noticed the jacket because it did not seem appropriate for our weather."

"Muntaka," I said, "that sounds like the Greek I saw in Zaria."

"You know him?" the commissioner asked.

Muntaka said only, "Perhaps. Perhaps not."

The commissioner escorted us to the gate, his arm around Muntaka's shoulders. He and Muntaka walked ahead, speaking in Arabic. As we reached the gate, the commissioner turned and shook my hand firmly, as he had before. "Let me give you some advice, young man. Do not let Mallam Muntaka lead you into any trouble." He put his arm around Muntaka again and said, "Muntaka, I have some advice for you also."

"Yes? And what is that?"

"Buy yourself some false teeth. It will improve your appearance." Muntaka smiled a broad, partially toothless smile and we rode off.

WE reached Daura in the late afternoon. The village was surrounded by a massive mud wall, some twenty feet high and crumbling at several points. The entranceway into the town was crowned by an arch, and the mud walls on either side were painted red, brown, and yellow in an intricate design I had seen in a number of small settlements in the north. Minarets appeared at several points along the top of the wall.

We drove directly to the emir's palace where the emir's legal advisor, Abdullahi, greeted Muntaka with considerable warmth. He was not, apparently, a reader of obituaries.

After the traditional exchange of greetings, each repeated three or four times by each man, Abdullahi said, "So, Muntaka, you are here. It is good to see you. This, I assume, is Mallam Stevens." I was startled that he knew my name. We shook hands and then Abdullahi patted me on the back. "It is a great pleasure to have you here, Mallam Stevens. I hope that you will enjoy your stay. My old friend Muntaka has brought you to the most important town in the north. It is here that the Hausa nation was born. But you are tired and hungry. After you have settled into your quarters we shall have a small supper."

Muntaka and I were given separate rooms. The dirt floor of my room was covered with rugs of deep reds and blues, and a small table carried a metal wash basin and pitcher of water. My folding cot and gear were brought in from the Land-Rover. After washing, I joined Muntaka and Abdullahi who were waiting in the anteroom drinking tea. Two bottles of Fanta had been opened for me and a brass bowl of ground nuts and kola nuts sat next to the drinks. As I reached toward the plate, a large cockroach surfaced from the ground nuts, sat for a moment on the edge of the dish, and then scampered across the table. Abdullahi swept the cockroach onto the floor and I heard the sharp crack of its back as Abdullahi stepped on it with his bare foot.

"It is good, Muntaka, that your assignment has brought you to Daura at this time. The emir is not well. I am afraid that we shall not have him with us much longer." Abdullahi paused and then said, "His mind wanders late in the day. You should not expect a lively conversation this evening. But tomorrow he will be more alert. You and I shall surely lose a good friend and companion."

"Alhaji Ahmadu and I have had many fine moments together. Allah is to be thanked for allowing this." Muntaka turned to me. "It is unfortunate, Mallam Stevens, that you did not have the opportunity to meet the emir in his full vigor. He was a remarkable man and an excellent traveling companion."

"You traveled with him, Muntaka?"

"On several occasions." Muntaka turned back to Abdullahi. "How is your work with the emir's court?"

"The court goes well. Last week we heard two cases involving allegations of witchcraft. In one the defendant dispatched an old woman whom he thought was exercising powers against him by shoving five unpeeled bananas up her rectum. To us the belief is irrational. But still it is difficult to condemn a man who is acting rationally according to his traditions."

The room was becoming dark and Abdullahi lit one of the kerosene lamps that sat on the small table. Then he rose, excused himself, and left the room. He returned shortly and announced that dinner was ready. We walked through several small rooms into a large one, about the size of the mortuary at the Katani prison. The only furniture was a long, dark table, placed in the middle of the room, and four armchairs with cathedral backs. They reminded me somewhat of Muntaka's chair in the funeral hut. There was a pewter dish and a glass of orange Fanta on the table at each place. In one of the chairs sat a huge man in a white robe. He wore wire-rimmed glasses that appeared too small for his face. Abdullahi took my arm, led me to the old man, and placed my left hand in the emir's right hand. The emir's skin was cold and there was almost no response, but he said softly, "Ka zo nan tare da Muntaka." *You have come here with Muntaka.* I spoke to him in halting Hausa and wished him prolonged life. I released his hand and, as I did, I realized for the first time that the hand had six fingers. The sixth finger hung loosely from the side.

Muntaka came forward, bent over, and embraced the old man warmly. He spoke close to the emir's ear; I couldn't hear what he was saying. The emir responded briefly, in a half-whisper. Abdullahi sat at one end of the table, opposite the old man, and Muntaka and I sat at the center of the table, facing each other. Four candles in silver holders provided the only light. The servant brought in a bowl of roasted chicken, yams, bread, and a pot of tea.

Abdullahi said, "The emir is now ninety-four. He is quite deaf and suffers from elephantiasis. His legs are swollen and he must be carried. It is not an easy task. He is six feet seven inches tall and still weighs over 250 pounds. He has been a great leader to our people."

No one spoke for the rest of the meal. Yet, as the three men exchanged glances, their thoughts became almost palpable. I found in my travels with Muntaka that the silences we shared with each other and which, together, we shared with others, were often more important than our conversations.

The next morning, after breakfast, we met with the emir again. The overnight transformation was startling.

"Abdullahi tells me, Muntaka, that you and the young man are traveling to the north. So, the time has come to carry on. You are going into Morocco?"

"It seems likely." Muntaka spoke loudly. "We shall, of course, have to proceed cautiously. If the manuscript is sold in Niger, it is possible that it will remain there for a substantial period—six months, perhaps, or a year. But my guess is that it will continue in transit. It depends very much on who now has the documents. If he has patience and private wealth, he may bide his time and remain in Niger. If he is impatient and lacks funds, he will move quickly. A stranger will be taking a risk to remain long in the territories to the immediate north. A thief with a stolen manuscript needs a more cosmopolitan setting."

I wondered how the emir knew about the manuscript.

The emir raised his hand slowly to his right ear and brushed away a fly. His sixth finger hung from the side of his hand like a large wart. "How long has it been, Muntaka, since we made the trip?"

"Thirty-seven years. I was somewhat younger than Mallam Stevens is now."

The emir turned his head slightly in my direction. "Muntaka has told you of our voyage together across the Sahara?"

I looked at Muntaka and then back at the emir. "No."

"What?"

"No." I shouted.

"So, Muntaka is attempting to repeat history but has not told you? You should know, young man, that in 1934 . . ."

Muntaka interjected, "Thirty-three."

"In 1933 we traveled together by camel into Algeria and Morocco. It was while my father was still alive. I became emir three years later. We were on the way to Mecca, for the *haj*. Travel, in that time, was more difficult than today." The emir paused and began coughing violently. Abdullahi put a handkerchief to the emir's mouth. I could see spots of blood on the emir's lower lip. Then he said, "You still have the book, Muntaka?"

"I have given it to Mallam Stevens."

"So, we have a new recruit to the Leo League?"

I looked at Muntaka. "Leo League?"

"Leo the African. It was in Fez that Alhaji Ahmadu came

across the book by Leo Africanus that is now in your possession. It is from that time that he and I became fascinated by the African. The emir has written several learned articles about Leo Africanus."

"I'd like to see them."

Abdullahi said, "There may be copies in the archives." He turned. "Speaking of which, Muntaka, the archives were broken into several weeks ago. We shall have to develop better security."

"Something was taken?"

"There is one box, filled with old maps, that was upset. It is possible that something was removed."

"Anything of value?"

"It is unlikely. Most of what has been left in these boxes are documents from the colonial period, and court records. I hope one day to survey the contents of the boxes but it will take time."

The emir coughed again, and again Abdullahi stood up and held a handkerchief to Alhaji Ahmadu's mouth. Then the emir said, "It no doubt occurs to you, Muntaka, that the entry into the archives may be connected to the theft at Jos."

"It has occurred to me."

Alhaji Ahmadu and Abdullahi clearly knew more about what was going on than I did. "Why do you think that, Muntaka?"

"Perhaps," Muntaka said, "I should let the emir explain."

"You have not told the young man about the significance of the manuscript?"

"I preferred that he hear it from you."

"So, young Leo, you have taken Muntaka on faith."

"I learned long ago that Muntaka puts faith first and facts second."

"The young man is perceptive, Muntaka. It is too bad that he is not a Moslem."

"Perhaps we can convert him."

"Like Pope Leo X converted Leo the African? It would be poetic." The emir's mouth twitched slightly, as if he were trying to smile, but the muscles were too old. It was unlikely that there was much feeling left in his face. For the last five minutes I had watched three flies parade along the top of his left ear.

The emir said, "We have in our archives several pieces of pottery dating from the thirteenth century. Several contain the impressions of Arabic script. Part of the name of the Prophet Mohammed may be seen on one fragment. Our archeologists have discovered what appears to be the remains of a great mosque and a great audience hall only a few kilometers from here. A bronze stamp found behind the mosque suggests that this area may have been the headquarters of a major government administration. And fragments of wall paintings and bronzes suggest that it was also the crossroads of the trans-Saharan caravans." The old man coughed. "Taken together, this evidence suggests that a great city may have existed here some six or seven hundred years ago. The city may have been a transfer point for men and goods traveling between the Niger, the Nile, and the Mediterranean. The script found on some of the fragments is a medieval dialect of Arabic. The pieces of the language which have been found are not yet fully understood."

The emir coughed again and his voice began to fade. He turned to Abdullahi. "Perhaps you should continue for me. My strength is gone."

"The significance of all this," Abdullahi said, "is that it has been thought, until recently, that no great cities existed in this part of the world until this century. If our findings are supported by other discoveries, we shall show the world that there flourished here an intellectual, commercial, and governmental center, important not only to the immediate area but also to the areas as far east as the Nile and as far north as the Mediterranean. Indeed, the black people and Islam may have influenced the civilizations of the Nile and the Mediterranean as much as those civilizations influenced ours. This is important to our nation. A people must know where it has come from. This knowledge helps us to set our course."

Muntaka said, "I have brought you here, Mallam Stevens, because I wanted you to touch the past of the Hausa nation and

Africa. You see, it is the story of thirteenth-century Daura which is recorded in the manuscript. When the manuscript is fully translated, we shall have the key that opens the door to Daura's history. And when that door is opened, we shall know something of Africa's past.''

''Muntaka, why hasn't this been revealed before?''

''As I have said, the manuscript has not been fully translated. What you have just heard is based in part on speculation.''

''Who's been working on the translation?''

''I have. In spare moments. With two assistants.''

''You? Hell, why not get every Arabic scholar in the world working on it?''

''There is one problem, Mallam Stevens.''

''What's that?''

''The emir, Abdullahi, and I have told you but part of the story. What we have not said is that there have been artifacts associated with the medieval Christian church found on the very ground where the mosque is thought to have stood.''

''So?''

Muntaka looked at the emir and Abdullahi. ''It is thought by some that the manuscript tells of the influence of Christianity in this region in the twelfth and thirteenth centuries; that Christianity, not Islam, was the moving force that gave birth and nourishment to the great intellectual and political center that thrived in this area. Such a discovery would, I am afraid, be a case of Allah giving with the right hand and taking with the left.''

''It is extremely doubtful,'' the emir said, ''that the manuscript is as some Christians believe. The church of the Christians did not penetrate westward from the Nile more than halfway to the river Niger by the thirteenth century. The history books cannot be wrong.''

I felt sorry for the old man and I knew that my next question was not going to make him happier. ''Where does the rabbi Meshiva fit into all this, Muntaka?''

Muntaka's face took on the same uncomfortable look that

68

crossed it at the commissioner's office. "Perhaps, Mallam Stevens, we should think about . . ."

The emir raised the trunk of his body and looked toward Abdullahi. "What did the young man say?"

Abdullahi looked toward Muntaka and then back at the emir. "He was asking to see the sword of Bayajida."

"Meshiva," the emir said. "You told him about the rabbi Meshiva, Muntaka?"

"The name came up in conversation with the provincial commissioner."

"It is unthinkable that it was the Jews who were instrumental in bringing Daura to its greatness."

I looked toward Abdullahi. "The commissioner called it the Meshiva manuscript."

"The theory is held, in some quarters, that it was the Jews who controlled this area in the thirteenth century, and that our people are the descendants of the black Berbers and Jews. There is no basis for it. The Arabs replaced the Jews in the western Sudan by the tenth century. The confusion has come because in many writings of the period the Jews and Arabs are referred to indiscriminately as Arabs." Abdullahi's face was grim. "The ruins we have found are of mosques, not Jewish temples."

I had to get it out on the table. "But you're not sure, are you, Muntaka?"

"I am unwilling to run the risk that the documents may fall into the wrong hands—Christian or Jewish."

"You'd suppress the manuscript if it came out wrong?"

"It is, Mallam Stevens, not my decisin. Still, such a revelation would do neither Islam nor Africa any good. You will see now why it is so important that we are successful in our quest."

DUST blew up from the saffron-brown landscape and Muntaka rolled up his window, leaving only two inches for air to penetrate the Land-Rover. "You and I, Mallam Stevens, are not unlike the great explorers of Africa—Barth, Mungo Park, Clapperton, Stanley. They sought to set straight the geography of a great continent. We, in a small way, are seeking to set straight a part of the history of this country and this continent. You will recall that the outside world, until Park's discoveries, believed that the river Niger flowed from east to west. Until the discoveries of Speke and others, it was believed that the great river Nile began in the Mountains of the Moon. Before these discoveries men created the geography their imaginations led them to create. You, of course, recall Pope's gentle couplet with the sword's edge:

> *Geographers in Afric Maps*
> *With Savage Pictures fill their Gaps*
> *And o'er unhabitable Downs*
> *Place Elephants for want of Towns.*

"That was Swift."
"I shall repeat it more slowly."

70

"I mean it was Jonathan Swift who wrote that. Pope wrote, 'To err is human, to forgive divine.' "

"It is unimportant. What is important is that you and I, Mallam Stevens, are embarked on a journey to map an important era in the history of Africa. For centuries men have believed that, before the arrival of the white man, Africa was nothing but savages and elephants and plains and forests. Africa is believed by many to have no meaningful history. Europe is everything. But a great urban center existed in this region in the thirteenth century and you and I must recover the key to its past. We are searching for nothing less than a lost city."

Muntaka smiled for the first time since beginning his discourse. "You, Mallam Stevens, are a twentieth-century Mungo Park and you do not appreciate it. Or a David Livingstone, if you prefer."

"I like it the way I am, Muntaka. If I remember right, Park died while trying to plot the course of the Niger and Livingstone left Africa as a corpse with his heart torn out. All in all, I'd prefer to leave the city lost and get back to the comforts of the Zaria rest house."

"There are some things which are greater than an individual's life," Muntaka said. "In any case, there is no danger."

Muntaka took a kola nut from his robe and chewed it. We drove in silence for several minutes. Then I said, "I'm surprised, Muntaka, that you give credit to the European explorers. I thought you would have considered them only the precursors of colonialism. What about the story you once told me of the African who, on being told that Livingstone had found a great falls, replied, 'I didn't know they were lost.' Park and Stanley and the others can hardly be heroes in Africa."

"You underestimate our ability to appreciate the spirit of adventure. To men like Baker, Clapperton, Park, Livingstone, and Stanley, Africa was the Great Unknown. Their coming here took much courage. They survived dysentery, malaria, suspicious peoples, even wild animals. These were adventurous men with a spirit I admire."

"Oh, come on, Muntaka. Livingstone was a fanatic and Park

71

and Stanley were egomaniacs. *They* had fortitude, but most of their companions didn't. Park took his men up the Niger in the middle of the rains after he had been warned about malaria. Most of them died. Stanley sacrificed some good men on the Congo. Livingstone lost more men in his search for the source of the Nile. Christ, even his wife had to be buried in Africa at an early age. It seems to me, Muntaka, that Livingstone and Stanley put more value on discovery and Park put more value on glory than any of them put on human life. I prefer a little less ego and a little more compassion. I'll take one of the humanitarians—like your Bishop Crowther.''

"It is true that Crowther, despite the fact that he was a Christian, was a great African. He did much for his people. His missionary expedition up the Niger in 1841 is of significance. But I personally prefer the adventurer. You are, of course, right about Park and Livingstone, and perhaps Stanley. They were complex men. No one will ever know what it was that drove David Livingstone to spend forty years of his life searching for the source of a great waterway. He was, as you know, both a missionary and a doctor, but he spent little of his life in either pursuit. He regretted his one notable conversion of an African chief to Christianity almost as soon as he accomplished it. His missionary career was, consequently, of short duration.

"For him, Mallam Stevens, the act of exploration was everything. It was in the search that he found fulfillment. His journals, you know, reveal that he was extremely fond of Stanley, whom he met at Ujiji, in what is now Tanzania, in 1871. He regarded him almost as a son. The reason, I believe, is not that he was "found" by Stanley. Livingstone, like the falls he came upon, was not lost. Rather, it is that Livingstone saw in the younger man the same love of the search that was within himself. For each of these men, it was the exploration, not the finding, that mattered. Livingstone, had he lived, would have taken great pleasure in hearing of Stanley's tracing of the great river Congo.''

"Are you the emir's Stanley, Muntaka?''

Muntaka put his left hand to his face and pulled gently on his nostrils. Then he said, "Perhaps, Mallam Stevens, I am your Livingstone."

We drove in silence for several minutes and then Muntaka began to doze. Thirty minutes later he was awake and talking as if there had been no interruption.

"Of course, Mallam Stevens, the greatest explorer of them all was not a white man. It is rather a man whose blood I share."

"Who's that?"

"It is the man whose book you have been reading, the man who has become known as Leo Africanus. His travels across the Sahara to the middle Niger came some three hundred years before Mungo Park. There was no man to compete with him as an explorer, geographer, and missionary."

"Missionary?"

"In the original sense of the word. He was sent on several important missions in northern Africa by the king of Fez. He was not, of course, a missionary of religion, like Livingstone. In fact, it was the African himself who ended up being converted. To Christianity." Muntaka took a bite of kola nut. Then he said, "To travel across the Sahara in the sixteenth century as he did was a brave act. And, by good fortune, he was not only a man of courage but, like myself, a scholar. He was a master of Italian and Spanish and was a teacher of Arabic. We have much in common."

"I'll ask you for an itemized list later."

"And he not only traveled through northern Africa. He was also an explorer of Arabia and the Upper Nile. He was, you know, captured by Sicilian pirates and presented to the Christian pope, Leo X, as a gift. That is how he acquired his name. It is the sort of adventure that Stanley would have liked. Stanley, you remember, created a story about being kidnapped by rogues in Constantinople, but it was not true. In any case, Leo the African's description of the continent from the Mediterranean to the Niger became a standard reference for three hundred years. This shows that others were fearful of traveling where he had been willing to go. Or else they lacked his scholarly instincts. But the book, I believe, was an afterthought. Like all of these men, it was the adventure that was important. Not the finding."

"And what about you, Muntaka? Are you more interested in the search or in finding the manuscript? I, for one, would like to keep the adventures to a minimum."

Before Muntaka could answer, the Nigerian border station loomed into view through the dust-filled air. The area north of Daura had quickly become little more than sand and scrub brush and the geography took on the timelessness of the desert as Muntaka and I exchanged views about the explorers of Africa. When the border station appeared on the horizon, it surprised me and, for some reason, a chill came over me. I could see Muntaka tense slightly. For both of us the border station seemed to represent a transition of some sort. My own feelings were complicated by the stories of the border killings that Worten had mentioned at the Katsina rest house and which the newspaper at the commissioner's office had reported. What Muntaka was thinking about at that moment I didn't know.

From Daura it had been less than two hours to the border. We saw few trees as we drove north and the sun seemed to become brighter and hotter. In sections where there was little growth the dust seemed to hang in the air. We saw no traffic in either direction except for a black Peugeot with Niger plates which had passed us at high speed heading north. As we approached the small house that served as the border station, we saw a small camel caravan—not more than six or seven camels—coming across.

"Carrying salt into Kano," Muntaka said.

We drove up to the border station and got out. It was very hot.

"May I see your visas and identification papers, please?" The young immigration officer spoke pleasantly. Dressed in blue shorts and gray shirt with epaulets, he maintained a brisk and efficient appearance, despite the battering of the hot sun and the heavy dust-laden air.

"Ah," said Muntaka, "we have something better." Reaching into his robes he pulled out the documents provided to us by the provincial commissioner. "I have here two Laissez Passers signed by the commissioner of Katsina Province." Muntaka handed them over casually. I had expected a slight flourish.

The young man studied them carefully, looking first at the front, with the handsome seal and sprawling signature of Alhaji Wadama, and then at the reverse side, on which nothing was written. He seemed to look longer at the back than at the front. The examination lasted for several minutes. Suddenly he raised his face to the sky, lifted his eyebrows, closed his eyes, and, in a voice of near desperation, said, "Allah be praised. How many times have I told the commissioner that these passes are worthless?" His eyes turned to me as if for an answer but I kept silent, feeling that it was still Allah, and not me, from whom he was seeking a response. I smiled wanly. We had been standing in the sun for four or five minutes by then and the little scenario had taken on an unreal appearance. There was Muntaka, a broad smile on his face. There was the young immigration officer telling us that the Laissez Passers were about as useful as a letter from Lord Lugard. There was the little house in the middle of nowhere and the little road to the north looking as though it led deeper into nowhere. And there was I standing in the hot sun, sweat pouring down my face, chest, groin, and legs, wondering what the hell I was doing there with Muntaka and those two pieces of paper. My head felt as if someone had stuffed it with sand.

Muntaka continued to smile, his orange teeth taking on a purplish cast in the sunlight. "You did not see the signature at the foot of the papers. They are signed by Alhaji Wadama!" Muntaka spoke exultantly.

"I know whose signature this is," the young man exclaimed, a little too loudly. "Of course it is the signature of Alhaji Wadama. Of course it bears the seal of the provincial commissioner. I have seen the signature and seal one hundred times. The signature is real. The seal is real. Only the document is worthless. Immigration is a national concern. A provincial paper means nothing."

Suddenly the scenario changed. Suddenly the young immigration officer was my passport out of this absurd trip with Mallam Muntaka. His words had a certain inevitability to them. It had not been in the cards for me to go tramping across the continent with Muntaka for God knows how long. Screw the manuscript. I had to get back to my law office and with luck I would be there in a week. The young officer looked at me and smiled. He appeared almost ethereal in the bright sunlight. I thought to myself that this was divine intervention. It was at that point that I fainted.

When I awoke I was lying on a metal cot at the rear of the small house. A woman somewhere between the age of thirty and fifty was wiping my forehead with a damp cloth. As my eyes focused I saw the young immigration officer, looking concerned, a police officer of about the same age as the immigration officer, also looking concerned, and in the far corner, Muntaka, drinking a bottle of orange Fanta and smiling.

"Well," said Muntaka, "if you are through resting, we'll be on our way north to Maradi."

Even in my stupor I could see that Muntaka had got the direction wrong. "You mean south to Katsina." My voice, despite my condition, had a slight ring of victory to it.

"No, we are in luck." Muntaka turned to the police officer. "This young officer says he recognizes you as the fellow who taught him all about homicides and assaults and other laws when we were working on the Central Hotel murder. He has convinced Officer Musa here that we are honest fellows and that since you taught Officer Dansanda the law, then perhaps the law should not be applied too strictly in our situation."

I snapped up, knocking over the pan of water held by the woman wiping my face. The police officer, seeing my rapidly improved condition, smiled broadly and saluted. "Lance Corporal Dansanda here. How are you, sir? Do you remember me from the police college?"

I didn't but I said I did. I had taught the law of crimes in my spare time at the police college, when I wasn't working on the Central Hotel case. I probably had taught Dansanda. At the moment I wished I hadn't. I had a headache. "It's good to see you again, corporal," I lied. "What are you doing way up here?"

The policeman smiled at my apparent recognition. "I have just been transferred up here from Bauchi. The corporal who served here before me was killed."

"Killed?" My head began to pound.

"Shot with a pistol. Mallam Musa was on duty at the time." He nodded toward the immigration officer. "We were lucky that Mallam Musa was not slain."

A chill came over my body. I knew what the answer was going to be, but I asked the question anyway. "How did it happen?"

Musa said, "A Peugeot pulled up to the checkpoint and Corporal Ibrahim went to the automobile to make a search. We had received word of the theft of documents from the museum at Jos. The police had been instructed to check all vehicles moving across the border. I was here in the house. I had just woken up and was putting on my shoes. I was about to go to the automobile to examine the driver's papers. As I came to the door, I heard a shot. I saw the corporal's body on the ground and I saw the Peugeot speed away. The boot of the automobile was open. The automobile was lost in the dust. I administered aid to the corporal but it was no use. Then I radioed Kaduna. We have no direct line to the Niger station, even though it is only two miles away. The call must be made to the Kaduna station which radios the message to Maradi. The call is transferred from there to the Niger border station. The automobile was not apprehended."

I looked at Muntaka and shook my head. "There was only one death?"

"So," Mallam Musa said, "you have seen the newspapers. They reported two, but there was only the one death. The other would have been me if I had had my shoes on." Mallam Musa gave a short laugh and then his face turned serious. "I had never seen a man shot before. It is a terrible thing."

Muntaka said, "Yes, it is a sad thing to happen. Were you able to see the driver?"

"No. Well, I saw him from the distance through the window. He was a European. His head did not seem to come far above the steering wheel, but perhaps he had lowered it. I could tell nothing else."

Muntaka turned to Corporal Dansanda. "I want you to be careful. One killing is enough."

"I shall be, sir."

Then Muntaka turned to me and said, "Well, Mallam Stevens, it is our good fortune that Corporal Dansanda recognized you. I shall mention his name to the military governor. And it is good that you are not accustomed to the African sun. Had it not been for you, we would be eating the dust of the road south."

I wondered whether I was going to regret my collapse at the Niger border.

Musa invited us to a lunch of roast chicken, yams, and thick soup, which Muntaka and I washed down with warm Fanta orange. The others drank water. I hoped we weren't consuming the last of their Fanta supply.

After thanking Musa's wife, Muntaka and I walked slowly to the Land-Rover, accompanied by Dansanda and Musa. Musa gave us directions. "The French border station is two miles to the north. About one mile—near the big baobab tree—you should begin driving on the right . . ."

I started up the Land-Rover and we drove off. Muntaka turned to me and said, "Well, see, you have paid your way already. Without you I would not have come this far. And I do not think those two young men are the type to accept a small gift to facilitate passage. We must say a good word to the governor for them when we return." Muntaka took out a small notebook and scribbled a few lines. Whether he was jotting down the names of the two officers or calculating how much he had saved in potential bribes I couldn't tell.

We drove in silence for a few minutes. I was thinking about the death of the police corporal. I expect Muntaka was too, but we didn't discuss it. "How do you say 'hello' in French?" Muntaka asked. I told him. "Ah, yes."

Just ahead I could see the outline of the Niger border house. A large black car, bearing French-style license plates bore down on us. I wasn't sure whether I had passed the imaginary spot where left becomes right, so I pulled over to the far left momentarily and the car, now nearly encased in dust, hurried past us. It was the same black Peugeot that had passed us earlier.

As we pulled up in front of the wooden gate blocking the road in front of the border house, a solid looking African of medium height, dressed in white shorts, white shirt, and a flat, brimmed hat came toward us. A leather belt encircled his waist and angled up to one shoulder. He carried a white holster at his hip, and wore a thin mustache. "Votre passeportes et documentation, s'il vous plait."

Muntaka reached into his robe, apparently forgetting the dialogue carried out two miles down the road just before my collapse in the sun. He brought forth, this time with a broad flourish, the two pieces of paper. "Bonjur," Muntaka proclaimed. "I have here two Laissez Passers from the Honorable Alhaji Wadama, provincial commissioner of the province of Katsina."

I interjected quickly, "Bonjour, Monsieur. Je suis Monsieur Stevens. Cet homme-ci est Monsieur Muntaka. Voila deux Laisser Passers du Chef du province de Katsina." I winced as I waited for the African-Gallic laugh to burst forth from the guard as he took the two pieces of paper.

The officer snapped his heels together, saluted and said, in French, "Fine, everything is in order. I must simply stamp the back of these forms; I shall return in a moment." Muntaka and I smiled at each other. "Well, Muntaka," I said, "what do you think did it—your little flourish, my brilliant French, or the two-pound note stuck between the two documents?"

"What two-pound note? Would I do such a thing? There is a Hausa saying, 'The chief receives greater praise over the hill than in his village.' Besides, the papers are written in English and our

79

friend there would not admit that he could not read it."

In a few minutes the officer was back and he handed the papers to Muntaka. He spoke, this time in Hausa, "Allah ya ba da sa'a." *May God take care of you.*

We drove off. I doubted there was an old Hausa saying about the reputation of chiefs over the hill. I wasn't sure what the hell it meant anyway.

MUNTAKA took a bite of a kola nut and pointed to the landscape with a small sweep of his arm. He said, "The route we are traveling now, Mallam Stevens, is one that was traversed by a number of the great explorers. Park, Clapperton, and Barth all traveled in this area. And, of course, my friend Leo the African."

"I don't understand your fascination with Leo, Muntaka. There's not much known about him, is there?"

"Therein lies the fascination. He was a man of great mystery. We are so much alike in so many ways."

"Yes, Muntaka, you told me. He was a great scholar, explorer, teacher, lawyer, adventurer, and geographer. And I assume that you think he was a great lover."

Muntaka ignored me. His mind was off and running.

"Leo, as you have seen, was quite faithful in his description of the great caravan routes and the people and settlements that he encountered in his travels across the Sahara. Yet history has not treated him well as a geographer."

"How so?"

"First, he described the city of Timbuktu—or Tomboto as you will see it called in his book—as a center of great wealth and learning. He wrote of libraries and scholars, doctors and lawyers.

And yet three centuries later, when Barth and Caillie and Laing, the European explorers, reached Timbuktu, they found little to substantiate what Leo had described. Instead of gold and splendor, Laing wrote that he found only dirt houses and arid plains.

"The answer to *this* mystery is, of course, that at the time that Leo wrote, in the early sixteenth century, Timbuktu *was* a splendid city, a center of learning and commerce—like our city of Daura three centuries earlier. And particularly in comparison with the sixteenth-century cities of Europe, it could have appeared very rich to Leo. Unfortunately, the city fell onto bad times. It had decayed by Laing's time. But it is well established that Timbuktu was, in the sixteenth century, a major crossroads in the movement of gold north from the area we now know as Ghana. No, he was no doubt accurate in his description of Timbuktu. It is the second mystery which is more puzzling and which may never be solved."

"What is that? Why he became a Christian?"

"There is little mystery there. He was captured by Christian corsairs at a young age and given to the Christian leader, Pope Leo X. His life may have been in danger. He would have had little alternative to abandoning his faith. It is difficult for me to accept, but I forgive him for that. The mystery of which I speak is this: He visited Timbuktu and Gao and other settlements along the river Niger and yet he wrote in his geography that the great river rose from a lake in the east and flowed *westward* into the ocean. How could he have made such a mistake? He saw the river. Any man could have seen that it flows eastward. And yet this is the story that he returned with. It was not until 1796, when Mungo Park arrived at Segou, on the Niger's banks, that the world learned of the river's eastward flow. Park had only to look. Why would the African have made such a mistake?"

"Maybe he never made it to the Niger. Maybe halfway across the Sahara he got cold feet—if that's possible in the Sahara—and decided to hole up with a beautiful Berber girl. Maybe his *Description of Africa* was the result of a very fertile imagination and a few good questions put to traders returning from the south."

82

"That may be what *you* would have done, Mallam Stevens, but it was not what Leo did. No. Too much of what he wrote has been confirmed by other sources as accurate. There is no question that he traveled to the river Niger. The only question is why he reported the flow of the river from east to west. He wrote that he went on the river by boat for several hundred miles. It has been argued that, because he was converted by the Christians, he was a man of weak commitment; that he was persuaded by others to change his story to conform to the reports made by respected medieval geographers centuries earlier. I cannot accept this. He was a man of spirit and adventure and a scholar of integrity. He must have had a reason for reporting as he did. It is a puzzle which only waits to be solved by the right man."

"Maybe, Muntaka, he thought that the facts would be more readily accepted if they were leavened with a little fiction. Maybe he thought that people would accept his description of Timbuktu and other places if he confirmed what they had thought all along about the Niger."

"Your idea is not without merit, Mallam Stevens. Who was it that wrote that history books which contain no lies are extremely tedious?"

"Napoleon? Ghengis Khan?"

"It doesn't matter. It doesn't apply in this case. Leo's histories were far from tedious."

"Maybe because they were full of fabrications."

"I've rejected that theory, as I said. You should do likewise."

Muntaka rested his head against the back of his seat and appeared to doze. After ten minutes, he said, "We shall spend the night in the village of Birnin Rabat. It is just south of Maradi. I am friendly with Hamdi, the village head, who also owns the bus service that runs from Maradi into Nigeria. We have had some small business dealings. He has not been unhappy with them. In the morning we shall go into Maradi to make some inquiries. Our quest will begin there."

Birnin Rabat was some ninety kilometers north of the border. It was seven-thirty in the evening when we arrived. We drove to the house of the village head, after asking directions. Hamdi was there. He was dressed in a brown robe with a red sash around his middle. He was tall, with sharp, angular features made more so by a small, perfectly triangulated beard. Muntaka and Hamdi greeted each other profusely. Hamdi was very pleased to see Muntaka. He spoke Hausa. "Muntaka, you fox, it is good to see you. You will, I hope, stay with us for some days. We have much to talk about."

"Unfortunately, we can stay only for one or two nights. Can you arrange a place for us to sleep?"

"Of course. You shall stay in my home. Mallam Stevens will no doubt wish more private accommodations. We cannot, I am afraid, give you all the comfort that you would like. Allah forgive us. Unlike the case of the shorn lamb, I am afraid that our hospitality has been tempered by the wind. During the last season of rains, the wind and water destroyed our guest house. Only a small mountain of dried mud and straw remains. I hope, Mallam Stevens, that you will join Allah in forgiveness if we shall ask you to spend the night in our schoolhouse. It is the only building available where you shall find privacy. It is warm. Only last month the men of the village filled all of the cracks in the walls with mud and dung, and sections of the roof were rewoven last year. It is a strong building. We shall have the benches moved to make room for your cot."

Hamdi turned to the young boy standing next to him and spoke in Arabic. The boy left the room. "Come, we shall share some wine made from grapes brought from Outat Oulid."

We drank wine and ate chunks of bread and chicken for over two hours as Muntaka and Hamdi shared stories, speaking first in Hausa so that I might be included, but lapsing into Arabic as the wine began to take effect. Several times the two men laughed heartily and I joined them although I had no idea what they were laughing about.

Then Hamdi said, speaking Hausa again, "Muntaka, your face is turning serious. I can see that you have come to my country for something other than a touristic trip for your young friend. What do you have on your mind?''

"You are right. Mallam Stevens and I have come here on a somewhat delicate matter. We have stopped at your village not only because of the hospitality that we could expect but also because I am respectful of your judgment and advice. Some time ago, a valuable manuscript, written in Arabic, was stolen from the museum at Jos. It is imperative that it be returned. It is suspected that it has been brought across the border into your country. Because of the increased security precautions on the airlines in these days, it is highly unlikely that the manuscript left my country by air. The border between your country and mine is wide and not easy to patrol. It would not be a difficult matter to have brought the manuscript into Niger without detection. Twelve pieces of parchment are easily concealed. Even had the manuscript been brought through the customs station, it is unlikely that it would have been detected. The border guards are trained to look for guns, or hashish, or young girls. There would be little difficulty in hiding the manuscript. It is our belief that the manuscript will change hands in Maradi, or Niamey, to be taken north to one of the great black markets, perhaps at Marrakech. It is there that the true value of the manuscript will be recognized. It is there that we are in danger of losing the manuscript forever.''

"So you have come to me for advice on where your search might begin."

"That is right. You must know where transactions of the sort I have described would take place."

"In Maradi there is but one man who is in a position to take possession of an item of antiquity which bears great value. Am I correct in assuming that we are speaking of an item worth forty or fifty thousand English pounds?''

"You are correct. Perhaps more. What the manuscript might bring if sold to the right person is impossible to guess.''

"You must visit the restaurant of Monsieur René Slabbinck. Monsieur Slabbinck's restaurant serves the finest French dishes south of Algiers. Monsieur Slabbinck himself is a connoisseur of African antiquities. He has one of the finest collections of the art of the Côte Ivoire, Senegal, and Mali. There is only one finer personal collection in all of west Africa, I am told. A Swiss in Monrovia. Monsieur Slabbinck's collection changes from day to day. He purchases an item here, he sells an item there. Many of the objects have been brought into Niger illegally. Many leave illegally. He is, no doubt, aware of every device for eluding the authorities. He is clever at seeing that the police do not pursue him too closely. A few francs in the right pocketbooks assist him greatly.'' Hamdi wiped his forehead with his handkerchief. As he did, the young boy entered and whispered something to him.

Hamdi turned to me. ''Your quarters, Monsieur Stevens, are ready. It is best that we continue our conversation in the morning. I wish you good night and may Allah bless you with untroubled sleep.''

The schoolhouse, from what I could see by the light of the lantern as we approached it, was indistinguishable from the rest of the buildings in the small village—mud walls, straw roof, small windows. The building was one room, about twenty-five feet long and fifteen feet wide.

In the shadow cast by the lantern, the benches piled high at the rear of the room resembled a herd of sleeping camels. I looked closely to make sure that they weren't and that I had ended up in the right building.

My cot had been set up just underneath a small blackboard. On the floor were three thick rugs and on the rug next to the cot was a straw mat of the type used by the Bedouins. Apparently I had been given my choice of sleeping accommodations. Or maybe it was assumed that no one could sleep in a canvas cot without falling out.

I undressed, put my lantern on the floor next to the cot and took my copy of Leo's *Geography* from my bag. The combined effects of the wine and the poor lighting made it difficult to read.

But returning againe to our purpose: The Anzichi who extend from the bankes of the river Zaire, even to the confines of Nubia, use circumcision, as also divers other bording people do, a thing that must necessarilie have been brought by the Iewes, & yet remayning in use, after the annihilation of the Mosaicall law amongst them. . . . On the other side, the Iewes being woonderfully increased in Sapine, passed one after an other into Affrick. . . . The Iewes encreased afterwards in Affrick. . . . They passe also by way of traffick even to Tombuto . . .

I began to doze and I closed Leo and turned off the lantern. In the pitch blackness of the room, I suddenly became aware of the stillness in the village. The chattering, the pounding of millet, the occasional drum beat were now gone and there was complete silence except for the light chirping of crickets nesting on the straw roof. My mind, hazed by the wine, drifted on the threshhold of sleep.

I lay there, half-awake, half-asleep, for either three minutes or three hours. Whichever it was, the knock on the door scared the hell out of me. I snapped up. In the blackness of the room I couldn't remember where I was. As my head cleared it became obvious that either some Arab was coming back for his camels or the town had been raided and I was to be taken into slavery. My throat was dry. I shook my head a few times. The knock came again. "Wa ne ne?" I asked in Hausa.

As I spoke the words, I couldn't remember whether I was saying "Who is it?" or "Where is it?" I felt panicky.

A quiet voice answered through the quiet night air. "I have been sent by Hamdi." I tilted my head back and let out a long breath of air, relieved by the friendliness of the voice. Hamdi must have sent his boy back with something.

I stumbled out of the cot through the darkness and opened the door. Standing in the soft light of an oil lamp held head high was a young woman. Her neck was slender, her dark face long, intelligent, aristocratic. Her body was covered by a soft blue robe. Her

87

eyes looked at me gently and then her lids lowered. "I have been sent by Hamdi," she repeated.

As this vision stood before me like last night's fantasy, and the implications of her presence cut through my wine- and sleep-clouded mind, a warm sweat broke out over my forehead and a cold shock broke through my groin. It dawned on me that I was standing there in my shorts.

I stepped back into the room to search for my trousers, which were lying somewhere on the floor. The girl moved softly into the room behind me and set the small, still-lit lantern in the corner. As I turned toward her with my trousers pulled half on one leg, her robe was falling to the floor. Light cast by the lamp played over her body, shadows caressing her breasts gently. She moved toward me slowly and I stood motionless, my hands still holding my trousers. I released them.

As her hands touched mine a small shock ran through my arms and body. She brought my hands to her breasts, which felt warm like the night air. Her hands moved to my shoulders and then slowly to the small of my back.

We floated down to the straw mat. She placed her right leg gently between mine and the softness of her thigh felt like the hot, smooth sand of the desert. Our bodies melted together just as the last light of the lantern flickered out. The intensity of the darkness seemed to push our bodies closer together. Her nearness enveloped me, and we were lost in each other like ancient travelers moving across unexplored desert. Christ, it was nice. No wonder Leo never made it to the Niger.

When I awoke the next morning there was no one beside me. My lantern stood by the cot but the lamp in the corner was gone. The sun streamed into the small schoolhouse windows. I could hear voices and, as I rose from the mat, I could see a small, closely-shaved head peering through one of the panes. The boy could not have been more than six or seven.

"What is he doing now?"

The boy turned his head. "He is just rising from sleep."

Suddenly aware of my audience, I slipped quickly into the trousers which had eluded me the night before. I walked over to the window. There the boy stood, perched on a small wooden box. From the window I could see a dozen small boys and girls lined up at the door of the house, each with a book or wooden tablet in his hand.

"What's going on?" I asked the boy at the window.

"We are waiting to enter the school. It is almost seven-thirty and our teacher shall be here soon. We are supposed to be seated when she arrives. If we are not, we shall be made to read extra lessons."

"Well, I wouldn't want to be the cause of that. I'll be cleared out of here in a minute." I made a quick job of washing up in the bucket of water left by Hamdi's boy, folding my cot and getting my gear together. My every move was announced, play by play, by the boy at the window.

"Come in," I said. "I'll give you a hand putting the benches back in place." The children poured into the room and we began to set up the benches. Two of the children rolled the mats and rugs and put them in the corner.

As the last few benches were being straightened, one of the children shouted, "Here she comes!" The children ran to their places. They were still settling down as she walked in.

She stood in the doorway in the soft light of the morning, books held gently against her breasts. Her black hair was pinned close to her head, which was gently tilted. A soft smile formed at her mouth. She was even more beautiful in the morning light.

She looked at the class. "I am afraid that you shall all have to do extra readings since you are not properly in your places." She did not look at me.

I swallowed hard and stared at the teacher. I spoke after a few moments of silence. "I'm afraid it's my fault. I had to use the school as a . . . a . . . rest house last night since the regular guest house was washed out in the last rains. I slept rather late and we could only now get the benches back in place. It's not the children's fault."

She turned her head toward me. Her eyes, brown in the morning light, met mine and we held each other's look.

"Well," she said, "in that case it would not be fair to punish the children."

I bent down and picked up my cot and bag.

"I hope," she said, so that the children could hear, "that you found your stay in the schoolhouse educational."

The children laughed. I walked out the door of the school, hoping that the eager young scholar at the window this morning had not been posted there all night.

As I walked away from the school toward Hamdi's house, I saw Muntaka standing by the Land-Rover.

His face was enveloped by a large smile. "Well," he said, "did you get enough sleep? I assume the accommodations provided by Hamdi were satisfactory."

I could feel my face redden. "Yes, it was very comfortable. Say, do you think I could get something to eat?"

"Hamdi's cook is waiting for us. Fresh eggs, fresh bread, and tea."

HAMDI poured himself a third cup of tea and said, "It would be best, Muntaka, if your young friend were to approach Monsieur Slabbinck alone." He looked at me. "You speak French?"

"Yes," I replied in French. "I should at least be able to order one of Monsieur Slabbinck's meals."

"Your accent is. . . ." Hamdi pursed his lips and tilted his head to the side. "How can I say this?" He raised his eyebrows. "It is like an untuned piano. Still, you will be understood. Your task would involve somewhat more than ordering a meal, however. It would be well if you could at first give the impression that you are interested in purchasing a piece of art. You must gain Monsieur Slabbinck's confidence. Do you know anything of African art?"

"Not much, but a little. I'm familiar with the Baoulé pieces from the Ivory Coast, the Benin bronze work, and the passport masks of central Liberia. Maybe a few other things."

"That should be enough for you to gain entry to Monsieur Slabbinck's collection. Your main job, however, will be to convince Monsieur Slabbinck of your interest in manuscripts. Your questioning must be done with care. You must give the impression that you are making inquiries on behalf of a wealthy American collector. Can you do this?"

I looked at Muntaka. "I'll do it if it's safe. I'm not about to play Miles Archer to your Sam Spade."

"Who is this Miles Archer?" Muntaka asked.

"He's dead."

"Ah, I see what you mean." Muntaka looked toward Hamdi. "There should be little danger to Mallam Stevens's person, am I not correct, Alhaji Hamdi?"

"You are no doubt correct. Yet, our young friend must exercise a certain amount of caution. I have not known Monsieur Slabbinck to deal in violence. Yet, if the items you seek are worth what you suggest, he may be tempted to alter his methods of operation. You must use care. That is all."

"Look, Muntaka," I said. "At the first sign of a problem I'm paying for my meal and taking off."

"There will be no problem. Mallam Stevens, you are a great worrier. You should relax. Hamdi, can we do something to help Mallam Stevens relax?"

"Perhaps after he returns."

I left the village at eight-thirty, alone. The drive to Maradi took less than an hour. I spent the time before lunch wandering on foot through the town and market. Maradi turned out to be considerably smaller than I had expected. And I was surprised to see the number of shops operated by Frenchmen. In Nigeria such stores would have been run by Nigerians or Lebanese. The British had not gone in for small shopkeeping. I purchased two short-sleeved white shirts with three button-down pockets and epaulets. The French like to button everything but the front of the shirt. I also bought a pair of white shorts. They were shorter than I was accustomed to, but I thought that they might be cool on the desert. I arrived at Monsieur Slabbinck's restaurant at twelve-thirty.

There were already several people in the restaurant. One man, in either police or military uniform, looked up at me as I entered, but only briefly. No one else paid attention. I was relieved.

There were about ten tables in the restaurant. Large green plants dominated the four corners of the room and on the walls were small, inexpensive white-framed prints showing scenes of Paris. Two overhead fans revolved fast enough to create a breeze and I felt sufficiently comfortable to order hot soup.

I had no difficulty identifying Monsieur Slabbinck. As a single waiter took and served orders, Slabbinck, a small man with glossy black hair, a pointed nose, pointed black shoes, finely manicured fingernails, and gold caps on his teeth, alternated between manning the cash register and talking with his customers. He spoke to the man in uniform at length. He seemed to know everyone in the restaurant but me. I was surprised when he came to my table.

"You are enjoying your meal, Monsieur?"

"Yes, very much. I'm amazed to find such food in the middle of Africa. It's delicious."

"I thank you for saying so. You are American?" *He* didn't seem to mind my accent.

"Yes. I'm on vacation and seeing a little of Niger."

"We do not get many Americans here. There is, I am afraid, little here to attract them. Perhaps when the country to the north, with the rock paintings that have been recently discovered, is opened up, we shall see more tourists. But that must await the construction of the railroad."

"Actually, one of the reasons I decided to come into Niger is that I understand that you have an interesting collection of African artifacts. I'm a collector—although on a very small scale. Is it true you have some items for sale?"

"I have a few pieces. What is it that interests you?"

I could see that Slabbinck was attempting to establish my identity as a bona fide collector. Whether he didn't like to waste his time on strangers who were looking for something to do on a hot afternoon, or whether he was cautious for other reasons, I couldn't tell.

"My own interest lies in Baoulé pieces and passport masks from Liberia."

"So, you like Baoulé?" Monsieur Slabbinck's voice became enthusiastic. "Perhaps I can show you a few pieces. As for passport masks, they interest me very little. Still, I have several hundred of them. They are small and the African traders find them easy to transport. Have another cup of coffee. If you can wait until two o'clock, once the restaurant is clear, I shall be glad to show you some of my collection.''

I had two more cups of thick coffee and a pastry. At two-fifteen Monsieur Slabbinck returned to my table.

''I am sorry to have kept you waiting. Come.'' We walked toward the back of the restaurant. Slabbinck reached behind a drape covering a window near the door, took something in his hand and led me outside and around the corner. We walked down a small flight of stone steps and through a gate with a sign, in French and Hausa, reading ''Beware the Dog.'' The house stood about ten yards behind the restaurant. Fences connected to the house and restaurant enclosed the walkway. Slabbinck unlocked the door to the house. The entrance opened into a living room dominated by a concert piano and a large, dark table covered with passport masks and finely carved dolls, six inches high, with large oval heads. No dog was in evidence.

The piano appeared to be well kept. It was highly polished. ''You play piano, Monsieur Slabbinck?''

''I do, but it is impossible to keep a piano of quality in this climate. The dust penetrates everywhere. Here, listen.'' He moved his left hand over several keys. ''It is out of tune,'' he said sadly. Then he smiled and said, ''By the way, Monsieur, where did you learn your French? Your accent is distinctive.''

I smiled back and shrugged my shoulders. To hell with him. I picked up one of the carvings.

''Fertility dolls. From Ghana. I leave them and the passport masks here because they are small and of no great value; the collection changes rapidly. You may look at them at your leisure later. My more valuable pieces are in the rear.''

We walked into another room which Slabbinck opened with a key. The room, about twenty feet long, had five shelves on each wall and each shelf was covered with carvings. Although I knew little of African art, the collection was impressive. They were obviously extremely fine pieces. Slabbinck took a carving from one of the shelves and showed it to me.

"This is the finest Baoulé piece in my collection. I purchased it two months ago. It is not for sale at this moment. I obtained it from a trader from Senegal, a Mandingo. The trader knew its worth. I paid several thousand francs for it."

"It's a beautiful piece. It has nice lines."

"You like it?"

"It has great power."

"Have you ever seen a Baoulé like this?"

"Only once. In Zurich." I was really rolling.

Slabbinck's voice softened. "Monsieur, you have never seen a Baoulé piece like this." Despite the softness of the voice, it had an edge of cruelty to it. "Because, Monsieur, it is a Bakongo piece from Central Africa. Even an amateur collector would know this."

As Slabbinck spoke, I could feel myself whiten. I felt like a hitchhiker who realizes he's made a mistake the moment he speeds away in a stranger's car. I was sure that Slabbinck could see deception and fear written all over my face and that my transparency was only making things irretrievable. I couldn't say, "I was only kidding. Of course it's a Bakongo." For all I knew it was a double trap and the damn thing was from New Guinea.

As I looked toward the door, Slabbinck said, "I should have known that you were a faker when you expressed interest in the passport masks. They are nothing. They are playthings. No serious collector seeks them out. What is it, Monsieur, that you have come to me for?"

I wondered whether I had translated *truqueur* correctly. *Faker.* Christ, I was no good at this sort of thing. The fact was, I had thought I would be able to carry off the charade with some skill. I just wasn't prepared for any detours. I had memorized my lines for a play, but the son of a bitch was changing the dialogue.

I had no choice. "To be honest, Monsieur Slabbinck, I know almost nothing about African art."

"So. That is difficult for me to believe, Monsieur." Slabbinck smiled maliciously.

"I'm serving as an emissary for an American collector. He is interested in rare books and maps. I have heard that occasionally you gain access to books and manuscripts that come to you . . . uh . . . outside of the . . . uh . . . normal course of trade." The moment I spoke I knew I was getting myself in deeper. I was calling the man some sort of criminal. I wanted to get out of there. I thought briefly about running.

Slabbinck smiled, this time with a trace of humor. My nearly accusing him of being a crook seemed to relax him. He put the Bakongo piece back on the shelf and then turned back to me.

"I do not see why you felt it necessary to resort to subterfuge, Monsieur. It is very difficult to simulate expertise when talking with an expert." He narrowed his eyes slightly. "I very rarely deal in books, manuscripts, or maps. It is not that I am averse to doing so. It is that in this part of the world one rarely sees anything in this line of any significant worth."

As he spoke, a bell rang and Slabbinck said, "You will have to excuse me. I shall return shortly." He left the room and I waited fifteen minutes. When he returned, he said, "The books that come to my attention are rarely more than one hundred years old and are typically from France or Britain. I am not interested in such things. From time to time I have seen a map of some interest. One map used by Heinrich Barth on his trip into Lake Chad in 1854 came into my hands several years ago. It brought a large sum. But such items are unusual. And I am not an expert in books and maps."

"My friend's interested in books and manuscripts in Arabic. He's asked me to make some inquiries on his behalf. He's willing to pay well for high quality items. Do you see much in the way of Arabic books?"

Slabbinck seemed to tense. It may have been my imagination. His right eyebrow tilted upward and for a moment he didn't speak.

Finally, he said, "I do have an item that might interest you. I doubt, however, that it is of much value."

"What is it?"

"An Arabic manuscript."

My heart doubled its beat as Slabbinck spoke, but I tried to appear calm. "I'd like to see it."

"Surely. I will be glad to get it. Wait here one moment."

Slabbinck left the room for about five minutes. He returned with a large leather case under his arm.

The case had obviously seen a good deal of use. It was worn thin in several places and was bound by a long leather thong. Slabbinck laid the case on the table and untied it. I swallowed hard as he drew out the thin volume of parchment-like paper bound together by dirty white string. He spread the sheets out on the table. It was then that I realized that I didn't have the foggiest notion of what the hell I was looking for.

In a manner that was as casual as I could muster, I asked, "Where is this from, Monsieur Slabbinck?"

"This manuscript was brought here from the west coast of Africa, in southern Senegal. It is an interpretation of the Koran. It is, perhaps, 125 years old. Maybe 150. Certainly no more."

I looked at the manuscript as closely as I could but I couldn't make much out of it.

"The person for whom I am acting is interested in items which are more unique. Have you nothing else?"

"No, there is nothing. . . . I agree; this manuscript is not of particular merit. A knowledgeable collector would not find it of special interest."

Slabbinck put the manuscript back in the leather cover.

"Well," I said, "thank you for taking so much time with me."

"It was a great pleasure. It is always gratifying, Monsieur, to speak with someone who appreciates my collection." I gave him an embarrassed smile. "Nevertheless," he continued, "it will be necessary for you to pay for your lunch. I operate on a small margin of profit." He smiled.

The guy must have thought I was a crook as well as an imposter. The fact was, I had forgotten about paying for the meal. I handed over the requisite number of francs and muttered something about the excellent quality of the food.

As we walked through the small dining area of the restaurant, I saw, in a corner, a man seated at one of the tables. His presence startled me because there had been no one in the room when Slabbinck and I left to view the collection. The man was cutting, with great precision, a piece of pastry. He didn't look up. He wore a green suit, green tie, and tinted glasses. It was the Greek I had seen at breakfast at the Zaria rest house and in the Zaria market. His camera hung from the side of his chair.

I arrived back at Hamdi's village about five o'clock. Muntaka walked toward the Land-Rover as I drove up in front of Hamdi's office. "Well, Mallam Stevens, what were you able to discover?"

I described my afternoon and the manuscript to Muntaka. He questioned me closely. I was surprised that I had noticed more about the manuscript than I had imagined.

"No," Muntaka said, "those pages are not the objects of our search. They are no doubt precisely what Slabbinck said they are. Now we must guess whether he was telling you the truth when he informed you that he had nothing else to show you. We must await Hamdi's return. He should be back shortly. Meanwhile, you can teach me a few of the magic tricks you have been practicing."

"What about the Greek, Muntaka? What do you think his presence means?"

"I am afraid, Mallam Stevens, that it means we must move very quickly."

HAMDI spoke as we ate dinner. "It is difficult to know whether Monsieur Slabbinck was telling the truth when he informed you that he had no other manuscripts in his possession. There is, of course, only one way to be certain."

"How's that?" I asked.

"His quarters must be searched."

I smiled. "Who are you going to get to do *that?*"

"I am afraid, Mallam Stevens, that it will have to be you."

"Me? Are you crazy?"

"You are the only one of the three of us who has been into Monsieur Slabbinck's residence. You know the rooms, the placement of the furniture. This is important, since you will have to search the place by night."

"I'm not searching Slabbinck's by day *or* night."

"Why do you protest? It is a simple matter."

"I protest for two reasons. First, I'm not too excited by the prospect of being shot at by Monsieur Slabbinck or being eaten by his watchdog. Second, I don't know what the manuscript looks like. Only Muntaka knows that." I pointed to Muntaka with the thumb of my left hand. "That's it. There's your man."

"With regard to your first point, there is no danger. Monsieur Slabbinck travels to Zinder each weekend. He will be gone by tomorrow evening. As for the dog, how big is he?"

"I didn't see any dog. Just a sign, 'Beware the Dog.' "

"Ah, as I expected. The climate is too hot for dogs. There are few of them in Maradi. Local businessmen buy the signs in the market to frighten potential thieves. You have nothing to fear."

"You're right, because I nominate Muntaka for the job. Do I hear a second?"

"Your second point may be more serious." Hamdi turned to Muntaka. "Do you think that Mallam Stevens will have difficulty in identifying the manuscript?"

"It is a simple matter. Any documents he finds in Arabic, he takes with him."

"Look, gentlemen," I said, "I'm not breaking into Slabbinck's and I'm not stealing Arabic manuscripts. Do you know what the penalty is for breaking and entering in Maradi? It's probably chopping off your hands. *My* hands. For theft it's probably my balls. No thanks."

Hamdi raised both hands to his shoulders, palms out. "I have connections with the police. If you are apprehended—an extremely unlikely event—I shall intervene. Besides, the Criminal Procedure Code has been revised. Penalties are less harsh than they once were."

"Swell. Maybe they'll take one ball instead of two."

"The chief of police is a friend of mine. You have nothing to worry about."

"Then get *him* to search the place."

"He is a person of discretion. It is something that he will not do." Hamdi turned to Muntaka. "I am beginning to believe, Muntaka, that the task of searching Monsieur Slabbinck's residence will require knowledge possessed by both you and our young friend. Mallam Stevens knows the geography of Monsieur Slabbinck's shop and home. You are familiar with the manuscript. Your knowledge will save time in the search. Perhaps it is best if you both examine Monsieur Slabbinck's quarters tomorrow evening."

Muntaka rubbed his nostrils with the back of his right hand and then ran the first two fingers of each hand along the sides of his nose. Then he said, "Perhaps you are right. There should be no more risk in two entering than one." Muntaka turned to me and smiled. "Mallam Stevens, I shall be at your side to protect you."

Hamdi said, "There is no need for protection. As I say, there is virtually no risk."

"What do you mean 'virtually'?" I asked.

"There is, Mallam Stevens, always, of course, the small chance that *something* can go wrong."

I had had visions of ladders and breaking glass, but that was out of the question. All of the windows were covered with iron bars, to keep out "t'ief men"—like Muntaka and me. Instead, we entered the front door. The key came courtesy of Mallam Audou, the chief of the Maradi Fire Brigade. All of the European shopkeepers in town left keys with the fire brigade to keep zealous firemen from chopping down valuable and scarce doors. Mallam Audou was, of course, a friend of Hamdi's and was obligated to Hamdi in some mysterious way that Hamdi did not bother to explain.

We had left the Land-Rover at the Ministry of Public Works, parked near a dozen other Land-Rovers and trucks. Most of the other vehicles had "Public Works—Maradi" markings, but at that hour of the night the absence of markings on ours would make no difference.

I had turned the headlights off just before we reached the public works building and killed the motor at the edge of the lot. Muntaka got out and made his way among the trucks and cars. He found a spot for our vehicle well inside the parking area, between two trucks.

It was darker than I thought it would be. There were no street lamps and only a few lanterns flickered at various places away from the main street. The moon, in crescent, gave off little light. There was no traffic. The public works building was on the edge of town, some five blocks and two left turns from Slabbinck's restaurant. It is unlikely that we were seen by anyone.

The key worked. The front door opened quietly and we entered

101

and closed the door, locking it. We didn't use our flashlights in the restaurant. I led the way and Muntaka placed his left hand on my shoulder as I traced a path among the tables. The room was pitch black. We moved slowly and avoided tripping over chairs. At the rear door I moved my hand along the wall to the drape and reached just above my head. I felt for the keys I knew Slabbinck had taken from there the day before. A moment of panic set in. They weren't there.

I whispered to Muntaka, "The keys. They're gone."

"What do you mean they are gone? Do you feel the hook?"

The hook. I hadn't felt a hook. I moved my hand along the wall area under the drape. No keys. No hook. Now I wasn't sure Slabbinck had gotten the keys from behind the drape. We did have an alternate plan. We could bust the two locks. Muntaka had a small chisel-like instrument tucked into his belt inside his robe. But smashing the locks would leave evidence of the break-in. We were anxious not to do that. We would have to smash the front door lock also, to protect Mallam Audou.

"The mother's not here, Muntaka."

"Use your flashlight. The drapery will conceal the light as you search underneath it."

"I'm not worried about someone in here seeing the light. It's the people out there I'm worried about."

"Move the drape against the edge of the window and cover your light with your handkerchief."

"I don't have a handkerchief."

"Then use mine." Muntaka was getting testy.

I bunched the drape up against the edge of the window and covered the head of the flashlight with Muntaka's handkerchief. I felt the monogrammed *M* and smelled a slight trace of perfume. I ran the light systematically up the wall from the floor, covering the six-inch area that had been concealed by the drape. Then I saw it—a small button built into the one-inch sash of the window. I pressed it and a slender, oblong piece of wood popped up from just below the button. Three keys were hanging one on top of the other on a small nail.

"Okay, Muntaka, I've got them." I turned off the flashlight. We moved along the wall to the door. The second key fit, and I moved gingerly around the corner and down the steps. Muntaka's left hand was again on my shoulder. I was relieved to see that there were no lights on in the house. I had guessed that the distance between the shop and the house was fifteen steps. In the darkness it was twenty-three. The first of the two remaining keys opened the door to the house. Muntaka and I entered and we stood just inside the room. Muntaka was slightly behind me, to my right.

I whispered to Muntaka. "There's a table about ten feet to the right. For God's sake don't bump into it. It's covered with small masks. A piano is on the left, about eight feet from here. The room with the art work is straight ahead. If we keep on the rug, we'll be on a dead line for the doorway. There are two windows in there. The room that Slabbinck entered when he went for the manuscript is just off the right of the next room."

We glided slowly across the rug and into the room with the two windows, then through a second doorway to the right. I guessed that there were no windows in the second room and I risked the flashlight. I was right. Muntaka closed the door behind him and I switched on a lamp sitting on a large wooden desk. I was relieved to see that there was no safe in the room. If there had been, no doubt our manuscript would have been in it.

There were several unlocked metal boxes on a shelf behind the desk. They were large enough to hold the twelve pieces of parchment and Muntaka started with them. I rummaged through the pile of papers on Slabbinck's desk and then opened the large vertical drawer at the left side of the desk. It was there that I found the leather case containing the manuscript Slabbinck had shown me the day before. I showed the contents to Muntaka.

"Yes, Slabbinck was telling the truth. These manuscript pages are of no particular value. There is nothing else in the drawer?"

"Nothing."

While Muntaka examined the contents of the third metal box, I sat down at Slabbinck's desk and looked into the center drawer.

There were several business cards sitting loosely on top. "L. Wells, Tribal Arts" was the first. "G. Kontos, Importe-Exporte" was the second. The others were cards of two French food purveyors.

The news clippings were just under the cards—four of them, each neatly trimmed and dated. The first, from a Hausa newspaper, bore the date of April 13. It told of the theft of "valuable documents" from the Jos Museum. The second, also in Hausa, was dated April 27 and was the news item I had seen at the office of the provincial commissioner. The third clipping, dated April 30, was in French and was a word-for-word translation of the second news item, except that for the Hausa word *mutuwa*, killing, there was substituted the French word *meurtre*, murder. The fourth clipping, dated April 25, was bordered in black. It was in Hausa and was about a half-column long. It was Muntaka's obituary.

Aside from the news clippings, which I showed to Muntaka and replaced in the drawer, we found nothing of interest.

"Do you think we should search the upstairs, Muntaka?"

"We have come this far. It would be foolish not to."

We turned off the light and moved slowly through the African art room, into the living room. A small staircase began just behind the piano. The staircase was an open one that spiraled gently to a small balcony overlooking the living room. We moved quietly, avoiding both the piano keys and the passport masks. At the top of the stairs I turned on my flashlight and ran it along the wall. There were two doors and a large carving of an antelope's head between them. I cut the light and opened the first door. I felt my way along the wall. Muntaka stayed in the hall. I felt a sink and backed out, then moved along the wall to the second door. I opened it slowly and stood at the entranceway blinking my eyes, hoping that I could get some bearing on the room without having to move along the wall. There were windows to the left. A small amount of night light made the bars of the windows barely visible. I was just about to move into the center of the room when Muntaka tightened his grip on my right shoulder. A small beam of light was shining through the four- or five-inch space under a raised window and a slender pole was being pushed slowly through the open space. The light revealed the full length of the pole—about seven feet—and a small hook at the end. The light glistened off the top and bottom edges of the pole. In a few moments the pole was being retracted, and a pair of trousers hung from the hook on the end. The pole stopped halfway between the back of the chair on which the pants had been hanging and the window. For a few seconds the legs of the trousers danced wildly, like the rubber legs of an old-time vaudevillian. Then they continued their journey to the window.

It was at this point that the man in the bed snapped up, shouted in French, and catapulted forward. I dove toward him but I was too late. He grabbed the pole and let out a scream that I associated with a man being run through the stomach with a saber. He had been too slow in releasing his hand from the strips of razor blades that ran along the two edges of the pole.

Muntaka turned on his flashlight. Blood was gushing from the man's right hand. He was moaning and holding his arm against his chest with his left hand. Blood ran down his bare stomach. The flashlight went out but in seconds Muntaka was back with a bunch of towels. It was only then that I thought to turn on my own flashlight. Muntaka wrapped two towels around the man's hand, as I held my light on the two of them. Then I found the lamp by the bed.

The man spoke French. "Cauterize. The wound must be cauterized. There is a black bag near the bed."

I reached for the bag and opened it. It contained medical supplies and instruments.

"I am a doctor." The man moaned, as if his being a doctor made the situation worse. "There is antiseptic. In the green bottle. In the white box is a cauterizing powder. They both must be poured into the wounds."

I poured large amounts of each on the two long gashes that ran along the palm and fingers. The flesh of the fingers had been cut widely and as I pushed back the end of the hand to pour in the antiseptic, I could see the bones of each finger. The man had placed one of the towels between his teeth with his left hand. The towel muffled his moans. Then he removed the towel and said, "You must sew the wounds." He made a sewing motion with his left hand. "There is a needle and cat gut thread in the plastic bag."

I was about to vomit. "I don't think I can do it."

The man looked at Muntaka. Muntaka looked at the hand, shrugged, and said, "Why not?" We helped the man to the bed. Muntaka threaded the needle and the doctor-patient gave directions, which I translated for Muntaka.

The sewing took forty-five minutes. When it was finished Muntaka went into the bathroom. The man closed his eyes. His back was resting against the wall. When Muntaka returned, he had a glass of water which he placed in the man's left hand. The man drank from it slowly. Then the glass slipped from his hand and crashed against the floor. The noise seemed to bring him to life. He sat up straighter and looked at the two of us with narrowed eyes.

Then he said, "I am very grateful to you. You have no doubt saved my life. Still, your presence here is quite illegal. I am afraid, gentlemen, that I must telephone the police."

I was just about to make for the exit when Muntaka said, "I am afraid that you make a mistake. We *are* the police."

The man looked confused. "The police? This is absurd. It is clear that you are not of Niger. You do not even speak French. And this man, he is an American. Do you take me for a fool?"

"My associate and I are on secondment to the police force of Niger. We are assisting the police in establishing a laboratory of scientific investigation. My associate is a lieutenant with the police of New York. I am with the Nigerian police."

"What are you doing here?"

"I have just told you. We are on secondment."

"I mean in this house."

"We were returning to our quarters. We saw a suspicious light. So we entered to investigate."

"How?"

I was interested in hearing Muntaka's answer. Instead he said, "I am afraid, sir, that it is now time for us to ask *you* a few questions." Muntaka turned to me. "You have your notebook?"

The man said, "You will not need a notebook. I am, as I said, a doctor. I am myself on secondment—from the French Ministry of Public Health. I arrived in the country just today. I am on my way to Agadez where I shall be stationed for three months." He looked at his hand. "I am afraid now that my services will be somewhat limited. Still, it could be worse."

"What are you doing in this house?" Muntaka asked.

"It was arranged for me to stay in Monsieur Slabbinck's residence until Sunday, when I shall fly to Agadez. Monsieur Slabbinck is away for several days."

"Yes," Muntaka said, "we know. The police keep a close eye on the comings and goings of the residents." Muntaka looked at me quickly and then turned back to the doctor. "Well, I am glad that we could be of assistance to you. Do you have a second pair of trousers? We could have a pair sent to you."

"That is most kind. I have others. Fortunately, my wallet was not in the trousers that disappeared out of the window. It was under my pillow. With my gun."

"Gun?" Muntaka asked. "You carry a gun?"

"Not in Marseilles. But in Africa, yes. It can be a very dangerous place. Unfortunately, I forgot that the gun was under the pillow."

"It would not have been worth killing a man for a pair of trousers."

"Perhaps not."

Muntaka and I went directly to bed when we got back to Hamdi's village and we didn't see Hamdi until the morning.

"The news clippings," Hamdi said, "are no doubt significant. Still, I now believe that Monsieur Slabbinck was speaking the truth when he informed you that he had no other manuscript in his possession. Were he still to have it, he would, I believe, at least have made an effort to check your background. He made no

107

arrangement to contact you if he wished to do so. He is not one to pass up the opportunity to make a sale as quickly as he can. Had I thought more carefully, I would have known that searching Monsieur Slabbinck's quarters would not have yielded the manuscript.''

"Now you tell me," I said. "We could've been killed."

"Muntaka, you are right," Hamdi said. "Mallam Stevens does not approach these matters in the right spirit. Mallam Stevens, what you do not appreciate is that life must be treasured for offering us the unexpected. It is true that you did not find the manuscript. But you have found evidence that links Monsieur Slabbinck to it. And what is more important, Allah gave you the opportunity to save a man's life. You should be grateful for this opportunity. It does not come to many men.

"In any case, gentlemen, it now seems clear that Monsieur Slabbinck has never been in possession of the manuscript, but would like to be, or he has been in possession of it and has transferred it to someone else. After breakfast I shall make some inquiries on your behalf. It is best, perhaps, that you, Alhaji, do not appear in Maradi.''

"Mallam Stevens and I will be content to rest here in the village. How do you plan to proceed?"

"There are two possible sources of information. Several acquaintances of mine who live in the old city make their living, shall we say, in a not entirely honest manner. They are aware of the traffic of illicit goods into and out of the city. While they tend to specialize in hashish, guns, and radios, they may be of some assistance to us. My other source is the chief of police. We have been friends for many years. We trained together at the government college in Niamey. At that time we were both going to become teachers. In fact, we both taught for several years, in different parts of the country. There is little that escapes his attention, either officially or unofficially. He should not be reluctant to provide the information we seek, if he has such information.''

Hamdi left the village at nine o'clock that morning. As Muntaka and I were finishing second cups of tea Muntaka said, "You never showed me the translation of the torn

108

pages found on the Levantine's body."

"I forgot all about it. It's in my bag. Wait here, I'll get it."

When I returned I laid the torn pages and the priest's scribbled translation on the table in front of Muntaka. He pressed the paper out with his hands and read the translation slowly. Then he looked up at me.

"You know, of course, where this comes from?"

"The priest said that it looks like it comes from the journal of a missionary. I suppose he's right."

"He is quite right. But not a Christian missionary. And not a religious missionary. I have read these passages many times. But only in the English. It is unfortunate that I do not know Latin. These passages, Mallam Stevens, were written by our old friend Leo the African. If you search the middle of the book I gave you, you will find a perhaps more proper translation. But the priest's effort seems quite accurate. It is strange, though."

"What's that, Muntaka?"

"I wonder what the Levantine Simhani was doing with pages from the Latin version of the African's book?" Muntaka paused and raised his eyebrows. "Leo's journal was originally written in Arabic. He later translated it into Italian, his adopted tongue. The original Arabic and Italian manuscripts are now lost. The Italian version was translated into Latin by a man called Florianus, in 1554. The Latin translation has, for the last four centuries, been regarded as the standard version. This page may come from a very old edition of the Latin translation. Perhaps as much as four hundred years old." Muntaka was thoughtful for a moment. "It is a shame to destroy a book of such value."

Muntaka studied the translation again for several minutes. Then he said, "It would be interesting, Mallam Stevens, to compare the priest's translation with that of the translator who prepared the version I gave you."

I stood up. "Just a minute. I'll get the book. It's in the Land-Rover."

After a bit of searching through the book, we found the relevant passages and we laid Father Nunn's translation alongside. Muntaka studied them.

Nor am I unaware how much my own credit is questioned when I myself write so homely of Africa, unto which country I stand indebted for the best part of my education. Although in this regard I seek not to excuse myself, but to appeal to the duty of an historiographer, who is to set down the plain truth in all places, and be responsible for the flattering or favoring of any person.

But all men do most adopt that place, where they find least damage and inconvenience. For my own part, when I hear the Africans spoken evil of, I will confirm myself to be a man of Granada; and when I see the nation of Granada disapproved, then I will profess myself to be an African. But herein the Africans shall be more obligated to me; for I will only record their principal and well-known vices, omitting their smaller and more tolerable faults.

in the time of my youth. Likewise I will set down my last voyages to Constantinople, from Constantinople to Egypt, and from there to Italy, in which journey I saw diverse and sundry islands. All which my travels I mean (by God's help) to be returned forth into my own country.

Neither am I ignorant how much mine owne credit is impeached, when I my selfe write so homely of Africa, unto which countrie I stand indebted both for my birth and also for the best part of my education: Howbeit in this regarde I seek not to excuse my selfe, but onely to appeale unto the dutie of an historiographer, who is to set downe the plaine truth in all places, and is blame-worthie for flattering or favouring of any person.

But that all men doe most affect that place, where they finde least damage and inconvenience. For mine owne part, when I heare the Africans evill spoken of, I wil affirme my selfe to be one of Granada: and when I perceive the nation of Granada to be discommended, then will I professe my selfe to be an African. But herein the Africans shall be the more beholding unto me; for that I will only record their principall and notorious vices, omitting their smaller and more tolerable faults.

in the time of my youth. Likewise I will set downe my last voiages to Constantinople, from Constantinople to Egypt, and from thence into Italie, in which Iourney I saw divers and sundry Ilands. All which my travels I meane (by Gods assistance) being returned forth of Europe into mine owne countrie.

"Your priest, Mallam Stevens, must possess a good knowledge of Latin. His translation is excellent. But you will notice that he has omitted a phrase at the beginning."

"What's that?"

"Here. In the English edition the translator writes, 'Africa unto which countrie I stand indebted both for my birth and also for the best part of my education.' "

"The priest writes, 'Africa, unto which country I stand indebted for the best part of my education.' "

I looked at the Latin page. It read, 'Afric et vitae initium et educationis meae bonam partem debeo."

I said, "The priest forgot to translate 'vitae initium.' "

Muntaka looked at each translation again. Finally he said, "You know, Mallam Stevens, these passages, taken together, are of some interest. There has long been some mystery concerning where Leo passed his last days—in Europe, the Near East, or Africa. If one assumes that Leo was born in Africa, the last sentence of our Latin pages, 'All which my travels I mean (by God's help) to be returned forth into my own country,' suggests he returned to Africa. The omission in the priest's translation suggests that Leo was born in Europe and returned *there*."

"Why does it matter where Leo died?"

"It is of interest, Mallam Stevens, to those of us who are true scholars. Besides, it has long been thought that Leo left a manuscript or letter—some sort of legacy or will—at the place of his death. Until now, no such legacy has been discovered. If one knew where he spent his last years, it would be easier to locate such a document." Muntaka paused for a moment and rubbed his nose with the fingers of his right hand. Then he said, "The mistranslation by the priest is interesting. It is strange that the translation is otherwise so very near that done by the translator in the book you have."

"Well, he did it quickly and I didn't tell him it had to be perfect. You think he deliberately mistranslated?"

"I have no reason to suspect so, but it is odd, nevertheless. Did he say anything of significance to you?"

111

"No. It's funny, though. The priest acted a little peculiar when he first saw the passages. Or maybe it was my imagination. When he asked where I got the pages he seemed almost accusatory. I thought maybe they were pages from the Bible and that he considered me some sort of blasphemer."

"It is interesting, Mallam Stevens. I wonder what it is we have here?"

Hamdi returned at three o'clock.

"What have you learned?" Muntaka asked.

"From my acquaintances in the old city I have learned nothing of relevance to your quest. They are unaware of the movement of anything of the value you indicate from your country into Niger. They say that, with the reduction of tariffs here, even the traffic in illicit manufactured goods has decreased to a mere trickle. The traffic in antiquities, I am told, is equally thin. They say that, with so little to watch and participate in, it is unlikely that items of great value would escape their attention. They have heard of nothing that would interest you—at least in your quest for the manuscript. Yet, they are not infallible. And one moving an item of such value would take more than the usual caution."

"And were you able to speak with the chief of police?"

"Mallam Moussa and I took our lunch together. It is always invigorating to be with him. He knows of everything that occurs in this *rondissement*. Or nearly everything. To take lunch with him is to live one hundred lives in one hour. And for every intrigue of another, he has an intrigue of his own. He has an unquenchable thirst for women. It is remarkable that he is able to find time to perform his duties. Yet, I assume that he learns much from the women whom he comes to know. Women often learn of things that do not come easily to the ears of men. There is one woman, from Zinder, whom he has described to me. She . . ."

Muntaka broke in impatiently. "Was he able to tell you anything about the manuscript?"

"No. He knows nothing of it."

Muntaka sighed and ran his hands over his face. "I am afraid that our search, Mallam Stevens, is going to be much more difficult than I had anticipated. I do not know what our next step should be."

Hamdi raised his hand slightly. "Do not become discouraged yet. You did not let me finish my story."

"I am sorry. Proceed."

"Mallam Moussa knows nothing of your manuscript. He has, however, something to say about Monsieur Slabbinck which may be of interest to you."

"Continue."

"Mallam Moussa informs me that Monsieur Slabbinck, ten days ago, traveled to Dakoro where food and other supplies are being loaded on camels to be carried to drought victims in remote areas of our country. Monsieur Slabbinck is not known for being a man of humanitarian instincts. It is doubtful that he had gone to Dakoro to assist with the operations there."

"What has this to do with us?"

"Mallam Moussa informs me that when he first learned of Slabbinck's trip he believed it was for the purpose of inducing one of the caravan leaders to smuggle merchandise across the border into Mali. Since much of the food and supplies are destined for Mali and Chad as well as the northern sections of our country, a number of the caravans will cross international borders. Because of the nature of their mission, they are unlikely to be the object of intensive search by border guards. Indeed, the guards on both sides of the Mali and Chad borders have instructions not to impede the travels of these camel trains. Mallam Moussa, at the time of learning of Slabbinck's trip, believed that items of considerable value were involved. He now believes that it is your manuscript which caused Slabbinck to travel to Dakoro. Your manuscript may now be hiding in a sack of millet strapped to the back of a camel crossing the border into Mali."

"How far north will these camels travel?"

"They are likely to go as far as Tanezrouft. No further."

"Where the hell is Tanezrouft?" I asked.

"It is in north central Mali, not far from the southern edge of

Algeria. It is a journey, by camel, of some fifteen days."

Muntaka looked contemplative. Then he asked, "What do you suggest we do? Will it be useful to track the caravan? Are we likely to be able to trace the manuscripts before they reach Tanezrouft?"

"It is perhaps most important that you travel to Dakoro to determine whether what we suspect has in fact occurred. If it has, it may be useful for you to track the caravan. You would have to be prepared to pay a large sum of money to the chief of the camel train for the return of the manuscript. Of course, the train may have left too long ago for there to be a hope of catching it before it arrives in Tanezrouft."

"What will happen to the manuscript there?" I asked.

"I am afraid," Hamdi said, "that it will not remain there long. Tanezrouft is not a market for such items. It will be brought into Morocco. There will be camel caravans with relief supplies coming from the north as well as from the south. Tanezrouft will be a crossroads for relief caravans. If the manuscript is brought to Tanezrouft from the south it will be taken from there to the north. Unless you can intercept the caravan, your goal will be Morocco, not Tanezrouft."

Muntaka and I looked at each other.

"If you must make the trip," Hamdi continued, "it will not be a pleasant one. You will not, I am afraid, find many Taureg settlements to the north. The great drought of the last few years has laid waste to many Taureg villages. Where oases once existed, you will now see only graves. I suggest that you move quickly through northern Niger and Mali. The cemeteries can only bring sadness to one's mind. The Tauregs were once a noble warrior tribe. Those who have survived have moved south into the cities and towns and into new settlements which are being irrigated to create fertile land. The cemeteries you will find represent not only the death of individuals; they symbolize the death of a people's way of life. The carcasses of camels, cattle, sheep, and goats will remind you why the desert people have had to travel into southern Niger. Many remained in their oasis communities too long.

The walk of several hundred miles destroyed many families. In the refugee camps, it is not unusual to see twenty persons die each day. The blue veils of the desert people have been replaced by the black veil of death.''

"We shall take your advice," Muntaka said. He laid out a map from his bag. "We shall attempt to move quickly through the north of your country. We shall cross here at Tilbouk and proceed to Anefis-I-n-Darane and Toufourine. We shall cross Algeria where it knifes into southern Morocco and then proceed to Taroudannt and Marrakech. I had hoped to show Mallam Stevens something of the life of the desert but we are, I'm afraid, some years too late."

I HAD no idea of the scene we would intrude upon in Dakoro. The moment our Land-Rover came to the edge of town, Muntaka and I were shaken by what we saw. Hundreds of children and women, and some men, were huddled under makeshift tenting sprawled over the desert terrain outside the city gates. The dark tents, opened at one side and shaped like lean-tos, stood out against the sandy background like cockroaches on a kitchen floor.

Many of the refugees were lying down. I learned later that, despite the supplies of food that had entered Dakoro, many of the refugees from the north were too weak to move. There were few men in sight and I remarked about this to Muntaka.

"This is strange. It is likely that the men have remained with what is left of their herds or have brought their herds southward to the grazing lands in Nigeria." He paused as we drove through the gates, and we saw more refugees scattered under tents along the street. "I have never seen anything like this. We have never, Allah be praised, suffered famine in Nigeria. That so few miles can make such a difference is remarkable."

We drove along in silence for several minutes. Muntaka pointed out a truck with United Nations markings and asked me to drive up alongside of it. We got out of the Land-Rover and Muntaka spoke in Hausa to one of the men standing by the truck. They exchanged formal greetings.

"What is the situation here now?"

The man, about twenty-five, was himself Nigerian, from Sokoto. He was seconded to the relief effort from the General Ministry of Health. His name was Assufu. "There is sufficient food for those in Dakoro. We have two problems now. Many of the people here have been ravaged by the famine, and rats have followed men and women here in search of food. The rats have brought disease. The refugees are in need of medical care. They must be nursed back to health. The second problem is getting food to the north. Many of the men remained with their herds—what is left of them. Others—men, women, and children—were too weak to make the trip south. The roads, as you may know, are not good. We must rely mostly on camels. It is difficult to find enough healthy ones to make the long trips. And we face the problem of black marketeers. Only half of our supplies are reaching the people in the north. The remainder is taken by camel drivers and others and sold here on the black market. Much of the food is going to those who need it least."

Muntaka's eyes reflected the sadness and torment of the refugee camp. "Is it possible, Mallam Assufu, for Mallam Stevens and me to be of some assistance? We shall be here for a few days perhaps."

The U. N. man excused himself and walked over to another man. They talked briefly. He walked back to us.

"If you are serious in your offer, we could use the two of you in helping to take a census of the refugees. We began several days ago, but it is a long process. We must learn what we can of the health of each person. We must learn the name of the village or section he has come from and the names of relatives left behind. We must determine when each person will be ready to return north. Each person must be asked to wear one of these tags so that we do not interview anyone more than once. If you could assist us for a few days, it would speed our work. You have been inoculated for cholera?"

"I have." Muntaka rubbed his arm and looked at me. I nodded. "Mallam Stevens and I shall be glad to assist. We should no doubt

117

work closely together since Mallam Stevens speaks Hausa and French, but not Arabic. I imagine that we may have some language difficulty.''

"Yes, but you will find men who speak Hausa in most of the camp areas. They can interpret if necessary. Will you need a place to stay?''

"I assume," Muntaka said, "that there is no rest house available. We have some tenting in our car. We shall put it up where you recommend."

"There is space near the tent where we have established our headquarters. I shall drive with you and show you the location.''

By ten o'clock the next morning, the heat and the smell of human waste through the refugee camp were nearly overwhelming. We had attempted to work fast, to cover as many persons as possible. I had seen at least a dozen rats and the sight sent chills through me each time. By noon Muntaka and I were both exhausted but wouldn't confess it to each other. We worked without lunch. I had no appetite, and to have returned to the Land-Rover for a meal would have seemed a sacrilege in the midst of the decimated bodies we were interviewing. The decimation existed even though there now appeared to be enough millet and sorghum to feed everyone in the town. It would be months before many of these people would return to health.

The evening of the first night we took our meal with Assufu and several others involved in the relief effort.

"Once we have solved the immediate problems," one of the men said, "there will be much reconstruction to be done. We must improve the resources for increasing village water supplies. Herds of cattle, camels and goats must be reconstituted. An adequate road network must be developed in this region and northwards. Large-scale forestation is needed to help stem the advance of the Sahara. Water-drilling brigades must be formed to try to deepen existing wells to reach depths where water may still be available. All this will take much time. We must pray for rain until we are prepared.

"The change in government has helped us. There was much corruption in the previous regime. Food supplies were sold on the black market by government officials. Now the military has taken control and the distribution of international aid proceeds more smoothly."

"What about the resettlement of refugees?" I asked.

"This will not be a simple problem to solve. The government is giving first attention to the settlement of refugees from the north of Niger. The Tauregs from Mali, however, will be the most difficult problem. Many will have to remain here and in other camps for one or two years before they are able to go back. What is more, many are not anxious to return to their homelands. The relationship between the Tauregs and the government of Mali has not been a warm one. Conflict between the two is not uncommon. Many Tauregs, after one or two years here, will not wish to return home. Shall we force them to do so? We can now provide the refugees with the basic needs for minimal survival. It costs somewhat over two hundred francs a week to feed each person. This provides a kilo of millet or rice, a half kilo of milk, one hundred grams of sugar, fifty grams of salt and ten grams of tea. We also provide soap and cooking oil. Each person receives one bar of soap a month. One of the agencies has provided each person with a blanket."

At dinner the second evening Muntaka asked directions to the area where millet and sorghum were being loaded on the camels for the trips north. One of the men drew us a rough map showing the direction to the northern edge of the town.

The next morning we were at the loading point at seven-thirty. Several camels snorted and poked their noses at the backsides of the females. Others were either in *flagrante delicto* or lying down. A number of Tauregs, blue masks covering their faces, sat in a circle off to one side, eating.

"These camels look pretty healthy, Muntaka."

"Yes, I expect that they have been brought up from the camel markets of Nigeria. One can make much money these days if one owns a healthy camel."

Muntaka spoke to several men and was finally directed to the manager of the loading area. The head man was seated at a desk in a small office made of corrugated tin. The tin was undoubtedly protection against the strong winds of the Sahara, but the interior of the hut was like a dusty oven. Everything in the room was covered with sand. The hand-painted sign nailed to the desk read, "Chef des Operations." On the wall behind the desk were two calendars, both four years out of date. One showed a young black woman, naked from the waist up, drinking milk. Beneath the picture was a caption advertising powdered milk of French manufacture.

Muntaka greeted the man in Hausa. The man returned the greeting, but in a desultory fashion. Muntaka introduced himself as a representative of the Nigerian Ministry of Health and me as a Red Cross representative. The man didn't ask for credentials.

"I have heard only good things about your efforts in moving grain to the north," Muntaka said.

The man did not respond.

"I understand," Muntaka continued, "that you are given much credit for the efficiency of the relief operation."

No response.

"Such work," Muntaka went on, "must build a great thirst in a man of your size during the course of the day. We have several bottles of beer in our car. Could we share a bottle or two with you?"

The man continued to say nothing. Finally he said, in English, "Why not?" He looked at me to see what effect the fact that he could speak English had on me. I tried to look impressed.

I went out to the Land-Rover and took three bottles of moderately cool beer from the cold chest. I set the bottles on the desk and opened one. The chief of loading operations took it and drank the contents in two swallows. I immediately opened the other two.

"Really, of course, a man needs more beer in a job such as this," he said, still speaking English. "Beer is just hard to get, really. We have had no beer in the town for a month."

Muntaka motioned to me and I returned to the Land-Rover for

three more bottles. I put them on the desk and the chief of loading operations put them in a drawer.

He drank from the second bottle, more slowly than the first. "What is it that I can do for you?"

"I can see that you are a man of straight speaking," Muntaka said. "I shall come directly to the point of our visit. A Frenchman from Maradi visited here not too long ago. His name is Slabbinck. We believe that he may have sought assistance in transporting an item of value to the north. We wonder whether you may have seen him."

"Is he missing?"

"No. We would simply like to know if he was here and if he arranged for the transport of the item."

"There are just many people who come here, really. It is difficult to recall individuals. My job, really, is to see that grain is loaded on the camels for the trips north. I do not have time to talk idly with Frenchmen." He took a swallow of beer. Then he said to me, "It is amazing, really, that you can keep the beer so cold in your motorcar."

"She's got an ice chest."

"A nice chest?" The chief of operations smiled and half-turned toward the wall behind his desk. "So you like my calendar? If you can send me more like it I just would like, really, to have them."

"I'll see what I can do."

Muntaka was getting restless. "Monsieur, you cannot see many white men here, unless they are with the relief program. Describe him, Mallam Stevens."

"He's short. About five feet three inches. He has shiny black hair. His nose is rather sharp. He has all of his teeth . . ."

"Unlike your friend," the chief of camel operations interrupted. He laughed at his joke.

". . . capped in gold," I concluded.

Muntaka said curtly, "Have you seen him?"

"Captain Gold?"

Muntaka let out a breath. "Monsieur Slabbinck. There is no Captain Gold."

"But your friend said . . ."

121

"Forget what my friend said."

"He won't send me the calendars?"

"He'll send you the calendars. Have you seen Monsieur Slabbinck?"

"As I say, it is just hard to recall, really. I just see so many persons."

Muntaka turned to me. "You, perhaps, should take a look to see that the Land-Rover is safe. I do not trust those Tauregs."

I shrugged and said, "Okay," and left the office. When I returned, the chief of camel operations had a large grin on his face. He was animated and he was talking rapidly.

"Yes, your Monsieur Slabbinck was here on the fifth of the month. He was not alone."

"Who was with him?"

"Another white man. A priest of the infidels, really."

I looked at Muntaka. "What's that supposed to mean?"

"He means one of the Christian missionaries."

The chief of camel operations continued. "Your Monsieur Slabbinck spoke with me and asked that items be transported north by way of Mali. He just paid very well for our services, really. The items were neither hashish nor weapons. I just have no interest in what they are."

"What is the destination of the package?"

"El Mraiti in central Mali."

"And from there?"

"Marrakech."

We spent the remainder of the day continuing our inventory of the refugees. We planned to leave Dakoro early the next morning.

At dinner Assufu said, "I am sorry that you must leave us tomorrow, but we are grateful that you have broken your journey to assist us. The two of you have covered a considerable amount of territory in the camp. You have made our task easier."

Muntaka said, "Our contribution is very small compared to the work being done here by you and your associates. If you would not mind, I would like to say a word on your behalf to the minister of health when I return."

Assufu smiled. "The reward of assisting in this effort is enough. Still, your speaking with the minister can do no harm. By the way, I hope that you will join us later this evening. We are arranging a small entertainment for the children in this sector of the camp. Each of us will perform. Perhaps, as a condition of permitting you to leave tomorrow, we should require you to participate. Do you sing, Mallam Muntaka?"

"I have been known occasionally to hum to myself but I do not count being a troubadour among my talents. I will, however, be glad to narrate some poetry if you think it appropriate."

"An excellent idea. We are, I am afraid, somewhat limited in what we can offer to the children. And what about you, Mallam Stevens?"

"I'm afraid you're out of luck."

"Mallam Stevens," Muntaka said, "will be delighted to perform a series of magic tricks for the children."

"You are a magician, Mallam Stevens?"

"Mallam Muntaka is joking."

"Joking?" Muntaka asked. "You seem to be spending all of your spare time practicing the magic you purchased in the Zaria market." Muntaka turned to Assufu. "He is getting quite good with a number of them. You cannot take no for an answer."

"So," Assufu said, "it is settled."

I shrugged. "I suppose if Muntaka is willing to become a performer, I should be too. I insist, however, on following Mallam Muntaka. I'll look better after his performance."

Assufu laughed. "Good. I expect that we shall enjoy this more than the children, but children provide an excuse to do things that we would not otherwise do."

About a hundred yards from our tent, twenty or so skinny children ranging in age from six to fifteen sat in a semicircle illuminated by a dozen lanterns. From somewhere someone had produced cookies and cherry-colored soft drinks in paper cups. The children took small bites of the cookies and sipped their drinks as if they wanted them to last forever.

Two French missionaries, probably in their fifties, sang a series of French ballads. It reminded me that I had not seen Father Nunn at the camp. The camp was large and he might have been working in another sector. The missionaries were followed by Assufu playing a small reed harp of the type that I had seen on sale in the Zaria market. The music had a soft, lilting quality that seemed oddly appropriate for the quiet Saharan night. Assufu was followed by his driver who performed on the harmonica, a medical assistant who played the flute, and three young men from Zinder who danced a number of uncoordinated jigs.

When Muntaka's turn came he stood up, bowed deeply, swept his arms out to his sides, and began half-talking, half-singing a poem in Arabic. It went on for a long time. The children, and the men, were captivated by the performance and, despite the fact that I couldn't understand any of it, so was I. As I watched Muntaka in the light cast by the lanterns, a strange sense of timelessness swept over me. We could have been in the century that produced the manuscript for which we were searching, or in the century that produced Leo the African, or any of the centuries in between or after.

I thought of Leo the African at that moment because I had read, just the evening before, of Leo's travels to "Hadecchis, a towne of Hea" where he entertained a priest who was "exceedingly delighted with Arabian Poetrie . . . which he accepted so kindly at my hands, that he would not suffer mee to depart without great and bountiful rewards. From hence I travelled unto Maroco." I wondered if Muntaka remembered that Leo, among his many accomplishments as a lawyer, judge, notary, merchant, diplomat, and scholar, had also been a troubadour.

When Muntaka finished, a large folding table was placed at the opened end of the semicircle, close to the children, and several of the lanterns were placed on the table to illuminate my performance. In a nearby tent, Assufu had wrapped a turban around my head and I had put on a white robe borrowed from Muntaka.

"Presenting," Assufu announced in Hausa, "the Great Stevensa."

I bowed deeply, mimicking Muntaka, and said, "I am about to show you a few feats of legerdemain." The Hausa, "mai saurin hannu," had a nice ring to it. "Have you seen magic before?"

The children advised that they had not. I began with the easiest trick. I pushed open the small match box and showed the matches to all of the children. I then waved my hand over the box, muttered the "haba, babba, ba ka ba ni babba taba ba" that I had heard in the Zaria market, and quickly converted the matches to peanuts.

The illusion was greeted with laughter, wide eyes, and applause. Encouraged, I caused a match stick ("one of the few that I have that has not been turned into a peanut") to jump from hole four to hole two of the flat balsa stick. More applause. I then performed the other tricks, producing four sponge guinea fowl where there had been two, making a small rubber ball disappear into a handkerchief, turning a small red wooden ball into two small red wooden balls, and making three paper blackbirds disappear and reappear on the tips of my fingers.

My repetoire was quickly exhausted, but I was asked to repeat the performance and I did. At the end the children shouted and clapped their hands. It was then that I realized that I was in the wrong profession. I bowed and turned to Muntaka, who was smiling broadly. I wondered for a moment whether it was he or I who was becoming a latter-day Leo the African. I had the peculiar feeling that it was both of us.

The show finished about nine o'clock and, since we planned to leave at five the next morning, Muntaka and I said our good-byes to Assufu and the others. We walked back to our tent slowly, guided only by the light from Muntaka's lantern.

"I am very much impressed by your sleight of hand," Muntaka said. "You will have to teach me. I am much interested in illusions. It is remarkable that we are all so willing to let our minds be deceived. I think there is something to be learned from the techniques of the magician."

I didn't have a chance to respond.

We were about five yards from our tent when someone came hurtling out of it directly into Muntaka and me. The three of us went sprawling to the ground and I heard the crash of Muntaka's lantern. I could see neither Muntaka nor the other person, but in seconds I heard someone running away from us toward the center of the camp. In the darkness I couldn't have followed him if I had wanted to.

"Are you all right, Muntaka?"

I could hear him brushing off his robe. "I am all right. What do you suppose that was?"

"I think it was a man. What do you suppose he was doing in our tent?"

"I do not know, but we shall find out shortly."

Muntaka and I made our way into the tent and Muntaka found the flashlight that he had left by his cot. He lit our second oil lamp and raised it head high.

"It appears, Mallam Stevens, that our cases have been searched." Muntaka placed the lamp on our small folding table. Several of Muntaka's robes and my shirts were scattered near our suitcases.

I kneeled down and looked through my bag.

"Nothing seems to be missing, Muntaka."

"Nor from my bag. But we shall need the morning light to make a complete inventory. Strange. Perhaps someone entered our tent by mistake. It would be easy to do in the darkness."

Muntaka took the oil lamp and walked to the front of the tent. He held the light chest high and moved it back and forth in front of him. Then he ran it along the ground. He walked several paces away from the tent, bent down, and then returned.

"What do you have there, Muntaka?"

"This is quite strange, Mallam Stevens. Quite strange. Here, you will want this back."

Muntaka handed me the object he had picked up from the front of the tent. It was my copy of Leo's *The History and Description of Africa.*

"What the hell would someone want with this, Muntaka?"

"I do not know, Mallam Stevens, I do not know." Muntaka scratched his right ear and then ran his hand over his face. "It looks, however, as if our intruder is interested in African history."

THE caravan bearing millet, sorghum, and Monsieur Slabbinck's package had left the loading grounds five days
before. The chief of camel operations had given us the name of
the camel driver leading the caravan and we were shown, on
Muntaka's map, the route he would take. With luck and speed,
we could overtake the caravan before it reached the border with
Mali.

We left at dawn. The road north was paved for less than eighty
kilometers. Then it became nothing more than a trail, and then,
three hours out of Dakoro, it became nothing more than the faint
memory of tire tracks.

Muntaka spoke. "You have not said a word in the last half
hour. Are you thinking of a beautiful woman?"

The Land-Rover moved in and out of long ruts like a skier who
had stayed on the slopes for one run too many. I held the steering
wheel as though it were going to fly off and my fingers were
beginning to feel numb. A dull pain spread from the lower part of
my neck into my back. What I had been thinking about was Leo.
The experience of the night before, in the shimmering light of a
dozen kerosene lamps, as Muntaka and I and Assufu and the
others played at being minstrels, lingered in my mind like a fog
settled over a marsh. It was becoming difficult for me to distin-

guish what I had read of Leo's travels from what was happening to me. I was moving back and forth in time.

"At the very same time when mine uncle was sent ambassadour from the king of Fez to the king of Tombuto, I my selfe also travailled in his companie. . . . And hither are brought divers manuscripts or written bookes out of Barbarie, which are sold for more money than any other merchandize. . ."

When Muntaka spoke I was pulled forward four centuries. Suddenly, there I was in the middle of the Sahara and I couldn't remember the road, the landscape, or the passage of time.

"Christ, Muntaka, this driving is worse than I expected."

"You do look somewhat preoccupied."

"Preoccupied is not quite the right word."

"Intense. You are, Mallam Stevens, too intense." He chuckled softly. "You should get on well with the Berbers. They are in tents too." He chuckled again.

Leo had been wrong.

"Neither shal you finde in these countries any places apt to bring forth corne, notwithstanding they have dates in abundance."

"Funny, Muntaka. Look, do me a favor and cool it with the jokes. I've got a splitting headache and my eyes are falling out of my head. Jesus, I don't know why we haven't ended up in a sand bank before now."

"I wish that I could assist you. I have never been inclined to drive a motorcar, but perhaps I should take instruction. Would you like some aspirins?"

Muntaka handed me the tablets and I popped two into my mouth. Then I reached for the canteen hanging from the dashboard, and within ten seconds it was all over. I lost control of the steering wheel and the Land-Rover began to slide. We skidded to the left and were off the track, bumping up and down over solidified sand that felt like rocks under the tires. For a moment it was almost exhilarating. Then I heard the tires blow, one by one. The rear of the Land-Rover swung around, made a 180-degree turn, and came to a standstill.

I was sitting straight up, holding onto the wheel. I could feel a small trickle of blood above my eyebrow where my head hit against the door. I let out a long breath. I turned to look at Muntaka. I couldn't see his face. The top part of his body was completely covered by his prayer rug, which he held down with his left hand, and his right hand clenched the passenger handle on the dashboard. He was muttering in Arabic. After a few seconds he peered out. He was not smiling.

"Well, Muntaka," I said with the exaggerated ease of someone who had been in this situation many times before, "here we are in 250-degree heat, our tires all blown to hell, the axles probably smashed, and a hundred miles from the nearest living thing. And, even assuming that the nearest living thing is human, chances are a hundred to one that he's a bloodthirsty Taureg who would love to get his hands on all that junk we have stashed in the back. To say nothing of your Laissez Passers. They say those Taureg shivs work very quickly. You hardly feel a thing."

"Mallam Stevens, you do not approach life with the right attitude. You worry too much. So, we have been temporarily halted in our travels. It is willed by Allah. You should look upon this as an opportunity to learn more about the world. And you exaggerate. Let us look at the damage."

We both got out. My legs wobbled momentarily and my head ached, but it could have been worse. I walked around the Land-Rover to look at Muntaka. He was down on his hands and knees looking at what had been the front right tire.

"I know nothing of motorcars," Muntaka announced. "I would say, however, that, based on the casual observation of the man in the street—or should I say man in the desert—this tire is no longer serviceable."

My head began to pound. Damn.

We walked around the Land-Rover and checked out the other three tires. Actually, the first one we looked at was the only one that was completely decimated. The other three tires had gaping holes in them, but at least they resembled tires. We had one spare, but no way to repair the others. I sat down on the sand, my knees up, my elbows on my knees, my chin in my hands, and my mind on an air-conditioned theater showing *Beau Geste*.

"Well, Muntaka, what do you suggest? Shall we cable the Ministry of Works to come get us?"

"We are in the hands of Allah, Mallam Stevens. There is nothing we can do but wait. And perhaps we can build a fire."

"In this heat? Are you kidding? This isn't the Antarctic, you know. We're in the middle of the goddamned Sahara." I squinted my eyes and looked at him closely. "Are you sun-stroked, Muntaka?"

"You are not one to speak of persons affected by the sun. My thought is to build a fire that might emit smoke. Despite your imagination, we cannot be far from a settlement. Someone will see smoke. Do we have anything to burn? Do you have an extra pair of trousers?"

"You're going to burn a pair of my pants? How about one of your robes?"

"I think we may need both." Muntaka went to his case and pulled out a gray robe. I took a pair of bush pants from mine. We laid them in a pile and poured on a small amount of gasoline from one of the spare cans. Muntaka threw down a match and the pants and robe burst into flame, but they gave off less smoke than a cheap cigar. The smoke couldn't be seen for twenty yards, much less twenty miles.

"Quick," Muntaka said, "gather up some of the pieces of rubber."

I did, and threw them into the flames. If the smoke didn't attract attention, the smell surely would. The stench was almost as unbearable as the heat. I doubted that, even if someone saw our signal, he would be tempted to head in our direction. He probably had already started north on a fast camel.

For three hours we waited, throwing more gasoline and rubber on the pile, eating Spam sandwiches, and sitting alternately in the Land-Rover, on the running board, and on the sand. No matter where we sat, there was no escaping the heat.

"I am reminded, Mallam Stevens, of the remark of Lady Holland's father as recorded in her *Memoirs*. 'The heat, ma'am. It was so dreadful here that I found there was nothing left for it but to take off my flesh and sit in my bones.' "

"Christ, Muntaka, will you clam up with those damn quotations. You're going to be sitting in your damn bones soon enough. As soon as those vultures get tired of flying, they'll be paying us a visit."

"Vultures seek only dead meat."

"They don't have long to wait."

"Those vultures are probably flying over a dead camel. And they are, in any case, some distance away. You can lock yourself in the Land-Rover if you wish."

"Moreover in sixe or seven daies journey they have not one drop of water, but such is brought unto them by certaine merchants upon camels backes. And that especially in those places which lye upon the maine road from Fez to Tombuto, or from Tremizen to Agad. . . . But in the way which leadeth from Fez to Tombuto are certaine pits environed either with the hides or bones of camels. Neither does the merchant in sommer time passe that way without great danger to their lives . . ."

I was about to say something when I saw three figures on horseback heading toward us. I felt neither fear nor excitement. I felt numb and completely drained of strength. I was prepared to accept Muntaka's claim that we were in the hands of Allah.

As the three horsemen approached, Muntaka spoke to them in Arabic, spilling out a stream of greetings, the sounds of which were familiar to me. The three men answered. They sounded moderately friendly.

"They say they come from the settlement at Sidaouet. It is only some five kilometers from here. Two of the men shall remain here with our motorcar. We shall use their horses and return to the village with the other one. The horses will be brought back for them."

Despite Muntaka's earlier disclaimers at horsemanship, he rode well and the trip to the settlement was easy. The village was a mixture of mud huts, tents, palm trees, camels, and sand. We were brought to the house of the village headman.

He was standing at the door as we rode up and dismounted. He spoke in Arabic and Muntaka responded. They clasped arms and embraced each other. Muntaka turned to me and spoke.

"Alhaji Bayero says that he welcomes us here as brothers. He says that his village is ours while we are here. He will have our motorcar repaired for us."

I looked around. "I think I missed the Land-Rover dealership on the way in, Muntaka. How?"

"It would be impolite to ask. Come, he has invited us in."

Alhaji Bayero's house was furnished in a tacky elegance that either belied or betrayed the fact that we were in the middle of nowhere. The dirt floor was bare but several leather chairs that could have come from a London club were placed around the room and a large mahogany table that could have come from my Aunt Margaret's sitting room stood at the far end. Next to the table was a console radio, some four feet high, on top of which lay a lace shawl and a white porcelain vase. The radio had a silky walnut finish and intricately carved wooden latticework over a cloth-covered speaker. There was no evidence of electricity in the village and I was prepared to wager that the last program that had come through the speaker had been sponsored by Ovaltine. On a small stand just inside the doorway were two bowls of fruit and a pitcher of what might have been goat's milk.

The headman spoke to Muntaka. "It is remarkable that you have come here. It is sometimes years before travelers chance upon our settlement. And yet we have had four strangers here within the course of a few days."

"There have been others here?"

"Two men—Levanters from the eastern Mediterranean—spent a night with us two days ago."

"Probably," I said, "with one of the international relief agencies."

"No, Mallam Stevens. These were men on a mission of their

own. A strange pair to be traveling the desert. And an even stranger quest."

"What were they looking for?"

"They were, if they were telling the truth, in pursuit of a camel caravan."

Muntaka and I looked at each other. Then Muntaka said, "Very odd. What in the world for?"

"They didn't explain. They asked whether any caravans had been through here in the past week and whether we could give information on the route of the caravans. Perhaps they are dealers in hashish. There is much hashish carried across the desert by the caravans. But the purchases are usually made in the cities to the far north."

"Can you describe the men?" I asked.

"They were quite unprepared for desert travel. One was wearing a western business suit. He was about your height, Alhaji Muntaka. His hair stood out from his head. He wore dark glasses." Bayero watched our faces. "You know him?"

Muntaka pursed his lips and tilted his head. "It does not seem likely."

"As I say, they were quite unprepared for desert travel. They will be forced to turn back soon or die in the desert. Their petrol could not last long. We sold them some provisions." Bayero pointed to a table in the corner. There was an expensive-looking thirty-five-mm. camera on it. "One of the men left his photo box. They departed in haste, at first light. Perhaps he will return for it. If he is still alive." The leather case next to the camera looked like it contained a telephoto lens.

"If they do return, Alhaji Bayero, you would do us a favor by not mentioning our visit. Or to others who may appear in your village."

"As you wish. But come, we talk too much. Try some of this fruit. It is fresh. It was brought down from the north only three weeks ago."

133

The next morning we were able to get to the problem of our Land-Rover.

Muntaka spoke to Bayero. "Your hospitality has been a great gift. But we must continue our journey to the north. Do you have facilities here for the repair of our motorcar?"

"We are a small village. We see very few motorcars. You must go to Oued Haouach, some 140 kilometers from here. They shall be able to replace your tires."

Muntaka and I looked at each other. Muntaka asked, "Do you have a suggestion as to how we should proceed? Could we use some of the camels of the village to tow us? For payment, of course."

"There will be no need. We shall be able to provide a temporary repair of the tires, enough to take you to Oued Haouach. Your motorcar is being brought here now."

"But I thought you have no repair shop here. Do you have old tires perhaps?"

"No. What we shall do is repair your tires in the manner of the desert. With *kashin rakumi*."

"Camel dung?"

"Of course."

"How do you use it?"

"We shall take your torn tires and pack them tightly with camel dung. After the dung is mixed with mud and allowed to dry inside the rubber, it shall itself have the consistency of rubber. It will not, of course, take you to your destination, but it shall be sufficient to take you to Oued Haouach. It is the science of the desert."

Muntaka and I looked at each other in slight disbelief. I shrugged my shoulders and Muntaka said, "We shall be delighted to see this magic. How long shall it take?"

"The collection of the dung, the mixing with the mud and the packing into the tires shall take less than a day. The drying and settling of the dung inside the rubber shall take no more than three days."

"Three days? It cannot be done more quickly?"

"To be done well, it must have the correct amount of time to settle and harden to the proper consistency. In the meantime, you shall continue to be my guests. I am, Monsieur Stevens, in any case, much interested in learning about the country you come from. You shall have several days in which to improve my education. Perhaps you would like to learn about the desert?"

At the end of the fourth day, the chief declared that the tires were ready. Two of his men and I mounted them on the Land-Rover. The car sat in about the same manner as it would on normal tires. I drove the car around the village. It drove well. In fact, I thought the tires seemed more comfortable than before. I wondered whether Goodyear was aware of the camel dung process.

We left at eight-thirty the next morning, while it was still cool. The chief had asked two of his camel riders to escort us part way. Fifteen minutes outside the settlement I heard three loud explosions. The car swerved, almost running into one of the camels. Camel dung flew in every direction. A large glob clung to the windshield. I held the wheel fast and was able to bring the Land-Rover to a stop.

The smell of hot camel dung permeated the car. It was overwhelming. I looked at Muntaka whose brown-black hands, clenching the passenger handle, were as white as they would ever be.

I jumped out. All but one tire were completely demolished. The camel dung had ignited inside the rubber like dynamite.

The two camel riders looked on contemplatively. One spoke. "We shall return to our village for horses for you. The motorcar will be towed to the settlement."

An hour and a half later we were back in Bayero's village.

"Well, Muntaka, what do you suggest we do now? Maybe we could settle here. Let's see. We could set up a law firm."

"The situation is serious. We have now wasted too much time and we cannot wait for tires to be brought up from Zinder or down

135

from Oued Haouach or from Agades. We must return to Dakoro."

"How do you propose we do that?"

"We shall go by camel."

"You can go by camel. I wouldn't travel to my grandmother's funeral on one of those things. I don't know anything about camel riding, Muntaka."

"You ride a horse. You shall learn."

"And what'll we do with the Land-Rover?"

"We shall sell it."

"I haven't seen too many used-car dealers in the area."

"Perhaps Bayero is interested. We shall speak with him."

"Do you think he can drive?"

"He can learn."

"What'll he use for tires? Oh yes, I forgot, he can stuff old tires with camel dung."

"They can be brought down from Agades. You, Mallam Stevens, think too much."

The next morning Muntaka and I approached Bayero's office and we were invited in. Tea was brought. We exchanged greetings for a few minutes. Then there was silence. Then we exchanged greetings again. Again silence. Finally, Muntaka spoke. "Alhaji, I have a proposition for you."

"Yes? What is that?"

"Mallam Stevens and I wonder whether you might be interested in purchasing our motor vehicle."

Bayero showed no interest. "And what would I want with your motor vehicle?"

"It would be useful for making trips to Agades or Niamey. A man in your position should have a motorcar."

"I have many camels. And three wives. I do not need a motorcar. If you were to sell it, what would the cost be?"

"Two thousand pounds or eight hundred thousand CFA francs."

"Eight hundred thousand francs?" Bayero laughed. "So, you are only joking about wishing to sell your motorcar."

"I am serious. What price do you think would be fair?"

"Since I am not really interested, I would pay no more than four hundred thousand francs. Even that is too much."

"But, have you inspected our motorcar closely? It is a beautiful object. Come outside."

Bayero shrugged his shoulders in an exaggerated show of indifference. "Why not?"

He walked around the Land-Rover several times. "How can I be interested in this? It has no tires and it smells of camel dung."

"That is your fault, not mine."

"I am only responsible for the smell, not the condition of the tires. Tires must be very expensive. And I must have them transported from Agades. More expense."

"But have you seen the fine quality of the leather seats? Here, run your hand over this cushion."

Bayero did.

"The dust is thick."

"It can be washed. Here, have you seen these tools for repairing the motorcar? A complete set."

"What do I need tools for? Does it need repair often?"

Muntaka retreated rapidly. "Oh no. Occasionally, however, one must tighten a bolt. Is that not so, Mallam Stevens?"

"Leave me out of this," I said.

"Well," Muntaka said, "What do you think, Alhaji?"

"I would pay no more than four hundred fifty thousand CFA francs for it."

Muntaka took out a piece of paper and a pen and jotted down some figures. "It would be impossible to sell it for less than six hundred thousand francs."

"My last price," Bayero said, "is five hundred thousand francs."

Muntaka said, "That is too low. I cannot go below five hundred seventy-five thousand francs."

"I shall give you a final price. Five hundred twenty-five thousand francs."

"You force a hard bargain, Alhaji. Because of your hospitality, we shall accept your offer."

The two men shook hands.

"Of course," Muntaka said, "the supplies in the motorcar will cost you extra should you want them."

"What? I thought that they are included in the price."

"For an additional fifty thousand CFA francs, the whole load, except for Mallam Steven's suitcase and mine, is yours."

"I can pay no more than twenty thousand francs."

"It is yours. Mallam Stevens, give him the keys."

I motioned Mallam Muntaka to one side. "Don't you think we should draw up a purchase and sale agreement?"

"This is no time for a lawyer. Once we have the money, we shall be gone. A contract could only be of benefit to Bayero, not us. Besides, we have entered a gentleman's agreement. It would be an insult to ask for an agreement in writing."

Muntaka turned back to Bayero. "There is one other thing. There is one other exchange that we would like to arrange."

"And what is that?"

"If you will teach Mallam Stevens how a camel is to be ridden, he shall teach you how the car should be driven."

"You are to leave here on camels?"

"Yes."

"I shall be glad to rent two camels to you. Fifty thousand CFA francs."

I had hoped that Bayero would start me out on a short camel but I was out of luck. There is no such thing as a short camel.

The process began with deceiving simplicity. My camel lowered itself to the ground, with its legs folded underneath it, as if it were a yogi beginning contemplation. Its face was impassive. Bayero cinched the saddle and instructed me in positioning myself. When I was theoretically set, the camel unfolded itself like a carpenter's ruler, in three stages. At the first stage I was thrown back and I had to snap myself forward; at the second stage I was thrown forward, and I found myself with my arms around the camel's neck; at the final stage I was thrown back again. The effect was very much like a rocking chair out of control. The unfolding completed, I was a hell of a lot higher off the ground than I would have liked to have been.

The first half-day was spent simply being led around the small village by one of Bayero's camel men. I felt completely foolish. The attention I got suggested that I was the major attraction of the year. The second half-day the camel man put the camel under my command, such as it was. We didn't move above a walk. Muntaka was impatient with the rate of progress but Bayero told him that camel riding could only be learned in this way.

"How long do you expect this process of instruction to take?" Muntaka asked.

"Your young friend is neither the best nor the worst student I have had. We shall need two more days."

Muntaka exhaled a long breath. "We are wasting much time."

The evening of the first day of my instruction was spent listening to Bayero philosophize about the camel.

"What I am telling you, Monsieur Stevens, is as important as the instruction you received today. The camel must be understood not only physically but also spiritually. The camel knows when a rider understands its soul. If you do not understand him intellectually, he may turn on you."

"Swell."

"The camel has played an important role in the history of the African and Arab worlds. It has played a role in international trade similar to the role played by the great sailing craft of the last century. It is for this reason, perhaps, that the camel is called the ship of the desert. The camel can carry as much as two hundred kilos across the great desert. It is made for the desert, as you and I are not. Its eyelids are transparent and will, by reflex, fall to cover the eyes in a duststorm. Its nostrils close as its mouth does. Its feet are wide and soft, and flatten when it moves on the soft sand. In short, your mount is well adapted to the trip you will make. You need not worry about his physical or mental condition. It is the rider who is apt to face difficulties."

"What do you mean?" I asked.

"The desert landscape changes little. You must take precautions to keep your mind occupied and to avoid the sun. I shall provide suitable body and head covering." Bayero looked at Muntaka. "It shall cost you nothing. It is a gift."

139

Muntaka spoke. "The Alhaji is correct. The desert landscape, while it possesses a special beauty, can be unrelenting. One may see nothing but sand and small brush. But the desert has seen much. It has been the canvas for great battles, great explorers and great caravans. One must attempt to recall these great moments to capture the true magic of the desert. What the desert leaves unsaid, one must improvise."

Bayero was impressed. "Mallam Muntaka, you speak with the tongue of the poet. I could not have stated it better than you have done."

Muntaka smiled. Then he turned to me. "Your lessons must begin early tomorrow. Time is passing swiftly. With each day's passing, our quest becomes that much more difficult. We should take some sleep now."

At the end of two more days Bayero pronounced me competent to ride. Muntaka and I left at five-thirty on the morning of the third day. Bayero waved us off just after taking our pictures with the Greek's camera.

Muntaka wasted no time. He rode with a fierceness and speed that surprised me. His white robe billowed out like the sail of a clipper ship. I wondered if Bayero had had this in mind when he described the camel as a ship of the desert.

I had decided to take the advice of Bayero and Muntaka seriously and to keep my mind occupied with what I had read of the desert—the golden trade of the Moors, Lawrence of Arabia's charge against the Turks in World War I, Rommel in World War II, General Khalid Ibn el-walid's eastward attack against the Persians with camel-borne shock troops, Gordon at Khartoum, Leo Africanus on his way to Timbuktu. In fact, I had decided the night before we left that I would spend the first half of the trip in the role of Lawrence and the second as General Khalid. But Muntaka's pace didn't permit it. He was clearly in command. Instead, I felt alternately like Little Beaver, Teddy Roosevelt's aide-de-campe at San Juan Hill, and a cockboat in the wake of a British man-of-war.

The trip back to Dakoro took three days. My lessons in camel riding had come from a master. I felt more comfortable on the camel than I ever imagined I could be. Nevertheless, I was exhausted when we arrived in Dakoro. And my ass was sore as hell. Muntaka did not appear any better off, despite his protestations that he could ride across the Sahara if necessary.

At Dakoro we headed immediately to the makeshift headquarters set up by the U. N. We were given directions to the place where we could find Assufu. He was surprised to see us.

Muntaka spoke. "We are in need of assistance. It is most urgent that we arrive in Marrakech as soon as possible. We wish to inquire about the possibility of finding a ride with one of the airplanes at the landing strip on the outskirts of town. Are any of them flying north?"

"There are several small transport planes which have brought powdered milk from France. They are being unloaded now and will leave here tomorrow morning. They will make a refueling stop in Casablanca or Rabat, I believe. I shall write a letter of introduction for you. Hand it to one of the pilots. If you are prepared to pay the pilot a fee, I should think it could be arranged."

We were, finally, like the two books Muntaka gave me back at the funeral hut, Morocco bound. The French pilot of the World War II cargo plane accepted a small donation and Muntaka and I sat paratrooper style on long benches that folded down from the inside of the cargo section.

Two hours into the flight the engineer brought us a lunch of cheese, bread, and Vichy water.

"Muntaka, when we get to Casablanca I want to buy a white suit. I've always wanted to wear a white suit."

"A white suit? You do not seem to understand that we must move as quietly and darkly as possible. In a white suit you will be as a cockroach on a pillow."

"In Casablanca everyone wears a white suit—Greenstreet, Lorre . . ."

Muntaka shrugged. "If it is your wish, it shall be done. When we arrive in that city we shall make the purchase."

"What happens when we get to Casablanca?"

"We shall rent a motorcar and you shall drive us to Marrakech." Muntaka pulled a map from inside his robe and spread it on his lap. He traced the road from Casablanca to Marrakech with his finger. "The trip is not a long one. Three or four hours perhaps."

"Marrakech must be a pretty big place. Have you any idea where to begin the search?"

"There are two possible starting points. The first is the camel market. If we are lucky, we can find the man who brought the manuscript into Morocco. If we are unlucky, the manuscript was lost in El Mraiti or was carried to Tangiers or elsewhere. Or we shall not be able to find our camel driver. We must then search out the dealers in antique books and manuscripts. Marrakech is not, in fact, a large city. It is a town of perhaps two hundred thousand people. It should not be hard to find the important dealers. In addition, the Nigerian police were able to give me the name of a man with knowledge of items taken illegally from below the Sahara. He calls himself Rakman."

THE Marrakech camel market was on the edge of the town in a vast, open area where the relentlessness of the sun couldn't be escaped. Many of the several hundred camels stood, motionless. Others lay on their sides. As a camel changed position a cloud of dust would rise, hang in the air, and settle either on Muntaka or me. By mid-morning of our first day of questioning my nostrils and ears were filled with sand.

A dozen or so Tauregs, their faces covered by protective blue cloths, watched over the camels. Other Tauregs were deep in conversation, haggling over the prices for which various camels were to be sold. The market was both a place for trading camels and a terminal for goods carried across the Sahara. The bargaining, and the unloading and loading of goods, were constant, and Muntaka and I found it difficult to find men willing to speak with us. Most of our questions elicited no response. When someone did respond it was to say, "I know nothing." Without exception the camel men were unfriendly.

In the late afternoon of our second day of questioning we finally found a young man, about twenty, who was willing to talk. He was a supply clerk and his job was to check the items being loaded on and off camels. He spoke French. "Yes," he said, "the camel caravan you speak of arrived here three days ago. It came up from El Mraiti in Mali with a small load of leather. The driver of that caravan, Moulay Ismael, left here the night he arrived. He has returned to his home at Foum el Hassane. I don't know when he shall return here."

"We must speak with him," I said. "How far is Foum el Hassane?"

"It is over five hundred kilometers. The trip is a long one. The roads are not good. Besides, it would not be wise for you to go there. The southern Berbers are not friendly. They were among the last tribes to be subdued by the French in the 1930s. They killed many French soldiers and many legionnaires between 1910 and 1930. They are more peaceful today, but still not friendly. Besides, you will not speak their language. Moulay speaks only Shilha."

I translated this to Muntaka.

"Well, Mallam Stevens, what do you think? Should we make the trip to Foum el Hassane?"

"Are you out of your mind, Muntaka? The roads are terrible, the people are unfriendly, and when we get there, if we get there, we'd be speaking to ourselves."

"Perhaps you are right. Our first road has led us nowhere. All we have learned is that the objects of our search may have arrived here three days ago. Or they may be in Foum el Hassane. If we are lucky, there has been no time for them to leave the country. Perhaps, Mallam Stevens, we should pursue our second road and see where it leads. We shall visit Monsieur Rakman tomorrow morning."

Two days earlier, Muntaka and I had rented a Citroën in Casablanca and had enjoyed a pleasantly cool trip along the coast before turning south onto the sun-baked road leading to Marrakech. I stocked the car with Vichy water, both with and without gas, several loaves of bread, and several large hunks of cheese. I was glad I had done so since there were no cold stores on the route. We stopped only twice. Once for Muntaka to make a purchase from a man selling black eggs and once to "liberate," as Muntaka termed it, the aftereffects of the black eggs and Vichy water.

We had taken separate rooms in a small, inexpensive hotel in Marrakech, and had spent the better part of the afternoon of the day of our arrival soaking in tubs to rid ourselves of the dust of the Sahara. The evenings of our second and third days in Marrakech were spent soaking off the dust of the camel market.

Muntaka went off by himself on the morning of the fourth day. He didn't tell me where he was going and I didn't ask. He returned for lunch and by mid-afternoon we set off to look for Monsieur Rakman. His office, we learned, was behind the Great Market.

I had no desire to drive the large Citroën through the hundreds of people, horsecarts, donkeys, and oxen crowding the narrow streets. We decided to leave the car in the parking area of the central plaza and walk to Rakman's office. Though it was almost four o'clock, the sun was still hot and its reflection from the white buildings surrounding the central plaza was almost blinding. I put on my sunglasses. Muntaka pulled his blue turban farther down on his forehead.

The Avenue d' El Fitr was far from being an avenue. It was no more than twenty feet in width. On either side were stalls covered by various colored awnings. A heavy smell of spices dominated the air and it didn't seem that anything other than spices was sold in the various sidewalk shops. I could identify the cinnamon, peppercorns, salt, oregano, and a few others. Muntaka named several more for me.

"Each street here specializes in a particular commodity," Muntaka said. "Around the corner we may find a street lined with various cloths, baskets, meats, fruits, or medicines. Each seller begins to specialize in his product from the time he is a boy and he may sell it for the whole of his life. For that man over there, for example, the cinnamons, peppers, and mints are his whole existence. But each of his products he knows with a special intimacy. For him, you might say that spice is the variety of life."

Behind us a horse-drawn cart came up the middle of the street where we were walking and we were forced to the side. I bumped into a woman dressed in a brown robe. A white veil covered her face. She paid no attention to me and continued to argue over price with the shopkeeper. In front of me two men with angular faces and white beards and dressed in white robes and white turbans were engaged in conversation, their beards almost touching. Each looked very much like the mirror image of the other. I mentioned this to Muntaka.

"Arabs cherish closeness more than you Americans. We are not afraid to come close to one another or to hold hands with one another. You Westerners must always keep a few paces between you when you talk. Closeness for us is the lifeblood of conversation. We cherish the breath of words as well as the words themselves."

As we rounded the corner, a narrow four-story building shot out from the stall-cluttered street. Four brass nameplates shone brilliantly in the sun. The first plate read, "Essam El Melahi, Censeur et Expert Fiscal." The third plate read, "Nafir Rakman, Exporte-Importe-toisième étage." It was just above a plate reading, "Bernard Lallouche-Avocat-Notaire—deuxième étage."

The stairway came almost to the front door. We walked up three flights of stairs and along the small hallway. Monsieur Rakman's nameplate was on the door. We knocked.

A voice responded, "Entrez."

The small office contained three large red leather chairs, a wall cabinet, a safe, a ceiling fan, and a wooden desk, behind which sat a man dressed in a Western business suit. His pale blue shirt was decorated by small flecks of white embroidery and crimson cuff links that matched a large ring on his right hand. His dark, square face rested on a thick, short neck.

"Oui? Que voulez vous?"

Muntaka spoke, in Arabic. I didn't understand what he said except for the words, *Muntaka* and *Stevens*.

The man behind the desk rose. I was surprised to see that he was no taller than Muntaka and me. He said something in Arabic

146

which I didn't understand, but a translation was unnecessary. He bent over slightly, opened the top, middle drawer of his desk, and took out a small, grayish pistol which he pointed in the direction of our stomachs.

We raised our hands. I had never had a gun pointed at me before, but I knew pretty much what I was supposed to do with my hands. Those grade-B Saturday afternoons hadn't been wasted. I reacted otherwise much as I would have expected under the circumstances. Reading from top to bottom, the blood drained from my face, my mouth and throat went dry, my stomach muscles knotted and my legs weakened. I had to take a piss. I turned my head toward Muntaka and began to speak, but I found that I had to accumulate a little saliva and swallow twice. Then I whispered, "Muntaka, what the hell have you got us into?"

Muntaka smiled. Speaking loudly, he said, in English, "No need to worry. Monsieur Rakman is merely being cautious. I have told him of our mission. If we are no more dangerous than we appear, Monsieur Rakman will find no need to keep a weapon pointed at us. Am I not right, Monsieur?"

"Of course." Rakman's English startled me. "I must apologize for this impoliteness but one cannot be too circumspect these days. This is most embarrassing for me. Would you both kindly empty the contents of your pockets on the desk. Thank you. You should do so with caution."

I placed my wallet, passport, vial of Enterovioform tablets, Swiss Army knife, and Moroccan change on the desk. Muntaka reached into his robes and extracted three kola nuts, his small leather purse, our Laissez Passers, his passport, and a small vial containing some sort of powder. I was disappointed. I had always viewed Muntaka's robes as some sort of cornucopia filled with an endless variety of useful objects. The meager offering didn't seem quite right. Rakman, apparently, had the same idea.

"Ahmed!" A thin young man of about twenty stepped from behind the curtains to the left. He moved toward us in quiet, catlike steps and ran his hands over each of us. As he ran his hand up my thigh, the little grasshopper squeezed my balls. Finding nothing to interest Rakman, he stepped back and disappeared behind the curtains again.

"Well, now we can talk in relaxation. None of us need worry. You may collect your worldly goods." As Rakman spoke, he replaced the gun in the top drawer of his desk and walked around to the front. I was surprised to see that he walked with a limp and that his left arm was slightly paralyzed. The combination gave him a vulnerability that softened the toughness of his broad shoulders and solid build. He sat in one of the leather chairs and motioned us to sit in the two similar chairs facing him. He chewed on the stub of an unlit cigar.

"By the way, Mallam Muntaka, what is it that you carry in the small vial? It is not hashish, I hope. It is quite illegal here, you know."

"Nothing so uncivilized. The vial contains powder from the horn of the bull-ox. It provides a degree of extra power." Muntaka smiled.

"Ah, you Nigerians. You are always concerned with increasing your sexual and physical power. Here, we rely on our inner strength. Of course, from time to time it does no harm to take a little essence of desert root. But we do not carry it with us in a vial! And you, Monsieur Stevens, are those tablets which you carry to assist you in increasing your power?"

"In a way. They're for dysentery."

Rakman laughed. "I am sorry. Well, in any case, you shall not need them here. Our mint tea will take care of you. On the other hand, perhaps you should borrow some of Mallam Muntaka's powder. Our women are very beautiful and are much even for a man in good health."

Muntaka smiled broadly. "I know. They are, indeed, quite potent."

"Ah, so you have been to Morocco before, have you?"

"Yes. I came here in 1952 on my way to Mecca for the pilgrimage. It was a brief stop, but not without its compensations."

"What? Can it be? 1952?"

"Why not?"

"Why, that is the very year in which *I* made the *haj!* So we are brothers! We must take a drink to mark this occasion." Raising his voice only slightly, he said, "Ahmed."

Ahmed appeared through the curtains like an eel moving through water. He gave me a quick, insipid smile. Rakman spoke to him rapidly in Arabic and Ahmed disappeared once again. He reappeared quickly, carrying a large tray with two decanters, six glasses, and a bowl of grapes.

"You must take from each bottle. These are the finest wines in the world. The taste of each wine enhances the taste of the other. The taste of the raw grape will bring the two wines to even fuller life." Ahmed poured each of us two glasses of wine and departed.

We drank slowly, saying nothing. Then Rakman spoke. "Well, Alhaji Muntaka, so we made the *haj* together and never knew it. But there were, of course, many thousands of us. Seventy-five persons died during the *haj,* Allah take them." He took a sip of wine. "So, you have come about an Arabic manuscript?"

Muntaka spoke. "Yes, Alhaji Rakman. I am an expert in Arabic manuscripts. I understand that you, yourself, have some knowledge in this area."

"It is so. But I come to the subject only recently." Rakman started to say something else but he paused, put the cigar stub in a small copper ashtray, and took a short, fat cigar from a box on the table next to his chair. He didn't offer the box to Muntaka or me. He lit the cigar and took several long, slow puffs, as if he were giving himself time to think. Then he said, "I shall look forward to learning from you, Alhaji Muntaka. And from you, Monsieur Stevens. But, for today, we should not speak of business. In my country it is impolite to do so in the first meeting. Today, we shall celebrate our brotherhood. Here, you must both take more wine."

Two bottles and two life histories later, Rakman was saying, "So, Monsieur Stevens, you have found a most interesting traveling companion. You are most fortunate, most fortunate."

Muntaka said, "It is kind of you to say so."

"Perhaps the three of us shall be able to take some leisure together. Are you familiar with guns, Monsieur Stevens?"

"Guns?" I looked quickly toward Muntaka and then back at Rakman. "What do you mean?"

Rakman rested his cigar in the ashtray, stood up, and walked to the cabinet hanging on the wall behind his desk. The wood was a rich mahogany and the fixtures were of a highly polished brass. He took a ring of keys from his pocket, unlocked the cabinet, and revealed a small arsenal of rifles and shotguns.

"On occasion I enjoy going into the high Atlas Mountains to hunt game and birds. Perhaps, if time permits, you will join me. You have hunted, Monsieur Stevens?"

"Muntaka and I have done some shooting together in Nigeria."

"You were successful?"

"Muntaka is better at guns than I am. I'm a poor shot."

"I began shooting at an early age. My father was an accomplished huntsman," Rakman said. "I shall be delighted to teach you what I know. You will undoubtedly be luckier in the high Atlas. I shall teach you the elements of the hunt. You should be able to shoot a brace of mountain foxes. I have a friend who is a taxidermist. Perhaps you could have them mounted."

"Or at least shaking hands."

Rakman squinted his eyes. "What?"

Muntaka shook his head and spoke to Rakman in Arabic and English.

Rakman laughed. "I like your wit, Monsieur Stevens."

Muntaka said, "Do not encourage him, Alhaji Rakman. He is less interested in using words to communicate than he is in the sounds of words."

"Words," Rakman said, "are seldom used for direct communication, Alhaji Muntaka. Your young friend realizes that men seldom say what they mean. It is the hidden meaning in language and gestures that one must pay attention to. Perhaps it is, after all, the sounds that are the most important." Rakman smiled. "However, Monsieur Stevens, we may discuss that at another time. It is late. We shall meet again tomorrow. If you have nothing better to do, you may wish to visit the Great Plaza this evening. There are many attractions. You should not miss the 'Girl in the Cup.' She appears in a tent near the Hassan Umaru Gate. It is quite amazing. Quite amazing.''

"What is it?" I asked.

"It is difficult to explain. But I have a feeling that it will appeal to you, Monsieur Stevens. It is best that you see for yourself. Ahmed will now drive you to your hotel.''

"There is no need to have your driver take us," Muntaka said. "Our car is parked only a short distance away. We are at the Hotel d'Essouira.''

We shook hands with Rakman and walked down the stairs. Once outside I said to Muntaka, "I thought you told me that you made the pilgrimage forty years ago.''

"1932, 1952. It is all the same." Muntaka shrugged.

I wondered how Muntaka had known that Rakman had made the trip in 1952. The fact that he had been prepared for the "coincidence" bothered me. I also wondered why Rakman had shown us the guns. I doubted that he planned to take us hunting in the high Atlas, or, if he did, that he was interested in shooting foxes. Muntaka and I walked the rest of the way to the car in silence, back down the street of spices.

151

BOTH Muntaka and I were anxious to taste more of Marrakech than the camel market, and that evening, at eight-thirty, we arrived at the tent advertising the "Girl in the Cup." There was a small line of people standing in front of a man selling tickets for fifteen dirhams each. Inside we found about thirty men and women packed three-quarters of the way around a roped-in, circular area about twelve feet in diameter. There were no chairs. The ring, which had a curtained entrance at the back, was empty. The woman standing next to us smelled of garlic, and Muntaka and I made our way to the opposite side. As we waited, another dozen or so people came into the tent and pushed themselves into the crowd. It was becoming very hot.

We waited for twenty minutes. Then the lights dimmed and suddenly we were in total darkness. There were several gasps and one loud female shout in Arabic, which Muntaka translated for me as "Pig!" I felt a hand on my left hip and I turned slightly and jammed my elbow into the stomach of the man standing directly behind me. I heard a moan and some guttural sounds in Arabic. I had moved my wallet to a front pocket before we entered the tent so the man's efforts were wasted anyway. When the lights reappeared, the man who had been selling tickets was in the middle of the ring standing next to a large object, about five feet tall. The object was completely covered by a large blue cloth.

"Ladies and gentlemen," he said in French, "what you are about to see is unmatched by anything in the world. What you see tonight you shall never forget. Never. As long as you live. It will haunt your memory in the day and night alike. If you are squeamish, if you become ill easily, if you are unable to control your emotions, you should leave the tent now. Your money will be refunded to you. The young woman you are about to see was discovered by me in Tangiers at the age of six months. She had been placed in a large jar. I found her only by hearing her cries. I have raised her as a daughter. But, as you will understand, this has not been easy. You see, ladies and gentlemen, my daughter, Balara, has only a head and shoulders. She was born without a torso."

As the man said this, he pulled aside the blue cloth, revealing a table about three and a half feet high, a large cup-shaped container of clear glass on the table, and the upper quarter of a girl of about eighteen, in the container. The bottom of the table was open and the man ran a stick back and forth under it to show that there was nothing there. The girl had long dark hair, brown eyes that did not move or blink, and perfectly formed naked breasts. I heard Muntaka suck in his breath. At first I thought that what we were seeing was a mannequin, but then slowly, almost imperceptibly, the girl smiled. I stared at her, looked at Muntaka, and then turned back to the girl. "Holy shit," I said. A chill shot through my body.

Then the man spoke. He stood just to the right of the girl. "Balara, greet the people."

Balara's eyes moved slowly to the left, and then to the right. "Good evening. I am very glad that you have come." She spoke slowly, deliberately.

"Would you like a drink of water, Balara?"

"Yes, please, I am thirsty." Her eyes stared straight ahead.

The man took a pitcher of water and a glass from the dirt floor behind the table. He poured the water elaborately. Then he put the glass to the girl's lips and she drank. The man turned the glass over to show that it was empty. Then he asked, "Does anyone in the audience have a question for Balara?"

A woman behind me said, "Yes. Balara, how do you live without a body? Where does the water go?"

Quietly the girl responded. "It is a mystery. I have lived for eighteen years with only the part of my body that you see now. My father has cared for me. He does everything for me." The man smiled and put his left hand on the girl's head. He smoothed the girl's hair and moved his hand over the back of her bare shoulders. Then he put his right hand just below her chin. He moved the hand slowly up and down along the girl's neck and then softly down across each breast. Her nipples hardened and she gasped softly. "I, in turn," the girl continued, "try to be as kind to my father as I can be." Saying this, she opened her mouth and shaped her lips into an oval. She moved her tongue slowly, first to the left and then to the right side of her lips, and then in a circle.

With that the lights dimmed again. There were more gasps. When the lights came on, the table, the girl and the cup were gone. The man, still standing in the ring, said, "What you have seen is nothing compared to what you will see in a few minutes. For fifteen dirhams more you will see one of the most amazing sights in the world. Here, in this very tent, a young woman will be converted, right before your eyes, into a pigeon. After the conversion has been completed, the pigeon will speak to you in French, Arabic, and Spanish. Please leave the tent now and purchase your tickets on the outside. The performance will begin in ten minutes."

Forty-five minutes later the show began. There had been no question in Muntaka's mind that we should stay. He was fascinated by the first illusion but neither of us could figure how it was done. There appeared to be no false bottom to the table. The girl had obviously been real. We were still discussing the first act when the lights were turned out. When they reappeared the man was again standing in the center of the ring. Next to him a young woman stood on top of a small, light, four-legged stool about two feet high, surrounded on three sides by a hinged screen. Over her head was what looked like a black parasol. Under the table was a silver candelabra with four white candles burning evenly. The young woman's hair was piled elegantly on the top of her head and she wore dark eye shadow and bright red lipstick. Despite the look of mature beauty that contrasted sharply with the almost childlike innocence of Balara, the two women had similar facial characteristics. The woman on the table was wearing a gossamer-thin gown of white and nothing else. Her nipples could be seen clearly beneath the gown, as well as the small patch of dark hair above her long, slender legs.

The man put his right hand on the woman's left ankle and moved his fingers slowly, gently, along her leg to just below her left buttock. The woman closed her eyes and began to sing softly. When she finished her song, three persons from the audience were invited to stand behind the screen, presumably to confirm that the woman could not escape behind it. The woman began to hum. Then the man pulled a string hanging from the parasol and a curtain dropped around the woman. The man drew a gun from his pocket. I flinched. The audience gasped. He fired the pistol and smoke burst out from under the curtain. A few seconds later he raised the curtain and the woman was gone. Sitting on the small stool in her place was a white pigeon cooing softly.

What happened next had not been part of the program. It was all over in seconds but at the time it seemed like minutes. The pigeon had appeared on the table. I turned toward Muntaka and saw a man, a Moroccan just behind Muntaka, raise his arm and bring a knife over Muntaka's left shoulder. I shoved Muntaka with my right arm and threw my left hand up to catch the Moroccan's wrist before the knife made contact. Muntaka fell to the floor and I fell on top of the Moroccan. The knife was still clenched in his hand. People were jammed around us and there was nowhere for me to roll off or escape. My hand held his wrist momentarily but the knife would have been in my chest if someone hadn't stepped on his face. I heard the crunch of the bone of his nose and then his scream. He dropped the knife and put both hands to his face. Blood ran down his chin and arms. We were both still on the ground and my body was lying half across his.

Suddenly he pushed me aside and jumped to his feet. He shoved his way through the crowd, under the rope, into the ring. I followed and tackled him just as he reached the pigeon sitting on the stool. He fell forward onto the stool and what turned out to be a triangular box covered with mirrors. The pigeon flew past my face and the stool fell over, revealing a trap door in its top. I noticed that the stool had only two legs and that the candelabra had only two candles. One of the mirrors broke against the man's head. Blood was now streaming from his left ear as well as his nose. He got up again and pushed over the three-sided screen. I grabbed him and tore off most of the left side of the jacket. He headed through the curtained exit at the rear of the ring. I followed, but before I could catch him he was out of the tent and into the crowd and the darkness.

As I came back into the tent the illusionist was shouting, the young woman's head was peering up through the trap door in the floor, and several men were pointing at the table, candelabra, and mirrors and apparently demanding their money back. Muntaka was standing inside the ring. There was blood on Muntaka's robe, at the shoulder. Either he had rolled into the blood from the Moroccan's broken nose or the wound from the shot he received in the market in Zaria had reopened. He was holding the Moroccan's knife and torn jacket in one hand. With the other he was feeling inside the pocket of the jacket. His hand emerged with a matchbook, a prophylactic, and a photo of the two of us sitting on camels. In the background of the picture was our Land-Rover with three flat tires.

WE were at Rakman's office just before eleven the next morning.

"Well," he said, "I am glad to see you both. Here, sit down. The mint tea is just about ready. I hope you shall join me." He poured three cups.

We drank in silence for a few moments and then Muntaka said, "We visited the young girl in the cup last evening."

Rakman raised his eyebrows and smiled. "So, you took my advice. It is a remarkable phenomenon, is it not?"

"Yes," Muntaka said, "remarkable. It is, of course, an illusion." Muntaka looked at me and then back at Rakman.

"You think so?"

"How could it be otherwise?"

"I have seen the young girl seven times. Each time I study a different aspect of the presentation. I do not see how she can be anything less—or, I should say more—than is represented."

"Mallam Stevens and I may have to return to view her again."

"Perhaps," Rakman said, "we should go together." Then Rakman turned to me and smiled. "You enjoyed it, Monsieur Stevens? I myself find the young woman strangely erotic."

"All in all," I said, "it was a pretty stimulating evening." I gave Muntaka a quick, thin smile and he began to look uncomfortable. He reached over and put his hand on my arm.

"Mallam Stevens is himself something of an illusionist, Alhaji."

"That is so, Monsieur Stevens?"

"My law firm thinks I do a great disappearing act. And I was able to hypnotize two camels in Niger into thinking that Muntaka and I could ride them."

Muntaka closed his eyes and began to tap the arm of his chair. Rakman's face was impassive.

"You came here by camel?" Rakman asked.

"In a fashion. Our Land-Rover needed to be retired. Fortunately we ran into a used camel dealer."

Rakman raised his eyebrows and smiled. "I have a feeling, Muntaka, that our young friend is an illusionist with words."

"In a manner of speaking. But he attempts also to give double meanings to objects. Can you show Alhaji Rakman a bit of sleight of hand, Mallam Stevens?"

"I'll take a stab at it." Muntaka shook his head and let out a long breath.

I pulled the small box of matches from my pocket and displayed the top with the three-star design, the plain blue bottom, and the sides. "Here, Alhaji Rakman, I have a simple box of matches." I pushed one end of the box and revealed the full length of the small wooden matches. "But what good are matches if you have nothing to cook?" I closed the box, gestured over it with my left hand, and pushed the box open again, revealing the peanuts in the shell.

Rakman laughed. "An impressive conversion, Monsieur Stevens, a most impressive conversion. Perhaps, Alhaji, we should arrange for a tent for Monsieur Stevens in the Great Plaza."

"Perhaps."

Rakman poured more tea and then said, "But you did not come here this morning to speak of illusions. You have come to discuss Arabic manuscripts with me, Alhaji Muntaka."

"That is so."

"As I have said, I have not had long experience in this field, but in recent months I have taken more than a casual interest in the subject. This is a matter of professional interest for you, Alhaji?''

"I am concerned with Arabic manuscripts for their religious and historical value. I am not a collector, but from time to time I assist our small government museum in the north in authenticating various documents. It is, unfortunately, something I can do only in my spare moments. I have seen many documents which I myself would like to own. Many of them are works of art. The calligraphy of the sixteenth-century mallams is of particular beauty.''

"Nor am I a collector," Rakman said. "At least for myself. But, from time to time, I become aware of manuscripts which are of interest to the dealers in Paris and Geneva. It is worth my while to know something of their value. Only last week I was able to facilitate the purchase and sale of a seventeenth-century manuscript. But, I am afraid that my knowledge is not extensive. I am, as one says, simply a 'middleman.' I assist the buyer and seller in reaching an agreement. Sometimes I am in fact the agent of the seller. Sometimes of the buyer. It is occasionally profitable.''

Muntaka spoke. "I have, from time to time, played the role myself. One finds that, occasionally, it is the man in the middle who may wield the most power. You are familiar with the story of the tortoise and the tug of war?''

"I do not think so.''

"Perhaps not. It is a story told often in the villages near the place where the Niger and the Benue rivers meet. I shall tell it.''

Rakman smiled. "Please do.''

"The tortoise believed himself to be someone of importance and he was not hesitant to inform others of his greatness. He would tell passers-by, 'The elephant and the hippopotamus and I, we are of equal importance. We are equal in authority and power.' His boast was heard by the hippopotamus and the elephant and they dismissed it as the rantings of one with delusions of grandeur. Their reaction was carried to the ears of the tortoise, who became angry. 'What? They do not believe me? I shall show them.' He traveled to the river and found the hippopotamus wallowing in mud. 'Hippopotamus, I the tortoise am here. How are you, my friend?' The hippopotamus looked up in surprise. 'What? You call me your friend? Why, I could trample you with ease. Go before I get angry.' The tortoise did not move. 'But I am equal to you in power. Would you call me friend if I proved that I am as powerful as you?' The hippopotamus laughed. 'And how would you do that?' The tortoise replied, 'I have a test for you. We shall have a tug of war. You shall hold the end of this great vine in your mouth. I shall hold it at the other end. Tomorrow, on signal, we shall both pull.' The tortoise went off with the other end of the vine, which was very long. He carried it to the elephant at the edge of the forest. He told him the same story.

The next day the tortoise stood at the middle of the vine and moved it gently. The elephant and the hippopotamus each began to tug his end. The tortoise sat back and laughed to himself. By evening the elephant and the hippopotamus were still tugging. Then the tortoise took his knife and cut the vine. Each competitor fell back with a crash, the elephant to the ground, the hippopotamus into the water. The tortoise then went to the hippopotamus who said, 'Who would have thought you are so powerful. You are my friend.' The two of them then went to the elephant who said, 'So, tortoise, we are equal. We shall be friends.' Thereafter, the three were considered to be of equal authority.''

Rakman laughed. ''You are correct. Power is often enhanced by the imagination—and ignorance—of one's antagonist. It is fortunate for those of us who are tortoises. Or are you playing the role of the elephant in this game, Alhaji?''

Muntaka smiled but said nothing. Rakman continued to speak. ''Well, Alhaji, it is perhaps time that we come to business. What is it that you have in mind?''

I wondered how much Muntaka was prepared to tell Rakman.

''I shall be frank with you, Alhaji Rakman. Some time ago an Arabic manuscript was withdrawn from the government museum at Jos. The manuscript is of great value to the government and people of Nigeria. It dates from the thirteenth century and is a record of a part of the history of the north. You can perhaps appreciate the significance of such a document to my people. It must be recovered.''

Rakman sat silently for what seemed like several minutes. He sipped his mint tea and then lit a small cigar. He puffed on it briefly and then balanced it on the edge of his copper ashtray. He sat back in his chair, put the tips of his fingers together, and brought them to his face. Then he spoke.

''I shall be frank with you, as you have been with me, Alhaji. I do not know the location of the manuscript. But what you say brings significance to a rumor that I heard just two days ago. It was told that an item or items of unlimited value had arrived in Marrakech and that a purchaser was being sought. At the time I had thought that the objects were rare coins which were stolen from the museum in Alexandria some months ago. But now I think that they include the item you seek.'' Rakman picked up the dead cigar and held it in the palm of his right hand, as if he were weighing it. He was weighing something.

Finally, Rakman said, ''It will be necessary for me to make some inquiries. For the moment, I suggest that you do nothing. I have assistants who are able to move unobtrusively throughout the city.'' He smiled. ''I expect, in any case, that you could use some relaxation. It is most important to take relaxation from time to time. You shall begin by taking dinner with me this evening. My driver shall come for you at eight o'clock. Tonight you shall have a meal like no other you have seen.''

Muntaka and I were in the hotel lobby at seven fifty-five and Rakman's driver came through the front door just as we were about to sit down. He led us to a black Peugeot 403. Rakman was sitting in the back seat. Muntaka sat with him and I sat in front. The car was air-conditioned and the blast of cold air was a shock after the heat of the Moroccan night.

Rakman said to me, ''That's a handsome suit you are wearing this evening, Monsieur Stevens.''

"I bought it in Casablanca."

"Ah, Casablanca. White suits are not worn much in Marrakech anymore. But, in Casablanca, everyone wears a white suit. My brother, my cousin. . . . I hope that you will enjoy the evening. I have arranged for you to have one of the finest meals in the world tonight. I hope, Monsieur Stevens, that you are fond of lamb."

We drove for about twenty minutes, through crowds of people and animals. Suddenly away from the main streets, we turned down a dark, narrow passageway just wide enough for the Peugeot. The only light came from the headlights of the car and an occasional lamp in a doorway. After about two hundred yards, we stopped in front of a large gateway. Rakman spoke.

"We are here." The three of us got out. The driver rolled down his window and Rakman spoke to him quietly in Arabic. The car disappeared into the night and the three of us stood there in pitch blackness.

"I am sorry that there is not much light here, but it is kept dark to discourage tourists. Please follow me."

We walked through the gates into a small courtyard. To the left was a red light. We walked toward it. A tall Moroccan, dressed in red robe and red turban, a sword in a sheath at his side, came toward us. His sudden appearance startled me.

"Assalamu Aleikum."

"Aleikum Assalam."

The red Moroccan led us through a series of four or five doorways. The last opened onto a large room that looked a quarter the size of a football field. At the very center was a large fountain, and colored lights played against the cascades of water. In each corner of the room was a small table surrounded by cushions. The walls, some twenty-five feet high, were covered by curtains of deep red.

The only other people in the room were three Moroccans seated at a distant table. They were drinking wine and appeared to be playing cards or tiles.

"So," Rakman said, "we have arrived. We shall sit over there."

A young man brought water in a shallow brass pan shaped like a camel's foot and held it in front of Rakman. Rakman washed his hands and wiped them on a thick orange towel. Muntaka and I followed suit. The meal consisted of seven courses accompanied by countless flasks of wine from different regions of the country. The last course consisted of grapes the size of goat's eyes.

"The skin of these grapes is very tough and not good for your digestion," Rakman said. "It is best if you remove the skin and eat only the meat."

The room was strangely silent. It was midnight. There was no sound except for the peeling of grapes and distant bells. I felt bloated, foggy and content. Three hours had passed since the dinner had begun.

Rakman wiped his mouth and lit a cigar. "Now comes the dessert."

"You must be joking," I said. "I can't eat another thing. Dessert? What about these grapes?"

"This dessert of which I speak you eat only with your eyes. . . . At least for now. Look."

From the far end of the room, which by that time seemed like several miles away, came five young women in soft-colored diaphanous gowns. Accompanied by lilting music, they moved to the center of the room, close to the fountain, and began a slow, hypnotic dance. For the first ten minutes they remained near the fountain. Then, one by one, they moved toward our table.

The first dancer, dressed in a film of light green, was one of the most beautiful women I had ever seen. Or so it seemed through the haze of soft light, Rakman's cigar smoke, and my wine-clouded mind. I was captivated and couldn't take my eyes off her—until I saw the second dancer. The gown of soft blue revealed slim, dark legs and breasts that glistened with perspiration. Her hips undulated in a slow, fluid motion while her breasts rose and fell gently with a steady breathing. Long dark hair came to the small of her back.

As the music began to increase in tempo, the movement of her hips changed imperceptibly from side to side to back and forth.

163

My throat went dry and I swallowed hard. The dancer's eyes seemed to fasten to mine and a warm feeling spread over my body. I began to sweat. My head was pounding and I could feel myself sway slightly. The music reached a crescendo and then, suddenly, the dancing stopped and the young women were no longer in front of the table.

I let out a long breath and pressed my hands against my temples. My head was killing me. I turned to speak to Rakman. Rakman wasn't there. Neither was Muntaka. A mild wave of panic swept over me until I saw, just behind Rakman's cushion, the young woman in blue. She held her right hand out to me. I took it and she gently pulled me to a standing position.

Saying nothing, she led me by the hand through the curtains directly behind us, through two sets of doors and into a small, dimly-lit room that smelled heavily of perfume. In one corner was a porcelain tub and, in the opposite corner, a large sheepskin rug and several cushions. In the center of the room was a small table on which sat a rectangular stringed instrument and a glowing stick of incense. Next to it was a chair and next to the chair was the young woman in green.

The woman in blue led me to the side of the tub and began to unbutton my shirt. In a matter of moments I was in the hot, scented water and the two young women were washing me gently with pieces of purple soap. It occurred to me that they may have needed a bath more than I did, but I didn't protest.

The woman in blue spoke to me for the first time. "So," she said in French, "you are Leo."

Damn. I wished I hadn't drunk so much wine. "What?"

"You are Leo. You are a handsome young man of independence and forcefulness. You like excitement. You are kindhearted and there is a poetic side to your nature. You are an adventurer. You are romantic. You are a gentle lover. You are Leo." She rubbed the soap across my chest and down my stomach.

That's what I thought she said. Jesus, maybe I *was* Leo. I looked at her through eyes clouded by the passage of time. "What century is this?"

"What century?"

"Yes."

She looked at the woman in green, who was massaging the back of my neck, smiled, and raised her right eyebrow slightly. "We are in the twentieth century."

I felt relieved. "In that case, I'm not Leo. My name is James Stevens. What's yours?"

"I was not stating your name. I am talking of your astrological sign."

"Sign? Oh. Well, I'm afraid you're wrong. I'm a Virgo."

"Virgo? That is unfortunate."

"Why?"

"Nadia and I are Gemini. Virgo and Gemini are incompatible. Particularly in matters of romance. Leo and Gemini, on the other hand, are very compatible. Well, perhaps we can talk. Nadia and I are studying existential philosophy at the University. We are now reading Kirkegaard and Satre. Are you familiar with. . .?"

For my owne part when the Africans are spoken evil of I shall confirm myself to be a man of Granada and when the Granadians are discommended, then I will profess to be an African. "Actually, now that I think of it, I *am* Leo. I was thinking of my friend Muntaka. *He's* Virgo."

The woman in blue smiled. "I thought so. Are you early or late Leo?"

What the hell was she talking about? "Late."

"That is unfortunate. The moon is now in crescent. While you are compatible with Gemini, you are slightly out of phase. It is dangerous to mix two Gemini and a Leo."

Damn. It was too late to say early. I was pressing my luck.

"Still, however, the time could not be better for Leo and one Gemini." The young woman in green stood up and walked to the chair. She sat down, placed the dulcimer in her lap, and began plucking at the strings.

The young woman in blue—or rather the young woman who had been in blue—made love with the athletic power and feminine grace of a dancer and the gentleness, sensitivity and mystery of

165

an existentialist. Halfway through, she murmured something to the effect of "Existence precedes essence." I was in no position to argue.

When I awoke, the haunting tones of the dulcimer had disappeared and the room was pitch black. The smoothness of another's skin touched my arm and I turned over and put my arm around her. She was lying on her stomach. Surprisingly, the texture of her skin and hair seemed different. It was as if someone had substituted one woman for another to see if I could tell the difference. To test the conversion, I ran my hand softly from the shoulders of the woman who had been in green—or was it the woman who had been in blue?—to the small of her back, and she stirred. She turned over and pulled me to her. We made love for the first—or was it the second?—time.

The second time I awoke a small lamp illuminated one corner of the room and I could make out a young woman in the chair next to the table. Her hair was pulled back and she was wearing a full-length brown dress, cut modestly to just above her breasts. Her eyes, two shades darker than the dress, dominated her small oval face. She looked so innocent that I had a difficult time relating her to the sexual embraces of a few hours before. In fact, I realized that I couldn't be sure that she *was* one of the two women.

"So, you are awake." She spoke French. "Perhaps you should get dressed." She pointed to my clothes piled neatly behind my head.

I stood up, naked, and she stood facing me.

"You had a pleasant evening?" She smiled gently. There was no condemnation in her voice. Nor any hint that she had spent the night with me.

"Yes. Nice. Very nice." I felt like a soldier reporting to his commanding officer. Was I embarrassed because she was one of the women I made love to or because maybe she wasn't? Her eyes inspected me from toe to head.

I turned and picked up my clothes and placed them on the table. Then I got dressed.

She took my hand and led me through a maze of corridors until

166

I felt the cool early morning air. A horsecart appeared and the girl spoke quickly to the driver in Arabic. As she turned to me, I noticed, for the first time, the thin silver chain that hung from her neck. At the center of the chain was a plain, silver six-sided star.

"Please get in, Monsieur Stevens. We are going to take a short ride."

"You're going with me?"

"*You* are going with *me*."

"Where're we going?"

"You are going, Monsieur Stevens, to meet my father."

THIRTY minutes later the horsecart pulled up in front of a nondescript concrete building in a section of the city I hadn't seen before. The young woman and I said nothing to each other as we drove. I wondered, momentarily, why I was going with her. Not why she wanted me to go with her, but why it had not occurred to me to say no. It did occur to me that I might have just accompanied the young woman through some Moroccan rites of sexual passage, and that the capstone of the ritual might be her taking the young man in marriage. I was confident, however, that her father would reject me out of hand once we came face to face and he learned that I was a jobless, impoverished, footloose adventurer. That is, if her father was an understanding sort. It was only halfway through the brief voyage that it occurred to me that the capstone of the ritual might involve human sacrifice.

But the truth is that the reason the young man did not protest or jump out of the horsecart at any stage of the ride was that he was being swept along by the warmth and memory of a long erotic night. And by one of the most beautiful women he had ever seen. She was not beautiful in the classical sense. Nor, during the long moment we sat side by side, did she even seem particularly sexual to me. I still couldn't relate her to the body or bodies of the night before. Perhaps it was the self-confidence with which she had moved and spoken that drew me like a magnet.

The young woman paid the driver. The early morning street was deserted. As I looked left and right to get some sense of where we were, I saw that there was something rather odd about the small shops and houses that lined the street. At first I couldn't identify what it was. Then I realized that there were no signs on the shops and no street numbers on any of the buildings. It was as if the shops and houses were all in hiding, afraid to proclaim their existence.

The young woman led me into the concrete building and up a long flight of narrow stairs. We walked along a dark corridor that gave no evidence of who the occupants might be. The anonymity of the passageway was suggestive of an entry to a whorehouse, but, setting aside the events of the late night and early morning, I found it difficult to associate my companion with a brothel. Maybe, I thought, it was a Dickensian factory employing child labor. At the end of the corridor the young woman turned to me and put a finger to her lips. As she opened the door, I heard what I thought was a low moaning.

The room might, indeed, have been a factory at one time. It was long and narrow and there were exposed beams and pipes running from one end of the high ceiling to the other. But it wasn't a factory. The room was filled with long benches, occupied by a hundred people or so. The men wore black skullcaps and white shawls and the man at the front of the room, standing just to the left, on a slightly raised platform, was speaking, alternately, Hebrew and French. The young woman took my hand and led me to a bench five rows from the back. She placed a skullcap on my head.

"Bless all who enter this sanctuary in search and in need; all who bring to this place the offering of their hearts. Then our tradition shall endure as son becomes husband and daughter becomes wife."

What the hell were we doing in a synagogue? I looked back at the door and two men, shawled and tough, stood on either side. The young woman took a prayer book from the back of the bench in front of us, opened it, and put the left side of the book in my right hand. It was in French. Suddenly I found myself talking responsively, together with everyone else, to the rabbi. The words were not registering but I was strangely swept up in the rhythm of the communal recitation. We stood up, we sat down, we stood up again. As we sat down for the second time, and as the rabbi spoke, I looked at the young woman. As her eyes moved from the book to the rabbi and back to the book, I examined her profile—her hair, her eyebrow, her nose, her chin, her neck, her shoulder, her breast, her arm, the outline of her thigh and calf.

"Forgive us, our Creator, when we have sinned; pardon us, our King, when we transgress; pardon us, oh mighty Redeemer, when our thoughts are impure; for you are a forgiving God."

I couldn't make the association. I thought for a moment of reaching over and touching her arm, to see if the feel of her skin would convey evidence that we had made love. I moved my side of the prayer book to my left hand, moved my right hand toward her arm, and then, without touching, drew back. I tried to imagine the texture and scent of her hair and I leaned to the right to capture her fragrance, but it was no use. Maybe, I thought, I should just whisper to her, "Did we, uh, make love last night?" It was just the sort of question one was trained in law school *not* to ask. It was okay if, in fact, we *had* made love, but if we hadn't, it would be ridiculous. What was she going to say? "No, I'm sorry, you must be thinking of someone else." Or, "I don't *think* so. What time was it?" Damn.

I liked the thought of sitting there next to her, having made love to her the night before. But the longer we sat there, the more certain I was that we had not. And if we hadn't, what the hell was I doing there? She had the type of breasts that, fully covered, caused a sensation of warmth to flow through the male body. It was a fullness that tread the thin line between wanton sexuality and putative motherhood. What would she be like unclothed?

"Days pass and years vanish and we walk sightless among miracles. Lord, fill our eyes with seeing and our minds with know-

170

ing; let there be moments when the lightning of Your Presence illumines the darkness in which we walk.''

As we stood for the third time, I looked around the room. It was then that I saw Muntaka and Rakman standing on the other side of the aisle, three rows back. I didn't know whether they had just come in or whether they had been there for some time. Muntaka saw me and nodded. I nodded back and wondered what the hell this was all about.

"Help us to keep far from sin, to master temptation, and to avoid falling under its spell. May our darker passions not rule, nor heathen companions lead us astray.

"And better it is to wait at the doorstep of Your house than to be an honored guest among the wicked.''

Four men climbed the low platform, moved toward the area behind the rabbi, and stood on either side of a large wall hanging that appeared to be made of camel's hair. The design looked oddly familiar to me. A series of straight lines formed squares of brown, purple, and yellow, and stick figures with large round heads and arms standing straight out from the bodies were grouped together in one corner. It seemed a strange motif for a synagogue. I wondered where I had seen the design and colors before. Then it dawned on me—it was the pattern that decorated either side of the gate leading into the emir's palace at Daura. The stick figures were similar to the fertility dolls I had seen at René Slabbinck's.

The camel's hair cloth was lifted by two of the men and the other two carried the parchment scroll from the ark and walked with it along the center aisle. Several men in the audience, standing next to the aisle, touched the scroll with their shawls.

"O House of Jacob: come, let us walk by the light of the Lord. Blessed is the Lord our God, Ruler of the Universe, who has given us a Torah of truth.''

Twenty minutes later the last of the congregation drifted up the aisle and I sat with my companion, not moving, as the room emptied. Then the young woman took me by the hand and led me

171

to the front of the room. I looked back and saw Muntaka and Rakman still sitting, alone. The rabbi came toward us and said to the girl, "This is the young American?"

"Yes. This is Monsieur Stevens."

I looked back again toward Muntaka and Rakman, then at the rabbi, and then at the girl. Suddenly it occurred to me that Muntaka had set me up once more and that the whole episode was a charade designed to exceed in absurdity Muntaka's funeral. But there was no irony in Muntaka's eyes. My God. Maybe I *was* about to be married and Muntaka and Rakman were the witnesses. They wouldn't do this to me. Or would they?

I looked back at Muntaka and Rakman for the third time, raised my eyes in a look of exaggerated exasperation, and shook my head. Muntaka and Rakman looked at me quizzically. The young woman said, "Monsieur Stevens, permit me to introduce my father." The rabbi held out his hand.

At first I felt relieved. Then I wondered whether her father was about to render some ancient form of Judaic retribution. But his handshake and eyes were warm and I wondered what I was supposed to say. *Your daughter and I really had a nice time last night. But I'm not prepared to marry her. I'm not at all religious. She should have someone from her own faith.* Or, *Look, I'm really sorry. I had no idea she was a rabbi's daughter. I thought she was a Moslem. Or a Christian.* Damn.

"So," he said to his daughter, "you have found them."

"Yes," she said, "it was not difficult. They were at the Maison Rouge behind the old quarter."

"So, Monsieur Stevens, you are fond of oriental dancing?"

"Uh, yes. Your daughter is, uh, very good."

"My daughter?"

The girl looked at me. "What are you saying Monsieur Stevens?"

"I, uh, thought, that, uh . . ."

The girl laughed. Then she spoke to her father in Hebrew. He

172

looked at me with wide eyes and then *he* laughed. "You thought, Monsieur Stevens, that my daughter dances at the Maison Rouge?"

Jesus. "Well, sir, your daughter is, uh, very beautiful. She has the gracefulness of a dancer." I thought it was a nice recovery.

"The Maison Rouge, Monsieur, as you no doubt know, is not simply an establishment for eating and dancing." He turned to his daughter. "At what time did you locate the young man?"

"Early this morning."

"He had spent the night?"

"Yes."

"As I suspected. So, Monsieur, you slept with a woman and thought it was my daughter. The lighting and your senses must have been quite dull. You think, Monsieur, that my daughter is a woman of less than full virtue?"

"I apologize, sir, but you see, she was sitting there as I woke up and. . . ." Jesus. The rabbi's daughter.

The rabbi laughed and winked at me. "It is no matter. My daughter is a beautiful young woman. Were I your age, my eyes would no doubt be turned to her. But she is quite pure. You would have to be patient." He spoke to the girl. "Are those the other two men?"

"Yes."

The rabbi motioned to Muntaka and Rakman and they came forward, down the aisle. As they came alongside I said to the rabbi, "This is Monsieur Mohamed Muntaka. From Nigeria. This is Monsieur Nafir Rakman. He is a countryman of yours."

"I am sorry, gentlemen, for the secrecy in bringing you here. But we thought it best that we contact you at night and bring you here in the early morning. You enjoyed the service?"

"At the Maison Rouge?" Muntaka asked.

"Here, in the synagogue."

"Oh." Muntaka looked at Rakman and then at me. He was uncomfortable. He shrugged.

"You have been in a synagogue before?"

"We have no Jews in Nigeria."

"You are Moslem?"

"Yes. Of course."

"From the north?"

"Yes."

"The history books teach us that we may have common blood."

Muntaka winced. He didn't respond.

"Your religion and mine, they have much in common."

"I would not know. You have something to discuss?"

"You do not know why I have asked you to come here?"

"I am uncertain. I have suspicions."

"Then I shall speak directly. I have learned that you three gentlemen are searching for the Meshiva manuscript. I would like to have it."

"I am afraid, sir," Muntaka said, "that the rabbi Meshiva had nothing to do with the manuscript for which we are looking."

"You know this?"

"It cannot be otherwise."

"You wish, perhaps, that it is not otherwise. But the history of my people in Africa suggests it is. We know, Monsieur Muntaka, that the manuscript taken from your museum tells the story of the role of the Jews in your part of Africa. I suspect that you know this already."

"I know nothing. The manuscript is untranslated."

"But it could be the case."

"There are some who think so. I am not among them."

"I shall pay you ten thousand dollars, on behalf of my people, if you will hand the manuscript over to me."

Muntaka looked around the spare, unpainted, almost pathetic synagogue. "You would pay ten thousand dollars for the manuscript?"

"It is a matter of great importance to my people. We are a poor congregation. We live in fear. But it is important that the manuscript come into our possession."

174

Muntaka thought for a moment, raised his left eyebrow, and ran his right hand across his face. "Even, sir, if we accept, for purposes of argument, that the manuscript is as you suggest, I would not be able to transfer it to you. It is the property of my government. And it is, of course, worth much more than you suggest. Moreover, if you will permit me to say so, you are making a grave mistake. If you accept my advice, you will forget about the manuscript. It is almost certain that the manuscript will unveil the history of our city of Daura. This will be of great importance to my country. A people must have a past. But Africa is not ready for a revelation that it was with the aid of the Berber-Jews that Daura was transformed into a great commercial and political center." Muntaka paused and looked around the synagogue. "Do you not see? This is the worst thing that you could do to your people—and mine. It would cause resentment in black Africa. Not admiration. Not affection. Not gratitude. Africa is not ready for such news. In fifty, maybe a hundred years, things might be different. But now, you would do best to have your people pray that the Jews had nothing to do with Daura and that the rabbi Meshiva had nothing to do with the manuscript. Use the money for your people. Paint your synagogue."

"I do not intend to make such a revelation."

Muntaka looked at him quizzically. "I do not understand."

"It is my *fear*, Monsieur Muntaka, that the manuscript reveals what I have said. And it is my fear that the manuscript will fall into the hands of our enemies. It is they, you see, who will reveal the role of the Jews in Africa, to create new jealousies and contempt. They may claim that it is a Jewish plot to undermine the black people of Africa. You see, we want the manuscript so that its contents are *not* revealed. As you say, black Africa is not prepared for such a revelation. If you do not mind my saying so, I can see that *you* are not prepared to receive such information. Am I not correct?"

Muntaka avoided the question. "You would pay ten thousand dollars for a document that you would destroy?"

"It may be destroyed. Or, as you suggest, we may wait fifty or one hundred or two hundred years. My people are accustomed to waiting. Perhaps in a hundred years the world will have changed and will welcome this information." The rabbi turned and walked up the small flight of stairs to the ark. He pulled back the camel's hair cloth and opened one door. He turned and held a small black bag in his hands. He walked back to us and raised the bag chest high. "There are ten thousand dollars here. The money is yours if you hand the manuscript to me."

As Muntaka was about to respond, a figure shot out from a small doorway just to the right of the raised platform. His face was covered by a white cloth and only his dark forehead was visible. He carried a pistol in his right hand. He ran toward us and shoved the rabbi against the platform with his elbow and shoulder as he grabbed the black bag with his free hand. The rabbi sprawled backwards. The gunman fired a warning shot into the ceiling, turned, and ran back toward the door. None of us moved. At the doorway he stopped momentarily as if he had forgotten something, pivoted, and aimed his gun at the rabbi, who was lifting himself from the floor. Suddenly Muntaka rushed forward and threw himself against the rabbi. The pistol fired and the shot ricocheted off the base of the small pulpit about three inches above Muntaka's head. The man disappeared and I started to follow, but Rakman pulled me back. "It is not worth losing your life, Monsieur Stevens."

The rabbi's daughter rushed to her father's side and put her hand under his head. "I am not hurt," he said. "He has taken the money?"

"I am afraid so," Rakman said.

"It will be necessary," the rabbi said, "for us to begin again." He looked toward Muntaka. Both men were still sitting on the floor. "You must give us time. When the manuscript is found, you must let us know. My people are accustomed to reversals." Then he said, "It was a brave thing you did."

Muntaka looked at Rakman and then at me. He didn't respond. I wondered what he was thinking.

176

I WAS sitting down to breakfast just as Muntaka walked in. We were the only two in the dining room.

"So, you have decided to greet the day. I have just taken my morning walk."

"What's the agenda?"

"Rakman has asked that we meet with him. Take a look at this note. Oh, I am sorry, it is in Arabic. I shall read it to you. 'Alhaji, after many greetings, I wish to inform you that I have, perhaps, had some success in connection with the search which is of mutual interest to us. I shall expect you at my office at ten-thirty. Prepare to spend the day with me. Allah be with you. Rakman, 14 June.' "

"What do you think he's got, Muntaka?"

"I do not know, but we shall find out shortly. You had first, however, best put a good breakfast into your stomach. The liver and kidneys are to be recommended."

I had the steak and eggs.

We arrived at Rakman's office at ten forty-five and he was seated at his desk as we entered the door. Ahmed brought in three glasses of tea and some biscuits.

Rakman took a bite of one of the biscuits. "I shall come immediately to the point of interest," he said. "I have located the camel driver, Moulay Ismael, whom you sought some days ago.''

"You sent someone down to Foum el Hassane?'' Muntaka asked. "I thought that it was more than five hundred kilometers away.''

"Your camel driver, Mallam Muntaka, is just on the outskirts of Marrakech, in a small Bedouin settlement. It is not more than two hours' drive from here.''

"But,'' I said, "the boy in the market said that he was in Foum el Hassane.''

"He was, Monsieur Stevens, uh . . . um, how does one say this in English? I shall have to say it in Arabic. You will excuse me, Monsieur Stevens. *'Beyat kalim kalam fadi.'* You may translate it for Monsieur Stevens, Alhaji.''

Muntaka said, "I am unsure of the English myself. In Hausa, Mallam Stevens, one would say, 'Ya yi magangannu daga dubura.' You catch my meaning?''

I laughed. "You mean, Monsieur Rakman, that the young man in the market was talking through his ass?''

"Precisely, Monsieur Stevens. You see, Alhaji, you were too quick in accepting his word. He was either paid to mislead you or he was simply giving a story so that he could appear to be helpful. But he was conversing through his backside. In any event, we know where our Moulay Ismael is. We shall proceed there immediately. We shall take my car.''

Five of us—Rakman, Muntaka, Ahmed, Rakman's driver, and I—got into Rakman's Peugeot. Rakman sat in front. I made sure that I sat next to a window, with Muntaka sitting between me and Ahmed.

As we were getting into the car I asked Rakman, "By the way, does anyone speak Berber?''

"They all speak Berber in Moulay's village.''

"I don't mean them. I mean us.''

"Oh, no. But perhaps someone will know Arabic, or Hausa.''

Muntaka said, "Do not mind Mallam Stevens. He worries too much.''

The drive to the Bedouin village took two and a half hours. The first half-hour of the drive, after we left the area behind the Great Market, was through a residential section. At one point Rakman asked the driver to pull up alongside a car just moving away from the curb. Rakman leaned out of the window and greeted the driver of the other car, in Arabic. The other man answered. He had a thin face, a thin moustache, thin eyebrows, and big teeth. He smiled, and then laughed. Rakman returned the laughter. The two men touched fingers and our car drove off. Thirty seconds later, the air conditioner died.

Gradually the large houses turned to small ones huddled together and then to houses and small shops huddled together. With the change in scenery came a change in traffic. We no longer had the street virtually to ourselves. We were surrounded by honking horns, diesel smoke, cars, buses, trucks, horse carts, donkey carts, men pulling wagons, men pushing wagons, camels, motorcycles, and bicycles. It was eleven forty-five; the heat from the sun and the surrounding traffic were becoming unbearable.

"I am afraid," Rakman said, "that we shall make little progress now until we reach the desert road. The heat will only become worse. Our driver will try to do the best he can by weaving in and out of the traffic and attempting to pass the slowest-moving vehicles. From long experience I have found that it is best not to look. One should either sleep until we get to the desert road, or pretend to do so. To watch is madness."

With that Rakman threw a cloth over his head and slouched down in his seat. As he did, the traffic began to clear just enough for the driver to begin to attempt to pass around various slow-moving objects in front of him. The road was wide enough for two and a half vehicles, and if there were a few yards separating our car and on-coming traffic the driver would use the opportunity to pass. On the first three such occasions he missed the on-coming truck or car by no more than two feet. On the fourth occasion he skimmed the edge of a wagon. On the fifth occasion there was absolutely no hope that we could avoid a collision with a bus moving north. I shouted for the driver to look out but he kept going. He had judged the speed of the bus perfectly and we missed it by inches. From that point on, I took Rakman's advice and attempted to sleep. I must have dozed for some time because I was awakened suddenly, not by the traffic noise, but by its absence. As I looked around I saw that we were on the edge of the desert. The buses, trucks, and cars had disappeared.

"We are nearing our destination," Rakman said. "The driver informs me that the village we seek is only a few kilometers from here. We had better stop for a moment."

The driver pulled the Peugeot over very close to a man carrying a large container of water on his back. The container was decorated in red and gold and a long spout led from the container along the man's side. Several brass cups hung from his belt.

We all got out of the car, stretched, and pulled sticky shirts and robes away from our bodies. The sun was high in the sky now and it would have been impossible to stand in it for more than a few minutes. Rakman purchased four cups of water from the man and handed three of them to Muntaka, Ahmed, and the driver.

"Monsieur Stevens," he said to me, "I shall give you a choice between a cold cup of this water and a bottle of warm Vichy. I expect that this water may not sit well on your stomach. One must have an African stomach to enjoy it."

"I appreciate your thoughtfulness, Monsieur Rakman. I'll take the Vichy water."

"I thought so." He returned to the car and reached into his bag, pulling out a large bottle. Ahmed, Muntaka, Rakman, and the driver each took two more cups of water and I finished the Vichy. Then, almost as if on signal, we each moved to a different section of the Peugeot, turned our backs to the car, and pissed. A viewer from overhead might have been fascinated by the kaleidoscopic symmetry of this aquatic performance. But he would have had to look quickly. The urine evaporated almost before it hit the ground.

It was another half-hour before we reached our destination. For the full thirty minutes there had been nothing on the landscape except endless desert, endless desert road, and the miragelike image of the high Atlas Mountains in the distance. Then, suddenly, like cardboard rabbits in a shooting gallery, two camels popped into view. I half-expected them to disappear back into the sand. Then more camels appeared on the horizon, forming a pattern of waves against the desert sky. As we came closer to the herd of camels, I could see a black tent, some twenty or thirty feet long, supported by poles about ten feet tall. The tenting was rolled up and one could look through to the other side where still more camels stood against the horizon. Sitting under the tent were several persons, all dressed in black robes and white headdress. Rakman spoke to our driver and the Peugeot pulled up near the tent. Rakman got out, spoke to one of the men, and then returned to the car.

"The headman can be found in the cement block building in the center of town. We must go there to inquire about our friend, Moulay Ismael."

We left our car and driver near the tent and walked into the small settlement, which couldn't have contained more than fifty buildings, many made of mud. The remaining thirty or so structures were made of tenting, except for the headman's office, which sat in incongruous cementy splendor in the exact center of the community. Rakman exchanged greetings in Arabic with several persons as we walked along.

The village headman greeted us with a warmth that I had not expected. Nor had I expected him to be wearing a Western business suit. He was about five feet tall, with a thin face and a small beard that looked like it had been pasted onto his chin. Large grapelike eyes, bright and brown, dominated his face. His suit was a size too large for him and the arms of the jacket came to the middle of the palm of each hand. By reflex I rubbed my wrists against my sides to push back imaginary sleeves.

"My name is Idrisi. It is a great pleasure for me to welcome you to our village. We receive few visitors here." The headman spoke in Arabic and then repeated his words in French for my benefit. He rang a small bell on his desk, as Rakman had done when we first visited his office. A boy of twelve or thirteen appeared. The headman spoke with him. The boy disappeared briefly, and then reappeared with five bottles of Fanta. I broke my vow of never drinking another bottle of Fanta and finished mine in two swallows, as did the others, except for Idrisi. More Fanta appeared. Rakman and Idrisi spoke in Arabic for some time. They spoke seriously but concluded their conversation with loud laughter.

"Alhaji Idrisi informs me that our Moulay Ismael returned here some days ago after travels across the desert from the French territory. He carried millet and sorghum north into the desert communities as well as leather from Nigeria. Alhaji Idrisi informs me that Monsieur Moulay Ismael is known to be willing to transport other items from time to time. Alhaji Idrisi will take us to Moulay."

Idrisi led us through a maze of tents, camels, children, chickens and goats. After we had gone about fifty yards, he held up his hand and we stopped. He stood in front of a closed tent. "Moulay Ismael," he said loudly, "Idrisi." A head peered out of the tent. The head looked at Idrisi, then at us.

Idrisi spoke to him again. The language wasn't Arabic. The man drew his head back, untied the flap of the tent, and walked out.

Moulay was wearing white boxer shorts. He looked first at Idrisi and then narrowed his eyes as he looked at Rakman, Muntaka, Ahmed, and me. Idrisi spoke to him again, with some animation. Moulay, a big man with sinewy, muscled arms and legs, towered over Idrisi. The fact that he was standing in his shorts, talking to a man in a business suit, didn't seem to bother him. He wasn't to be easily convinced that he should talk with strangers and some fifteen minutes passed before Idrisi came over to us.

"He is willing to speak with you but he says that you are spoiling his . . . uh . . . afternoon sleep. He would like that you make your visit brief."

"Tell him," Rakman said, "that we shall not take long."

Idrisi returned to Moulay and spoke to him briefly. Moulay opened the curtain to his tent and motioned us in.

182

The tent was spacious and the ground was covered by remarkably fine oriental rugs. Several leather hassocks, a small table with a wash basin, a metal cot, and a mat covered with sheepskin were the only furnishings. Idrisi offered one of the hassocks to me but I declined and squatted on the floor. Ahmed sat next to me. Rakman, Muntaka, and Idrisi sat on the hassocks. Moulay sat on the mat covered with the sheepskin.

Idrisi said something to Moulay and Moulay shouted several words. A woman appeared through the rear curtain of the tent. Moulay spoke to her. She left and then reappeared a few minutes later carrying a large tray of dates. She offered them first to me. The dates were clustered together on a thick stem and I cut off several bunches with my pocket knife. I took one bunch and the rest were passed around to the others.

Idrisi spoke. "Moulay speaks only Berber. It will be necessary for me to translate your questions for you, Alhaji Rakman."

Rakman spoke to Idrisi in Arabic and Idrisi translated into Berber for Moulay. Moulay's answers were translated by Idrisi into Arabic for Rakman. Muntaka translated the Arabic into English for me so that I could know what was going on. I could hear a few French words scattered among Idrisi's and Moulay's Berber and Idrisi's Arabic. Like many persons of north and west Africa, the three men constructed their sentences from several languages at once.

"We understand, Monsieur Moulay, that on occasion you are able to transport across the Great Desert various items of special value."

"It is perhaps so."

"My colleague, Alhaji Muntaka, who sits here at my right hand, informs me that you were in the town of Dakoro in central Niger some weeks ago."

"It is possible that that is so."

"Alhaji Muntaka informs me that you may have received, in addition to your regular cargo, some items which would not have been a great burden to your camels."

"And what are these items of which you speak?"

"Alhaji Muntaka informs me that they are papers which some-one may have wished transported across the Great Desert into Morocco."

"What is the interest of your friend in these papers?"

"He is interested in them for his government. He is able to offer you a small payment for them."

Moulay said nothing for a few moments. Then he said, "What does your friend mean by a small payment?"

Rakman spoke with Muntaka and then turned to Moulay. "Alhaji Muntaka, a man of Islam like yourself, would be willing to discuss the matter with you and reach a fair price."

Moulay was quiet again. Then he spoke to Idrisi, who didn't translate. Then Moulay said, "it is true, as you say, that I have carried a packet of papers across the desert. They were to be handed by me to a person who has not yet appeared in this village. This person was to come here two days ago."

"Who is it that was to retrieve the papers?" Rakman asked.

"I was told that it would be a religious person."

"An imam?"

"No, a person of a foreign religion. It is for this reason that I am willing to speak with you. I do not like the idea of dealing with an infidel. You are men of Islam. I would prefer to deal with men of my own faith. Still, I am also a man of business. You must be willing to pay me a fair price for my goods."

"What do you consider a fair price?"

"I was to be paid eight thousand dirhams on delivery. From you I shall need twice that figure, sixteen thousand dirhams."

Rakman spoke briefly to Muntaka and then said to Moulay, "That price is too high. Why are you not willing to receive eight thousand dirhams for your services? It is what you would have received from the infidel and you will have the satisfaction of assisting a man of your faith."

"I shall, Allah excuse me, receive greater satisfaction from the sixteen thousand dirhams."

"It is too much."

"It is not too much. I am asking you to pay me not only for my services of transporting the papers. I must also receive payment for breaking my pledge with the man who delivered the papers to me. It is possible that if it is learned that I have broken my trust, I shall lose another opportunity to transport items of special value. It may take me a year, perhaps two, to recover my good name. The news of such things travels quickly into the market and across the great caravan routes. As I speak, I am beginning to believe that I am asking too little. Twenty thousand dirhams may be necessary to save me from future losses."

Rakman spoke once again to Muntaka and then said, "The Alhaji is willing to make you a final price of ten thousand dirhams. It is the limit of his purse."

Moulay took a bite of date and then spoke to Idrisi. Idrisi then turned to Rakman and said, "Moulay believes that it is too little money. Yet, he is willing to accept it because he considers you and Alhaji Muntaka to be men of strong religious faith. He would, however, like two other things."

"What is that?"

"He would like your assistant."

"Ahmed?"

"Yes, he would like you to leave Ahmed here when you depart."

"It shall be done."

I couldn't believe what Muntaka translated to me. "Sure, Muntaka," I said. "Give him Ahmed. Why not?" Then I said, to Rakman, "What the hell do you mean we'll leave Ahmed here? You can't just deposit him with Moulay. What does Moulay want with him?"

"There is no need to worry, Monsieur Stevens. It shall only be for a few nights. Moulay finds Ahmed attractive. This is one of the things for which I pay Ahmed. He shall find his way back to Marrakech in due time. Alhaji Muntaka will reimburse him for his time, I am sure." Ahmed sat still. I looked at Muntaka in disbelief.

"And, Monsieur Moulay, what is the second item which you would like?"

"The white stranger . . ."

Oh my God.

"The white stranger's knife."

"He would like your knife with the many blades, Monsieur Stevens."

"My Swiss Army knife? Damn. I've had that knife for fifteen years. Does he know that I'm an infidel?"

"He shall no doubt wash the knife before putting it to use."

"Oh, swell."

"You can purchase another."

I shrugged. "If you're willing to sacrifice Ahmed for the damn manuscript, I guess I'm willing to sacrifice my knife. Are you sure he doesn't want the Peugeot?" I handed the knife to Moulay. "Tell him to write me in a year if he hasn't found the tweezers and toothpick."

Moulay examined the knife and spoke to Idrisi. Rakman translated. "He says he likes the scissors."

"Maybe he can set up a Berber shop."

Muntaka took a large number of bills from his leather purse and laid them in front of Moulay. Moulay handed them to Idrisi, who counted them carefully.

"Now, Alhaji Idrisi," Rakman said, "we would like to see the papers."

Moulay stood up and walked to the corner of the tent. He moved his cot, lifted a rug and then brushed away a quantity of dirt. He pulled a small metal box, about two feet long and two feet wide, from the ground, lifted the cover and drew out a package wrapped in brown paper and heavy string. He handed the package to Muntaka who walked to the small table, removed the wash basin, and set the package down gently. He took the Swiss Army knife from Moulay, cut the string, and unwrapped the package, revealing a large, handworn leather case. Muntaka wiped his hands on his robe and opened the case carefully. He extracted two pieces of parchment and laid them gently on the table. He stared at them for several minutes and said nothing.

"Well, Muntaka," I said, "can I make reservations for the trip home?"

"I am afraid, Mallam Stevens," Muntaka said, turning, "that this is the second wild turkey that we have pursued. These parchments are not the manuscript. They are maps."

"M APS?" I said in disbelief.

"Come here and see for yourself. These are maps, not manuscript pages. They are, to be sure, of some antiquity, but they are not what we are seeking. I am afraid, Alhaji Idrisi, that it shall be necessary for us to retrieve the ten thousand dirhams and Monsieur Ahmed. Monsieur Moulay may keep the Swiss Army knife."

"What do you mean he can keep the knife?" I asked. "It's *my* knife."

"Was. Moulay was attempting to be helpful. You have eaten his dates. You should be generous." Muntaka's face showed his disappointment. He walked to the entrance of the tent and stood looking out.

I said nothing. I turned and looked at the maps again. Rakman, who was now standing next to me, said, "These maps appear to be very old. They are both of northern Africa and the old Soudan. How old do you suppose they are, Monsieur Stevens?"

I looked closely at the maps for the first time. They were, as Rakman had said, both maps of the northern tier of Africa and what used to be called the western Soudan—the area of west Africa between the Atlantic and Nile. They were extremely primitive. There was writing on both of them. The first seemed to be in

Arabic script. The other was in Latin or some medieval form of French or Spanish. I asked Rakman if he could decipher either of them.

Rakman took a small magnifying glass from his pocket and looked closely at one map and then the other. He traced several lines on each map with his finger and felt the texture of the parchments carefully. He placed his thumb along one of the maps, appearing to measure distances. He called Muntaka over to the table and he spoke to us out of the hearing of Idrisi and the others.

"I have a small collection of maps myself," he said. "And I have, from time to time, collected them for others. My expertise in this area is limited, but I believe that this first map is not without some interest. It was, as you see, drawn by a man literate in Latin. It shows here the mountains we call Atlas. This break in the lines is undoubtedly part of the route taken by merchants from the Mediterranean traveling to the south, into the Sahara. You know Latin, Monsieur Stevens?"

"A little, from high school days."

"What are these words here, toward the center?" Rakman handed the magnifying glass to me.

The words were *patria gentis nigri.*

"It looks," I said, "like 'the father's knees gathering clouds.' "

"What?" Rakman looked at me skeptically. "That can't be correct."

Damn. I looked at it again.

"Wait," I said, recovering. "It's something like 'the territory of the black man.' "

Rakman nodded. "You will notice, Alhaji, that there are included here the names of several places: Ciutat de Mali; Tenbuch, which, as you know, is the ancient name for Timbuktu; and Sijilmassa. They are quite accurately located. And the west African gold mines are indicated. This information sets the earliest possible date at about 1350. It is the absence of other information which sets the limits at the other end. It suggests a date of no later than the beginning of the fifteenth century. The map, if I am not mistaken, dates from no later then 1380. If I am correct, this map was prepared by the Jewish cartographer, Abraham Cresques of Majorca. If this is the case, this map may be of considerable value."

I thought about the rabbi Meshiva and looked at Muntaka to see his reaction. His face was tense.

"As you may know," Rakman said, "it was only the Christians who were prevented from coming into the area beyond the littoral controlled by the men of Islam. Travel by Jews was permitted. Abraham Cresques is famous for his great Catalan map of 1375. This map before us is very much like it. It was undoubtedly done by Cresques or one of his pupils."

"Mallam Stevens and I are familiar with the history of the Jews in Africa. Perhaps, Alhaji Rakman, we should take the map. Monsieur Moulay shall keep the ten thousand dirhams and you shall keep the map for your collection, or you may sell it, as you wish. You should be compensated for your trouble in assisting us."

"You have missed what I am saying, Alhaji. Here, look at this second map. It has been prepared by an Arab, or a Moor. The writing is in Arabic script, but it is different in some respects from the Arabic that you and I know. It contains more information than the first. If I am correct, it dates from the early sixteenth century. Look closely at both maps. Do you notice something of interest on each?"

Muntaka and I stared at the maps. "They're primitive, but beautiful pieces of work," I said. "If they're as old as you say, they must be worth something."

"I do not know what you mean, Alhaji," Muntaka said.

"Perhaps I have a finer eye than I believed. Do you not see here on this map, and here on this one, these place names and the caravan route leading to them? You will notice that the names are written in large characters. The place is obviously one of great importance. If my translations are correct, we are looking at maps which show the city for whose past you are searching. On each of these maps the great caravan routes find their crossroads at your city of Daura. You have here, Alhaji, a key to the mystery of Daura's past. Together with the manuscript for which you search, they will tell a story that cannot be refuted."

"Alhaji Rakman, if it is as you say, then you have already proved of great value to us. Mallam Stevens and I would not have had the eyes to see what you have seen. If these maps are what you say, they will not only help us to unveil the mysteries of the past, but they may lead us also to the manuscript we seek. For I believe now that these maps must have been sent north by the same person or persons who sent the manuscript north. We must now find who it is that was to retrieve these maps. We must pursue further questions in Marrakech. Tell Idrisi that we shall take the maps and that Moulay may keep the money and Ahmed."

Then it dawned on me. "Muntaka," I said, "I wonder if these could be the maps that Abdullahi mentioned back in Daura. The ones that were stolen from the emir's archives."

Muntaka sucked in his cheeks and ran a hand over his mouth. "It had not occurred to me. You may be right, Mallam Stevens. It is not unreasonable that maps such as these would have found their way into the archives of the emir's palace. But it is strange that Abdullahi had been unaware of their significance."

"He said he hadn't had time to catalogue the contents of the boxes in that room, much less examine them for historical significance."

Muntaka turned to Rakman. "Do you have any doubt about the authenticity of the maps?"

"As I say, I am not as skilled in these matters as I would wish. Still, they appear to be what I have said. The first map was drawn no later then 1380. The second no later then 1525. The parchment is very old. I have no doubt about the age of either map. And, if I am correct about the age of each map, there is every chance that they are accurate in what they report. Cresques was one of the most careful and reliable cartographers of his time. He recorded nothing on his maps which was based on mere speculation. He interviewed merchants who traveled into the desert and beyond. He was able to interview men of his own faith. Men whom he could trust. If it is his map, and I am quite confident it is, then what he reports about your city of Daura is no doubt accurate."

"But what of the second map?" Muntaka asked.

"Of its parentage I am even more certain."

"How's that?" I asked.

"You will see here at the lower left-hand corner these faded words in Arabic script. They become clearer through my glass. Look." I bent over, close to Rakman. "It is the name of the maker of the map. It is Al-Hassan Ibn Mohammed e al Wazzan al Zayyati, one of the outstanding recorders of African geography of all time."

"I'm afraid," I said, "that I've never heard of him."

"I expect that you have," Rakman said. "You probably know him by the name which he received when he took the Christian religion. He was known as Giovanni Leoni, or Leo the African."

Muntaka, who had been standing behind us as Rakman and I used the magnifying glass, interrupted. "Alhaji, what is it you have said?"

"If I am not in error, this is a map prepared by Leo the African."

"What? Leo the African? I have never heard of such a map." Muntaka moved in between Rakman and me.

"Look here for yourself at the lower left-hand corner." Rakman handed Muntaka the magnifying glass.

"Dear Allah. Alhaji, we have found something here!" Muntaka stared at the name for several moments. Then he handed the glass back to Rakman who examined the map again. He moved his finger toward the middle of the map and traced some lettering.

"There is here, Alhaji Muntaka, some writing in Arabic. It is too faint for me to decipher. I can, if you wish, show the map to a friend of mine, an art dealer who maintains a shop in the Great Market. Farouk has instruments which permit him to bring the

192

words to life. He is a man of considerable knowledge in this field. I have learned much from him. He can also confirm our beliefs concerning the age and parentage of the maps.''

"My dear Alhaji, as Mallam Stevens knows, I am much interested in Leo the African. This is a remarkable discovery. I would be grateful to you for the assistance of your friend. I shall, of course, pay him for his time.''

"There shall be no need for that. He and I are very close. To offer money would be an offense.''

"As you wish.''

We turned away from the table and sat down again. Rakman spoke to Idrisi. "These are not, unfortunately, the items which Alhaji Muntaka has traveled to our country to recover. Still, he is not anxious for Monsieur Moulay to suffer a loss. Consequently, he is willing to pay Monsieur Moulay as we have agreed. It will be necessary, however, to ask Monsieur Moulay several more questions. Is he willing to contribute his time to the brotherhood of Islam?''

"Monsieur Moulay will speak with you a short time more. He states that he needs sleep and has other matters to deal with.''

"We shall take little more of his time. He says that the package was to be retrieved from him two days ago?''

"That is so.''

"Was he given the name of the person who was to retrieve them from him?''

"Monsieur Moulay states that he is not accustomed to the names of Westerners. He states, nevertheless, that the name was Nunn.''

"He was given no other name? Only Nunn?''

"That is so.''

Muntaka turned to me. "What kind of name is that, Mallam Stevens?''

"Nunn? It's Irish. You know, Muntaka, that was the name of the priest I met at the Katsina rest house the night before we left for Daura—the one who translated the Latin passages for me.

Father Cornelius Nunn. He told me that he was going into Niger to assist the drought victims. But why the hell would he be interested in these maps?''

''Maybe he is not averse to making a small income on the side.''

''Muntaka, priests don't steal maps—or anything else for that matter.''

''Who knows about the private life of the priest? Perhaps he has become disillusioned. Perhaps, seeing the corruption in government around him, he has been influenced by it. Who knows what motivates men? And who, Mallam Stevens, is to say what motivates men of religion? It is an interesting question. But there is another question which is, at the moment, more interesting.''

''What's that?''

''It is whether our priest was attempting to mislead you with his translation of the Latin text.''

''Jesus, Muntaka, it fits. If this map is the document left by Leo, and the priest thought we were on to something, he might have tried to throw us off the track.''

''Nunn. Is it a common name?''

''I've met only two people in my life with the name. But I imagine Ireland is full of them. You know, Muntaka, the priest did speak about wanting to get his hands on a sizable sum of money.''

''The coincidence is very strong. I think, Mallam Stevens, your drinking beer in the Katsina rest house bar has been of some value to us.'' Muntaka turned to Rakman. ''Alhaji, is it possible for you to have some of your associates undertake a search of Marrakech for a priest by the name of Nunn? We are fortunate that Mallam Stevens can provide us with a description of the man we seek. If I am not mistaken, the Catholic priest is in possession of the manuscript or he knows where it is. I sense, gentlemen, that we are close to the end of our search.''

MUNTAKA and I spent the next three days taking long walks, reading, and discussing Leo Africanus. We took turns narrating the description of sixteenth-century Morocco from Leo's book. There was little we could do in connection with the search for Father Cornelius Nunn. Rakman felt that the search should be left to his men. He was afraid that inquiries by Muntaka or me might scare off our prey. Rakman informed me that, once the manuscript was in hand, and Muntaka's business relations with him had been terminated, we would return to the night club to which he had taken us earlier. It seemed like a good idea.

On the evening of the third day we received a message from Rakman, at the hotel. It was in French and Muntaka handed it to me for translation.

" 'Alhaji, we are without success in gaining word of the manuscript. But it is early. It is too soon to despair. My friend Farouk, however, has had somewhat more success with the script from the map of Leo the African. It appears to be of minor interest, but should you wish to learn what he has learned, I shall be in my office shortly after eight o'clock in the morning. We can proceed from there. Rakman, Wednesday evening, 18 June.' "

Muntaka and I agreed to meet at breakfast. He wanted to spend the rest of the evening reading. I was restless and went for a walk alone through the Place Djemaa el Fna, just outside the great wall that embraced the hundreds of little shops inside the medina. Acrobats tumbled in one spot, jugglers performed in another, musicians, in another. My attention was caught by a sign announcing the presence of a magician. It showed a man with a top hat and wand. Maybe I could pick up a few tips. In front of the sign the magician was in the middle of his performance. He changed the ace of spades into the three of diamonds, he turned a four-dirham piece into a two-dirham piece, he poured a pink liquid into his hat and put the hat on his head, with no appearance of the pink liquid. I put five dirhams into the container in front of him and moved away. To the left of the magician was a storyteller surrounded by children and adults. I couldn't understand what he was saying, but I stood there watching him for twenty minutes.

I stayed in the plaza until almost midnight and then headed back to my room. About a half-block from the hotel a figure stepped from the dark alleyway. The man, thin and somewhere between fifty and sixty years old, was wearing a suit that looked like it hadn't had a day off for a month. He handed me a piece of paper and spoke in French.

"You want nice girl? Can give you nice office girl for whole night. Very cheap. Nonoffice girl cheaper. You not like girl? You like young boy? You like show? Man-woman. Man-man. Woman-woman. Woman-dog. What you like, mister? Moving pictures is cheaper. Best pictures from Algiers. Guarantee top quality, lowest price."

I shoved the piece of paper into my pocket. I should have kept walking, but I didn't. Had he suggested any one of the services in isolation, I would have continued on to the hotel. But the orgiastic suggestiveness of the offerings intrigued me. Did he really have access to everything he mentioned or was he talking ragtime?

"How much for the whole package?" I asked.

"Whole package?"

"Office girl; nonoffice girl; man-woman; woman-woman;

man-man; woman-dog; blue movie. Have I left anything out?"

The man took out a notebook and pencil and made a few calculations. "Five hundred dirhams. Plus forty dirhams for me." Then he looked at me quizzically. "You want office girl and nonoffice girl together or in separation? Can give you very nice combination."

I looked at my watch. "It's too late tonight. Maybe later in the week."

I turned in the direction of the hotel. It was then that I was hit behind the left ear with something resembling a sledgehammer.

I had never been knocked unconscious before and when I came to it felt as if my head was full of blood and was ready to explode. I was lying on a cheap metal cot with a thin mattress. My jacket was on the floor. A woman was wiping my face with a wet cloth, as Mallam Musa's wife had done back at the Niger border crossing. Only this woman was about twenty years old and was wearing nothing but a pair of beige panties with delicate lace at the legs. In other circumstances this would have been an interesting way to wake up, but as I started to raise my head a sharp pain shot through my skull. I put my head back on the pillow. I took the girl's hand and placed it and the cold cloth behind my left ear.

The girl floated from the side to the top end of the cot and began to massage my temples gently. She moved her hands to my neck, where she pressed softly on the veins just below the chin. Then her hands reached down to my shoulders, chest, and stomach. As they did, her breasts, slightly perfumed and smooth as talcum powder, brushed against my face. After a few minutes she stopped and moved once again to the side of the cot. She stood straight, took a deep breath, threw her shoulders back and, with her right hand, pressed on the small of her back. A mole appeared under one breast as she did. I tried to focus on the physical layout of the room, but I was too groggy to absorb much of anything.

Then the girl drifted away from the cot. As she did so, I saw the figures of two men moving into the room. One stood close by the door. It was the Arab who had confronted me near the hotel. The other took a small wooden chair and pulled it alongside the cot.

He looked vaguely familiar, but I couldn't place him.

It was only as I heard him say, "I hope you are not too uncomfortable, Monsieur Stevens," that I realized it was the Lebanese I had met at the Zaria rest house. Daboul. Georges Daboul.

"I am sorry, Monsieur Stevens, that it was necessary to have brought you here by force, but I had no alternative. You have a small cut behind your ear, but it is not serious. Here, take these." He handed me a bottle of aspirin. I poured five into my hand and put them in my mouth. The girl put a glass of water to my lips.

"You will feel better soon. Now, Monsieur Stevens, I shall tell you why you were brought here. I would like to have the manuscript."

I was having a difficult time focusing on what he was saying. "What?"

"I would like the manuscript."

"What manuscript?"

"This is not a time for playing a game, Monsieur Stevens. I am aware that you and Monsieur Muntaka have come to Marrakech in pursuit of the manuscript taken from the museum in Nigeria. I know that you have taken possession of it from the man who led the camel caravan from Dakoro."

"We don't have it."

"You don't have what?"

"The manuscript."

"Let us avoid the bullshit, Monsieur Stevens." Daboul seemed to have a good command of the English language. "I am willing to pay a fair price for the manuscript."

"What do you want with it?"

"I shall resell it."

"To whom?"

"A collector, a museum, the Vatican, the Israeli government, the Nigerian government, an Arab government. . . . There are endless possibilities."

Jesus. He probably knew more about the manuscript than I did.

"At a small profit, of course. See, Monsieur Stevens, I am being honest with you."

"What were you telling me about selling your business and returning to Lebanon?"

"I am making a slight detour. What about it, Monsieur Stevens? I shall pay you well."

"We don't have the manuscript, Daboul. And we're not about to sell it to you if we do get it. It's going back to the museum at Jos."

"Cut the crap. Your friend Muntaka is too smart for that. Where's the manuscript?"

"We don't have it. I wish we did. I'd like to get the hell out of Marrakech." I touched the back of my head and winced.

"Moroccans have a way of making people speak the truth."

I felt a knot in my stomach. "And of silencing them?"

"What do you mean?"

"You know what I mean, Daboul. The son of a bitch you sent to kill Muntaka."

"You mean the Moroccan with the broken nose?"

"You know what I mean." My head was beginning to pound. Suddenly it occurred to me that it wasn't a very bright idea to bring up the subject of the Moroccan.

Daboul smiled. "You will be pleased to learn, Monsieur Stevens, that the Moroccan with the broken nose is in the next room."

I knew it was now or never. I rolled off the bed, stood up, and raced for the door. I got about three feet and keeled over. Daboul and the Arab who had been standing near the door each took an arm and raised me to my feet. The room was out of focus.

The two men led me toward the adjoining room. I wondered whether there would be pain as the knife entered the body or whether the pain comes after. I remembered the scream of the doctor back at Slabbinck's bedroom and my whole body shuddered.

The Arab opened the door. As he did, Daboul turned his head toward the girl, who was making the bed, and said, "Leave enough sheet to permit us to cover his head." Damn.

The second room, like the first, had a cot and one chair. Only this room didn't have a beautiful girl. Instead, on the cot was a man with a large bandage covering the middle of his face. He was bigger than I remembered. He made no movement as we entered. He was stretched out like a corpse.

"This, Monsieur Stevens, is Hassan Ali. He is the man who attempted to ah . . . ah, assassinate your friend, Alhaji Muntaka. I understand that you interfered with his plan. His failure was a disappointment to him. And to me. Your friend was able to retrieve the manuscript."

"Is he dead?"

"That is wishful thinking, Monsieur Stevens. He is merely drugged."

"Drugged?"

"The pain connected with the injury to his face is, as he describes it, excruciating. He takes large doses of pain-killer. Some of the medication has a sleep-inducing effect. But it does not last long. Perhaps you would like to tell me about the manuscript."

"I don't have it."

"Your friend does."

"Nobody has it."

"I shall give you one more chance. We know of your trip to the Berber village."

"I'm telling you, Daboul, we didn't find it."

Daboul motioned to the Arab and the Arab shook the Moroccan by the shoulder. The Moroccan moaned. The Arab shook him again and the Moroccan raised his head slightly.

Daboul shouted to the Moroccan. "Hassan, there is a friend of yours here. It is Monsieur Stevens. From the side show."

The Moroccan raised his trunk quickly and looked toward me. He let out a loud moan and held the sides of his head. Then he reached under his pillow and pulled out a short dagger.

"Put the knife down, Hassan. We are not ready to kill Monsieur Stevens yet." Daboul turned toward me. "What about the manuscript, Stevens?"

200

"Jesus, Daboul, we don't have it."

Daboul let out a breath and motioned to the Moroccan with his head. The Moroccan stood up. The bandage covered most of his face and he looked like something out of *The Prisoner of Zenda*. He came toward me slowly. He raised his right hand and I put my arms in front of my face. As I did, his left hand plowed into my stomach, just below and between the ribs. I fell backwards, onto the floor and tossed part of my dinner. My mouth tasted like rancid green peppers. My stomach felt like it had been stepped on by an elephant. I started to push myself off the floor, but I was only halfway up when the Moroccan's right foot slammed into the side of my face. I fell back again and just lay on the floor. I wanted to go to sleep. Maybe I did. When I opened my eyes, I saw Daboul, the Arab and the Moroccan standing in a row. Daboul had his arm in front of the Moroccan.

I thought the violence was all over and I raised myself slowly and stood up.

"The manuscript, Stevens."

I started to talk and realized that there were peppers on my tongue. I spat them out and said, "I can't take any more of this Daboul. But I don't have the manuscript. If I had it, I'd tell you."

Daboul lowered his arm and the Moroccan came at me again. Suddenly I decided that I was not going to spend the rest of the day getting the shit kicked out of me. Two years earlier I had taken a judo lesson from a Japanese stockbroker in a Greenwich Village loft and it was all coming back. The Moroccan was inches from me and I faked a thrust with my left foot. The Moroccan stepped back and I wrapped my right leg behind his left leg and reached for his right arm. I missed and the Moroccan's left foot made solid contact with my gonads. I screamed, fell to the floor again, and threw up the rest of my dinner. My hands were between my legs. I looked up and the Moroccan was standing over me. He was holding his dagger.

As he stepped toward me, I heard the faint voice of a woman. "Wait, Georges. Look at this."

I looked toward the doorway. It was the girl in the beige panties. She had a piece of paper in her hand.

"I found this in the pocket of his jacket." She paused. "I was, . . . ah . . . looking for cigarettes."

It was the note that Rakman had sent us earlier that evening. Daboul read it. He looked at the girl, then at me, and then at Hassan Ali. "Put the knife away, Hassan. What is this reference to a map, Stevens?"

"That's what I've been trying to tell you, Daboul. We didn't find the manuscript. All we got from the camel driver was a map."

"Shit." Daboul's face was covered with contempt. He looked at the note again. "So you were telling the truth."

I was still on the floor. "Look, Daboul, I'll make a deal with you."

"You are not in a good position for deals."

"You let me go. If and when we get the manuscript, I'll sell it to you for fifty thousand dollars."

Daboul laughed. "Fifty thousand dollars?"

"Okay, forty thousand dollars."

"You've got nerve, Stevens. Why should I pay you anything? And why should I believe you would transfer it to me?"

"I need the money. You need the manuscript."

Daboul thought for a moment. The Moroccan said, "Let me kill the little bastard."

Daboul motioned to the Arab and the Moroccan. They lifted me to my feet and held me up by the armpits. "We shall make a deal, Monsieur Stevens. Ten thousand dollars. If you do not deliver, I shall see that Hassan gets his wish."

I wondered if the ten thousand dollars was a coincidence. Surviving the beating from the Moroccan made me light-headed and reckless. "The money you stole from the synagogue?"

"What are you talking about?"

"Ten thousand dollars was stolen from the Marrakech synagogue. The rabbi was almost killed."

"Ten thousand dollars is penny-ante stuff, Stevens. Why would I want to kill a rabbi?"

"Who knows? Maybe you think he'll beat you to the manuscript."

"He wants it?"

"It's the Meshiva business."

Daboul didn't bat an eye. "Not that it makes any difference, Stevens, but I had nothing to do with the rabbi. I didn't even know there are Jews in Marrakech."

"If it wasn't you, who was it?"

"I'm not a clairvoyant, Stevens. How do I know? Maybe it was a small-time crook. Marrakech is full of them."

"The money was in a black bag. The rabbi was handing it to Muntaka. It could have been someone who thought he was handing over the manuscript."

"You think that there's someone else who wants the manuscript?"

"Jesus, you said yourself that half the world's interested."

"Interested, yes. But I had not thought that there were others besides you and your friend in close pursuit."

"What about the Greek?"

"The Greek?"

"You were with him in Niger."

"Oh. Yes. . . . Monsieur Kontos. . . . Yes. Monsieur Kontos and I are . . . uh . . . cooperating. We are, uh, pooling our resources. . . . At least for the moment. I doubt that it was he who was involved in the assault at the synagogue." Daboul narrowed his eyes and pushed out his lower lip. "Still, of course, one cannot be sure. Partnerships are always fragile things at best, whether it is business or otherwise. Trust must be developed over time. When did the attack take place?"

"A few days ago."

Daboul ran a hand through his hair. Then he nodded toward the doorway. The two men brought me into the first room and threw me on the bed. The Moroccan slammed his fist into the small of

203

my back as he let me go. My head was swimming and I almost blacked out.

Daboul said, "You say you are prepared to cooperate. Perhaps I believe you. But if you double-cross me, you shall not live to regret it. Meanwhile, to show my good faith and to minimize your discomfort, I shall delay your departure for a few hours." Daboul nodded to the girl.

As he, the Arab, and the Moroccan left the room, the girl began to unbutton my shirt.

THE next morning I woke up in a cold sweat. My head felt as if I had slept on a concrete pillow and my stomach and groin ached each time I took a breath. The last thing I remembered was dreaming that I was in the Maison Rouge. At the middle of the room was a coffin. Seated around the coffin were five men: Georges Daboul in shorts, sandals, and sunglasses; the Englishman Worten trying to convince Daboul to purchase a 1910 geography of the British Empire; the Levantine Simhani, naked except for the words "Laissez Passer" stamped on his stomach; and Muntaka and Rakman, playing chess. Worten would periodically stand and announce, in solemn tones,

> *Whatever happens we have got*
> *The maxim gun and they have not.*

The last rites were being given simultaneously in Hebrew and Latin by the Marrakech rabbi and Father Cornelius Nunn. Off to the side was Kontos in a sequined tuxedo, layered with camera equipment. In the background were three women, singing softly and looking like dryads in diaphanous gowns: the girl from the cup, the rabbi's daughter, and the school teacher from Hamdi's

205

village. Suddenly the body in the coffin sat up, looked around, and collapsed back into the box. It was me.

The lump behind my ear was the size of a gum ball and didn't stand much touching. I could feel a small amount of blood caked in my hair. After showering and dressing I went to Muntaka's room and knocked on the door. There was no response. I went down to the breakfast room and found Muntaka eating liver and tomatoes.

"You're up early, Muntaka." I took the chair opposite him.

"We should see Rakman early, before he is distracted by other matters." Then Muntaka stopped talking. He looked at me closely. "Is it your eyes or mine that are unfocused? Are you all right?"

I turned my head sideways and showed Muntaka the area behind my ear and the bruise on my cheek where the Moroccan kicked me.

"Good heavens." Muntaka stood up and walked over to me. He felt the lump. I winced. "What happened?" he asked.

I told Muntaka about the Lebanese, the Arab, and the Moroccan. I didn't bother to mention the girl.

"We are fortunate that you had Rakman's note with you and that your honesty is so transparent." Muntaka paused. Then he said, "I am sorry that this happened. I had hoped that we would not encounter violence."

I was about to mention the fellow who jammed into my bike after I left Father Nunn's mission school, the fellow who shot Muntaka in the market behind the emir's palace, and the Moroccan who tried to stab Muntaka at the sideshow. I decided the hell with it.

"Still, your experience last evening tells us that the manuscript may still be at large." Muntaka was quiet for a moment. Then he said, "And, of course, it tells us who one of our adversaries is."

We arrived at Rakman's office at eleven-fifteen and sat drinking mint tea with him. Rakman told us of the efforts his men were making. Two leads which Rakman had thought would be promising proved to be false.

Rakman went to his safe and opened it. He took out the leather case and withdrew one of the maps. He placed it on his desk and put a piece of paper next to it.

"Farouk informs me that there is no question of the authenticity of both maps. He has large magnifying instruments. And his eyes see much more than yours or mine. This map was prepared by Leo the African. Farouk has examined these words here. While the last several words . . . here . . . are worn by time, he believes that he has identified the words, if not their meaning. Here, to the left, is the Arabic for "the river Niger." Under this line, which one must presume traces the river, are these in Arabic. If they are as Farouk says, they translate thus: 'Herein lies the true course of my faith.' "

Muntaka examined the Arabic script that Farouk had copied onto the sheet of paper. He turned to the map and then back to the copy of the script. Suddenly, he threw his right hand to his forehead, "Allah be praised! Mallam Stevens, look here at this map. There is, of course, no doubt that this is the river Niger?"

"No, of course not. In fact, it seems very accurately located. I didn't realize that Leo had done such a careful job in tracing the river."

"But look here. Don't you see? These small lines. He has drawn this river flowing from west to east!"

"Jesus, Muntaka, that's got to be what those lines mean. Look, Monsieur Rakman, he's got the goddamned river flowing eastward. But his *Description of Africa* said that the river flows westward. What the hell do you make of it, Muntaka?"

"Mallam Stevens, it has all become clear to me. How could I have been so witless? How could I have believed that the African had made such an amazing mistake? The answer is that he did not make a mistake. He knew what he was doing when he wrote that the river flowed westward."

Rakman and I looked at each other. Rakman said, "I am afraid, Alhaji, that you shall have to explain this to Monsieur Stevens and me. We are, perhaps, somewhat slow."

"You are in good company. Look, here, at the words brought

to life by your friend Farouk. 'Herein lies the true course of my faith.' Don't you see?''

"I am afraid not," Rakman said.

"The evidence was before me and I was blind to it. I knew that he was, like myself, a scholar, a man of the law, and an adventurer. I knew that he, like myself, was careful in his work. It could not have been possible for him to have made the mistake attributed to him."

"You mean that someone changed his text?" I asked. "The translators into Latin and English?"

"That was one possibility which I and others rejected many years ago. No. It is not that. And I am such a fool for not having seen it. Leo was, as I have said, a man of adventure, scholarship, and skill. What has escaped me until now is that he was also a man of humorous spirit. Unlike almost all of the other great explorers of Africa, he did not take himself too seriously. His mind was mischievous. Perhaps not unlike yours, Mallam Stevens." Muntaka slapped me on the back. "Perhaps there is a bit of Leo in both of us. Do you remember what he wrote? It is one of the passages in Latin found on the body of the Levantine. 'For mine owne part, when I hear the Africans evil spoken of, I will affirm myself to be a man of Granada. When I perceive the nation of Granada to be discommended, then I will profess myself to be an African.' Men have long interpreted this to reflect cynicism, or worse, weak will. But it was said as a jest."

"So?"

"With these words, 'herein lies the true course of my faith,' he is thumbing his nose at the Christian leader, the pope, Leo. The true course of his faith was eastward—*toward Mecca*. He is telling the world here that his partaking of the Christian religion was a sham; that he was, after all, a true believer, a Moslem." Muntaka held both hands out to the sides, palms up, and smiled. "It fits so well. It has long been thought that he reconverted to Islam in his old age. But little is known of his later life. You see, he never, in his mind, became a Christian."

I wasn't keeping up. "What the hell does all this have to do with the course of the Niger?"

"Do you not see? He knew that in later times men would learn the true path of the great river. He also knew that men would be perplexed as to why he stated that it flowed to the west. He must have planned to have this map released after his death, to show the world the river's true course and to evidence his own faith. He knew that such an amazing blunder would attract the attention of the world and that this map would draw even more attention to the river's course and his faith in Islam. It is a stroke of genius by a man with a love of language and a sense of the mischievous. What he did not foresee was that the true course of the Niger would remain a mystery for three hundred years after his own travels, and that this map would be lost, until this very moment."

"Muntaka," I said, "If you're right, this map is of tremendous value. And it may be an important document for the people of Islam. But the pope isn't going to like it."

Rakman offered to hold the two maps in the floor safe behind the desk in his office. He informed us that he would call the hotel, or send a messenger, as soon as he had any leads concerning Father Cornelius Nunn.

On our return to the hotel we walked through the square outside the wall to the Great Market. Traders were setting out their wares and hawkers were beginning to announce the arrival of acrobats, magicians, and dancers. Muntaka was in high spirits. The discovery of the Leo Africanus map and the information it contained had elated him. He quietly sang a little song.

> *If I were a cassowary*
> *On the plains of Timbuctoo*
> *I would eat a missionary*
> *Cassock, band and hymnbook, too.*

Muntaka smiled at me. "That, Mallam Stevens, was Samuel Wilberforce, the bishop of Oxford. A man with a fine wit."

"Maybe that's what happened to our missionary. Maybe Father Nunn ran into a cassowary. What the hell's a cassowary?"

"Who can say? I believe it is some sort of vulture, not unlike the ones you saw flying on the desert."

Muntaka sang the verse again, and then began humming it. We stopped in front of a young woman performing with snakes. She was light skinned, wore a brief, sequined outfit, and was surprisingly attractive. Her name, painted on the back of the small stage on which she was standing, suggested that she was probably East European. At the moment Muntaka and I stopped she was in the middle of her act. A large snake, resembling a green mamba, was wrapped around her rib cage. Its head came up the middle of her chest, between her breasts, and rested just under the woman's chin. A second snake was wrapped around the woman's right leg. It's head had come around the back of her thigh, up between her legs and rested near her navel.

Muntaka was fascinated. "That, Mallam Stevens, is remarkable. Do you think you could do that?"

"Sure, if you get those snakes out of there."

We walked on, past three jugglers, a sword swallower, and a group of small white dogs standing on their hind legs. I was surprised to see that we had come to a carousel. It was the only mechanical device that I had seen in the square.

"What," Mallam Muntaka asked, "is that?"

"It's called a merry-go-round. You find them with carnivals in the United States and Europe."

"Have you ever been on one?"

"When I was a boy."

"I must try it."

"Are you serious? It's for children, not grown men. You'd look ridiculous."

"To whom? No one knows me here. Except you. And you can join me."

"I'm not getting on a merry-go-round."

"Yes, you are." Muntaka walked over to two small ragamuffin boys who were standing a few feet away staring at the machine.

210

He swept one up under each arm and returned. He handed one of the boys to me. "Here, take one of these. They shall need our assistance in riding the small horses." Muntaka handed several coins to the attendant and walked back among the wooden horses. He placed his boy on one of the horses and he mounted the horse next to him. My boy and I took the two horses directly in front of Muntaka and his companion. The youngsters, who could not have been more than five or six years old, were bewildered. But as soon as the calliope sounded and the merry-go-round began to move, the face of the boy next to me broke into a wide grin. I looked back and the second boy was also grinning. Muntaka's robe was billowing out as it had done on our camel ride to Dakoro. Muntaka held onto the post with one hand and held down his small cap with the other. He was beaming. The calliope was playing something resembling "Camp Town Races," and it occurred to me that, for the first time in my travels with Muntaka, I was in the lead. But we were going in circles.

After we dismounted, Muntaka gave each of the boys three dirhams. They took the coins and ran off. Muntaka and I continued our walk.

Muntaka stopped to investigate a number of gold and silver pocket watches spread out in front of an old Moroccan who sat on a mat, fingering a string of red beads.

Muntaka took one of the watches in his hand and the Moroccan followed each of Muntaka's movements with his eyes. Muntaka rubbed the back of the watch on his robe and stared at the reflection of his nose and right eye.

"This, Mallam Stevens, is a handsome object," he said. It was a man's gold watch, in a hunter's case. A stag deer was embossed on one side. Under the deer were the initials "M. M." in fine script. Muntaka wound the watch carefully and held it to his ear. "If one were interested in knowing the precise time, this would be a fine object to own. I, however, have never been inclined to carry a timepiece. Were I so inclined, I would carry one such as this, not one that you strap to your wrist, Mallam Stevens."

"Why don't you buy it anyway, Muntaka? How often are you

going to find a watch with your initials on it?''

Muntaka turned to the old man and spoke in Arabic. He translated for me. ''I am not much interested in this piece. If I were, what would you charge me to relieve you of it?''

The Moroccan answered with elaborate casualness.

''He tells us, Mallam Stevens, that this is an exceptionally fine piece, admired by many, and that it keeps precise time. He says he will give us a special price of two hundred dirhams.'' Muntaka turned back to the old man. ''The piece has someone else's initials on it. Look here.'' He put the watch in front of the old man's face. ''And how do I know that it will keep precise time unless I stand here for the whole day?''

The old man took the watch and looked at it carefully front and back. ''This watch,'' the old man said, ''is so fine that one should be willing to change his name to match the inscription. Still, I shall accommodate you. One hundred seventy-five dirhams.'' He handed the watch back to Muntaka.

''One hundred.''

''I am sorry, one hundred fifty is my last price. You make take it or refuse it. It makes no difference to me.''

Muntaka offered one twenty-five but the old man wouldn't budge. Muntaka returned the watch to the place on the blanket where he found it and began to walk away. I expected the old man to call us back, but he didn't.

''Why not pay the one-fifty, Muntaka, if you really want it?''

''I would lose face. The man is stubborn. He should be willing to yield somewhat more.''

''Who cares about losing face? You're going to lose the damn watch. You'll never see the old codger again.''

''It is a matter of principle.''

I shrugged my shoulders and looked back at the old man. He was polishing a watch on a piece of cloth. Muntaka and I walked on and headed back to the hotel.

As we entered the lobby the hotel manager, who had been standing at the desk, came toward us. In a near whisper, he drew us aside. ''I am afraid, gentlemen, that something terrible has happened. I am very sorry.''

212

My heart pounded from my toes to my ears. "What is it?" I asked.

"I am sorry. The attendant for your floor informed me an hour ago that your rooms were entered by a stranger. It appears that they have been searched. I directed the attendant to touch nothing. I am sorry. Nothing like this has ever happened in our hotel. It is our fault. Our floor attendants are placed there to keep strangers from entering. I am sorry. I shall have a fine bottle of wine sent to each of you in your rooms."

Muntaka said, "That will not be necessary. Let us see what has been done."

Our suitcases had been overturned and the clothes scattered. Dresser drawers were opened and the rugs pulled back. The mattress in Muntaka's room was on the floor.

As we stood in my room, the manager wiped his hands on his jacket. "Will it be necessary to call the police?"

Muntaka put his hand on the manager's shoulder and maneuvered him to the door. "That will not be necessary. Nothing of value has been taken. Do not worry. These things happen." Muntaka opened the door and pushed the manager out, gently. Then Muntaka shut the door and turned to me. "Whoever came into our rooms was, of course, looking for the manuscript. It is, perhaps, just as well that we were in the market."

We didn't hear from Rakman for three days. During some of the afternoons, when the sun was too hot for walking, Muntaka and I sat on large pillows in the hotel tea room, sipping mint tea and eating dates and figs.

We were the only two in the room on Tuesday afternoon at three o'clock when the Greek walked in. I was seated facing the doorway and Muntaka's back was to the door. When the Greek appeared, I recognized him immediately. He was wearing the same heavy green suit he had been wearing when I saw him at breakfast in Zaria and at Slabbinck's in Maradi.

"Muntaka," I said quietly, "it looks as if we have company."

The Greek walked slowly but directly to our table. He spoke to Muntaka, who had not turned around. "You are the Alhaji?"

"I am known as Alhaji Mohamed Murtala Muntaka. I am also known as the Mutawali."

"My name, sir, is Kontos. Permit me to give you my card." He reached into his jacket and pulled out a small leather case. He handed a light green card to Muntaka. Muntaka looked at it and handed it to me. It read simply, "G. Kontos, Importe-Exporte." It was a copy of the card I had found in the desk drawer at Slabbinck's. "You would not be offended if I were to join you for a small conversation?"

Muntaka pointed to one of the cushions. "Sit here. I shall order you some tea." Muntaka rang the bronze bell in front of him and a waiter appeared with three cups of tea and more dates.

"May we share this tea in health," the Greek said. He took a sip and then wiped his mouth and nose with a handkerchief. "I shall come directly to the point. I am an emissary for a man of some wealth who would like to obtain the Arabic manuscript that is in your possession. He will pay you appropriately for the papers as well as for the time you have spent in your travels. That will include the young American." He nodded to me and ran the handkerchief over his upper lip.

Muntaka took a bite of fig. "So, sir, you are now willing to pay for the manuscript. It had been my impression that the use of money was not part of your methodology. It was, of course, you who searched the rooms of Mallam Stevens and myself. I would have thought that you were more accustomed to the techniques of the thief."

"You are a blunt man, Alhaji."

"There is no need for indirection. We have both traveled too far to play the game of cat and lizard."

"Then you are willing to sell the manuscript."

"I do not have it."

"I shall be able to pay a substantial amount."

"Your search of our rooms revealed nothing because, unfortunately for both of us, the manuscript has not yet come into my possession. And, it seems likely now that it will not."

"Am I to believe you?"

"You have no choice. However, if you were to think for a moment, you would realize that my friend and I would be unlikely to be sitting here sipping mint tea if we had the manuscript."

Kontos rose. "You have my card. Should you wish to conduct business with me, you may contact me at the Alhamda Hotel." Kontos nodded to me and left. Muntaka picked a piece of fig from a back tooth with his finger.

"Well, Mallam Stevens, we know two things. We know who one more of our adversaries is, and that he has been no more successful than we. I am beginning to believe that we shall not find the manuscript here."

O N the seventh day after our return from Moulay Ismael's village Rakman was waiting for us in the breakfast room of our hotel. He was reading a newspaper.

As we sat down he said, "I am afraid, Alhaji, that I have bad news for you. My men have searched every hotel in Marrakech and every corner of the city in which our priest might be. We have found nothing. I have even been in touch with the Immigration Service in Rabat and with friends of mine connected with Air Maroc. There is no sign of Monsieur Nunn. My men are clever. They seldom fail in quests of this type. You will recall the speed with which they located Monsieur Moulay."

"You have no leads at all?" I asked.

"None. There was a moment in which I thought that we had found our quarry, but I was mistaken. I am afraid that my men have caused some inconvenience to an Italian bishop in transit from Libya to Venice. To rectify our mistake, I had a case of excellent wine sent to him at his hotel. The bottle we found in his room was of the lowest quality. I hope he was not too disturbed. It is a mistake that I much regret."

"You will add the price of the wine to our bill," Muntaka said.

"No. The mistake was ours. The Italians and the Irish are very much alike to my men. This will serve as a lesson for them to be more careful."

"What does this mean then?" Muntaka asked.

"I am fearful that we are at a dead end. I do not know what to suggest now. I have also, of course, made inquiries of persons who are likely to make contact with items of the type we seek. They have seen nothing."

"Well, Alhaji Rakman," Muntaka said, "we are most grateful for the assistance you have given us to this point. I shall reimburse you for the expense that you have incurred on our behalf."

"I shall accept no payment at this time. If we are ultimately successful in recovering the manuscript, I shall, naturally, require appropriate payment."

"Naturally."

"But, if we fail, I shall expect nothing from you. It is one of the risks of my business."

"Mallam Stevens and I are, nevertheless, very grateful to you. We shall remain in Marrakech some days more. If nothing appears, we shall have to consider our next move."

"If anything comes to my attention, I shall contact you," Rakman said. "I hope that you will see me in any case before you go."

"Of course."

That evening Muntaka told me that he would be going out alone. He didn't tell me where and I didn't ask. I ate dinner at the hotel and then walked to the square.

I stopped briefly to watch an old man, squatting in the center of a cement slab, ironing clothes. The man wore no shirt. His arms were long and thin and his ribs appeared and disappeared as he moved the iron back and forth. He looked up and smiled, showing fewer teeth than Muntaka had. Next to him was a bed of hot coals. From time to time he removed ashes from the iron and replaced them with new coals, which he picked up with his bare hands. At his right was a water jug. The old man drank from the jug, filled his cheeks, and then sprayed the water onto the cloth he was ironing. The spray was as thin as mist, just sufficient for the old man's purposes. I wondered whether he had been better or worse at this when he had teeth.

I found the man selling watches, and picked up the pocket-watch that Muntaka had looked at.

"You want this for the old man you were with the other day?" The man spoke French. I was surprised that he remembered me. I smiled at his characterization of Muntaka as an "old man." He was a good ten years older than Muntaka.

"Yes."

"You should buy it now. It may be gone tomorrow. There is no time like the present. How much did I offer to sell it to the old man for?"

"One hundred and fifty dirhams."

"You may have it for one hundred twenty-five."

I paid the money and the man polished the watch on a piece of cloth. He handed it to me and smiled. I smiled back and dropped the watch into my jacket pocket.

"There is," I said in English as I turned to leave, "no present like the time."

I returned to the hotel at ten-thirty and was told by the desk clerk that my key had been picked up by a friend who was waiting in my room. I felt a shock of excitement. I guessed that Muntaka had come on to something. The caged elevator seemed to take forever getting to the third floor and I swore at myself for not racing up the stairs. I ran down the hall and, before I had fully opened the unlocked door, said, "Well, Muntaka, what've we got?"

Muntaka didn't respond, because it wasn't Muntaka. It was a woman. She was sitting primly in a straight-backed chair, next to the window, facing the door. She stood up as I barged in. She was, to put it as plainly as I can, extremely beautiful. She was about five feet six, her skin was light, and her deep brown eyes were large, lively and intelligent. She was perfect. Except for one

218

thing. She was wearing a small white cap with a cloth falling to her shoulders, something in the manner of the headgear worn by the French Foreign Legion, without the brim. She wore a black top with a white collar and a small cape. Her black skirt came just below her knees. What I could see of her legs was terrific, but I knew I should get my mind onto other things.

"Monsieur James Stevens?" She pronounced my first name gently, in a manner I had never heard before. The *J* was soft, almost as if it were *shh,* and the *a* was elongated. She said it as if she were caressing a cat. "I am Sister Monique Blanc-Jouvan of the Holy Order of St. Francis. I am sorry to intrude in this way. I am not accustomed to such behavior. But it was important that I speak with you as soon as possible."

I stood just inside the room, moderately dumbfounded. The door was still open and I closed it. I turned and looked at Sister Monique. I knew that the episode in the schoolhouse was a once-in-a-lifetime thing, and that no man could expect a beautiful woman to walk into his room every few weeks. But a fugitive from a convent seemed, somehow, a little cruel. Particularly one that looked like this.

I walked over to her and held out my hand. "I'm Jim Stevens. I'm happy to meet you, Sister. Here, please sit down."

Then I did something which I almost never do. I walked over to my suitcase, took out my bottle of bourbon, and said, "Sister, would you like a drink?"

"Yes, thank you. A drink would be pleasant. I would like a little water if you do not mind."

Did she mean just a glass of plain water or water with bourbon? What the hell. I threw caution to the wind and poured her a light one. Then I took the other straight chair in the room and sat opposite her.

"Well, Sister Monique, if you're seeking contributions for the convent, I'll be happy to give something. I didn't realize that there are convents in Morocco. But isn't it rather late in the evening to be . . . uh . . . soliciting?"

Sister Monique took a sip of her drink and then put the glass down on the small table beside her. "I shall speak to the point. I have what you are looking for."

My God, I thought. What kind of a woman is this, anyway. The French convents must be a hell of a lot more liberated than I thought. My imagination and my blood raced, ending up in a dead heat.

"Aaa, what do you mean exactly, Sister?"

"I have here, Monsieur Stevens, the manuscript in Arabic for which you have come all the way from Nigeria."

"You've got what?"

"I have the manuscript you seek. It is in medieval Arabic script. It dates from the thirteenth century. I am going to return it to you." She leaned to the side of her chair and lifted a large dossier case to her lap.

I needed another drink quickly and I went to the table to pour myself one. As my back was turned to her, I heard the sound of a zipper. I closed my eyes momentarily and then turned slowly. Sister Monique had opened the dossier case and had drawn out a package wrapped in the same kind of brown paper and heavy twine that the maps had been wrapped in. She untied the string and pulled the paper back, revealing a leather case. She drew twelve pieces of parchment from the case and handed them to me.

They appeared to be just what Muntaka had described. The parchment was very old and the script was clearly some form of Arabic. The writing was beautifully done. Aside from that, I could tell nothing.

"If this is the manuscript, Sister, how in heaven's name did it come into your possession?"

"It was sent to me."

"Sent to you? You mean from Niger?"

"Yes, by way of Mali. It was put into the custody of a camel driver named Moulay to be transported to Marrakech."

"Moulay?"

"Yes."

The son of a bitch, I thought to myself. What the hell kind of game was he playing?

"*You* retrieved the manuscript from Moulay?"

"Yes."

I slapped the heel of my left hand against my forehead. "Oh, my God. *That's* what he meant. Moulay said he was to expect a religious person and that the name would be Nunn. Or that's what Muntaka heard and translated to me. Moulay meant a *religieuse, une nonne,* a nun. I thought he meant a priest by the name of Cornelius Nunn. We've had people looking for him for almost a week. Rakman is going to be sore as hell."

"I'm sorry," she said. Then she laughed. "I am sorry," she said again, still laughing. "But it is rather amusing."

Then I laughed. "Son of a bitch," I said, shaking my head. "Muntaka will never let me forget this. He tells me that I hear things differently from other people. But the one time that it could be put to some use, I make a complete boff of it. I feel ridiculous."

"Please do not blame yourself for your failure to recover the manuscript before now. It is not often that a sister becomes involved in such things. The manuscript was, after all, stolen."

"Jesus Christ, don't tell me *you* stole the manuscript?"

"My dear James Stevens, your language is abominable. And how dare you suggest such a thing?"

"I dare suggest such a thing because you are, at the very least, in possession of stolen goods."

"Monsieur Stevens, I have not come into possession of the manuscript for criminal purposes. If it were so, would I be here now to return the manuscript to you?"

"I'm sorry, Sister. Would you like another drink?"

"If it is not an inconvenience, a small one would be appreciated. A little water, as before."

222

Sister Monique took a sip of her drink and said, "The manuscript came into my possession ten days ago. It was delivered to me here in Marrakech by the camel driver Moulay."

"How did you locate Muntaka and me? How did you know we were looking for the manuscript?"

"I am afraid that I shall not be able to answer that for you now."

"Look, Sister, it seems to me you have a lot of explaining to do. There's been a lot of time and money wasted on the search for this manuscript. I think you had better start at the beginning and work your way forward. The Vatican isn't going to be too keen on one of its nuns running around with stolen merchandise."

"Monsieur Stevens, I am here with the permission of my superiors. I have not, as you say, been 'running around,' and this is not stolen merchandise. It is a manuscript. I shall, however, tell you how it comes to be in my possession." Sister Monique was becoming a little edgy.

"I'm sorry, Sister. I didn't mean to snap at you. But you have to admit that the situation is a little strange."

"Perhaps. I shall try to explain. The manuscript, as you point out, was stolen from a museum in Nigeria. By whom I do not know. But in May it was brought into Niger and carried into Maradi. It found its way to the refugee center at Dakoro. It is my impression that the manuscript changed hands at least twice before reaching Morocco. Once at the border between Nigeria and Niger, where two men were killed, and once in Dakoro where Father René Henrot obtained them from a Levantine who had died of cholera."

I didn't bother to correct her. "Who's Father René Henrot?"

"Father René is a French missionary who has spent most of his life in Niger. He is now quite an old man. He may be eighty. He has spent much of the past year working with the refugees in Dakoro and elsewhere in Niger. He is quite well known in my country for his educational and humanitarian work in French Africa. For many years he worked with a leper colony near Lake Chad."

"And what's he got to do with the manuscript?"

"As you may know, the drought of the Sahel has brought much misery to that area. People have come in great numbers from the desert toward the river Niger. Dakoro is one of the refugee centers. The people from the desert were followed by rats. The rats brought disease. There has been much death from many diseases, including cholera.

"Yes, I know. My friend Muntaka and I spent several days there."

"One of the victims of the cholera was a Levantine. Father René thought that he might have been Lebanese. Father René was asked to administer last rites of the Catholic faith to the Levantine." Sister Monique paused. "Are you Catholic, Monsieur Stevens?"

"No."

"Oh." Sister Monique shrugged her shoulders. "Well, it is no matter. As I have said, Father René was asked to administer last rites to the Levantine. He had an opportunity to examine the Levantine's personal effects. He came upon the manuscript in the Levantine's suitcase. It did not appear to be of particular significance to him, but he decided that it would be best to determine whether it was of any value. Father René was familiar with an art dealer in Maradi. A Monsieur René Slabbinck."

"I met Slabbinck. I visited his restaurant and shop."

"I know that."

"How?"

"Let me continue. Monsieur Slabbinck's children had been baptized by Father René. This created a bond between them. The fact that the two men had been christened the same first name must have strengthened that bond. In any case, Father René sent a message to Monsieur Slabbinck, asking him to travel to Dakoro. Monsieur Slabbinck did so. He was shown the manuscript. Father René and Monsieur Slabbinck concluded that it was potentially of great value, and great significance. Although Monsieur Slabbinck was familiar with Arabic, he was not familiar with the particular dialect used in the manuscript. It is a type of medieval idiom that is known to few persons today."

"My friend Muntaka has told me."

"But Monsieur Slabbinck and Father René were able to glean what they thought was part of the significance of the manuscript. They determined that it is possible that the manuscript tells of the influence of Christianity in the western Soudan in the twelfth or thirteenth century. As you may know, it has not been thought that the Church had moved much further than halfway between the Nile and the Niger by the thirteenth century. A discovery of this sort, bringing the Church well beyond the Nile in this early period would be of great importance to Christianity. It might even indicate some influence of Christianity on the Islamic religion in that area. There has been some belief on the part of Christian historians that several of the assembly halls discovered through archeological explorations in the area north of the Niger were, in fact, churches. Or, and this fact would be of great importance, these buildings may have served as mosques and churches simultaneously."

"Jesus, that's just what Mallam Muntaka was afraid of. If he brings the manuscript back to Nigeria, he'll be excommunicated from the Islamic faith. If they do such a thing in the Islamic faith."

Sister Monique rubbed her eyes. "Your vulgarisms are needless. This manuscript, unfortunately, or fortunately, depending on your point of view, does not in fact prove the presence of Christian churches in the western Soudan. The gleanings of Father René and Monsieur Slabbinck were incorrect."

"How do you know that?"

"Because, Monsieur Stevens, I have translated it. It tells the story of Daura as a great center of the southern Sahara and the northern black territories. The manuscript is of much historical significance. It is, no doubt, of commercial value. That is why at least two men have died attempting to bring it out of Africa. Three, if you include the Levantine." Sister Monique reached into her case and extracted a sheaf of papers. "This is the translation." She handed the papers to me.

"*You* translated it?"

"Why does this surprise you?"

"A Catholic nun? That in itself will be enough to get Muntaka excommunicated. You know Arabic?"

"I have studied medieval and modern Arabic for fifteen years, since I was sixteen. I have studied it at the Sorbonne, at Cairo University, at the University of Tangiers, and at the London School of Oriental and African Studies. You see, Monsieur Stevens, it is because of my expertise in this field that Father René cabled me in Lyon and asked me to retrieve the manuscript."

"How long did the translation take you?"

"Four days."

"Four days? My God, Muntaka had been working on the translation for four *years*. He's not going to like this."

"I shall give him my translation. No one need know that I did it. Tell Monsieur Muntaka that this is a gift from my church to his."

"What was all this business with Moulay? Why didn't Father René simply mail the manuscript to you?"

"Father René knew, after speaking with Monsieur Slabbinck, that the manuscript was stolen. Once he discovered what he thought was its significance, he felt that it should not be allowed to fall into non-Christian hands. He knew that the customs and postal authorities throughout west and north Africa would be alerted. Thus he asked Monsieur Slabbinck to arrange for transport across the desert by camel caravan. It was a good idea. It succeeded."

"And Slabbinck told the camel driver at Dakoro that the manuscript would be picked up by 'une religieuse, une nonne.' "

"Yes."

"And you were willing to hold on to the manuscript, knowing that it belonged to the Nigerian government?"

"I am returning it to you," she said curtly. "Am I not?" She was silent for a few moments. "In any case, Father René did the right thing. Monsieur Slabbinck had told him of your visit to his restaurant. Slabbinck at the time did not know who you were.

And, as he told Father René, another man, a Greek, came close on your heels. Father René felt that the manuscript needed protection. He sent it north.''

"There's no mention of the Jews in the manuscript?''

"The Jews? So, you are familiar with the legend of the rabbi Meshiva?''

"Legend?''

"It is nothing more. There is no mention of the Jews in the manuscript because by the thirteenth century the Jews had been driven from west Africa. The Jewish kingdoms collapsed several centuries before. The Jewish people have made great contributions to the world, but the nurturing of the city of Daura was not one of them.''

I looked at my watch. It was eleven-thirty. We had been talking for an hour. I decided that Muntaka should be informed. I excused myself and walked down the hall to Muntaka's room. I knocked several times, loudly, but there was no response. Muntaka was either in deep sleep or he hadn't returned to the hotel. I went back to my room. Sister Monique was lying on her side on the bed, her head on the pillow. Her skirt was lifted slightly above her knees and her right arm rested between her thighs. She was sound asleep. I covered her with a blanket. The manuscript and the translation were on the table. I put them into Sister Monique's dossier case and placed the case on a shelf in the closet. Then I took a spare blanket from the closet, and within five minutes I was asleep, sitting up in the one soft chair in the room.

At seven-thirty the next morning I woke to a knocking at the door. I got up, unfolding myself from the chair, and opened the door. It was Muntaka. He peered in.

"What, Mallam Stevens, is that in your bed?''

"It's a Catholic nun.''

"May Allah have mercy. Have you no decency? A Catholic nun?''

"It's not what you think, Muntaka. She's given me something that you'll be interested in.''

Muntaka held up his right hand, fingers outstretched, palm toward me. He shook his head. "Not I, Mallam Stevens. I draw the line first at Christians and second at nuns. 'Sow a habit and reap a destiny,' as the poet says."

"Muntaka, will you listen to me. This woman has brought the manuscript."

"What manuscript?"

"What do you mean *what* manuscript? The manuscript we've been running our asses off for all over northern Africa."

"You mean *the* manuscript?"

"No. I mean the manuscript of your grandmother's latest novel. Of course I mean *the* manuscript."

"What in Allah's name are they doing in the possession of a Catholic nun?"

"It's a long story."

As we spoke, Sister Monique sat up in bed and smiled. She rubbed her eyes like a child.

"Sister Monique," I said, "this is my friend Mallam Mohamed Muntaka. Muntaka, this is Sister Monique."

Thez nodded to each other. Then I said, "Muntaka, perhaps we should give Sister Monique a chance to wash up. We can have breakfast together." I went to the closet and took out Sister Monique's case. I handed it to Muntaka. "Here, you can look this over downstairs. If you have trouble with the Arabic, there's a translation included."

23

MUNTAKA, the nun, and I sat at a corner table in the dining room. Sister Monique, between sips of tea and bites of toast, repeated the story she had told me the night before. Muntaka said hardly anything during the course of Sister Monique's narrative and he didn't ask anything further about Slabbinck, Father René, or the camel driver. It was the translation he was interested in. He began to question Sister Monique about particular Arabic words. Gradually the conversation moved from English to a mixture of English and Arabic and then to only Arabic. I was cut out of the dialogue completely and neither of the others seemed to notice or mind.

Muntaka was clearly fascinated by the nun. The fact that she was able to translate the manuscript with such speed and apparent accuracy amazed him and he seemed truly in awe of her achievement. I ordered more tea and toast to keep myself occupied, while Muntaka continued to quiz her on the meaning of specific words. He became more excited with each revelation.

Finally, after half an hour, Muntaka turned to me, as if I had been in on the conversation all along. "This is a remarkable woman we have here, Mallam Stevens. I have never met a person who knows more of Arabic scholarship than myself. She is truly remarkable."

Shortly thereafter, Muntaka turned to me again, still oblivious of the fact that I didn't have the foggiest notion of what they were talking about.

"Mallam Stevens, you know the word *jema'a?* It is the same in Hausa and Arabic."

"Sure."

"The word appears as *jum'maha* in the manuscript. As you know, its most basic meaning is 'assembly place.' By association it also means 'mosque,' 'a place of meeting together,' and 'Friday,' the day of assembly for prayer. Sister Monique thought at first that it might have meant a Christian church in the manuscript, but she now believes it connotes only a mosque, not a church." Muntaka turned to the nun.

"It is a marvelous word. It has so many associations in our language. There is a phrase that Hausa children enjoy. It is one of the first sentences I taught Mallam Stevens some years ago. Do you remember it, Mallam Stevens?"

" 'Akwai jema'a a jema'a a jema'a Jema'a?' Will there be people at the assembly in the mosque on Friday?"

Sister Monique laughed. "It is the great economy of the Arabic and Hausa languages that permits one word to do so much," she said.

Then Muntaka and the nun returned to their conversation in Arabic. I nibbled some more toast and studied Sister Monique's eyes. They were beautiful. Finally, after forty-five more minutes of discussion, Muntaka returned to English.

"Well, Sister Monique, our travels have led us to our manuscript. For this we are very grateful. I wonder what we can do to thank you and compensate you for your work?"

Sister Monique's face turned somber. She looked at Muntaka, then at me, and then once again at Muntaka. "You can give me the Leo Africanus map."

Muntaka and I reacted in unison. "What?"

"You can hand over to me the Leo Africanus map."

I looked at her in disbelief. "You know about the maps?"

"The maps were to be delivered to me by the camel driver Moulay. You arrived at his village two days before I did."

"What are you talking about?" I asked. "You got the manuscript from Moulay. You told me that yourself."

"I received the manuscript from the camel driver Moulay Abubakar. He delivered it to me here in Marrakech, as I told you."

"I thought you meant the camel driver Moulay Ismael."

"I know."

"You mean there were two Moulays?"

"There are many. Nearly everyone from that area is named Moulay. It is a village name. Monsieur Slabbinck and Father René handed the manuscript over to Moulay Abubakar and the maps to Moulay Ismael. It was thought best not to entrust all of the items to one driver. I was to obtain the maps from Moulay Ismael in Marrakech but he had arrived in Marrakech and left for his village before I arrived here myself. I was unable until a few days ago to obtain transport to his village. I could not find a driver who was willing to take me there. Whether it was because I am a woman or because I am a white woman, or because I am a Christian, I do not know. I do not drive well and consequently could not think of renting a car. Finally, two days ago, upon payment of a large sum to a taxi driver, I was able to make the long trip to Monsieur Moulay Ismael's village."

"So that's how you found out about Muntaka and me."

"Yes. The head person, Monsieur Idrisi, informed me that you had been to his village and had taken a package away with you."

Muntaka intervened. "But why do the maps interest you now that you know that the manuscript says nothing about Christianity in Daura?"

"Not maps, Monsieur Muntaka. Map. I am interested only in the map prepared by Leo Africanus."

"But it says nothing about Christianity."

"This is no time for games, Monsieur Muntaka. I am aware of the African's purported disavowal of the Christian faith."

Muntaka said, "You know about that?"

"Since the time of Pope Marcellus II in 1555 there have been rumors of a document secreted by Leo in Africa. The Vatican has for centuries attempted to trace such a document. With no success. When Father René communicated with me I guessed immediately the significance of the map.

"As an Arabic scholar I have taken an interest in Leon l'Africain. The Vatican has consulted me on the subject on a number of occasions. Leo's *History and Description of Africa* was, of course, written in Arabic originally." Sister Monique paused and lowered her eyes, as if embarrassed that she was revealing too much of herself. Then she continued. "The maps no doubt came from the section of Africa near Katsina. It has long been suspected that Leon l'Africain had placed clues to his true religious beliefs in several sections of his *History and Description of Africa*. Some Christian scholars had discovered some passages which were suggestive in this regard, but nothing which could be pointed to as definitive. You no doubt know, Monsieur Muntaka, that there are several points at which the African apparently extols Christianity and slanders Mohammedanism. Yet these passages are written with a fine, and, perhaps, mischievous touch, bordering on irony. The Italian and French translations capture this apparent spirit much better than the English version does. One cannot be sure about the African's state of mind.

"It has also long been suspected that the African intended to return to Africa and to leave a message for later generations concerning his faith. There is a passage in his book, for example, which says something like 'I intend to be returned forth from Europe back into my own country.' By which, of course, he meant Africa. Until recently there has been no evidence to support this suspicion. Some Christian scholars believed that Leo, in his later years, returned to visit the emir of Katsina and left with him some sort of will or legacy.

"Four months ago it was discovered that one of the three Latin versions of Leo's geography in the Vatican library had been damaged. Three pages had been torn from the book. I was shown the book when I last visited the Vatican. A comparison of the muti-

232

lated book with another copy revealed that the pages which had been removed contained passages which scholars regarded as clues to Leo's true beliefs. The first passage concerned Leo's birth in Africa. It is interesting, however, that this fact appears in one of the two unscathed Latin versions but not in the other. One speaks of 'vitae initium et educationis,' the other simply 'educationis.' The first passage also reveals Leo's willingness to profess whatever is convenient to him at the time: 'When Africans are ill spoken of, I profess to be a man of Granada.'

"The second passage concerns his desire to return to his home country. If one accepts the version of his book which proclaims Africa as his home, this passage suggests a return to Africa. The third page torn from the book includes Leo's infamous statement concerning the course of the Niger.

"When I received word from Father René that a map prepared by Al-Hassan Ibn Mohammed e al-Wezzan al-Zayyati had been discovered in Dakoro, I knew then that it was the map that included the African's statement of faith.

"The discovery of the mutilation of the book in the Vatican library was made by a priest from Genoa. Because each person using materials from the library's treasure room must show personal identification, the name of the reader who last used the book before the priest is known. But he was no longer in Rome. The address he had given was that of a *pensione*. In any event, there is no way to prove that the borrower before the priest from Genoa was the person who defiled the book."

Muntaka said, "Do you remember the name of the person?"

"The name was that of a Levantine. It was, I believe, 'Simhani.' "

Muntaka and I looked at each other but said nothing.

"It is to be wondered," Sister Monique said, "whether the theft of those three pages had anything to do with the emergence of the Leo Africanus map."

"What is it you want us to do, Sister?" I asked.

"If the map were to be made public, it would be a great disappointment to my faith. The pretended conversion to the Christian faith by Leon l'Africain, if revealed, would benefit no one."

Muntaka said, "You do not see the irony in what you are saying?"

"Irony?"

"You were prepared to reveal to the world that Christianity played a role in the creation of the great center at Daura. This would have been as much a blow to the faith of Islam as the revelation concerning Leo the African."

"I do not know what we would have done with the information from the manuscript if it had been as we suspected."

"History cannot be denied," Muntaka said. "The truth must be told. Unfortunately, the truth that emerges from the manuscript and maps is not as your church wishes. I am sorry for that. But the secret of the Leo Africanus map must be revealed. It solves a mystery which has baffled geographers and historians for two hundred years."

"You are not content with the satisfaction it gives you personally? You must share it?"

"It would be selfish to do otherwise."

"But you would offend many persons of my faith by revealing the significance of the map. I would prefer that the map not be made public." Sister Monique looked directly into Muntaka's eyes. "You would do this favor for me? It is I, after all, who translated your manuscript. And it was the manuscript, not the maps, which brought you to Morocco. The maps are a gift of God."

"Yours or mine?"

"We can discuss that at another time."

Muntaka sat silently, his eyes staring off into space. He rubbed his ears, his nose, and his chin. Sister Monique said nothing. And I was not about to say anything. Christ, I was in the middle of a goddamned religious war.

Then Muntaka spoke. "It shall be as you request. Not only have you brought the manuscript to us, you have provided a translation of the highest quality. I never expected that I would say this to any person, particularly not a woman—or a Christian—but the translation is. . . ." Muntaka pressed his lips together and tilted his head slightly to the side. "The translation is, no doubt, better than I would have accomplished." Muntaka's eyes met mine and I looked away. He looked at Sister Monique again. "We owe you a great deal. Moreover, you are a person of charm, dedication, and honesty, qualities which I admire. You are a person of great substance. Perhaps Mallam Stevens and I shall never again meet someone just like you. For these reasons, I shall abide by your request. The manuscript translation is a gift from your church to Islam. In return, I shall see that the map of Leo the African remains locked in a vault at the archives at Daura. I shall share the discovery with only one other person, the emir of Daura, from whom the map was stolen."

"You will not give the map to me?"

"I promise that it shall not leave the archives at Daura."

Muntaka rose and took Sister Monique's hand. He held it briefly and then released it. He looked down at the nun. "Our travels have led us to the manuscript. For this, we thank you. And we thank you for permitting us to discover things we did not expect to find." Muntaka turned to me and said, "You had best put the manuscript in the hotel safe until we can make better arrangements for it." Muntaka folded the translation, put it inside his robes, and walked out of the room.

Sister Monique and I left the dining room ten minutes later. I handed the manuscript to the desk clerk, for the hotel safe. He handed me a note. It was from Muntaka.

Mallam Stevens,

I shall see you tomorrow morning. There will be a package for you to give to Sister Monique this evening. I shall have it left at the desk. You should learn where she is residing in Marrakech. I assume that she will not spend another night in your room.

Muntaka

I read the note to Sister Monique.

"I must return to Lyon this evening. I have a reservation for an eight o'clock flight."

235

"I hope you'll let me take you to the airport."

"The hotel has arranged for transport. What are your plans this afternoon?"

I swallowed hard. "Why do you ask?"

"I would enjoy showing you the mosques of Marrakech. They are very beautiful. I have made a small study of them. You should not leave Marrakech without seeing them."

"Okay," I said, relieved, "you're on."

Five hours and nine mosques later we were sitting in a small outdoor café. When the sandwiches and citron pressé were finished we ordered cups of the thick, black Moroccan coffee. We sat in silence for a few minutes and I examined Sister Monique's large brown eyes, her cheekbones, and the ridge of her nose. She didn't look away. Then I said, "Sister, may I ask you a question?"

"Of course."

"Do you ever think about making love to a man?"

"Monsieur Stevens, what kind of a question is that to ask a nun?"

"I ask the question because you *are* a nun. Do you ever regret that you can't experience love with a man?"

"Monsieur Stevens, a nun is not supposed to think of such things."

"I'm a lawyer but that doesn't mean that I don't occasionally go through a red light."

"District?"

"No, traffic."

"Oh. Well, the analogy is not a very appropriate one. In any case, Monsieur Stevens, I am able to find complete fulfillment in my work for God, and in my scholarship. In whatever profession one chooses, one must sacrifice something. Except, perhaps, your friend Monsieur Muntaka. He seems to be able to live many lives and practice many professions at once. It is quite remarkable. He is, you know, very much like the man he admires, Leon l'Africain, in this respect."

I laughed. "I'll tell Muntaka you said so. Your observation will endear you to him forever." Then I said, "Sister, you are really something."

"Something?"

"Someone. You are an exceptional woman—and beautiful."

She looked down shyly and said, "I thank you for saying so."

I wanted to say more, but I didn't.

Shortly before six, we returned to the hotel where Muntaka and I were staying. A package was waiting for me at the desk. It was wrapped in brown paper and tied with a string. I opened it. Inside there was another small package with Sister Monique's name on it, four hundred dollars, and a note. She looked disappointed. She may have hoped that Muntaka had relented on turning the map over to her.

Mallam Stevens,
    Please give the small package and this money to our friend, the nun. The money is to cover her expenses.
                                                    Moh. Muntaka

Sister Monique opened the package and extracted a small gold cross, about an inch long. It was attached to a thin gold chain. For a moment she was quiet. Then she said, "This is very beautiful. Have you ever seen such a delicate cross? Where do you think your friend was able to find such a thing in Marrakech?"

"It looks handmade. Muntaka must have spent the whole day getting it for you."

"It will be a great treasure to me."

I drove Sister Monique to her hotel. I opened the car door for her and we stood looking at each other for several seconds. Then she said, "Monsieur Stevens, thank you for spending the afternoon with me."

I felt like a high school boy on a first date, awkward, self-conscious, anticipating God knows what. "I hope you have a pleasant journey. And I hope, Sister, that . . . uh . . . I shall see you again sometime."

Sister Monique looked into my eyes. Then she said, "You, my

dear James Stevens, you, also, are really something." There was, I thought, just a trace of sadness in her voice. "I am afraid, however, that we shall never see each other again." She put her right hand gently on my arm and kissed me on the cheek. It was the first time that I had been kissed by a nun. And it will probably be the last.

MUNTAKA was not at the hotel when I got back, and I had dinner alone. After dinner I went directly to my room, undressed, took a long shower, and went to bed. At twelve-thirty there was a knock at the door.

"Who is it?"

"Muntaka. I must speak with you."

I turned on the light and opened the door. Muntaka said nothing, came in, shut the door behind him and sat down in the chair that Sister Monique had occupied the night before.

He ran his hands over his face. Then he said, "The maps have been stolen."

"Stolen? How?"

"Rakman's safe was broken into. He and I spent the afternoon and evening together. We returned to his office at eleven o'clock to settle our account. The door to his office was unlocked, the safe was open, the maps were gone."

"Was anything else taken?"

"Rakman states that he had a small amount of money in the safe. That money was not touched. Other papers were not removed."

"Damn. Does Rakman think there's any chance of recovery?"

"His men are searching Marrakech now. He has suggested that

someone might try to hold the maps for ransom, but he does not really believe this. It is his belief and mine that the maps have been taken by, or on behalf of, someone who wants permanent possession of them.''

"Who do you suspect?''

"I am afraid, Mallam Stevens, that the most likely suspect is your friend, the nun. I am afraid that she did not believe me when I said the Leo map would be locked in the archives at Daura.''

"Sister Monique? You've got to be joking. She's a nun, Muntaka. She's not a thief. Besides, she was with *me* all afternoon.''

"Oh? . . .Well, you forget that she was willing to receive stolen goods. We do not know what she would have done with our manuscript had it turned out as she suspected. As for her being with you this afternoon, what time did you leave her?''

"About five forty-five.''

"The maps could have been stolen anytime between four and eleven.''

"She was going to catch a plane to Lyon.''

"Do you know what time it left?''

"I'm not sure. I think about eight.''

"Rakman checked with a security agent at the airport. Sister Monique's flight departed at ten-thirty. There would have been sufficient time for her to enter Rakman's office before leaving for the airport. I am sorry to say, Mallam Stevens, that she may have spent the afternoon with you to divert suspicion away from herself.''

"She's not a safecracker, Muntaka.''

"She is a woman of many talents. It would not have taken a man to have opened the safe. Of course, it is quite possible that she did not enter Alhaji Rakman's office at all. The theft could have been done by an associate.''

"How do we know it wasn't one of Rakman's men? Sure, *he* was with you, but he could have had one of his men stage a break-in. Christ, Muntaka, he was the only one besides us who knew where the maps were kept. What do we know about him, anyway?''

"I rely on my judgment of him."

"And I rely on my judgment of Sister Monique. What *do* you know about Rakman, Muntaka? Your taking the *haj* together was too much of a coincidence."

"Special branch of the criminal investigation division in Kaduna gave me his name and some data. Alhaji Rakman has been known to be familiar with the passage of illicit goods. It is not known that he has engaged in facilitating such passages. As for the rest, you know as much as I. I do not believe that I have judged him incorrectly."

I pressed my lips together. Then I said, "I wish I were as confident of that as you."

"There is nothing more we can do tonight. I'll see you in the morning. Good night."

Muntaka was nowhere to be found when I went down to the dining room, and I ate breakfast alone. The desk clerk informed me that Muntaka had left the hotel at seven o'clock. There was no message. I took a cab to Sister Monique's hotel and was there at nine-thirty. The manager, after some inducement, informed me that Sister Monique had checked into the small hotel one week ago, that she shared the room with no one, and that she was most courteous. She paid her bill and stole neither towels nor ashtrays.

"Did you see her with anyone?"

"She came and went alone. And she ate alone. She did spend one night away from the hotel."

"Oh yes."

The manager smiled knowingly and raised his eyebrows. "You were with her?"

I winked and walked out.

My next step was to check on Rakman. I decided that it would be foolhardy to try to check his reputation among the antique dealers in the old market, but that the Frenchmen operating antiques shops in the new quarter might be helpful. Only one of the three French dealers knew Rakman.

"He has a reputation for shrewdness," he said in French. "He

241

comes into possession of books, manuscripts, and related items of considerable value. It has been suspected that he does so in a not entirely legal manner, but I have no evidence of this. I do know that he is very knowledgeable in my field. His judgment is highly respected. It is all the more amazing for the fact that antique books, maps, and manuscripts seem only to be a hobby of his. I understand that he is engaged in a general import-export business.''

"What does he import and export?"

"I do not know."

"Can you suggest anyone else who might know anything about him?"

"Only the police."

I had nothing to lose so I took the suggestion. In forty minutes I was at the headquarters of the Marrakech branch of the Moroccan police. The police guard at the entrance escorted me to a policeman sitting at a large wooden desk on which there was a telephone and a book marked "Visiteurs."

He spoke to me in French. "Who do you wish to see, please?"

"I would like to speak with the chief of police."

"Do you have an appointment?"

"No. But I have some information which I believe he'll find useful."

"I shall refer you to an assistant."

"I'll reveal my information to no one but the chief of police."

The policeman pressed a button on the phone and spoke in Arabic. For a brief period he said nothing into the phone. Then he hung up and said, "Please sign your name and the time." The policeman pressed a button located at the side of his desk and another policeman appeared. He motioned me down the hall and we stopped in front of a door marked "Commandant." The policeman knocked, someone announced "Entrez," and the policeman opened the door for me and then left.

The commandant sat behind an ornately-carved desk placed in the middle of a large, carpeted room. He had a thin, tapered moustache, broad shoulders, and a braided jacket with several

242

small service bars above the left chest pocket. He motioned me to a chair. I sat down.

"I do not usually see visitors without an appointment. Since the officer said you are a European, I considered that your information may be of some importance. Europeans seldom come here on their own volition. The police headquarters frightens them. What is your information, Monsieur?"

"I'm afraid that the officer misunderstood. I'm seeking information from you."

"I see." The commandant changed neither the tone of his voice nor his expression. "May I examine your passport?"

I showed it to him. He looked at it carefully and scribbled a few notes. He handed it back to me.

"What is it you wish to know, Monsieur Stevens?"

"I am seeking information about a man named Rakman. Nafir Rakman."

"What is it you wish to know about him?"

"Do you know him?"

"Answer my question, Monsieur Stevens."

"I'm interested in learning about his reputation. I want to know whether he has ever been involved in illegal operations."

"And why are you interested in this information?"

"A friend of mine and I left an item of some value with him. The item has disappeared. Monsieur Rakman alleges that it was stolen."

"I see."

"Can you help me?"

"I am somewhat familiar with Monsieur Rakman. Have you taken lunch, Monsieur Stevens?"

"No, I haven't."

The commandant smiled for the first time. "Will you do me the pleasure of dining with me? I was about to leave for my noon meal. There is a small café just across the street. We can talk there."

The offer surprised me. "That's very kind of you. I'd be delighted."

243

"Good." The commandant picked up his phone and gave a number to the operator. He carried on a brief conversation in Arabic. He replaced the receiver and stood up. "Come. The café serves excellent soups."

We sat in the open air. The brightness of the sun reflected blindingly off the white tablecloths, but we were protected from the sun's heat by a small table umbrella. The commandant sipped a glass of red wine and said, "So, you are interested in Monsieur Nafir Rakman?"

"Yes."

"You have had dealings with him?"

"He's been purporting to assist my friend and me in locating some items of value. As I said, one of the items disappeared from his office. What I want to know is how trustworthy he is."

The commandant took another sip of wine and put the glass back on the table with great deliberateness. He did not speak for several moments. Then he said, "Monsieur Rakman is well known to the police. Not only in Marrakech, but in Casablanca, Fez, Rabat, and elsewhere. His operations are, shall we say, both within and without the law. You understand what I mean?" He didn't wait for an answer. "He is, as you know, in the import-export business. There are many men in this country who use such operations as a curtain to hide illicit activities. Smuggling is rampant here. It is ruining the economy. The accounting devices used by the operators of so-called import-export businesses are difficult for our government agencies to decipher. It is not just a matter of the smuggling of goods. It is the evasion of exchange-control regulations and the establishment of overseas bank accounts which are protected from Moroccan tax. The illegal importation of drugs, weapons, and consumer goods is a matter of major importance."

He paused and took a sip of wine. I took the opportunity to say, "What do you know specifically about Rakman?"

"He is shrewd. He is quick to gain the confidence of men he deals with. He has a number of trusted associates who are his eyes and ears. He knows a great deal about many things. What he

244

does not know, he can find out about quickly.''

"But has he ever been arrested? Has he ever been convicted of theft or smuggling?''

The commandant smiled, took another sip of wine, and said, "Perhaps, Monsieur Stevens, you should ask him that question yourself.'' Saying that, the commandant stood up. I looked over my left shoulder. There, standing at my side, were Rakman and Muntaka.

The commandant said, "I believe you know each other. Monsieur Rakman, I hope you and your friend will join Monsieur Stevens and me. We have nearly finished our lunch but perhaps you would like some wine or Vichy water.''

As Rakman and Muntaka sat down my stomach sank. I tried desperately to figure out an explanation for the inevitable question. The question never came. Instead, the commandant said, "I apologize, Monsieur Stevens. I have had a bit of fun at your expense. Monsieur Rakman and I are old friends. The call I made back in my office was to him. I described you to him and he knew, of course, who it was.''

It was the first time since our search began that I felt like an outsider. I wondered whether there was something between Muntaka and Rakman that I didn't know. I felt like I had been set up. I could feel myself redden. But before I could think of something to say, Rakman said, "It is fortunate, Monsieur Stevens, that we have found you. We have some good news.''

"What is it?''

"The maps have been returned.''

"Returned? What the hell do you mean?''

Muntaka said, "As Alhaji Rakman and I sat in his office this morning, we were visited by your Greek friend, Mallam Kontos. He was a most disappointed gentleman. He confessed to breaking into the Alhaji's office and taking the maps. What he thought he was taking was a leather folder containing the manuscript. He has no interest in the maps and knows nothing of their significance.''

Rakman said, "He stated that he did not wish to spend the rest

245

of his life on the continent of Africa. He had reached a dead end. He returned the maps to show his good faith and to make a precise offer for the manuscript. One hundred and fifty thousand dollars. He is not certain, of course, that we have the manuscript, but he is a desperate and hopeful man.''

''Yes,'' Muntaka said, ''a most hopeful—and wealthy—man.''

Then Rakman said, ''It was resourceful of you, Monsieur Stevens, to attempt to solicit the assistance of the police in our search for the maps.'' Rakman smiled at the commandant. ''It is one less problem for the police to worry about.''

THAT evening, while I was drinking beer in the hotel bar, I found the piece of paper Daboul's henchman had given me just before I was knocked unconscious. I was wearing the bush jacket I had worn that night and the paper was in the left-hand pocket.

It was an advertisement, eight and a half by eleven, written in five languages: Japanese, German, Arabic, French, and English. The English read:

Live Sex Show. Coming from Skandanavia.
Luxery Serroundings. Being Best Performance
in North Africa.
24 number rue Kouba ed-Debbagh
Continuance showing

It was nine-thirty. If the surroundings were luxurious, it would no doubt be safe enough. I found a cab just outside the hotel and gave the driver the address. I tried to act like I was heading for a business meeting.

"You going to see fuck show?" The cabbie spoke French.

"Uh, no, I'm meeting the commercial attaché from the German embassy."

The cabbie turned part way around. He was a wispy-looking man with a long, angular nose and a moustache that covered only the dimple in his upper lip. "At 24 Kouba? I can take you to better place. More action. Girls come right into audience. Give blow jobs."

"I'm not interested in any action. Just take me to 24 Kouba ed-Debbagh."

The cabbie shrugged and was silent for the rest of the journey. Twenty-four Kouba was farther than I had expected. The drive took a good half hour into an area of the city that was completely unfamiliar to me. The streets were narrow, dirty, and deserted. The building at 24 Kouba ed-Debbagh had a small light over the door but there was no sign and the front windows were covered with boards. I considered having the driver take me back to the hotel, but before I could make up my mind, the back door of the cab opened and a Moroccan was saying, "Welcome to House of Pleasures. New show beginning just now."

I stepped out of the taxi and looked around. There were no other taxis in sight—or any other cars, for that matter—and I decided that I should have the cabbie wait. He must have read my mind, because before I could say anything he said, "I better wait for you, mister. This is not a safe place to walk. Not many taxis. I stay here. Fifty dirhams for waiting."

I started to take out my wallet but he said, "You pay me later, mister. I wait."

I followed the doorman up a flight of stairs into a small theater with about fifteen chairs facing onto a stage. I knew the place wasn't going to be Lincoln Center, but I hadn't expected this. The room smelled awful and there was hardly any light. I could make out one Oriental sitting at the far left and six or seven other men, apparently Moroccan.

For fifteen minutes nothing happened. Then the doorman circulated around the room collecting 125 dirhams from each customer. After another fifteen minutes a movie screen was pulled down at the back of the stage and the small light went out. For ten minutes we watched a "farmer's wife" in various postures with a cat, a pig, and a Great Dane. I assumed that the last episode was the Scandinavian reference on the announcement.

When the light went on, the screen went up and a young woman, who was not bad looking, and a man about twice her age appeared on the stage. The man began to unbutton the woman's blouse. He had about three buttons to go when the lights went out. The room was pitch black and my heartbeat doubled. I moved my wallet to a front pocket. Then, on stage, a beam of light appeared and I heard the doorman's voice.

"The electricity in this sector of the city has failed. We regret the inconvenience. Be patient. The lights will reappear soon."

Twenty minutes later we were still sitting in darkness and I decided to get the hell out of there. I groped my way out of the room and down the stairs. The doorman was standing at the bottom with his flashlight.

He said, "You should stay. I have nice girl upstairs. One hundred dirhams for two hours. Lights will be back by then. Two hundred for whole night."

I couldn't see my taxi.

"Better you go upstairs spend night with young girl. Very nice skin. Very clean."

"Have you seen the taxi I came in?" I asked.

The doorman turned around and flashed the beam to the right of the building. The cab was parked about fifteen yards away. The car windows were open but I couldn't see the driver. I took a box of hotel matches from my pocket, lit one, and leaned in the front window. He wasn't there. I got into the cab and pressed the horn. Then, from the back of the cab came a low moan and a stream of Arabic words that sounded like cursing. I felt for a ceiling light and found the switch. Stretched out in the back seat was the skinny taxi driver.

"What the hell are you doing?" He sounded drunk.

"I want to go back to my hotel."

"Then go find a taxi."

"You said you'd take me back."

"I have a headache."

"I'll give you a good tip."

"My head feels like a camel has stepped on it. Do you have any aspirin with you?"

"No. But I have some in my hotel room. If you drive me to the hotel, I'll get you some."

"My head is splitting. Can you drive?"

"Yes."

"Then you take the wheel. I am remaining back here."

I flipped up the meter flag, started up the little Renault, and headed down the street. I drove slowly. There was no traffic and the street was dark, except for our headlights. The cabbie was still stretched out in the back seat but he muttered periodic directions that got us back to the hotel in thirty-five minutes.

I cut off the motor, turned, and said, "Hey, Mac, we're here. That'll be fifteen dirhams."

The voice in the back said, "This is no time for a joke. My head is killing me. If you get me the aspirin, I'll charge you only sixty dirhams." The man raised his head and then sat up. His hands were pressing against his temples. "Shit. I have never had a headache like this." He opened the rear door and got out. He looked like he was going to keel over so I grabbed his arm and held him up as we walked into the well-lit lobby. The hotel must have had an auxiliary power system.

Once into the room he went straight for the bed and sprawled forward. He lay on his side and pressed against his eyes with his left hand. I went into the bathroom, took four aspirins from my kit, and poured a glass of water. I held a washcloth under the faucet. When I came back into the bedroom he was sitting on the straight-back chair Sister Monique had used. I handed him the aspirins, the water, and the washcloth. He looked at the aspirins as if he couldn't decide what to do with them. He shrugged, popped them into his mouth and drank the water. He put the glass on the table next to the chair and then washed his face with the cloth. Then he reached inside his jacket and took a pack of cigarettes from his shirt pocket. He lit a cigarette and took two puffs. Finally, he reached into his jacket pocket, pulled out a large revolver, and said, "Monsieur Stevens, it would be convenient if you would now hand me the package given to you by the French woman."

The headache routine would have been laughable if the gun hadn't been pointed at my belt buckle.

"What the hell are you talking about?" My stomach muscles began to tighten.

"The package handed to you by the nun. I would like you to hand it over to me."

"I don't know any nun and I don't have any package."

"Monsieur, I have been observing you for a week. I know everywhere you have been and everyone you have seen. I sat five tables away from you in the dining room as you, your friend, and the French woman examined the contents of the package. I know that the package is with you."

"Go ahead and search the room. You won't find anything."

"In that case, we shall ask the desk clerk. I know that you have placed the package with the management." With his gun he motioned me toward the door. He stood up and pressed the revolver into my back. I had no reason to think he wouldn't pull the trigger if he had to. As we walked down the hall he removed his jacket and placed it over his arm and hand, hiding the gun. "I am prepared to shoot you if you make any attempt to run or warn anyone. I want you to ask the desk clerk for the package that you left in the hotel safe."

I realized then that the situation was serious. Unless the clerk was smarter than I thought he was, the taxi driver would walk out of the hotel with the manuscript. I felt completely helpless. The journey in the caged elevator from the third floor to the lobby, which normally seemed to take an eternity, went too fast. I couldn't think of anything I could do. In five minutes the manuscript was out of the safe and under my arm. The desk clerk acted as though there was nothing strange in asking for a package from the safe at one-thirty in the morning. I didn't even bother to try to signal him. I knew it would go right over his head.

The taxi driver maneuvered me toward the front door of the

hotel and we stood next to his cab. He said, "I shall take the package now." I handed it to him. "And I am afraid, Monsieur, that it will be necessary for you to continue your career as a chauffeur." He chuckled. "I shall return to the back seat."

"Where are you taking me?"

"I am afraid I must consult with my employer to determine what is to be done with you. I cannot leave you here. You would undoubtedly call the police, if you could convince the idiot at the desk to let you use the telephone."

He walked to the driver's side with me and waited for me to get in. He held the gun to my head. Then he opened the rear door and got in the back. I started the car and he gave me directions.

In the darkness I soon lost all sense of where we were heading. Along the streets small kerosene lamps flickered here and there but they didn't give sufficient light for me to recognize any of the buildings after the first few blocks. We drove for twenty minutes. Then I was told to pull over. My companion exited from the car and motioned me out. We entered a building and climbed two flights of stairs. The taxi driver knocked and then opened the door, not waiting for a response. In the room two lamps and three candles flickered feebly and didn't provide much light. But I could make out the form of a man sitting in a chair. He stood up and walked toward us. He smiled and his gold teeth reflected the light from one of the lamps. He said, "Well, Monsieur, we meet again." It was René Slabbinck.

"I hope, Monsieur Stevens, that you had an opportunity to learn more about African art since I last saw you. I am afraid you evidenced considerable ignorance." He smiled maliciously. "I must confess, however, that I at first thought you were a collector. Otherwise, I would not have wasted time on you." He looked at the taxi driver. "You have the package, Mahmoud?"

The man handed the package to Slabbinck and then stood by the door. He held the pistol casually. Slabbinck placed the package on a table. "Well, Monsieur Stevens, would you care for a drink?"

"What the hell do you want, Slabbinck?"

252

"I have what I want. Would you like some wine? Or Perrier water?"

I didn't answer. Slabbinck shrugged and poured a glass of wine for himself. He took a swallow and then said, "It is unfortunate that you were able to reach the young woman before I was. It would have saved us both much inconvenience." Slabbinck returned to his chair. He motioned me to another chair and I sat down.

"I don't suppose you want to explain any of this to me, Slabbinck?"

"What is there to explain? I wanted the package that the sister transferred to you. I now have the package. Now I have to decide what to do with you."

"What do you mean what to do with me? You got what you want. I'll never be able to find this place again."

"Whether you can find this apartment again is not significant. I do not plan to see this place again myself after a few hours. But I do plan to return to Maradi. The question is whether I shall be able to dispose of these documents quickly. The longer I hold on to them, the more I may be able to obtain for them. It is therefore desirable that they not be traced to me. The result, I am afraid, Monsieur, is that we cannot afford to have you remain alive. It is a shame. Neither Mahmoud, here, nor I really have the stomach for this sort of thing."

I needed time to think. I tried not to act frightened, but I was. "I don't understand, Slabbinck. You were the one who sent the package north to begin with. Why the hell didn't you just hold on to it?"

"At the time that I assisted Father René in transporting them north, I knew that the documents were of some value, but I did not know how much. The old priest believed that the manuscript said something about the role of Christianity in western Africa in the thirteenth century. If this were the case, the manuscript would be of interest to a number of potential purchasers, including the governments of several Moslem countries of Africa, and the Vatican. But the old priest is getting senile. It was impossible for me to put much stock in what he was saying. I humored him, and assisted in sending the documents to Morocco.

"But after your visit, and that of the Greek, Kontos, I began to suspect that the documents were more valuable than I had first thought. I decided to do some research with the assistance of an acquaintance of mine in Rome, a bishop. But I could learn nothing about the manuscript and its connection with Christianity in west Africa. The old priest is, as I say, out of touch with reality. His beliefs about the manuscript are a result of wishful thinking and foolish dreams. The manuscript is untranslated. After seven centuries it is unlikely that it shall ever be deciphered. The Arabic idiom is lost forever. It is nothing more than a curiosity, of no great commercial value.

"By chance, however, I was able to piece together the story of the map of Leon l'Africain. With the information provided by my friend in Italy, I realized the possible worth of the map. The second map may be of comparable value. Who knows? If I am able to obtain less than one million American dollars for the Leo map, I shall be surprised." Slabbinck took a sip of wine.

I wondered whether the French priest was the old fool that Slabbinck thought he was. It looked like Father René told Slabbinck too much about the manuscript and too little about the map. And he apparently didn't bother to mention Sister Monique's linguistic skills. It's just what a shrewd man would have done with someone he didn't trust.

Slabbinck continued talking. "The Vatican, of course, should be willing to pay much more. Perhaps several million. Perhaps I can arrange for the Vatican to bid against the Arabs. There is, of course, some risk in selling the map to the Vatican, but it is a risk that will be difficult to resist. The Vatican will, I suspect, be more interested in having the map than in knowing how it came into my hands."

"Then what do you want with this package?"

"Are you stupid, Monsieur? I have just explained."

"I'm afraid you had better brace yourself for a shock, Slabbinck. What you've got here isn't the Leo Africanus map. It's the manuscript.''

The brown paper and string were on the floor. The hand-worn leather case and the manuscript were on Slabbinck's lap. He sat staring off into space for a good five minutes. I poured myself a drink. Mahmoud, who somehow looked blanched, said nothing. Finally Slabbinck said, contemptuously, "Mahmoud, you are a fool."

Mahmoud continued to say nothing. He stared stupidly at the pistol in his hand. I wondered whether he would use it on Slabbinck. Then Slabbinck said, "It appears that I deal only with fools. I hope, Monsieur, that you prove to be smarter than the others. Although, I am afraid, there is nothing in your past performance to suggest this."

I thought that the last statement was somewhat gratuitous. I let it roll off.

"If you retrieve the Leo Africanus map for me, Monsieur, I shall pay you twenty thousand dollars."

"We don't have it, Slabbinck. As soon as Muntaka got hold of the maps, he sent them to the Nigerian embassy in Rabat. They're probably with the Nigerian police now."

"You are lying. You should know by now, Monsieur Stevens, that you do not lie well. I am afraid that I shall have to have this idiot return with you to your hotel to search your room and the hotel safe. Perhaps the package containing the maps is in the name of your friend."

"Go ahead, Slabbinck, but you won't find anything. The maps are in Rabat or Nigeria."

"If the maps have been sent to Rabat, how is it, Monsieur, that the manuscript is—or was—still in your possession?"

"Muntaka wants to return it to the museum himself. It's a matter of pride with him."

Slabbinck let out a long sigh. Then he shrugged his shoulders and said to Mahmoud, "Take the American back to his hotel."

Slabbinck handed me the manuscript. "I have no use for this."
He wiped his face with a handkerchief. "Perhaps, as an object of
art, it is worth two or three thousand dollars. Only a fool like the
Levantine Simhani would risk his life for so little. If I were to
keep these pieces of parchment, I would have to kill you. The risk
is not worth it to me." Slabbinck was silent for a moment. Then
he said, "The Leo Africanus map would have been worth it. You
are fortunate, Monsieur. Very fortunate. You came close to being
dead."

I WAS back at the hotel at two-thirty. I woke up Muntaka, told him about Slabbinck, and handed over the manuscript to him. Then I went to bed.

I lay in bed for an hour thinking about how close we had come to losing both the manuscript and the Leo Africanus map. Sister Monique got possession of the manuscript from the camel driver Moulay Abubakar but wanted the map, not the manuscript. The Greek Kontos stole the map from Rakman's safe but wanted the manuscript, not the map. Slabbinck, just a few hours before, had the manuscript in his lap but wanted the map. He had to be kicking himself for having helped the French priest, Father René, put the map on the camel train. Georges Daboul wanted the manuscript to sell to the highest bidder and the rabbi wanted the manuscript to bury for a hundred years.

I thought back to the body of the Levantine Simhani lying naked in the mortuary at the Katani prison and wondered what he would have done with the manuscript and map if he had made it out of Dakoro alive. I wondered if the Vatican would really have purchased the manuscript and map without asking questions. I expected they would have.

I slept for ten hours and didn't see Muntaka at all that afternoon or evening.

On the morning of the next day I was up at seven-thirty. As I passed the desk clerk on my way to the breakfast room, he called to me.

"Monsieur Stevens, there is a message for you." He handed me an envelope with my name on it. The message was from Muntaka.

Mallam Stevens,

I shall need your assistance this morning. Do not fail me. It is important that you arrive before eleven o'clock at the shop of Alhaji Rakman's friend Farouk, in the Great Market. To arrive there you must enter the Great Market by the Hassan Umaru Gate. Continue straight ahead, counting ten shops on your left. The last shop will be that of a leather dealer. Turn left into the passage running from the leather dealer's shop. Proceed straight ahead, counting seven shops on your right. Turn right at the seventh shop, that of a silversmith, and proceed into the passage running from the silversmith's shop. You will pass nine shops on your right. All of these shops will sell brass goods. At the end of the line of shops you will enter a small square with five passageways running into it. You should go to the passageway second on your right. The first shop will be that of a dealer in antique guns and knives. The fourth shop on your right will be that of Farouk, a dealer in old books and maps. I shall be there.

Moh. Muntaka

It was eight-thirty. I left the hotel at nine-fifteen and headed for the Hassan Umaru Gate. What was Muntaka up to?

The plaza was at the height of its morning activity. In the large square outside the gate the fortune tellers, magicians, traders, and petty thieves were already at work. I moved my wallet from my back pocket to a front one, read the beginning of the instructions, and entered the market.

Inside the tall-arched gate, I was transposed from the relative openness of the square into a world of hundreds of narrow alleys, hundreds of small shops, and hundreds of people searching for pots, rugs, spices, and a thousand other things. The atmosphere was, strangely, both festive and sinister. I moved to my left to be able to count the shops. A hand grabbed my shoulder. Started, I spun around.

"Monsieur, you are interested in some fine rugs? I can give you a good price."

"No, thank you." I brushed his hand off my shoulder.

"It is not necessary for you to buy. Come in for a glass of mint tea. We shall talk and relax."

I moved on. I came to the leather dealer and turned left. Again, hands on my shoulder, but I shrugged them off, counted seven shops, and turned right at the silversmith's. I soon came to the square. There were six passageways running into it, counting the one that brought me to the square. I thought the note had said five passageways. I reached into my coat pocket to reread it. It wasn't there. In semipanic I patted and dug into each pocket. The note was gone. I should have followed my instincts and picked a passage. Instead, I decided to look for the note. I backtracked along the line of shops selling brass. With the crowds, I was able to see only patches of ground. Nothing. At the end of the passage I turned left at a silversmith's shop. I searched past two more sets of shops and decided the search was foolish. Either the note was trampled into the ground or someone was using it for cigarette paper. I decided to go back to the small square with the six passages running into it.

After fifteen minutes, I knew I was lost. Lost is not the right word. I was trapped in a maze of passageways winding in dozens of directions. I felt that I was digging myself deeper and deeper into the market. I decided it was time to ask directions.

"I am looking for the antique dealer Farouk," I said in French to the person next to me. He didn't respond and he walked on. I repeated my statement to a second person. His reaction was the same. I then approached a dealer in one of the shops selling small pieces of hardware, locks, keys, and rope.

"I am looking for the antique dealer Farouk." The shopkeeper looked at me quizzically and replied in Arabic. I repeated my question in French and he again replied in Arabic. He picked up a padlock and showed it to me.

"Farouk, Farouk," I repeated. Suddenly, a look of comprehension on his face. He stepped to the front of his shop and pointed to the left. I saw a piece of paper and a pencil on his desk at the back of the small shop, grabbed them and handed them to him. He drew a map. I thanked him and left.

The map took me no more than two passageways and fifteen shops away. I stopped in front of the shop indicated on the map. As I moved through the curtained entrance, a bell sounded and a Moroccan in a steel blue robe and matching cap appeared through a door at the rear of the shop. The room was small and narrow and contained nothing but a bare wooden desk and a chair.

"Are you Monsieur Farouk? I am James Stevens. I'm looking for a Nigerian named Mohamed Muntaka."

Finally, recognition. The Moroccan spoke in Arabic, but he knew what I wanted. "Ahh, Farouk, Farouk," he said, smiling and nodding in assent. Relieved, I knew that this was the man I was looking for. He smelled of old books and his steel-rimmed glasses revealed the eyes of a scholar.

"Monsieur Farouk, I am looking for a man named Muntaka."

The man stepped aside and motioned me toward the door through which he had appeared moments earlier. I moved to the door, opened it, and stepped into a dimly-lit room that smelled not of old books and manuscripts but of baby oil and talcum powder.

"Holy shit," I said, as I looked around the room. I knew Muntaka wasn't there because, if he had been, he would have been quoting Descartes: "The greatest minds are capable of the greatest vices as well as of the greatest virtues."

On a cot to the left a girl of about fifteen straddled a fat Moroccan. To the right, two girls rubbed oil on the back of a man with large, gray, flat feet. Putting the philosopher before the whores, I turned to leave, but the man whom I had taken to be Farouk blocked the door. He began to push me against another girl, and put his hand on my left rear pocket. The girl began to unbuckle my belt.

I snapped my left elbow back into the man's stomach and pushed the girl away. She fell to the floor, sprawling spread-eagled on her back. I moved quickly to the other side of the room, knocking a small table and an oil lamp on top of the fat man on the cot. He shouted in Arabic. I plunged through a curtained doorway into an adjoining room and broad jumped over another cot bearing two women eyes to thighs with each other. A door on the other side of the cot led into a back alley. As I stepped outside, I tripped over two garbage pails and sprawled headlong into the alleyway. A rat the size of a football ran over my outstretched arms and stopped three inches from my left hand. He turned around and, for several long moments, stared at my face. Then he brushed his tail against my finger tips, and disappeared behind one of the overturned pails. I stood up and brushed myself off. The right leg of my trousers was ripped. I looked around. No one had followed me out of the shop. I took a deep breath, buckled my belt, and walked down the alley to a main passageway. I stood at the junction for a few minutes to get my bearings. I had no bearings. I looked up and down the passage and then walked directly ahead into a shop selling old eyeglasses and thin gold rings.

"I am looking for Farouk, the antique book dealer," I said, wiping sweat from my face with the sleeve of my jacket.

The shopkeeper smiled. He opened his arms wide in a gesture I didn't understand. The only word in his response that I understood was *Farouk*. He picked out a pair of eyeglasses and tried to place them on my nose. I was in no mood for it. I left the shop and walked into the crowd, letting myself be swept along.

Halfway up the passage I felt an object pressed against my back. At first I thought it was another aggressive rug salesman, but as I turned part way around I saw the skinny taxi driver. Next to him, right behind me, was Slabbinck. I grabbed an old lady coming in the opposite direction and shoved her between me and Slabbinck and his friend. I started running, and despite the crowd I was able to move pretty fast. I didn't look back. After five minutes I stopped to catch my breath. Then I decided to put more distance between me and my two pursuers.

At the next turn I was almost overwhelmed by the smell of dead animals. I was standing at the edge of a large open area containing two or three dozen vats of red, green, and black dye. Hanging from stalls along the outer edges of the area were animal skins, and three or four men were dipping them into the concrete tanks. I decided that it wasn't a good idea to stay in the open area for long and I ran along one edge. As I did, I saw the skinny taxi driver emerge from an alley about three vats from me. I turned to double back and saw Slabbinck emerging from the passageway that had just brought me into the area. He raised a handgun and pointed it in my direction. I dove down behind a vat. As I did, I heard a shot. I looked back in time to see the taxi driver grab at his face and fall headfirst into one of the vats. In seconds the upper half of his body emerged. He was screaming. The blood from the head wound was indistinguishable from the dye that covered his body. He looked as if he had been hit by a cannon. He brought his hands to his face and then sank slowly back into the vat.

I was about five yards from the nearest passage and, crouching over, I ran into it. After ten minutes of running I couldn't take any more. I looked around and saw no sign of Slabbinck. I leaned on a chair at the front of one of the shops and then sat down in it, holding the cramp in my side. I was drenched in sweat.

"You would like a letter written for you in Arabic?" I looked up. At the back of the shop was a large sign in four languages. The English read: "Letter and reference writer. Small prices." He had spoken English.

"I need some assistance. I'm looking for the shop of Farouk, the antique book dealer."

"One dirham, please." I handed it to him. "The antique shops are close by. I shall draw you a map and write you a letter. The

262

map will bring you to a square with six passageways running into it. At the square, present the letter to one of the dealers. I shall ask him to guide you to Farouk. Give him one dirham for his trouble."

I handed the letter writer two more dirhams and followed his map. In fifteen minutes I was back at the square with the six passageways running into it. I went into a shop selling brass lamps. I handed the letter writer's note to the dealer. He read it, smiled, and nodded his head. He called into the back of the store and a young boy came forward.

The dealer spoke to him in Arabic and the boy motioned me to follow him. We went up one of the alleyways and stopped at the fourth shop on the right. The sign over the shop read "Farouk— Antiquaire." In smaller letters, "cartes et libres." The young boy said to me, "dirham," and held up two fingers. I gave him five dirhams.

"Farouk—Antiquaire" was one of the few shops in the market with an enclosed front. As I entered, a bell over the door rang softly. There was no one in the front room, but in a few moments a man of about fifty-five, dressed in a black-and-red-striped djellabah and wearing a matching fez, walked through the blue curtains hanging at the back of the shop.

He spoke in French. "Yes, Monsieur, may I be of assistance?"

"I am looking for an acquaintance of mine, a Nigerian. I was to meet him here."

"A Nigerian? Hmmm. Are you sure that this is the correct shop? I have seen no Nigerian here today. He is black?"

"He is quite dark. He would be wearing a long robe and a small cap. His front teeth are missing. The others are orange."

"The other what?"

"The other teeth."

"I am sorry. He has not been to my shop." The man appeared impatient. "Is there something I can show you?"

"Are you the only shopkeeper named Farouk who sells antique books and maps?"

"There are many Farouks in the market. But there are few

persons who specialize in antique books and maps. One must be an expert.''

"This man would get along famously with Muntaka," I thought.

"Few men have the knowledge to operate a shop such as this. May I show something to you?''

I was unsure what to do. I could go back into the market and look for Muntaka elsewhere. Or I could return to the hotel—if I could ever find my way out of the goddamned place. The trouble was that I wasn't sure what the hell Muntaka was up to. Why did he leave me the note unless he wanted me here? As I turned to leave, Farouk said, "Who is it you are looking for?''

"A Nigerian called Muntaka.''

"Wait here, please.'' Farouk disappeared into the back of the shop. He returned in less than a minute.

"Come this way, please.''

Farouk led me through the blue curtains into an adjoining room cluttered with old books and papers. We walked through into a second room. It was dimly lit and it took a while for my eyes to focus. Farouk disappeared behind me. As my eyes adjusted I saw Muntaka sitting in a large leather chair. Sitting opposite him was Rakman, holding a gun. The man next to Muntaka was the Lebanese, Daboul. Next to him was the Greek, Kontos. I couldn't tell who Rakman was holding the gun on. He turned it toward me and motioned me into the room.

The room was lit by a bare bulb hanging from a wire in the corner. The walls were lined with dark shelves covered with papers. The papers were covered with dust and the room smelled of stale air. There were only four chairs. I stood to the left of Kontos, trying to figure out what was going on.

"So, Alhaji,'' Rakman said, "your young friend is here. Does he know the nature of your visit?''

"I am afraid that I have told him nothing.''

"No matter. I am sorry, Monsieur Stevens, that we have nothing to offer you in the way of refreshment. You look rather worn down." Rakman continued to hold the gun casually. "And I am sorry that we cannot even offer you a chair. But you are younger than the rest of us. Standing will do you no harm. I believe that you have met Monsieur Kontos and Monsieur Daboul before?"

I didn't answer. I still couldn't understand what was going on, or Rakman's relation to the three men opposite him. I didn't know whether he was prepared to shoot Muntaka, shoot Kontos, or shoot Daboul.

Turning to Muntaka, Rakman said, "It is best that we conclude our business quickly."

The Greek said, "Two hundred and fifty thousand dollars is out of the question. It is too much."

"Sir," Muntaka said, "you are, I believe, a man of Greece. Is that not so?"

"Yes, I am of Greek parents."

"Then you are familiar with the story which takes place during the Peloponnesian War. A courier was running to Athens with a message of urgency. As he traveled, he met an old shepherd. He stopped and asked him, 'How far is Athens from here?' The shepherd did not answer. The courier, thinking that the old man was perhaps deaf, asked the question once more. Again, no answer. The messenger started off, at a brisk trot. When he had gone about fifty yards, the shepherd shouted, 'Two hours away.' The messenger turned his head and shouted back, 'Why didn't you answer before?' The shepherd replied, 'How did I know how fast you run?' "

The Greek looked blank. "What is the meaning of that story?"

Good question, I thought.

"The shepherd was unable to judge the time to Athens without knowing how fast the messenger could run. But once he knew, he could give the answer. Had you and I met in Maradi, and had I been in possession of the manuscript, I would not have known how much you would be willing to pay for the manuscript. But now I have seen you run. I have seen how far you have been willing to travel for the manuscript. I can now judge how much I am able to extract from you. The price is two hundred and fifty thousand dollars. No more, no less."

"I shall pay it. First, I should like to see the manuscript."

"First," Muntaka said, "I should like to see . . . I am afraid there is no other word for it . . . the money."

"If you insist. Monsieur Daboul, give the envelope to the Alhaji."

The Lebanese reached into a carpetbag at his feet. He produced three thick, brown, stained manila envelopes. He handed them to Muntaka. Muntaka took the envelopes, opened one, and took out several large packets of bills. American dollars.

"I shall assume," Muntaka said, "that the two hundred and fifty thousand dollars are here." He riffled through one of the packets of bills. "As the poet said, 'money represents the prose of life, and which is hardly spoken of in parlors without apology but it is, in effects and law, as beautiful as roses.' I apologize, my dear Alhaji Rakman, for having to speak of money in your parlor."

"You shall have to apologize to my friend, Monsieur Farouk. Perhaps you could show Monsieur Kontos and Monsieur Daboul the manuscript?"

"Of course." Muntaka reached into his robe and pulled out the smooth, brown leather case. He handed it to Kontos. Daboul and the Greek looked at each other and smiled. Kontos opened the case and lifted the parchments out gently. He examined them with a magnifying glass and then handed them to Daboul.

I couldn't believe my eyes and ears. "Muntaka," I said, "what the hell's going on?"

"I have negotiated a small business matter with Monsieur Kontos and Monsieur Daboul. Alhaji Rakman and I are two tortoises attempting to play at being elephants."

"I am merely a tortoise in this matter, Alhaji," Rakman said. "You, it would appear, are a tortoise who has become an elephant."

Kontos eyed Muntaka suspiciously. "What is this talk of tortoises?"

266

Muntaka smiled. "So, you have not heard this story? It is one told . . ."

Rakman interrupted. "Alhaji, you had best save the story for another time. We should conclude our business."

"Perhaps you are right."

I looked at Rakman and then at Muntaka, the Greek, and the Lebanese. "Jesus, Muntaka, I can't believe you're doing this. This isn't a piece of airport art you're selling. It's your country's heritage."

"If this were a piece of art from the airport, Mallam Stevens, I would not be selling it for a quarter of a million dollars."

"But it's beyond valuing. You told me so yourself."

"They are merely papers. Whether they are returned to my country or not makes little difference. No one will die because they are gone. No one would live longer if they were returned. With two hundred thousand dollars perhaps *I* shall live longer."

The Greek looked up. "You are lowering your price?"

Muntaka raised his right hand shoulder high, palm out, and turned toward Kontos. "It is a manner of speaking." The Greek shrugged. Muntaka turned back to me. "Besides, I shall use some of the money for alms for the poor. Is it better that these papers sit in a museum or that a beggar receive a decent meal?"

"Or that you buy a dozen more Land-Rovers, a hundred fancy robes, and a lifetime supply of kola nuts. Damn it, Muntaka, it's not right."

"There are many things wrong in this world. One more thing will make no difference."

"Muntaka, you're not the same person I've known for four years. For me, you've just died. Only this time you won't be reborn. I no longer know you."

"As your Mark Twain said, 'Everyone is a moon, and has a dark side which he never shows to anybody.' Perhaps he was wrong, perhaps it is shown from time to time. I am sorry." Muntaka turned to Rakman. "Well, Alhaji, if Monsieur Kontos and Monsieur Daboul find the manuscript in order, we should perhaps leave."

It was then that I lunged at Daboul to grab the manuscript. I fell over the Greek's feet and landed in the center of the group with my body on top of parchments. Rakman grabbed me by the back of my jacket and pulled me up, his pistol sticking in my back. I dropped the manuscript pages. Daboul bent over to retrieve them and, as he stood up, I tried to kick him in the nuts. Rakman jerked me back with his bad arm, and my foot went up through the air.

Muntaka tied the envelopes of bills together with a string and put the package under his arm. He got up to leave and I followed. Rakman, who was behind me, kept the revolver pointed at Daboul and Kontos as he sidestepped through the doorway and pushed me along with his elbow. In seconds we were out of Farouk's shop by way of an exit that led to a small alleyway. About twenty yards from the shop I heard a shot behind us. It sounded as if it had come from inside the shop, but I wasn't sure. Muntaka looked back, but neither he nor Rakman said anything. I assumed that Farouk had been advised to get the hell out of there and that the shot represented the end of the Daboul-Kontos partnership. I guessed that it was the Greek who came away with the goodies.

Rakman, Muntaka, and I walked to a small cul de sac about two hundred yards away from Farouk's shop. Rakman's car and driver were waiting.

Rakman pocketed his gun. I could have broken away and run, but I didn't. Not because I didn't want to, or because I thought Rakman would take a shot at me, but because I knew I would never find my way out of that damned walled labyrinth. I quickly convinced myself that getting the hell out of Marrakech was more important than a dramatic gesture. So much for the good guys.

Rakman took the seat next to the driver. Muntaka and I sat in the back. The package of money rested on Muntaka's lap. The driver nudged the Peugeot through the crowd of people and into the street. As he did, I looked out the side window and saw Slabbinck hurrying in the direction of Farouk's shop. He didn't see us. I wondered whether he had thought it was the Leo map that was changing hands or whether he had discovered the value of the manuscript. Neither Muntaka nor Rakman saw him, and I said nothing.

As the driver maneuvered the car through the narrow streets, I sat there feeling despair and betrayal, wishing that it was all going to end differently, realizing that it wasn't, and realizing that, after all, I didn't know Muntaka. I should never have returned to Africa. I should have known that it wouldn't be the same as the first time. It never is. Africa had changed, and so had Muntaka. From what, to what? Who was Muntaka four years ago? Who was he now? I wasn't going to stick around to find out. The special bond that I thought had developed between us was the conceit of a naïve American.

A few minutes later I reached into my jacket and took out the pocketwatch I had bought for Muntaka in the market. I rolled down the window, looked at the watch briefly, and then threw it into the gutter that ran along the side of the street. Muntaka had turned as I pulled the watch from my pocket, moved forward slightly as I raised my hand to jettison it, but then pulled back. He pressed his lips together and said nothing. He drew the package of money closer to his body.

When we reached the hotel the three of us remained seated. No one spoke. Then I said, "Well, Muntaka, I guess we can say goodbye here." I opened the door and got out of the car.

Muntaka followed. "Wait. Let me walk to your room with you. There is something I must say."

"There's nothing to say. I'm getting out of here. Have a nice life. Thanks for all the crap about the search for a lost city."

Rakman leaned out of the car window. "Alhaji, I shall see you this evening at seven." The car drove off. Muntaka followed me into the hotel and onto the elevator. We ascended in silence. I headed to my room and Muntaka followed close behind. As I opened the door, I turned around and said, "Well, Muntaka, what is it?"

"Please, let me come inside." We entered and Muntaka closed the door. He placed the package of money on the end of the bed.

"Mallam Stevens, you do not really believe that I have sold the

269

manuscript. Do you not know me better than that?''

''Not only do I believe it, I saw it. What the hell are you talking about?''

''Here, let me borrow your Swiss Army knife.''

''My Swiss Army knife and I parted company in Moulay's village, just like you and I are about to do.''

''Oh, I forgot. You have a razor blade?''

''In the bathroom.'' I jerked my thumb over my shoulder.

Muntaka hurried into the bathroom and returned with my razor. He took out the blade and raised the bottom of his robe. He began cutting the thread at the top of a wide hem. He cut ten or twelve inches. When he finished cutting, he pulled out a packet and handed it to me.

''Here, open this.''

I did. I pulled out twelve pieces of thin parchment. ''Jesus Christ, Muntaka, this is the goddamned manuscript.'' I shook my head to clear my eyes. It *was* the manuscript. ''Muntaka, how the hell did you get this back? If you pulled a switch on those two men it was the neatest trick of the century.'' Then bewilderment turned to panic. ''One of those cut-throats is probably on his way here now.''

''I did not get it back.'' Muntaka took the manuscript and tossed it on the bed next to the package of money. ''This,'' he said, ''is the true manuscript. The manuscript I gave to Kontos and Daboul is a copy. A very good copy, but, nevertheless, a copy.''

''Copy? Where the hell did you get it?''

''It came to Morocco by way of the diplomatic pouch to Rabat. It was delivered to me here in Marrakech by an aide from the Nigerian mission. I cabled Colonel Ajisafe of the Nigerian police and requested that he obtain the copy from the museum at Jos. As I told you in the funeral hut, this manuscript, the original, was too valuable for us to display in the museum. We could not afford the elaborate protection that would be needed to safeguard it were it to be put on display. So we had a copy made. The copy took four years to complete. It is. . . . How can I say this? . . . Close to perfect. It will take a very clever eye to detect the forgery. No, forgery is not the correct word. The copy is itself a work of art. The age of the parchment could not, of course, be duplicated and an eye trained in such matters will become suspicious. But it would require much skill.

"In any case, Mallam Stevens, it did not occur to me until after we had begun our journey that it might be useful to have the copy with us. In fact, the idea came to me only at Dakoro, thanks to you."

"To me? What do you mean?"

"Your magic show for the children. I have simply demonstrated a variation on the theme of illusion."

"Son of a bitch, Muntaka. We're not dealing with children. You sold a forgery to Kontos and Daboul for two hundred and fifty thousand dollars. Christ, I can't believe that the *original* is worth that much."

"What? So now you are feeling sorry for the Greek? A short while ago you were feeling sorry for my country and its loss."

"It's you, and me, and Rakman I feel sorry for. When Kontos discovers that you sold him a forgery, he'll be after us before you can say, 'Allah be praised.' "

"There is no danger of that. Your reaction to the events at Farouk's shop lent the essential element of credibility to my actions. By the way, what took you so long?"

"I got lost."

"No matter. You appeared in time. As I say, your reaction produced the essential element of credibility, and the distraction that every creator of illusion needs. More important, the copy is, as I have said, a work of art. You see, Mallam Stevens, I created it myself."

"You?"

"In my defense, I would like it to be known that I did not spend the four years at translation only. I am sorry that I was unable to reveal this to the Catholic nun. In any case, Kontos does not possess the skill to see that the copy is not the true manuscript. Not until he shows it to someone trained in antiquities of this sort

271

will he learn of our deception. And Kontos, in any event, will leave here by morning, if he has not already departed. We have nothing to fear."

"Unless Slabbinck has ended up with the fake."

"Slabbinck?"

"He may have found out about the significance of the manuscript. He was heading for Farouk's shop as we were leaving. The bastard may be able to spot the forgery. Besides, he didn't have the benefit of your little play."

"Hmmmm. Slabbinck. I hadn't counted on that." Muntaka paused and bit into his lower lip. He tilted his head and raised his eyebrows. "My transcription is not without flaws."

"I thought you said it was a work of art, close to perfect."

"Close, yes. But not perfect. I am not a genius, you know."

"No, I didn't know."

Muntaka looked worried. He was not in a mood for banter. "After we have dined with Alhaji Rakman and paid him for his services, it is best that we leave Marrakech immediately."

"Uh, Muntaka, speaking of money, what, if you don't mind my asking, do you plan to do with the two hundred and fifty thousand big ones?"

"Big ones?"

"Dollars."

"Oh. The two hundred and fifty thousand dollars. Well, let's see. I could buy a dozen Land-Rovers, a hundred fancy robes, a lifetime supply of . . ."

"Sorry, Muntaka."

"There is nothing to be sorry about, Mallam Stevens. You did right. Your reaction was what I would have hoped from you. In any case," he continued, "it will be necessary to pay Monsieur Rakman a rather substantial commission. I shall take a small commission for myself."

"Can I make a suggestion, Muntaka?"

"Why not?"

"I think we owe something to Father Cornelius Nunn. Somehow I feel we did him an injustice. How about a small contribution to his mission?"

"It can be done."

"And a contribution to Sister Monique's order."

Muntaka raised his eyebrows and sucked in one cheek, causing his mouth to move directly under his right nostril. He ran the back of his left hand along the small stubble of beard under his chin. Then he rubbed his right eye and cheek with his right hand.

"Mallam Stevens, it is not my mission in life to subsidize the Catholic religion. I . . ."

Muntaka was interrupted by a knock at the door. Had the knock come minutes earlier, before Muntaka's revelation about the manuscript, I wouldn't have been so quick to open the door. But the atmosphere had cleared, I had become faintly light-headed, and, in the last seconds, I had forgotten about Kontos, Slabbinck, and Daboul.

I pulled the door open. As I did, a size ten or eleven dusty brown shoe was shoved against the door jamb and a small caliber pistol was shoved against my stomach. The instructions were precise and clear. "Please be careful, Mr. Stevens. I have never shot a man before, but I am prepared to do so now. Please step carefully into the room."

I backed in with my hands raised. Muntaka came forward and stood at my side, just as he had done back in Rakman's office. Our visit to Marrakech was ending as it had begun. Perhaps we had come full cycle. I felt neither surprise nor panic. I lowered my arms slightly and half-turned to my right. "Muntaka," I said, "permit me to introduce Father Cornelius Nunn."

"CUT the pleasantries, Stevens. The manuscript, where is it?"

Oh, my God. The manuscript. Involuntarily I looked to the foot of the bed where Muntaka had set down the manuscript and the package containing the two hundred and fifty thousand dollars. They weren't there. Muntaka must have moved them just as I was opening the door. But where were they?

"The manuscript, Stevens. I don't have much time."

I was sure that I had heard this dialogue before. Somewhere. In this very room. Sister Monique. No. She gave *me* the manuscript. Well, in any event, I had my catechism memorized. "What manuscript?"

"Don't be a bloody fool, Stevens. If you don't produce the Leo Africanus manuscript in the next twenty seconds, I'm going to blow a hole through your Isles of Longerhans."

"Manuscript?" I must have sounded like a babbling idiot. But the question was more for my own benefit than the priest's. What the hell did Leo have to do with the manuscript? My brain felt like it needed tuning. I turned my head toward Muntaka who gave me a look that was at once quizzical and warning. He was telling me in effect, "I don't know what he's talking about but don't give away too much."

"Don't play me for a bloody fool, Stevens. I know you have the manuscript. I know the story of the African, and I know you know. I also know that it'll make me a rich man. At least five men have been killed for the manuscript. I have no desire to make you number six."

I wasn't sure whether the priest would pull the trigger but I wasn't about to risk Muntaka's life or mine. Five men? The door was open about two inches, but since my room was at the end of the corridor, the likelihood of someone seeing what was going on was slim. I needed more time.

Wherever Muntaka put the money and manuscript, it wasn't going to take the priest long to find them. I looked toward the bed again. The blanket was pulled down to the bottom. The bed had been made when we walked in. Muntaka had covered the package and papers with the rumpled blanket. The stuff was sitting there like purloined letters.

Muntaka continued to say nothing. I had to say *something.* "It's not here. Why the hell do you want it anyway? It's unimportant. It's not worth more than a few hundred dollars. Right, Muntaka?"

"Perhaps," Muntaka said, "a bit more. Certainly not of a value to cause violence."

"Stevens, you are more of an ass than I first suspected. The theft of the manuscript was in every newspaper in Nigeria. A theft of something worth a few hundred dollars wouldn't have been reported. I know the reputation of your friend Muntaka. I know how far you have traveled. And, on your fortuitous visit to our small mission school, you provided me with evidence of the significance of the manuscript. The story of the legacy of Leo the African is one that is well known within the church. I merely put two and two together."

What he didn't know was that he had put two and two together and come up with three. But this wasn't going to do Muntaka and me any good. If we told him about the map, the son of a bitch might end up with the map, the manuscript and the money. He was three feet away from the last two. Rakman still had the maps but Nunn might figure that one out.

Muntaka said, "The manuscript, I am afraid, has been returned to Nigeria. You'll find nothing here."

"You are both poor liars. In my profession, one becomes quite skilled at detecting liars. It will be a simple matter to search the room. I shall start with the bed."

The priest moved toward the cot. Holding the gun toward us with his right hand, he reached with his left hand toward the blanket. As he bent sideways, Muntaka fell to the floor and rolled against the priest's legs. The priest kicked his foot against Muntaka's head and I heard Muntaka moan. I threw myself forward. My right shoulder went into the priest's stomach and my left hand pushed the priest's hand toward the ceiling. The gun fired. As I twisted Nunn's wrist, a large piece of plaster and the gun fell onto the bed almost simultaneously. I fell on top of the priest and we rolled between the wall and the bed, pushing the cot out about two feet. I scrambled up, but as I did the priest shoved his elbow hard against my stomach. He lunged for the pistol. His fingers were inches from the gun when I saw a black, pointed-toe shoe push against the bottom of the bed, moving it away from Nunn and me. At first I thought it was Muntaka's foot, but as I slipped from one bed to the floor I saw Muntaka lying unconscious. I looked up. The foot belonged to René Slabbinck. He was holding a gun of his own.

"Against the wall, gentlemen." Slabbinck motioned with his pistol.

The priest and I stood up together, between the wall and the bed, like targets at a side show. Our hands were raised. I looked at the end of the bed. The manuscript and money were still hidden under the blanket.

Slabbinck moved his head toward Muntaka. "What's wrong with him?"

"He's been kicked unconscious. I'd like to take a look at him."

"I shall take care of that, Monsieur. Slabbinck backed toward the small table and picked up a pitcher of water with his free hand. He poured the water on Muntaka's face. Muntaka moaned and then opened his eyes. He raised his torso, looked around, got to his knees and then stood up. Slabbinck motioned him to the wall, next to me.

"I am pleased to see that you have recovered, Monsieur Muntaka. It is essential that I have your attention. You know, of course, why I am here."

Muntaka was touching his left temple gently. He winced. "I am afraid not."

"Perhaps you are not thinking clearly at the moment. I shall not make a game of this. I should like to negotiate a small exchange. The manuscript for the map."

Slabbinck unbuttoned his jacket. Tucked in his trousers was the brown leather case that had contained the fake manuscript that Muntaka had sold to Daboul and Kontos. He withdrew the case with his left hand, threw it on the bed, and tightened his belt several notches. "Open it, Monsieur Stevens."

I picked up the case and considered momentarily the possibility of throwing it at Slabbinck's head or gun. The chances were that I would miss. I opened the case and pulled out the manuscript. I placed the case and manuscript on the bed, on top of the rumpled blanket. The priest said nothing.

Slabbinck smiled maliciously, flashing several gold teeth. "There, Monsieur Muntaka, is my part of the bargain. The next move in this little play is for you to produce the map."

I could see the priest eyeing the fake manuscript like a rat spotting a piece of cheese in a trap. The question was how he was going to obtain the object of desire without killing himself. Muntaka was pressing the area above his left eye with his raised hand It didn't look like he was prepared for an, more roll-on-the-floor, hit-him-in-the-stomach routines.

The priest was hungrier than I would have thought. As I was thinking of something to say to Slabbinck—I couldn't stand the silence in the room—the priest shoved his right elbow into the area just between my ribs. I moaned loudly and bent over. The priest lunged forward onto the bed, grabbed his pistol with his

277

right hand and fired it at Slabbinck. Slabbinck responded too late. A bullet from the priest's gun hit Slabbinck's shoulder, knocking him backward onto the floor. The bullet from Slabbinck's gun entered the wall at a point just to the right of where the priest had been standing. Slabbinck's gun skipped across the floor.

The priest moved quickly off the bed. He took the fake manuscript pages, placed them carefully into the leather case, took a last look at Slabbinck, and headed out the door. I ran to Slabbinck. The wound was bleeding but Slabbinck was breathing and conscious. I picked up his gun and put it in my pocket. Muntaka took the cover off the pillow and pressed it against the wound to stop the bleeding. Then he lifted the blanket and picked up the manuscript and money.

As he did, the door to the room swung open. I put my hand into my jacket pocket and wrapped my fingers around Slabbinck's pistol.

The manager looked around the room in alarm. He seemed more distressed by the holes in the wall and ceiling than by the body on the floor. "What has happened here?"

Muntaka stepped forward. "There has been a small accident. I should be grateful if you could telephone a man named Nafir Rakman and ask him to come here immediately. He is involved in export and import. Rakman will contact the police and a physician."

At the mention of the word *police* the manager became panicky. "The police? Why the police? The presence of police is not good for business."

"It shall be done quietly," Muntaka said as he maneuvered the manager to the door. "But unless you move quickly we shall have a dead man here."

Within an hour Rakman had contacted the commandant of police, a doctor had removed the bullet from Slabbinck's shoulder, the police had removed Slabbinck, and Muntaka had paid the manager the price of a new rug and two sections of plaster. Rak-

man accompanied the commandant to headquarters, promising to return to have dinner with Muntaka and me.

We stood at the foot of the bed looking at each other.

"Well, Muntaka, where were we?"

"You had just suggested that we make a small contribution to Father Nunn's mission."

"Maybe we should scrap that idea."

"And to Sister Monique's order."

With the money we're saving on the priest, there's nothing standing in the way of assisting the nun."

"I gave the nun funds for her travels. And a small, but rather expensive, religious necklace."

"A nice gesture, Muntaka, but I'm thinking about a few thousand dollars for the convent."

"A few thousand dollars?"

"Oh, come on, Muntaka."

Muntaka shrugged. "All right. It shall be done. How shall we get the money to her?"

"I'll deliver it."

"Mallam Stevens, I suggest that we mail it. I also suggest that you abandon any ideas of seeing the nun again."

"What about the rest of the money, Muntaka? Rakman's commission, and yours, and the contribution to the convent aren't going to make much of a dent in a quarter-million dollars."

"I have one other contribution in mind." Muntaka paused and ran his right hand along his nostrils. "The balance will go to support the museum at Jos. Perhaps we can install a new security system."

"What contribution, Muntaka?"

Muntaka's eyes avoided mine. "I am thinking, Mallam Stevens, of the ten thousand dollars stolen from the synagogue. Perhaps it would not be inappropriate to replace it, with perhaps a small addition."

"How much, Muntaka?"

"Do you think an additional five thousand dollars would be too much?"

"Make it ten, Muntaka. What the hell."

"It shall be done. Perhaps you would like to deliver it to the rabbi's daughter." Muntaka took a deep breath. "Well, Mallam Stevens, have we forgotten anyone?"

I laughed. "Only me, Muntaka."

"I have not forgotten you, Mallam Stevens. I am setting aside a small fund to cover your expenses."

"Expenses? What expenses?"

"Your expenses for the next several months." Muntaka smiled his partially-toothless grin. "Pack your bag, Mallam Stevens, the trip to Timbuktu is a long one."